Praise for
The Alexandria Link

"Fast-moving . . . nonstop action."
—*Boston Sunday Globe*

"Contemporary issues and page-turning thriller elements combine with history in shocking ways. Fans of this type of thriller and readers who have already discovered Berry will not be disappointed."
—*Library Journal*

"A fun read."
—*San Jose Mercury News*

"Berry, to the same degree as Michael Crichton and Clive Cussler . . . keeps writing and writing great mystery thrillers. . . . *The Alexandria Link* is one fast-moving bullet train and does not stop for any refreshments or intermission, so you had better be prepared for a lost day or two when you climb onto this high octane and well-conceived and researched thriller."
—*I Love a Mystery*

"Malone, a hero with a personal stake in the proceedings, is a welcome respite from the cold, calculating superspies who litter the genre."
—*Entertainment Weekly*

"Berry's riveting quest to locate a hidden treasure and uncover a plot that threatens national security is packed with nonstop action."
—*Romantic Times*

"Turbulent action sequences and striking locations."
—*Rocky Mountain News*

The Third Secret

The Romanov Prophecy

The Amber Room

THE
ALEXANDRIA
LINK

A Novel

STEVE BERRY

BALLANTINE BOOKS • NEW YORK

2007 Ballantine Books Mass Market Edition

Copyright © 2007 by Steve Berry
Excerpt from *The Venetian Betrayal* copyright © 2007 by Steve Berry
Interview with the author copyright © 2007 by Random House, Inc.

Published in the United States by Ballantine Books, an imprint of The Random House Publishing Group, a division of Random House, Inc., New York.

BALLANTINE and colophon are registered trademarks of Random House, Inc.

Originally published in hardcover in the United States by Ballantine Books, an imprint of The Random House Publishing Group, a division of Random House, Inc., in 2007.

ISBN 978-0-345-48576-2

Cover photographs: ruins © Bettman/Corbis; flames © Michael Simpson/Getty Images

Printed in the United States of America

www.ballantinebooks.com

OPM   9   8   7   6   5   4   3   2   1

For Katie and Kevin

Two shooting stars,
who drifted back into my orbit

ACKNOWLEDGMENTS

Writers should be careful with the pronoun *I*. A book is a team effort, and the team I'm privileged to be a part of is truly a wonder. So for the fifth time, lots of thanks. First, Pam Ahearn, my agent, who met a storm named Katrina but made it through. Next, to the wonderful folks at Random House: Gina Centrello, an extraordinary publisher and extremely charming lady; Mark Tavani, my editor, now a married man who remains far wiser than his years; Cindy Murray, who outdoes herself each time with publicity; Kim Hovey, whose marketing skills are beyond description; Beck Stvan, the talented artist with a great eye for covers; Laura Jorstad, who again copyedited with precision; Carole Lowenstein, who always makes the pages easy on the eyes; and finally to all those in promotions and sales—absolutely nothing could be achieved without their superior efforts.

One other individual deserves a special mention: Kenneth Harvey. At a dinner in South Carolina a few years ago, Ken pointed me toward a Lebanese scholar named Kamal Salibi and a rather obscure theory that eventually turned into this novel. Ideas spring up at the oddest times and from the most unexpected sources—a writer's task is to recognize them. Thanks, Ken.

Also, I have a new Elizabeth in my life who's smart, beautiful, and loving. Of course, my eight-year-old daughter, Elizabeth, continues to bring nothing but joy. Finally, this book is for my two grown children, Kevin and Katie, who make me feel both old and young.

History is the distillation of evidence surviving the past.
—OSCAR HANDLIN, *Truth in History* (1979)

Since the first Adam who beheld the night and the day and the shape of his own hand, men have made up stories and have fixed in stone, in metal, or on parchment whatever the world includes or dreams create. Here is the fruit of their labor: the Library . . . The faithless say that if it were to burn, history would burn with it. They are wrong. Unceasing human work gave birth to this infinity of books. If of them all not even one remained, man would again beget each page and every line.
—JORGE LUIS BORGES,
   regarding the Library of Alexandria

Libraries are the memory of mankind.
—JOHANN WOLFGANG VON GOETHE

PROLOGUE

GEORGE HADDAD'S PATIENCE ENDED AS HE GLARED AT THE man bound to the chair. Like himself, his prisoner possessed the swarthy skin, aquiline nose, and deep-set brown eyes of a Syrian or a Lebanese. But there was something about this man Haddad simply did not like.

"I'll only ask one more time. Who are you?"

Haddad's soldiers had caught the stranger three hours ago, just before dawn. He'd been walking alone, unarmed. Which was foolish. Ever since the British decided last November to partition Palestine into two states, one Arab, the other Jewish, war had raged between the two sides. Yet this fool had walked straight into an Arab stronghold, offering no resistance, and had not said anything since being bound to the chair.

"Did you hear me, imbecile? I asked who you are." Haddad spoke in Arabic, which the man clearly understood.

"I'm a Guardian."

The answer meant nothing to him. "What's that?"

"We're keepers of knowledge."

He was not in the mood for riddles. Just yesterday the Jewish underground had attacked a nearby village. Forty

Palestinian men and women had been herded into a quarry and shot. Nothing unusual. Arabs were being systematically murdered and expelled. Land that their families had occupied for sixteen hundred years was being confiscated. The *nakba,* the catastrophe, was happening. Haddad needed to be out fighting the enemy, not listening to nonsense.

"We're all keepers of knowledge," he made clear. "Mine is how to wipe from the face of this earth every Zionist I can find."

"Which is why I've come. War is not necessary."

This man *was* an idiot. "Are you blind? Jews are flooding this place. We're being crushed. War is all we have left."

"You underestimate Jewish resolve. They've survived for centuries and will continue."

"This land is ours. We shall win."

"There are things more powerful than bullets that can provide you victory."

"That's right. Bombs. And we have plenty of those. We'll crush every one of you thieving Zionists."

"I'm not a Zionist."

The declaration came in a quiet tone, then the man went silent. Haddad realized that he needed to end this interrogation. No time for dead ends.

"I've come from the library to speak with Kamal Haddad," the man finally said.

His rage bowed to confusion. "That's my father."

"I was told he lived in this village."

His father had been an academic, schooled in Palestinian history, teaching at the college in Jerusalem. A man big in voice and laugh, body and heart, he'd recently acted as an emissary between the Arabs and the British, trying to stop the massive Jewish immigration and prevent the *nakba*. His efforts had failed.

"My father is dead."

For the first time he spied concern in the prisoner's barren eyes. "I was not aware."

Haddad retrieved a memory he'd wanted to forever dismiss. "Two weeks ago he ate the end of a rifle and blew off the back of his head. He left a note that said he couldn't bear to watch the destruction of his homeland. He thought himself responsible for not stopping the Zionists." Haddad brought the revolver he now held close to the Guardian's face. "Why did you need my father?"

"He's the one to whom my information must be passed. He's the invitee."

Anger built. "What are you talking about?"

"Your father was a man due great respect. He was learned, entitled to share in our knowledge. That's why I came, to invite him to share."

The man's calm voice hit Haddad like a pail of water dousing a flame. "Share what?"

The Guardian shook his head. "That's only for him."

"He's dead."

"Which means another invitee will be chosen."

What was this man rambling about? Haddad had captured many Jewish prisoners—torturing them to learn what he could, then shooting what of them remained. Before the *nakba* Haddad had been an olive farmer, but like his father, he was drawn to academics and wanted to pursue further studies. That was now impossible. The state of Israel was being established, its borders carved from ancient Arab land, the Jews apparently being compensated by the world for the Holocaust. And all at the expense of the people of Palestine.

He nestled the barrel of the gun between the man's eyes. "I just made myself the invitee. Speak your knowledge."

The man's eyes seemed to penetrate him, and, for a moment, a strange uneasiness overtook him. This emissary had clearly faced dilemmas before. Haddad admired courage.

"You fight a war that is not necessary, against an enemy that is misinformed," the man said.

"What in God's name are you talking about?"

"That's for the next invitee to know."

Midmorning was approaching. Haddad needed sleep. From this prisoner he'd hoped to learn the identity of some of the Jewish underground, perhaps even the monsters who'd slaughtered those people yesterday. The cursed British were supplying the Zionists with rifles and tanks. For years the British had made it illegal for Arabs to own weapons, which had placed them at a severe disadvantage. True, Arabs came with more numbers, but the Jews were better prepared, and Haddad feared the outcome of this war would be the legitimacy of the state of Israel.

He stared back at a hard, unbending expression, into eyes that never drifted from his, and he knew that his prisoner was prepared to die. Killing had become much easier for him over the past few months. Jewish atrocities helped ease what little of his conscience remained. Only nineteen, and his heart had turned to stone.

But war was war.

So he pulled the trigger.

PART ONE

1

COPENHAGEN, DENMARK
TUESDAY, OCTOBER 4, THE PRESENT
1:45 AM

COTTON MALONE STARED STRAIGHT INTO THE FACE OF TROU-
ble. Outside his bookshop's open front door stood his ex-
wife, the last person on earth he'd expected to see. He
quickly registered panic in her tired eyes, remembered the
pounding that had awoken him a few minutes before, and instantly thought of his son.

"Where's Gary?" he asked.

"You son of a bitch. They took him. Because of you. They
took him." She lunged forward, her closed fists crashing
down onto his shoulders. "You sorry son of a bitch." He
grabbed her wrists and stopped the attack as she started crying. "I left you because of this. I thought this kind of thing
was over."

"Who took Gary?" More sobs were his answer. He kept
hold of her arms. "Pam. Listen to me. Who took Gary?"

She stared at him. "How the hell am I supposed to know?"

"What are you doing here? Why didn't you go to the police?"

"Because they said not to. They said if I went anywhere

near the police, Gary was dead. They said they would know, and I believed them."

"Who's *they*?"

She wrenched her arms free, her face flooded with anger. "I don't know. All they said was for me to wait two days, then come here and give you this." She rummaged through her shoulder bag and produced a phone. Tears continued to rain down her cheeks. "They said for you to go online and open your e-mail."

Had he heard right? *Go online and open your e-mail*?

He flipped open the phone and checked the frequency. Enough megahertz to make it world-capable. Which made him wonder. Suddenly he felt vulnerable. Højbro Plads was quiet. At this late hour no one roamed the city square.

His senses came alive.

"Get inside." And he yanked her into the shop and closed the door. He hadn't switched on any lights.

"What is it?" she asked, her voice shredded by fear.

He faced her. "I don't know, Pam. You tell me. Our son has apparently been taken by God-knows-who, and you wait two days before telling a soul about it? That didn't strike you as insane?"

"I wasn't going to jeopardize his life."

"And I would? How have I ever done that?"

"By being you," she said in a frigid tone, and he instantly recalled why he no longer lived with her.

A thought occurred to him. She'd never been to Denmark. "How did you find me?"

"They told me."

"Who the hell is *they*?"

"I don't know, Cotton. Two men. Only one did the talking. Tall, dark-haired, flat face."

"American?"

"How would I know?"

"How did he speak?"

She seemed to catch hold of herself. "No. Not American. They had accents. European."

He motioned with the phone. "What am I supposed to do with this?"

"He said to open your e-mail and it would be explained."

She glanced nervously around at the shelves cast in shadows. "Upstairs, right?"

Gary would have told her he lived over the store. He certainly hadn't. They'd spoken only once since he'd retired from the Justice Department and left Georgia last year, and that had been two months back, in August, when he'd brought Gary home after their summer visit. She'd coldly told him that Gary was not his natural son. Instead the boy was the product of an affair from sixteen years ago, her response to his own infidelity. He'd wrestled with that demon ever since and had not, as yet, come to terms with its implications. One thing he'd decided at the time—he had no intention of ever speaking to Pam Malone again. Whatever needed to be said would be said between him and Gary.

But things seemed to have changed.

"Yeah," he said. "Upstairs."

They entered his apartment, and he sat at the desk. He switched on his laptop and waited for the programs to boot. Pam had finally grabbed hold of her emotions. She was like that. Her moods ran in waves. Soaring highs and cavernous lows. She was a lawyer, like him, but where he'd worked for the government, she handled high-stakes trials for *Fortune* 500 companies that could afford to pay her firm's impressive fees. When she'd first gone to law school he'd thought the decision a reflection of him, a way for them to share a life together. Later he'd learned it was a way for her to gain independence.

That was Pam.

The laptop was ready. He accessed his mailbox.

Empty.

"Nothing here."

Pam rushed toward him. "What do you mean? He said to open your e-mail."

"That was two days ago. And by the way, how did you get here?"

"They had a ticket, already bought."

He couldn't believe what he was hearing. "Are you nuts? What you did was give them a two-day head start."

"Don't you think I know that?" she yelled. "You think I'm a complete idiot? They told me my phones were tapped and I was being watched. If I varied from their instructions, even a little, Gary was dead. They showed me a picture." She caught herself and tears flowed anew. "His eyes . . . oh, his eyes." She broke down again. "He was scared."

His chest throbbed and his temples burned. He'd intentionally left behind a life of daily danger to find something new. Had that life now hunted him down? He grabbed the edge of the desk. It would do no good for both of them to fall apart. If whoever *they* were wanted Gary dead, then he was already. No. Gary was a bargaining chip—a way to apparently gain his undivided attention.

The laptop dinged.

His gaze shot to the screen's lower-right corner: RECEIVING MAIL. Then he saw GREETINGS appear on the FROM line and YOUR SON'S LIFE noted as the subject. He maneuvered the cursor and opened the e-mail.

YOU HAVE SOMETHING I WANT. THE ALEXAN-
DRIA LINK. YOU HID IT AND YOU'RE THE ONLY
PERSON ON EARTH WHO KNOWS WHERE TO
FIND IT. GO GET IT. YOU HAVE 72 HOURS. WHEN

YOU HAVE IT, HIT THE NUMBER 2 BUTTON ON
THE PHONE. IF I DON'T HEAR FROM YOU AT THE
END OF 72 HOURS, YOU WILL BE CHILDLESS. IF
DURING THAT TIME YOU SCREW WITH ME, YOUR
SON WILL LOSE A VITAL APPENDAGE. 72 HOURS.
FIND IT AND WE'LL TRADE.

Pam was standing behind him. "What's the Alexandria
Link?"

He said nothing. He couldn't. He was indeed the only person on earth who knew, and he'd given his word.

"Whoever sent that message knows all about it. What is it?"

He stared at the screen and knew there'd be no way to trace
the message. The sender, like himself, surely knew how to
use black holes—computer servers that randomly routed
e-mails through an electronic maze. Not impossible to follow, but difficult.

He stood from the chair and ran a hand through his hair.
He'd meant to get a haircut yesterday. He worked the sleep
from his shoulders and sucked a few deep breaths. He'd earlier slipped on a pair of jeans and a long-sleeved shirt that
hung open, exposing a gray undershirt, and he was suddenly
chilled by fear.

"Dammit, Cotton—"

"Pam, shut up. I have to think. You're not helping."

"I'm not helping? What the—"

The cell phone rang. Pam lunged for it, but he cut her off
and said, "Leave it."

"What do you mean? It could be Gary."

"Get real."

He scooped up the phone after the third ring and pushed
TALK.

"Took long enough," the male voice said in his ear. He
caught a Dutch accent. "And please, no *if-you-hurt-that-boy-*

I'm-going-to-kill-you bravado. Neither one of us has the time. Your seventy-two hours have already started."

Malone stayed silent, but he recalled something he learned long ago. Never let the other side set the bargain. "Stick it up your ass. I'm not going anywhere."

"You take a lot of risks with your son's life."

"I see Gary. I talk to him. Then, I go."

"Take a look outside."

He rushed to the window. Four stories down, Højbro Plads was still quiet, except for two figures standing on the far side of the cobbled expanse.

Both silhouettes shouldered weapons.

Grenade launchers.

"Don't think so," the voice said in his ear.

Two projectiles shot through the night and obliterated the windows below him.

Both exploded.

2

VIENNA, AUSTRIA
2:12 AM

THE OCCUPANT OF THE BLUE CHAIR WATCHED AS ONE CAR deposited two occupants under a lighted porte cochere. Not a limousine or anything overtly pretentious, just a European sedan of muted color, a common sight on busy Austrian roads.

The perfect means of transportation to avoid attention from terrorists, criminals, police, and inquisitive reporters. One more car arrived and deposited its passengers, then headed off to wait among the dark trees in a paved lot. Two more appeared a few minutes later. The Blue Chair, satisfied, left his second-floor bedchamber and descended to ground level.

The meeting convened in the usual place.

Five gilded, straight-backed armchairs rested atop a Hungarian carpet in a wide circle. The chairs were identical except for one, which sported a royal blue scarf across its cushioned back. Next to each chair stood a gilded table that supported a bronze lamp, a writing pad, and a crystal bell. To the left of the circle a fire bristled inside a stone hearth, its light dancing nervously across the ceiling murals.

A man occupied each chair.

They were designated in descending order of seniority. Two of the men still possessed their hair and health. Three were balding and frail. All were at least seventy years old and dressed in sedate suits, their dark chesterfields and gray homburgs hanging on brass racks off to one side. Behind each stood another man, younger—the Chair's successor, present to listen and learn but not to be heard. The rules were longstanding. Five Chairs, four Shadows. The Blue Chair was in charge.

"I apologize for the late hour, but some disturbing information arrived a few hours ago." The Blue Chair's voice was strained and wispy. "Our latest venture may be in jeopardy."

"Exposure?" Chair Two asked.

"Perhaps."

Chair Three sighed. "Can the problem be solved?"

"I think so. But prompt action is needed."

"I cautioned we should not interfere in this," Chair Two sternly reminded, shaking his head. "Things should have been allowed to run their natural course."

Chair Three agreed, as he had at the previous meeting. "Perhaps this is a signal that we should leave well enough alone. A lot can be said for the natural order of things."

The Blue Chair shook his head. "Our last vote was contrary to such a course. The decision has been made, so we must adhere to it." He paused. "The situation requires attention."

"Completion would involve tact and skill," Chair Three said. "Undue attention would defeat the purpose. If we intend to press forward, then I recommend we grant *die Klauen der Adler* full authority to act."

The Talons of the Eagle.

Two others nodded.

"I've already done that," the Blue Chair said. "I called this gathering because my earlier, unilateral action required ratification."

A motion was made, hands raised.

Four to one, the matter was approved.

The Blue Chair was pleased.

3

COPENHAGEN

MALONE'S BUILDING SHOOK LIKE AN EARTHQUAKE AND swelled with a rush of heat that soared up through the stairwell. He dove for Pam and together they slammed into a threadbare rug that covered the plank floor. He shielded her as another explosion rocked the foundation and more flames surged their way.

He gazed out the doorway.

Fires raged below.

Smoke billowed upward in an ever-darkening cloud.

He came to his feet and darted to the window. The two men were gone. Flames licked the night. He realized what had happened. They'd torched the lower floors. The idea wasn't to kill them.

"What's happening?" Pam screamed.

He ignored her and raised the window. Smoke was rapidly conquering the air inside.

"Come on," he said, and he hustled into the bedroom.

He reached beneath the bed and yanked out the rucksack he always kept ready, even in retirement, just as he'd done for twelve years as a Magellan Billet agent. Inside was his passport, a thousand euros, spare identification, a change of clothes, and his Beretta with ammunition. His influential friend Henrik Thorvaldsen had only recently re-obtained the gun from the Danish police—confiscated when Malone had become involved with the Knights Templar a few months back.

He shouldered the bag and slipped his feet into a pair of running shoes. No time to tie the laces. Smoke consumed the bedroom. He opened both windows, which helped.

"Stay here," he said.

He held his breath and trotted through the den to the stairwell. Four stories opened up below. The ground floor housed his bookshop, the second and third floors were for storage, the fourth held his apartment. The first and third floors were ablaze. Heat scorched his face and forced him to retreat. Incendiary grenades. Had to be.

He rushed back to the bedroom.

"No way out from the stairs. They made sure of that."

Pam was huddled next to the window gulping air and coughing. He brushed past her and poked his head out. His bedroom sat in a corner. The building next door, which housed a jeweler and a clothing store, was a story lower, the roof flat and lined with brick parapets that, he'd been told, dated from the seventeenth century. He glanced up. Above the window ran an oversized cornice that jutted outward and wrapped the front and side of his building.

Someone would surely have called the fire and rescue squads, but he wasn't going to wait around for a ladder.

Pam started coughing harder, and he was having trouble breathing himself. He turned her head. "Look up there," he said, pointing at the cornice. "Grab hold and move yourself to the side of the building. You can drop from there onto the roof next door."

Her eyes went wide. "Are you nuts? We're four floors up."

"Pam, this building could blow. There are natural gas lines. Those grenades were designed to start a fire. They didn't shoot one into this floor because they want us to get out."

She didn't seem to register what he was saying.

"We have to leave before the police and fire rescue get here."

"They can help."

"You want to spend the next eight hours answering questions? We only have seventy-two."

She seemed to instantly comprehend his logic and stared up at the cornice. "I can't, Cotton." For the first time her voice carried no edge.

"Gary needs us. We have to go. Watch me, then do exactly as I do."

He shouldered the rucksack and wiggled himself out the window. He gripped the cornice, the coarse stone warm but thin enough that his fingers acquired a solid hold. He dangled by his arms and worked his way, hand over hand, toward the corner. A few more feet, around the corner, and he dropped to the flat roof next door.

He hustled back to the front of the building and peered upward. Pam was still in the window. "Come on, do it. Just like I did."

She hesitated.

An explosion ripped through the third floor. Glass from the windows showered Højbro Plads. Flames raked the darkness. Pam recoiled back inside. A mistake. A second later her head emerged and she hacked out violent coughs.

"You have to come now," he yelled.

She finally seemed to accept that there was no choice. As he'd done, she curled herself out the window and grabbed the cornice. Then she leveraged her body out and hung from her arms.

He saw that her eyes were closed. "You don't have to look. Just move your hands, one at a time."

She did.

Eight feet of cornice stretched between where he stood and where she was struggling. But she was doing okay. One hand over the other. Then he saw figures below. In the square. The two men were back, this time with rifles.

He whipped the rucksack around and plunged a hand inside, finding his Beretta.

He fired twice at the figures fifty feet below. The retorts banged off the buildings lining the square in sharp echoes.

"Why are you shooting?" Pam asked.

"Keep coming."

Another shot and the men below scattered.

Pam found the corner. He gave her a quick glance. "Move around and pull yourself my way."

He searched the darkness but did not see the gunmen. Pam was maneuvering, one hand clamped onto the cornice, the other groping for a hold.

Then she lost her grip.

And fell.

He reached out, gun still in his hand, and managed to catch her. But they both crumpled to the roof. She was breathing hard. So was he.

The cell phone rang.

He crawled for the rucksack, found the phone, and flipped it open.

"Enjoy yourself?" the same voice from before asked.

"Any reason you had to blow up my shop?"

"You're the one who said he wasn't leaving."

"I want to talk to Gary."

"I make the rules. You've already used up thirty-six minutes of your seventy-two hours. I'd get moving. Your son's life depends on it."

The line went silent.

Sirens were approaching. He grabbed the rucksack and sprang to his feet. "We have to go."

"Who was that?"

"Our problem."

"Who was that?"

A sudden fury enveloped him. "I have no idea."

"What is it he wants?"

"Something I can't give him."

"What do you mean you *can't*? Gary's life depends on it. Look around. He blew up your store."

"Gee, Pam, I wouldn't have known that if you hadn't pointed it out."

He turned to leave.

She grabbed him. "Where are we going?"

"To get answers."

4

DOMINICK SABRE STOOD AT THE EAST END OF HØJBRO PLADS and watched Cotton Malone's bookshop burn. Fluorescent yellow fire trucks were already positioned, and water was being spewed into the flame-filled windows.

So far, so good. Malone was on the move. Order from chaos. His motto. His life.

"They've come down from the building next door," the voice said through his radio earpiece.

"Where did they go?" he whispered into the lapel mike.

"To Malone's car."

Right on target.

Firefighters scampered across the square, dragging more hoses, seemingly intent on making sure the flames did not spread. The fire seemed to be enjoying itself. Rare books apparently burned with enthusiasm. Malone's building would soon be ash.

"Is everything else in place?" he asked the man standing beside him, one of the two Dutchmen he'd hired.

"I checked myself. Ready to go."

A lot of planning had gone into what was about to occur. He wasn't sure success was even possible—the goal was intangible, elusive—but if the trail he was following led somewhere, he would be prepared.

Everything, though, hinged on Malone.

His given name was Harold Earl, and nowhere in any of the background material was there an explanation of where the nickname *Cotton* had originated. Malone was forty-eight, older than Sabre by eleven years. Like him, though, Malone was American, born in Georgia. His mother a native southerner, his father a career military man, a navy commander whose submarine had sunk when Malone was ten years old. Interestingly, Malone had followed in his father's footsteps, attending the Naval Academy and flight school, then abruptly changed direction, eventually earning a government-paid law degree. He was transferred to the Judge Advocate General's corps, where he spent nine years. Thirteen years ago he'd changed direction again and moved to the Justice Department and the newly formed Magellan Billet, which handled some of America's most sensitive international investigations.

There he remained until last year, retiring early as a full commander, leaving America, moving to Copenhagen, and buying a rare-book shop.

A midlife crisis? Trouble with the government?

Sabre wasn't sure.

Then there was the divorce. That, he'd studied. Who knew? Malone seemed a puzzle. Though a confirmed bibliophile, nothing in the psychological profiles Sabre had read satisfactorily explained all the radical shifts.

Other tidbits only confirmed his opponent's competence.

Reasonably fluent in several languages, possessed of no known addictions or phobias, and prone to self-motivation and obsessive dedication, Malone was also blessed with an eidetic memory, which Sabre envied.

Competent, experienced, intelligent. Far different from the fools he'd hired—four Dutchmen with few brains, no morals, and little discipline.

He stayed in the shadows as Højbro Plads crowded with people watching the firefighters go about their job. The night air nipped his face. Fall in Denmark seemed only a quick prelude to winter, and he slipped balled fists inside his jacket pockets.

Torching everything Cotton Malone had worked the past year to achieve had been necessary. Nothing personal. Just business. And if Malone did not deliver exactly what he wanted, he would kill the boy with no hesitation.

The Dutchman beside him—who'd placed the calls to Malone coughed but continued to stand in silence. One of Sabre's unbending rules had been made clear from the start. *Speak only when addressed.* He hadn't the time or desire for chitchat.

He watched the spectacle for another few minutes. Finally he whispered into the lapel mike, "Everyone stay sharp. We know where they're headed, and you know what to do."

5

4:00 AM

MALONE PARKED HIS CAR IN FRONT OF CHRISTIANGADE, HEN-
rik Thorvaldsen's mansion that rose on the Danish Zealand
east coast adjacent to the Øresund sea. He'd driven the
twenty miles north from Copenhagen in the late-model
Mazda he kept parked a few blocks from his bookshop, near
the Christianburg Slot.

After finding their way down from the roof, he'd watched
as firefighters tried to contain the blaze roaring through his
building. He'd realized that his books were gone, and if the
flames didn't devour every last one, heat and smoke would
do irreparable damage. Watching the scene, he'd fought a
rising anger, trying to practice what he'd learned long ago.
Never hate your enemy. That clouded judgment. No. He
didn't need to hate. He needed to think.

But Pam was making that difficult.

"Who lives here?" she asked.

"A friend."

She'd tried to pry information from him on the drive, but
he'd offered little, which only seemed to fuel her rage. Before he dealt with her, he needed to communicate with someone else.

The dark house was a genuine specimen of Danish

baroque—three stories, built of sandstone-encased brick, and topped with a gracefully curving copper roof. One wing turned inland, the other faced the sea. Three hundred years ago a Thorvaldsen had erected it, after profitably converting tons of worthless peat into fuel to produce glass. More Thorvaldsens lovingly maintained it over the centuries and eventually transformed Adelgade Glasvaerker, with its distinctive symbol of two circles with a line beneath, into Denmark's premier glassmaker. The modern conglomerate was headed by the current family patriarch, Henrik Thorvaldsen, the man responsible for Malone now living in Denmark.

He strode to the stout front door. A medley of bells reminiscent of a Copenhagen church at high noon announced his presence. He pressed the button again, then pounded. A light flashed on in one of the upper windows. Then another. A few moments later he heard locks release, and the door opened. Though the man staring out at him had certainly been asleep, his copper-colored hair was combed, his face a mask of polished control, his cotton robe wrinkle-free.

Jesper. Thorvaldsen's head of household.

"Wake him up," Malone said in Danish.

"And the purpose of such a radical act at four in the morning?"

"Look at me." He was covered in sweat, grime, and soot. "Important enough?"

"I'm inclined to think so."

"We'll wait in the study. I need his computer."

Malone first found his Danish e-mail account to see if any more messages had been sent, but there was nothing. He'd then accessed the Magellan Billet secured server, using the password that his former boss, Stephanie Nelle, had given him. Though he was retired and no longer on the Justice Department payroll, in return for what he'd done for Stephanie recently in France she'd provided him a direct line of communication. With the time difference—it was still only ten o'clock Monday evening in Atlanta—he knew his message would be routed directly to her.

He glanced up from the computer as Thorvaldsen shuffled into the room. The older Dane had apparently taken the time to dress. His short, stooped frame, the product of a spine that long ago refused to straighten, was concealed by the folds of an oversized sweater the color of a pumpkin. His bushy silver hair lay matted to one side, his eyebrows thick and untamed. Deep lines bracketed the mouth and forehead, and his sallow skin suggested an avoidance of the sun—which Malone knew was the case, as the Dane rarely ventured out. On a continent where old money meant billions, Thorvaldsen was at the top of every wealthiest-people list.

"What's happening?" Thorvaldsen asked.

"Henrik, this is Pam, my ex-wife."

Thorvaldsen flashed her a smile. "Pleased to meet you."

"We don't have time for this," she said, ignoring their host. "We need to be seeing about Gary."

Thorvaldsen faced him. "You look awful, Cotton, and she looks anxious."

"Anxious?" Pam said. "I just climbed out of a burning building. My son is missing. I'm jet-lagged, and I haven't eaten in two days."

"I'll have some food prepared." Thorvaldsen's voice stayed flat, as if this kind of thing happened every night.

"I don't want food. I want to see about my son."

Malone told Thorvaldsen what happened in Copenhagen, then said, "I'm afraid the building's gone."

"Which is the least of our worries."

He caught the choice of words and nearly smiled. He liked that about Thorvaldsen. On your side, no matter what.

Pam was pacing like a caged lioness. Malone noticed that

she'd lost a few pounds since they'd last spoken. She'd always been slender, with long reddish hair, and time had not darkened the pale tone of her freckled skin. Her clothes were as frayed as her nerves, though overall she carried the same good looks from years ago, when he'd married her soon after joining the navy JAG. That was the thing about Pam—great on the outside—the inside was the problem. Even now her blue eyes, burned red from crying, managed to convey an icy fury. She was an intelligent, sophisticated woman, but at the moment she was confused, dazed, angry, and afraid. None of which, by his estimation, was good.

"What are you waiting for?" she spat out.

He glanced at the computer screen. Access into the Billet server had yet to be granted. But since he was no longer active, his request was surely being forwarded directly to Stephanie for approval. He knew that once she saw who was calling she'd immediately log on.

"Is this what you used to do?" she asked. "People trying to set you on fire. Shooting guns. This is what you did? See what it got us? See where we are?"

"Mrs. Malone," Henrik said.

"Don't call me that," she snapped. "I should have changed that last name. Good sense told me to do it in the divorce. But no, I didn't want my name different from Gary's. Can't say a damn thing about his precious father. Not a word. No, Cotton, you're the man. A king in that boy's eyes. Damndest thing I've ever seen."

She wanted a fight, and he half wished he had the time to give her one.

The computer dinged. The screen converted to the Billet's access page.

He typed in the password, and a moment later two-way communication was established. The words KNIGHTS TEM-

PLAR appeared. Stephanie's coded introduction. He typed ABBEY DES FONTAINES, the place where he and Stephanie had, a few months ago, found the modern-day remnants of that medieval order. A few seconds later What is it, Cotton? appeared.

He typed in a summary of what had happened. She answered:

We've had a breach here. Two months ago. The secured files were accessed.

Care to explain that one?

Not at the moment. We wanted it kept secret. I need to check some things. Sit tight and I'll be back to you shortly. Where are you?

At your favorite Dane's house.

Give him my love.

He heard Henrik snicker and knew that, like two divorced parents, Stephanie and Henrik tolerated each other simply for his sake.

"We're just going to sit here and wait?" Pam said. They'd both been reading over Malone's shoulder.

"That's exactly what we're going to do."

She stormed for the door. "You can. I'm going to do something."

"Like what?" he asked.

"I'm going to the police."

She yanked open the door. Jesper stood in the hallway, blocking the way. Pam stared at the chamberlain. "Get out of my way."

Jesper stood firm.

She turned and glared at Henrik. "Tell your manservant to move or I'll move him."

"You're welcome to try," Thorvaldsen said.

Malone was glad Henrik had anticipated her foolishness. "Pam. My guts are ripped up, just like yours. But there's zero the police can do. We're dealing with a pro who's at least two days ahead of us. To do the best thing for Gary, I need information."

"You haven't shed a tear. Not a hint of surprise, nothing from you at all. Like always."

He resented that, particularly coming from a woman who just two months ago calmly informed him that he was not their son's father. He'd come to the conclusion that the revelation meant nothing when it came to how he felt about Gary—the boy was *his* son and would always be *his* son—but the lie made a huge difference in what he thought about his ex-wife. Anger surged up his neck. "You've already messed this up. You should have called me the second it happened. You're so damn smart, you should have found a way to get in touch with me or with Stephanie. She's right there in Atlanta. Instead you gave these guys two days. I don't have the time or the energy to fight you and them. Sit your ass down and shut up."

She stood rock-still with a brooding silence. Finally she surrendered and sank limply onto a leather couch.

Jesper gently closed the door and remained outside.

"Tell me one thing," Pam said, eyes fixed on the floor, her face stiff as marble.

He knew what she wanted to know. "Why can't I give him what he wants? It's not that simple."

"A boy's life is at stake."

"Not a boy, Pam. *Our* son."

She did not reply. Maybe she'd finally realized he was

right. Before acting, they needed information. He was
stalled. Like the day after law school exams, or when he requested a transfer from the navy to the Magellan Billet, or
when he strode into Stephanie Nelle's office and quit.

Waiting, wishing, wanting, all combined with not knowing.

So he, too, wondered what Stephanie was doing.

6

WASHINGTON, DC
MONDAY, OCTOBER 3
10:30 PM

STEPHANIE NELLE WAS GLAD TO BE ALONE. WORRY CLOUDED
her face, and she did not like anyone, particularly superiors,
seeing her concerned. Rarely did she allow herself to be affected by what happened in the field, but the kidnapping of
Gary Malone had hit her hard. She was in the capital on business and had just finished a late dinner meeting with the national security adviser. Changes were being proposed by an
increasingly moderate Congress to several post-9/11 laws.
Support was growing to allow sunset provisions to lapse, so
the administration was gearing up for a fight. Yesterday several high-ranking officials had made the Sunday talk-show
rounds to denounce the critics, and the morning papers had
likewise carried stories fed to them by the administration's

publicity machine. She'd been summoned from Atlanta to help tomorrow with lobbying key senators. Tonight's gathering had been preparation—a way, she knew, for everyone to learn exactly what she intended to say.

She hated politics.

She'd served three presidents during her tenure with Justice. But the current administration had been, without question, the most difficult to placate. Decidedly right of center and drifting farther to that extreme every day, the president had already won his second term, three years left in office, so he was thinking legacy, and what better epitaph than *the man who crushed terrorism*?

All of that meant nothing to her.

Presidents came and went.

And since the particular anti-terrorism provisions in jeopardy had actually proven useful, she'd assured the national security adviser that she'd be a good girl in the morning and say all the right things on Capitol Hill.

But that was before Cotton Malone's son had been taken.

THE PHONE IN THORVALDSEN'S STUDY RANG WITH A SHRILL-ness that rattled Malone's nerves.

Henrik answered the call. "Good to hear from you, Stephanie. And I send my love, too." The Dane smiled at his own facetiousness. "Yes. Cotton's here."

Malone gripped the phone. "Talk to me."

"Around Labor Day we noticed a breach in the system that had occurred much earlier. Someone managed a look-see through the secured files—one in particular."

He knew its identity. "Do you understand that by withholding that information you've put my son at risk?"

The other end of the phone was silent.

"Answer me, dammit."

"I can't, Cotton. And you know why. Just tell me what you're going to do."

He knew what the inquiry really meant. Was he going to give the voice on the cell phone the Alexandria Link? "Why shouldn't I?"

"You're the only one who can answer that question."

"What's worth risking my son's life? I need to understand the whole story. What I wasn't told five years ago."

"I need to know that, too," Stephanie said. "I wasn't briefed, either."

He'd heard that line before. "Don't screw with me. I'm not in the mood."

"On this one I'm shooting straight. They told me nothing. You asked to go in, and I was given the okay to do it. I've contacted the attorney general, so I'll get answers."

"How did anyone even know about the link? That whole thing was classified at levels way above you. That was the deal."

"An excellent question."

"And you still haven't said why you didn't tell me about the breach."

"No, Cotton. I haven't."

"The thought that I was the only person on earth who knows about that link didn't occur to you? You couldn't connect the dots?"

"How could I have anticipated all this?"

"Because you have twenty years of experience. Because you're not a dumb-ass. Because we're friends. Because—" His worry was spilling out in a stream. "Your stupidity may cost my son his life."

He saw how his words had jarred Pam, and he hoped she didn't explode.

"I realize that, Cotton."

He wasn't going to cut her any slack. "Gee, I feel better now."

"I'm going to deal with this here. But I can offer you something. I have an agent in Sweden who can be in Denmark by midmorning. He'll tell you everything."

"Where and when."

"He suggested Kronborg Slot. Eleven AM."

He knew the place. Not far away, perched on a spit of bare land overlooking the Øresund. Shakespeare had immortalized the monstrous fortress when he set *Hamlet* there. Now it was the most popular tourist attraction in Scandinavia.

"He suggested the ballroom. I assume you know where all that is?"

"I'll be there."

"Cotton. I'm going to do all I can to help."

"Which is the least you can do, considering."

And he hung up.

7

WASHINGTON, DC
TUESDAY, OCTOBER 4
4:00 AM

STEPHANIE ENTERED THE HOME OF O. BRENT GREEN, THE ATtorney general of the United States. A car had just delivered her to Georgetown. She'd telephoned Green before midnight and asked for the face-to-face, briefly telling him what had happened. He'd wanted a little time to investigate, which she'd had no choice but to accept.

Green waited in his study.

He'd served the president for the entire first term and had been one of only a handful of cabinet members who'd agreed to stay for the second. He was a popular advocate of Christian and conservative causes—a New England bachelor with not a hint of scandal attached to his name, who even at this early hour projected a serious vigor. His hair and goatee were precisely groomed and smoothly combed, his spare frame sheathed in a trademark pin-striped suit. He'd served six terms in Congress and was the governor of Vermont when tapped by the president for the Justice Department. His frank words and direct approach made him popular with both sides of the political aisle, but his distant personality seemed to prevent him from rising any higher nationally than attorney general.

She'd never been inside Green's house and had expected a sullen, unimaginative look, something akin to the man himself. But instead the rooms were warm and homey—lots of sienna, taupe, pale greens, and shades of maroon and orange—a Hemingway effect, as one furniture chain in Atlanta advertised similar ensembles.

"This matter is unusual, even for you, Stephanie," Green said as he greeted her. "Anything further from Malone?"

"He was resting before heading to Kronborg. With the time difference, he should be on his way there now."

He offered her a seat. "This problem seems to be escalating."

"Brent, we've had this talk before. Somebody high on the food chain accessed the secured database. We know files on the Alexandria Link were copied."

"The FBI is investigating."

"That's a joke. The director is so far up the president's ass, there's no danger of anyone at the White House being implicated."

"Colorful, as always, but accurate. Unfortunately it's the only procedure available to us."

"We could look into it."

"That would bring nothing but trouble."

"Which I'm accustomed to."

Green smiled. "That you are." He paused. "I'm wondering, how much do you actually know about that link?"

"When I sent Cotton into the fray five years ago it was with the understanding that I didn't need to know. Not unusual. I deal with a lot of that sort of thing, so I didn't worry about it. But now I need to know."

Green's face cast a measure of concern. "I'm probably about to violate myriad federal laws, but, I agree, it's time you know."

MALONE STARED ACROSS THE ROCKY ELEVATION AT KRONBORG Slot. Once its cannons were aimed at foreign ships that traversed the narrow straits to and from the Baltic, the collected tolls swelling the Danish treasury. Now the creamy beige walls stood somber against a clear azure sky. Not a fortress any longer, merely a Nordic renaissance building alive with octagonal towers, pointed spires, and green copper roofs more reminiscent of Holland than Denmark. Which was understandable, Malone knew, since a sixteenth-century Dutchman had been instrumental in the castle's design. He liked the location. Public locales could be the best spots in which to be invisible. He'd used many during his years with the Billet.

The drive north from Christiangade had taken only fifteen

minutes. Thorvaldsen's estate sat halfway between Copenhagen and Helsingør, the busy port town that stood adjacent to the slot. Malone had visited both Kronborg and Helsingør, wandering the nearby beaches in search of amber—a relaxing way to spend a Sunday afternoon. Today's visit was different. He was on edge. Ready for a fight.

"What are we waiting for?" Pam asked, her face set like a mask.

He'd been forced to bring her. She'd absolutely insisted, threatening to make more trouble if he left her behind. He could certainly understand her unwillingness to simply wait with Thorvaldsen. Tension and monotony made for a volatile mixture.

"Our man said eleven," he noted.

"We've wasted enough time."

"Nothing we've done has been a waste of time."

After hanging up with Stephanie, he'd managed a few hours' sleep. He would do Gary no good half awake. He'd also changed clothes with the spares from his rucksack, Pam's cleaned by Jesper. They'd eaten a little breakfast.

So he was ready.

He checked his watch: 10:20 AM.

Cars were starting to fill the parking lots. Soon buses would arrive. Everyone wanted to see Hamlet's castle.

He couldn't have cared less.

"Let's go."

"THE LINK IS A PERSON," GREEN SAID. "HIS NAME IS GEORGE Haddad. A Palestinian biblical scholar."

Stephanie knew the name. Haddad was personally acquainted with Malone and, five years ago, had specifically asked for Malone's assistance.

"What's worth the life of Gary Malone?"

"The lost Library of Alexandria."

"You can't be serious."

Green nodded. "Haddad thought he'd located it."

"How could that have any relevance today?"

"Actually, it could be quite relevant. That library was the greatest concentration of knowledge on the planet. It stood for six hundred years until the middle of the seventh century, when the Muslims finally took control of Alexandria and purged everything contrary to Islam. Half a million scrolls, codices, maps—you name it, the library stored a copy. And to this day? No one has ever found a single shred of it."

"But Haddad did?"

"So he implied. He was working on a biblical theory. What that was, I don't know, but the proof of his theory was supposedly contained within the lost library."

"How would he know that?"

"Again, I don't know, Stephanie. But five years ago, when our people in the West Bank, the Sinai, and Jerusalem made some innocent requests for visas, access to archives, archaeological digging, the Israelis went berserk. That's when Haddad asked Malone to help."

"On a blind mission, which I didn't like."

Blind meaning that Malone was told to protect Haddad, but not to ask any questions. She recalled that Malone hadn't liked the condition, either.

"Haddad," Green said, "only trusted Malone. Which was why Cotton eventually hid him away and is the only one today who knows Haddad's whereabouts. Apparently the administration didn't seem to mind hiding Haddad, so long as they controlled the route to him."

"For what?"

Green shook his head. "Makes little sense. There's a hint, though, as to what might be at stake."

She was listening.

"In one of the reports I saw, written in the margin was Genesis 13:14-17. You know it?"

"I'm not that good with my Bible."

"The Lord said to Abram, lift up now your eyes and look from the place where you are northward and southward and eastward and westward, for all the land which you see, to you I will give it, and to your seed forever."

That she knew. A covenant that, for eons, had been the Jews' biblical claim to the Holy Land.

"Abram removed his tent and lived on the plain of Mamre and built there an altar to the Lord," Green said. "Mamre is Hebron—today the West Bank—the land God gave to the Jews. Abram became Abraham. And that single biblical passage goes to the core of all Mideast disagreements."

That she knew, too. The conflict in the Middle East, between Jews and Arabs, was not a political battle, as many perceived. Instead it was a never-ending contest over the Word of God.

"And there's one other interesting fact," Green said. "Shortly after Malone hid Haddad away, the Saudis sent bulldozers into west Arabia and obliterated whole towns. The destruction went on for three weeks. People were relocated. Buildings leveled. Not a remnant remained of those towns. Of course that's a closed part of the country, so there was no press coverage, no attention drawn to it."

"Why would they do that? Seems extreme, even for the Saudis."

"No one ever came up with a good explanation. But they went about it quite deliberately."

"We need to know more, Brent. Cotton needs to know. He has a decision to make."

"I checked with the national security adviser an hour ago.

Amazingly, he knows less about this than I do. He's heard of the link but suggested I talk with someone else."

She knew. "Larry Daley."

Lawrence Daley served as the deputy national security adviser, close to the president and vice president. Daley never appeared on the Sunday-morning talk-show circuit. Nor was he seen on CNN or Fox News. He was a behind-the-scenes power broker. A conduit between the upper echelons of the White House and the rest of the political world.

But there was a problem.

"I don't trust that man," she said.

Green seemed to catch what else her tone suggested but said nothing, staring at her with penetrating gray eyes.

"We have no control over Malone," she made clear. "He's going to do what he has to. And right now he's running on anger."

"Cotton's a pro."

"It's different when it's one of your own at risk." She spoke from experience, having recently wrestled with ghosts of her own past.

"He's the only one who knows where George Haddad is," Green said. "He holds all the cards."

"Which is precisely why they're squeezing him."

Green kept his gaze locked on her.

She knew her quandary was certainly being transmitted through suspicion she could not remove from her eyes.

"Tell me, Stephanie, why don't you trust me?"

8

OXFORDSHIRE, ENGLAND
9:00 AM

GEORGE HADDAD STOOD WITH THE CROWD AND LISTENED TO
the experts, knowing they were wrong. The event was nothing more than a way to garner media attention for both the
Thomas Bainbridge Museum and the little-praised cryptanalysts of Bletchley Park. True, those anonymous men and
women had labored in total secrecy during the Second World
War, eventually deciphering the German Enigma code and
hastening an end to the war. But unfortunately their story
wasn't fully told until most of them were either dead or too
old to care. Haddad could understand their frustration. He,
too, was old, nearing eighty, and an academician. He, too,
once labored in secrecy.

He, too, had discovered a great revelation.

He wasn't even known any longer as George Haddad. In
fact, he'd used too many aliases to remember them all. Five
years he'd been gone to ground and not a word from anyone.
In one respect, that was good. In another, the silence racked
his nerves. Thank God only one man knew he was alive, and
he trusted that person implicitly.

In fact, he'd be dead but for him.

Coming out today was taking a chance. But he wanted to

hear what these so-called experts had to say. He'd read about the program in *The Times* and had to admire the British. They had a flair for media events—the scene set with the precision of a Hollywood movie. Lots of smiling faces and suits, plenty of cameras and recorders. So he made a point of staying behind their lenses. Which was easy since the focus of everyone's attention was the monument.

Eight stood scattered across the estate gardens, all erected in 1784 by the then earl, Thomas Bainbridge. Haddad knew the family history. The Bainbridges first bought the property, hidden in a fold of Oxfordshire and surrounded by beech woods, in 1624, erecting an enormous Jacobean mansion in the center of six hundred acres. More Bainbridges managed to retain ownership until 1848, when the Crown acquired the title through a tax sale and Queen Victoria opened the house and grounds as a museum. Ever since, visitors came to see the period furniture and sneak a glimpse of what it was like to live in luxury centuries ago. Its library had come to be regarded as one of the best anywhere on eighteenth-century furnishings. But in recent years most visited for the monument, since Bainbridge Hall possessed a puzzle, and twenty-first-century tourists loved secrets.

He stared at the white marble arbor.

The top, he knew, was *Les Bergers d'Arcadie II, The Shepherds of Arcadia II,* an unimportant work painted by Nicolas Poussin in 1640, the reverse image of his previous work *The Shepherds of Arcadia.* The pastoral scene depicted a woman watching as three shepherds gathered around a stone tomb, pointing at engraved letters. *ET IN ARCADIA EGO.* Haddad knew the translation. And in Arcadia I. An enigmatic inscription that made little sense. Beneath that image loomed another challenge. Random letters chiseled in a pattern.

D   O.V.O.S.V.A.V.V.   M

Haddad knew that New Agers and conspiratorialists had labored over that combination for years, ever since they'd been rediscovered a decade before by a *Guardian* reporter visiting the museum.

"To all of you here today," a tall and portly man was saying into microphones, "we here at Bainbridge Hall welcome you. Perhaps now we will know the significance of whatever message Thomas Bainbridge left behind in this monument more than two hundred years ago."

Haddad knew the speaker to be the museum's curator. Two people flanked the administrator—a man and a woman, both elderly. He'd seen their pictures in *The Sunday Times*. Both were former Bletchley Park cryptanalysts, commissioned to weigh the possibilities and decipher whatever code the monument supposedly contained. And the general consensus seemed to be that the monument was a code.

What else could it be? many had asked.

He listened as the curator explained how an announcement had been published concerning the monument, and 130 solutions had been offered by a variety of cryptographers, theologians, linguists, and historians.

"Some were quite bizarre," the curator said, "involving UFOs, the Holy Grail, and Nostradamus. Of course, these particular solutions came with little or no supporting evidence, so they were quickly discounted. A few of the entrants thought the letters an anagram, but the words they assembled made little sense."

Which Haddad could well understand.

"One promising solution came from a former American military code breaker. He drew up eighty-two decryption matrices and ultimately extracted the letters *SEJ* from the sequencing. Reversed, this is *JES*. Applying a complex flag grid, he extracted *Jesus H defy*. Our Bletchley Park consultants thought this a message that denied the divine nature of

Christ. This solution is a reach, to say the least, but intriguing."

Haddad smiled at such nonsense. Thomas Bainbridge had been a devoutly religious man. He would not have denied Christ.

The elderly lady beside the curator stepped to the podium. She was silver-haired and wore a powder blue suit.

"This monument presented a great opportunity for us," she said in a melodious tone. "When I and others worked at Bletchley, we faced many challenges from the German codes. They were difficult. But if the human mind can conceive a code, it can also decipher it. The letters here are more complex. Personal. Which makes their interpretation difficult. Those of us retained to study all one hundred thirty possible solutions to this puzzle could not come to a clear consensus. Like the public, we were divided. But one possible meaning did make sense." She turned and motioned to the monument behind her. "I think this is a love note."

She paused, seemingly allowing her words to take hold.

"OVOSVAVV stands for *'Optimae Uxoris Optimae Sororis Viduus Amantissimus Vovit Virtutibus.'* Roughly, this means, 'a devoted widower dedicated to the best of wives and the best of sisters.' This is not a perfect translation. *Sororis* in classical Latin can mean 'of companions' as well as 'of sisters.' And *vir,* husband, would be better than *viduus,* widower. But the meaning is clear."

One of the reporters asked about the D and M that bookended the main clump of eight letters.

"Quite simple," she said. "*Dis Manibus.* A Roman inscription. 'To the gods of the Underworld, hail.' It's akin to our *Rest in Peace.* You'll find those letters on most Roman tombstones."

She seemed quite pleased with herself. Haddad wanted to pose a few pertinent inquiries that would burst her intellectual bubble, but he said nothing. He simply watched as the two Bletchley Park veterans were photographed before the monument with one of the German Enigma machines, borrowed for the occasion. Lots of smiles, questions, and laudatory comments.

Thomas Bainbridge was indeed a brilliant man. Unfortunately Bainbridge had never been able to communicate his thoughts effectively, so his brilliance languished and ultimately vanished unappreciated. To the eighteenth-century mind, he seemed a fanatic. But to Haddad he seemed a prophet. Bainbridge did know something. And the curious monument standing before him, the reverse image of an obscure painting and an odd assortment of ten letters, had been erected for a reason.

One Haddad knew.

Not a love note, nor a code, nor a message.

Something altogether different.

A map.

9

KRONBORG SLOT
10:20 AM

MALONE PAID THE SIXTY-KRONER ADMISSION FOR HIM AND PAM to enter the castle. They followed a group that had poured off one of three buses.

Inside, a photographic exhibit, which showed glimpses from the many productions of *Hamlet,* greeted them. He thought about the irony of the location. Hamlet had been about a son avenging his father, yet here he was, a father, fighting for his son. His heart ached for Gary. Never had he wanted him placed in jeopardy, and for twelve years, while he'd worked for the Billet, he'd always kept a clear line between work and home. Yet now, a year after he'd voluntarily walked away, his son was being held captive.

"This what you used to do all the time?" Pam asked.

"Part of it."

"How did you live like this? My guts are a wreck. I'm still shaking from last night."

"You get used to it." And he meant it, though he'd long ago tired of lies, half-truths, improbable facts, and traitors.

"You needed this rush, didn't you?"

His body was heavy with fatigue, and he wasn't in the mood for this familiar fight. "No, Pam. I didn't *need* it. But this was my job."

"Selfish. That's what you were. Always."

"And you were just a ray of sunshine. The supportive wife who stood by her husband. So much so that you got pregnant by another man, had a son, and let me think it was mine for fifteen years."

"I'm not proud of what I did. But we don't know how many of *your* women became pregnant, do we?"

He stopped walking. This had to end. "If you don't shut up, you're going to get Gary killed. I'm his only hope and, right now, playing with my head is not productive."

That truth produced a momentary flash of understanding in her bitter eyes, an instant when the Pam Malone he'd once loved reappeared. He wished that woman could linger but, as always, her guard flew up and dead eyes glared back at him.

"Lead the way," she said.

*   *   *

They entered the ballroom.

The rectangular hall stretched two hundred feet. Windows lined both sides, each set deep in alcoves of thick masonry, the oblique light casting a subtle spell across a checkerboard floor. A dozen or so visitors milled about admiring huge oil canvases that dotted the pale yellow walls, mainly battle scenes.

At the far end, before a hearth, Malone spotted a short, thin man with reddish brown hair. He recalled him from the Magellan Billet. Lee Durant. He'd talked with Durant a few times in Atlanta. The agent caught sight of him, then disappeared through a doorway.

He headed across the hall.

They passed through a series of rooms, each sparsely decorated with European Renaissance furniture and wall tapestries. Durant stayed fifty feet ahead.

Malone saw him stop.

He and Pam entered the room identified as the Corner Chamber. Hunting tapestries adorned plain white walls. Only a few pieces of furniture dotted the dull black-and-white tile floor.

Malone shook Durant's hand and introduced Pam. "Tell me what's happening."

"Stephanie said to brief you, not her."

"As much as I'd like for *her* not to be here, she is, so don't sweat it."

Durant seemed to consider the situation, then said, "I was also told to do whatever you ask."

"Glad to hear Stephanie's being so accommodating."

"Get to the point," Pam said. "We're under a deadline."

Malone shook his head. "Ignore her. Tell me what's happening."

"Access was gained to our secured files. No evidence of

hacking or forced entry through the firewalls, so it had to be by password. That's changed at regular intervals, but there are several hundred people with access."

"No traces to a particular computer?"

"Zero. And no fingerprints in the data. Which indicates that whoever did it knew what they were doing."

"I assume somebody is investigating."

Durant nodded. "The FBI, but so far nothing. About a dozen files were viewed, one of which was the Alexandria Link."

Which might, Malone thought, explain why Stephanie had not immediately alerted him. There were other possibilities.

"Here's the interesting part. The Israelis are super-hyper right now, particularly during the last twenty-four hours. Our sources tell us that information was learned yesterday out of the West Bank from one of their Palestinian operatives."

"What does that have to do with this?"

"The words *Alexandria Link* have been mentioned."

"How much do you know?"

"I was just told this an hour ago by one of my contacts. I haven't even fully reported to Stephanie yet."

"How is any of this helping?" Pam asked.

He said to Durant, "I need to know more."

"I asked you a question," Pam said, her voice rising.

His civility ended. "I told you to let me handle this."

"You have no intention of giving anything to them, do you?" Her eyes blazed and she seemed ready to pounce.

"My intention is to get Gary back."

"Are you willing to chance his life? All to protect some damn file?"

A group of camera-clad visitors wandered into the room. He saw that Pam had the wisdom to hush, and he was grateful for the interruption. Definitely a mistake bringing her.

He'd have to ditch her as soon as they left Kronborg, even if it meant locking her in a room at Thorvaldsen's manor.

The visitors wandered off.

He faced Durant and said, "Tell me more about—"

A bang startled him, then the ceiling-mounted camera in the corner exploded in a shower of sparks. Next came two more bangs. Durant lurched backward as blood roses blossomed from punctures in his olive-colored shirt.

A third shot and Durant collapsed to the floor.

Malone whirled.

A man stood twenty feet away, holding a Glock. Malone stuffed his right arm under his jacket to find his own weapon.

"No need," the man calmly said, and he tossed the gun.

Malone caught it. He gripped the pistol's stock, finger on the trigger, aimed, and fired.

Only a click came in response.

His finger worked the trigger.

More clicks.

The man smiled. "You didn't think I'd give it to you loaded."

Then the shooter fled the room.

10

STEPHANIE CONSIDERED BRENT GREEN'S INQUIRY—*WHY don't you trust me?*—and decided to be straight with her boss.

"Everybody in this administration wants me gone. Why I'm still here, I don't know. So I don't trust anybody at the moment."

Green shook his head at her suspicion.

"Those files were accessed by someone with a password," she added. "Sure, they scanned through a dozen or more, but we both know the one they were after. Only a few of us are privy to the Alexandria Link. I don't even know the details— just that we went to a lot of trouble for something that was seemingly meaningless. Lots of questions. No answers. Come on, Brent. You and I haven't actually been asshole buddies, so why should I trust you now?"

"Let's be clear," Green said. "I'm not your enemy. If I were, we wouldn't be having this conversation."

"I've had friends in this business say that to me many times and not mean a word."

"Traitors are like that."

She decided to test him further. "Don't you think we ought to bring more people into the loop?"

"The FBI is already in."

"Brent, we're operating in the dark. We need to know what George Haddad knows."

"Then it's time we deal with Larry Daley at the White House. Any road we take will lead straight to him. Might as well go to the source."

She agreed.

And Green reached for the phone.

MALONE HEARD THE PERSON WHO HAD JUST MURDERED LEE Durant scream that there was a man with a gun who'd shot somebody.

And he was still holding the Glock.

"Is he dead?" Pam muttered.

Stupid question. But standing with the murder weapon in hand was even more stupid. "Come on."

"We can't just leave him."

"He's dead."

Hysteria filled her eyes. He recalled the first time he'd watched someone die, so he cut her some slack. "You shouldn't have seen that. But we have to go."

A warning rush of heels on tile echoed from beyond the room. Security, he assumed. He grabbed Pam's hand and yanked her toward the opposite end of the Corner Chamber.

They scampered through more rooms, each like the next, sparsely furnished with period pieces, illuminated by dim morning light. He noticed more cameras and knew he'd have to eventually avoid them. He stuffed the Glock into his jacket pocket and brought out his Beretta.

They entered a room identified as the Queen's Chamber.

He heard voices from behind. Apparently the body had been found. More shouts and footfalls, coming their way.

The Queen's Chamber was an apartment. Three doorways led out. One to a staircase up, the other down, the remaining portal opening into another room. No security camera in sight. He scanned the décor trying to decide what to do. A large armoire towered against the exterior wall.

He decided to play the odds.

He rushed to the armoire and grabbed the double-door iron handles. Inside was spacious and empty. Plenty big enough for them both. He motioned at Pam. For once she came without comment.

"Get in," he whispered.

Before entering, he cracked open both stairway exits. Then he climbed in and eased the doors shut, hoping their pursuers assumed they went either down, up, or back into the castle.

STEPHANIE LISTENED AS BRENT GREEN BRIEFED LARRY DALEY about what had happened. She couldn't help wondering if the arrogant ass on the other end of the phone already knew every detail, plus more.

"I'm familiar with the Alexandria Link," Daley said through the speaker.

"Care to tell us?" Green asked.

"Wish I could. Classified."

"To the attorney general and the head of one of our most elite intelligence agencies?"

"For a select set of eyes only. Sorry, neither of you qualifies."

"Then how did someone else manage a peek?" Stephanie asked.

"You haven't figured that out yet?"

"Maybe I have."

Silence stung the room. Daley apparently received her message.

"Wasn't me."

"What else would you say?" she asked.

"Watch your mouth."

She ignored the jab. "Malone is going to give them the link. He won't risk his son."

"Then he'll have to be stopped," Daley said. "We're not handing that over to anyone."

She caught his meaning. "You want it for yourself, don't you?"

"Damn right."

She couldn't believe what she was hearing. "A boy's life may be at stake."

"Not my problem," Daley declared.

Calling Daley had been a mistake, and she could see that Green now realized that fact, too.

"Larry," Green said. "Let's help Malone out. Not make his task more difficult."

"Brent, this is a matter of national security, not a charity case."

"Interesting," she said, "how you're not the least bit concerned that someone accessed our secured files and learned all about this highly classified Alexandria Link—a matter of supposed national security."

"You reported that breach more than a month ago. The FBI is handling the situation. What are *you* doing about it, Stephanie?"

"I was told to do nothing. What did you do, Larry?"

A sigh came through the speaker. "You truly are a pain in the ass."

"But she works for me," Green made clear.

"Here's what I think," Stephanie said. "Whatever this link is, it somehow fits with whatever it is you geniuses at the White House have conceived as foreign policy. You actually like the fact the files were compromised and that somebody has this information. Which means you're going to allow them to do your dirty work."

"Sometimes, Stephanie, enemies can be your friend." Daley's voice had fallen to a whisper. "And vice versa."

A knot formed in her throat. Her suspicions were now fact. "You're going to sacrifice Malone's boy for your president's legacy?"

"I didn't start this," Daley replied. "But I intend to use it."

"Not if I can help it," she said.

"Interfere and you'll be fired. Not by you, Brent, but by the president himself."

"That could become a problem," Green said.

She caught the threat in his tone.

"You're saying you'd stand with her?" Daley asked.

"Without question."

She knew that this was a threat Daley could not ignore. The administration possessed a measure of control over Green's actions as attorney general. But if he quit, or was fired, then it would be open season on the White House.

The speakerphone sat silent. She imagined Daley sitting in his office, puzzling over his quandary.

"I'll be at your house in thirty minutes."

"Why do we need to meet?" Green asked.

"I assure you, it'll be worth your while."

The line clicked dead.

MALONE STOOD IN THE ARMOIRE AND LISTENED AS FOOTSTEPS rushed into the Queen's Chamber. Pam was nestled beside him, the closest they'd been to each other in years. A familiar smell rose from her, like sweet vanilla, one he recalled with a mixture of joy and agony. Funny the way smells triggered memory.

He still held the Beretta and hoped he didn't have to use it. But he had no intention of being taken into custody, not when Gary needed him. Surely one reason for killing Durant was to isolate them. Another had been to prevent them from learning any useful information. But he wondered how anyone had known of the meeting. They hadn't been followed from Christiangade, of that he was sure. Which meant Thorvaldsen's phones must have been monitored. Which meant that his going straight to Christiangade had been anticipated.

He couldn't see Pam, but he sensed her discomfort. Considering all the intimacy they'd once shared, now they were simply strangers.

Perhaps even enemies.

Voices outside grabbed his thoughts. Footsteps grew fainter, then became lost in silence. He waited, finger on the trigger, sweat breaking in his palms.

More silence.

No way to see anything without cracking the armoire's doors. Which could prove disastrous if someone remained in the room.

But he couldn't stand here forever.

He eased open the door, gun ready.

The Queen's Chamber was empty.

Down the stairs, he mouthed, and they rushed through the open portal and descended a circular staircase that hugged the castle's outer wall. At ground level they came to a metal door that he hoped wasn't locked.

The latch released.

They stepped out into a bright morning. A sea of shiny grass littered with swans stretched from the castle walls to the sea. Sweden loomed on the horizon, three miles across the gray-brown water.

He stuffed the Beretta beneath his jacket.

"We need to get out of here," he said. "But slowly. Don't draw attention." He could tell she was still rattled from the killing, so he offered, "You'll see it over and over in your brain, but it'll pass."

"Your concern is touching." Her voice was again filled with menace.

"Then chew on this. That's probably not the last person who's going to die before this is over."

He led the way across the ramparts that overlooked the sound. Few visitors milled about. They came to a spot he knew was Flag Battery, where ancient cannons once stood and where Shakespeare had allowed Hamlet to meet his father's ghost. A wall rose from the sea. He lobbed the Glock out into the choppy water.

Sirens wailed from beyond the grounds.

They slowly made their way to the main entrance. Seeing flashing lights and more police rushing onto the grounds, he decided to wait before heading out. Unlikely that anyone would have a description of them, and he doubted that the shooter had stayed around to provide one. The idea was surely not to have them arrested.

So he blended with the crowd.

Then he spotted the shooter.

Fifty yards away, heading straight for the main gate, strolling, not trying to attract attention, either.

Pam saw him, too. "That's the guy."

"I know."

He started forward.

"You're not," she asked.

"Couldn't stop me."

11

THE BLUE CHAIR WONDERED IF THE CIRCLE HAD COMMITTED itself to the proper course. For eight years *die Klauen der Adler,* the Talons of the Eagle, had dutifully carried out his assigned tasks. True, they'd collectively hired him, but on an everyday basis he worked directly under the Blue Chair's control, which meant that he'd come to know Dominick Sabre far better than the rest.

Sabre was an American, born and bred, which was a first for the Circle. Always they'd employed Europeans, though once a South African had served them well. Each of those men, including Sabre, had been chosen not only for his individual ability but also for his physical mediocrity. All had been of average height, weight, and features. The only noticeable trait about Sabre was the pockmarks on his face, left over from a bout with chickenpox. Sabre's black hair was cut straight and always held together with a dash of oil that added gleam. Stubble often dusted his cheeks, partly, the Blue Chair knew, to conceal the scars, but also to disarm those around him.

Sabre maintained a relaxed look, wearing clothes, usually a

size too big, that concealed a lean-limbed muscular frame—surely more of his effort to be constantly underestimated.

From a psychological profile Sabre had to endure prior to being hired, the Blue Chair learned that there was something about defiance of authority that appealed to the American. But that same profile also revealed that, if he was given a task, told the intended result, and left alone, Sabre would always perform.

And that was what mattered.

Both he and the Chairs could not care less how a given task was completed, only that the desired result be obtained. So their association with Sabre had been fruitful. Yet a man with no morals and little respect for authority bore watching.

Especially when the stakes were high.

As now.

So the Blue Chair reached for the phone and dialed.

SABRE ANSWERED HIS CELL PHONE, HOPING THE CALL WAS from his man at Kronborg Slot. Instead the strained voice on the other end belonged to his employer.

"How did Mr. Malone enjoy your initial greeting?" the Blue Chair asked.

"Handled himself well. He and the ex-wife crawled out through the window."

"As you predicted. But I wonder, are we drawing unnecessary attention?"

"More than I'd like, but it was necessary. He tried to call our bluff, so he had to see he's not in charge. But I'll be more discreet from here on out."

"Do that. We don't need law enforcement overly involved." He paused. "At least not any more than they are as of now."

Sabre was ensconced in a rental house on Copenhagen's north side, a few blocks inland from Amalienborg, the seaside royal palace. He'd brought Gary Malone here from Georgia on the pretense that his father was in danger, which the boy had believed thanks to falsified Magellan Billet identification Sabre had showed him.

"How is the lad?" the Blue Chair asked.

"He was anxious, but he thinks this is a U.S. government operation. So he's calm, for now."

They'd terrorized Pam Malone with a photo of her son. The young man had cooperated with that, too, thinking they were producing security credentials.

"Isn't the boy located too close to Malone?"

"He wouldn't have gone voluntarily anywhere else. He knows his father is nearby."

"I realize you have this under control. But do be careful. Malone may surprise you."

"That's why we have his son. He won't jeopardize him."

"We need the Alexandria Link."

"Malone will lead us straight there."

But the call from his man at Kronborg still had not come. For everything to work, it was critical that his operative perform exactly as he'd instructed.

"We also need this resolved in the next few days."

"It will be."

"From what you've told me," the Blue Chair said, "this Malone is a free spirit. You sure he'll stay properly motivated?"

"Not to worry. Right now more than sufficient motivation is being provided."

MALONE EXITED THE GROUNDS OF KRONBORG SLOT AND SPOTted his quarry strolling calmly into Helsingør. He loved the town's market square, quaint alleys, and timber-and-brick buildings. But none of that Renaissance flavor mattered today.

More sirens wailed in the distance.

He knew murders were rare in Denmark. Given that this one occurred inside a National Historic Site, it would surely make for big news. He needed to notify Stephanie that one of her agents was dead, but there was no time. He assumed Durant had been traveling under his own name—that was standard Billet practice—so once the local authorities determined that their victim worked for the American government, the right people would be contacted. He thought about Durant. Damn shame. But he learned long ago not to waste emotion on things he could not change.

He slackened his pace and yanked Pam alongside him. "We need to stay back. He isn't paying attention, but he could still spot us."

They crossed the street and clung to an attractive row of buildings that fronted a narrow walk facing the sea. The shooter was a hundred feet ahead. Malone watched as he turned a corner.

They reached the same corner and peered around. The man was plowing ahead down a pedestrian-only lane lined with shops and restaurants. A clutter of people milled about, so he decided to risk it.

They followed.

"What are we doing?" Pam asked.

"The only thing we can do."

"Why don't you just give them what they want?"

"It's not that simple."

"Sure it is."

He kept his gaze ahead. "Thanks for the advice."

"You're an ass."

"I love you, too. Now that we've established that, let's focus on what we're doing."

Their objective turned right and disappeared.

Malone hustled forward, glanced around the corner, and saw the shooter approach a dirty Volvo coupe. He hoped he wasn't leaving. No way to follow. Their car was a long way off. He watched as the man opened the driver's-side door and tossed something inside. Then he closed the door and started back their way.

They ducked into a clothing shop just as the shooter passed in front, heading back in the direction from which they'd come. Malone crept to the door and watched the man enter a café.

"What's he doing?" Pam asked.

"Waiting for the commotion to die down. Don't force the issue. Just sit tight, blend in. Leave later."

"That's nuts. He killed a man."

"And only we know that."

"Why kill him at all?"

"To rattle our nerves. Silence any information flow. Lots of reasons."

"This is a sick business."

"Why do you think I got out?" He decided to use the interlude to his advantage. "Go get the car and bring it around to over there." He pointed through an alley at the seaside train station. "Park and wait for me. When he leaves, he's going to have to go that way. It's the only route out of town."

He passed her the keys and, for an instant, memories of other times he'd handed her car keys rattled through his brain. He thought of years past. Knowing she and Gary were waiting at home, after an assignment, had always brought him a measure of comfort. And as much as neither of them wanted to admit it, they'd once been good for each other. He remembered her smile, her touch. Unfortunately, her deceit about Gary now colored all that pleasantness with suspicion. Made him wonder. Question whether their life together had all been an illusion.

She seemed to sense his thoughts and her gaze softened, like the Pam before bad things changed them both. So he said, "I'll find Gary. I swear to you. He'll be all right."

He actually wanted her to respond, but she said nothing.

And her silence stung.

So he walked away.

12

OXFORDSHIRE, ENGLAND
10:30 AM

GEORGE HADDAD ENTERED BAINBRIDGE HALL. FOR THE PAST three years he'd been a frequent visitor, ever since he'd convinced himself that the answer to his dilemma lay within these walls.

The house was a masterpiece of marble pavings, Mortlake tapestries, and richly colored decorations. The grand staircase, with elaborately carved floral panels, dated from the time of Charles II. The plaster ceilings from the 1660s. The furnishings and paintings were all eighteenth and nineteenth century. Everything a showpiece of English country style.

But it was also much more.

A puzzle.

Just like the white arbor monument in the garden where members of the press were still gathered, listening to the so-called experts. Just like Thomas Bainbridge himself, the unknown English earl who'd lived in the latter part of the eighteenth century.

Haddad knew the family history.

Bainbridge had been born to the world of privilege and high expectations. His father had served as the squire of Oxfordshire. Though his position in society had been fixed by generational affluence and family tradition, Thomas Bainbridge shunned the traditional military service and turned his attention to academics—mainly history, languages, and archaeology. When his father died, he inherited the earldom and spent decades traveling the world, being one of the first Westerners to intimately explore Egypt, the Holy Land, and Arabia, documenting his experiences in a series of published journals.

He taught himself Old Hebrew, the language in which the Old Testament had originally been written. Quite an accomplishment considering that the dialect was mainly vocal and consonantal, and had disappeared from common usage around the sixth century before Christ. He wrote a book published in 1767 that challenged the known translations of the Old Testament, calling into question much of his age's conventional wisdom, then spent the latter part of his life defending his theories, dying bitter and broken, the family fortune gone.

Haddad knew the text well, having studied every page in detail. He could relate to Bainbridge's troubles. He, too, had challenged conventional wisdom with disastrous consequences.

He enjoyed visiting the house but, sadly, most of the original furnishings had been long ago lost to creditors, including Bainbridge's impressive library. Only in the past fifty years had some of the furniture been found. The vast majority of the books remained missing, drifting from collectors, to vendors, to the trash, which seemed the fate of much of humanity's recorded knowledge. Yet Haddad had been able to locate a few volumes, spending time rummaging through the myriad of rare-book shops that dotted London.

And on the Internet.

What an amazing treasure. What they could have done in Palestine sixty years ago with that instant information network.

Lately he'd thought a lot about 1948.

When he'd toted a rifle and killed Jews during the *nakba*. The arrogance of the current generation always amazed him, considering the sacrifices made by their predecessors. Eight hundred thousand Arabs were driven into exile. He'd been nineteen, fighting in the Palestinian resistance—one of its field leaders—but it had all been fruitless. The Zionists prevailed. The Arabs were defeated. Palestinians became outcasts.

But the memory remained.

Haddad had tried to forget. He truly wanted to forget. Killing, though, came with consequences. And for him it had been a lifetime of regret. He became an academician, abandoned violence, and converted to Christianity, but none of that rid him of the pain. He could still see the dead faces. Especially one. The man who called himself the Guardian.

You fight a war that is not necessary. Against an enemy that is misinformed.

Those words had been burned into his memory that day in April 1948, and their impact eventually changed him forever.

We're keepers of knowledge. From the library.

That observation had charted the course of his life.

He kept strolling through the house, taking in the busts and paintings, the carvings, the grotesque gilding, and the enigmatic mottoes. Walking against a current of new arrivals, he eventually entered the drawing room, where all the antique gravity of a college library blended with a feminine grace and wit. He focused on the shelving, which had once displayed the varied learning of many ages. And the paintings, which recalled people who had privately shaped the course of history.

Thomas Bainbridge had been an invitee, just like Haddad's father. Yet the Guardian had arrived in Palestine two weeks too late to pass on the invitation, and a bullet from Haddad's gun had silenced the messenger.

He winced at the memory.

The impetuousness of youth.

Sixty years had passed, and he now viewed the world through more patient eyes. If only those same eyes had stared back at the Guardian in April 1948, he might have found what he sought sooner.

Or maybe not.

It seemed the invitation must be earned.

But how?

His gaze raked the room.

The answer was here.

13

STEPHANIE WATCHED AS LARRY DALEY COLLAPSED INTO ONE of the club chairs in Brent Green's study. True to his word, the deputy national security adviser had arrived within half an hour.

"Nice place," Daley said to Green.

"It's home."

"You're always a man of few syllables, aren't you?"

"Words, like friends, should be chosen with care."

Daley's amicable smile disappeared. "I was hoping we wouldn't be at each other's throats so soon."

Stephanie was anxious. "Make this visit worth our while, like you said on the phone."

Daley's hands gripped the overstuffed armrests. "I'm hoping you two will be reasonable."

"That all depends," she said.

Daley ran a hand through his short gray hair. His good looks projected a boyish sincerity, one that could easily disarm, so she cautioned herself to stay focused.

"I assume you're still not going to tell us what the link is?" she asked.

"Don't really want to be indicted for violating the National Security Act."

"Since when did breaking laws bother you?"

"Since now."

"So what are you doing here?"

"How much do you know?" Daley asked. "And don't tell me that you don't know anything, because I'd be really disappointed in you both."

Green repeated the little bit he'd already related about George Haddad.

Daley nodded. "The Israelis went nuts over Haddad. Then the Saudis entered the picture. That one shocked us. They usually don't care about anything biblical or historical."

"So I sent Malone into that quagmire five years ago blind?" she asked.

"Which is, I believe, in your job description."

She recalled how the situation had deteriorated. "What about the bombing?"

"That was when the shit hit the fan."

A car bomb had obliterated a Jerusalem café with Haddad and Malone inside.

"That blast was meant for Haddad," Daley said. "Of course, since this was a blind mission, Malone didn't know that. But he did manage to get the man out in one piece."

"Lucky us," Green noted with sarcasm.

"Don't give me that crap. We didn't kill anybody. The last thing we wanted was for Haddad to die."

Her anger was rising. "You placed Malone's life at risk."

"He's a pro. Goes with the territory."

"I don't send my agents on suicide missions."

"Get real, Stephanie. The problem with the Middle East is the left hand never knows what the right is doing. What happened is typical. Palestinian militants just chose the wrong café."

"Or maybe not," Green said. "Perhaps the Israelis or the Saudis chose the right one?"

Daley smiled. "You're getting good at this. That's exactly why we agreed to Haddad's terms."

"So tell us why it's necessary for the American government to find the lost Library of Alexandria?"

Daley applauded softly. "Bravo. Well done, Brent. I figured if your sources knew about Haddad, they'd deliver that tidbit, too."

"Answer his question," Stephanie said.

"Important stuff is sometimes kept in the strangest places."

"That's not an answer."

"It's all you're going to get."

"You're in league with whatever is happening over there," she declared.

"No, I'm not. But I won't deny there are others within the administration who are interested in using this as the quickest route to solving a problem."

"The problem being?" Green asked.

"Israel. Bunch of arrogant idealists who won't listen to a word anybody says. Yet at the drop of a hat they'll send tanks or gunships to annihilate anyone and anything, all in the name of security. What happened a few months ago? They started shelling the Gaza Strip, one of their shells goes astray, and an entire family having a picnic on the beach is killed. What do they say? Sorry. Too bad." Daley shook his head. "Just show a shred of flexibility, an ounce of compromise, and things could be achieved. No. It's their way or no way."

Stephanie knew that, of late, the Arab world had been far more accommodating than Israel—surely a result of Iraq, where American resolve was demonstrated firsthand. Worldwide sympathy for the Palestinians had steadily grown, fed by a change of leadership, a moderation in militant policies, and the foolishness of Israeli hard-liners. She recalled from the news reports the lone survivor of that family on the beach, a young girl, wailing at the sight of her dead father. Powerful. But she wondered what realistically could be done. "How do they plan to do anything about Israel?" Then the answer came to her. "You need the link to do that?"

Daley said nothing.

"Malone is the only one who knows where it is," she made clear.

"A problem. But not insurmountable."

"You wanted Malone to act. You just didn't know how to get him to do it."

"I won't deny that this is something of an opportunity."

"You son of a bitch," she spat out.

"Look, Stephanie. Haddad wanted to disappear. He trusted Malone. The Israelis, the Saudis, and even the Palestinians all thought Haddad died in the blast. So we did what the man wanted, then backed off the whole idea, moved on to other things. But now everyone's interest is piqued again and we want Haddad."

She wasn't going to allow him any satisfaction. "And what about whoever else may be after him?"

"I'll handle them as any politician would."

Green's countenance darkened with anger. "You're going to make a deal?"

"It's the way of the world."

She had to learn more. "What could possibly be found in two-thousand-year-old documents? And that's assuming the manuscripts survived, which is unlikely."

Daley cast her a sideways glance. She realized that he'd come to keep her and Green from interfering—so maybe he'd throw them a bone.

"The Septuagint."

She found it hard to conceal her puzzlement.

"I'm no expert," Daley said, "but from what I've been told, a couple of hundred years before Christ, scholars at the Library of Alexandria translated the Hebrew Scriptures, our Old Testament, into Greek. A big deal for the day. That translation is all we know of the original Hebrew text, since it's gone. Haddad claimed that the translation, and all the others that followed, were fundamentally flawed. He said the errors changed everything, and he could prove it."

"So what?" she asked. "How would that change anything?"

"That, I can't say."

"Can't or won't?"

"In this instance, they're the same thing."

"He has remembered His covenant forever," Green whispered, *"the word which He commanded to a thousand generations, the covenant which He made with Abraham, and His oath to Isaac. Then He confirmed it to Jacob for a statute, to Israel as an everlasting covenant, saying, 'To you I will give the land of Canaan as the portion of your inheritance.' "*

She saw that the words genuinely moved the man.

"An important promise," Green said. "One of many in the Old Testament."

"So you see our interest?"

Green nodded. "I see the point, but I question its ability to be proven."

She didn't grasp that, either, but wanted to know, "What are you doing, Larry? Chasing phantoms? This is crazy."

"I assure you, it's not."

The implications quickly became real. Malone had been right to chastise her. She should have immediately told him about the breach. And now his son was in jeopardy, thanks to the U.S. government, which apparently was willing to sacrifice the boy.

"Stephanie," Daley said, "I know that look. What are you planning?"

No way she was telling this demon anything. So she drank the dregs of humiliation, smiled, and said, "Precisely what you want, Larry. Absolutely nothing."

14

COPENHAGEN
12:15 PM

DOMINICK SABRE KNEW THAT THE NEXT HOUR WOULD BE CRITI- cal. He'd already watched on the Copenhagen television sta- tions as the shooting at Kronborg Slot was reported. Which meant Malone and his ex-wife were now on the move. He'd finally heard from the man he'd dispatched to the castle and was glad he'd followed orders.

He checked his watch, then stepped from the front parlor to the back bedroom where Gary Malone was being held. They'd managed to take the boy at school, using official cre- dentials and tough talk, all supposedly in the name of the U.S. government. Within two hours they'd left Atlanta on a charter flight. Pam Malone was approached while they were en route and told precisely what to do. All reports painted her as a difficult woman, but a photo and thoughts of harm com- ing to her son had ensured that she'd do exactly what they wanted.

He opened the bedroom door and crafted a smile on his face. "Wanted to let you know that we heard from your dad."

The boy was perched by the window reading a book. Yesterday he'd asked for several volumes, which Sabre had obtained. The young face brightened at the news about his father. "He okay?"

"Doing fine. And he was grateful we had you with us. Your mom is with him, too."

"Mom is here?"

"Another team brought her over."

"That's a first. She's never been here." The boy paused. "Her and my dad don't get along."

Knowing about Malone's marital history, he sensed something. "Why's that?"

"Divorce. They haven't lived together in a long time."

"That hard on you?"

Gary seemed to consider the inquiry. He was tall for his age, lanky, with a head of auburn hair. Cotton Malone was a study in contrast. Fair-skinned, thick-limbed, light-haired. Try as he might, Sabre could find nothing of the father in the boy's face or countenance.

"It'd be better if they were together. But I understand why they're not."

"Good you understand. You have a level head."

Gary smiled. "That's what my dad always says. You know him?"

"Oh, yes. We've worked together for years."

"What's happening here? Why am I in danger?"

"I can't talk about it. But some really bad guys have targeted your dad and they were going to come after you and your mom, so we stepped in to protect you." He could see that the explanation didn't seem to totally satisfy.

"But my dad doesn't work for the government anymore."

"Unfortunately his enemies don't care about that. They just want to cause him pain."

"This is all really weird."

He forced a smile. "Part of the business, I'm afraid."

"You have any kids?"

He wondered about the boy's interest. "No. Never been married."

"You seem like a nice man."

"Thanks. Just doing my job." He motioned and said, "You work out?"

"I play baseball. Season's been over awhile, though. But I wouldn't mind throwing a few."

"Hard to do in Denmark. Baseball is not the national pastime here."

"I've visited the past two summers. I really like it."

"That the time you spend with your dad?"

Gary nodded. "About the only chance we get together. But that's okay. I'm glad he lives here. It makes him happy."

He thought he again sensed something. "Does it make you happy?"

"Sometimes. Other times I wish he was closer."

"You ever thought about living with him?"

The boy's face scrunched with concern. "That would kill my mom. She wouldn't want me to do that."

"Sometimes you have to do what you have to do."

"I've thought about it."

He grinned. "Don't think too hard. And try not to be bored."

"I miss my mom and dad. I hope they're all right."

He'd heard enough. The boy was pacified. He wouldn't be a problem, at least not for the next hour, which was all Sabre would need.

After that, it wouldn't matter what Gary Malone did.

So he stepped toward the door and said, "Not to worry. I'm sure this is all going to be over soon."

MALONE STOOD ON THE STREETS OF HELSINGØR AND WATCHED the café. A steady stream of patrons had flowed in and out. His target was sitting at a window table, sipping from a mug. Pam, he assumed, was with the car, parked at the train station, waiting. She'd better be. When this guy made his move, they'd only have one chance. If his adversaries were somewhere nearby, and he firmly believed that to be the case, this might be his only route to them.

Pam's appearance in Denmark had rattled him. But then she'd always had that effect. Once, love and respect bound them, or at least he'd thought that the case; now only Gary drew them together.

His mind replayed what she'd said to him in August. About Gary.

> *"After years of lying to me, you want to be fair?"*
> *"You were no saint yourself years ago, Cotton."*
> *"And you made my life a living hell because of it."*
> She shrugged. *"I had an indiscretion of my own. I didn't think you'd mind, considering."*
> *"I told you everything."*
> *"No, Cotton. I caught you."*
> *"But you let me think Gary was mine."*
> *"He is. In every way except blood."*
> *"That the way you rationalize it?"*
> *"I don't have to. I just thought you should know the truth. I should have told you last year when we divorced."*
> *"How do you know he's not my son?"*

"Cotton, run tests. I don't care. Just know you're not Gary's father. Do with the information what you please."

"Does he know?"

"Of course not. That's between him and you. He'll never hear it from me."

He could still feel the anger that had flooded him as Pam remained calm. They were so different, which might also explain why they were no longer together. He'd lost his father young but had been raised by a mother who adored him. Pam's childhood had been nothing but turmoil. Her mother had been a flighty woman with conflicting emotions who'd operated a day care center. She'd squandered the family savings not once but twice. Astrologers were her weakness. She never could resist them, eagerly listening as they told her exactly what she wanted to hear. Pam's father was equally troubling, a distant drifting soul who cared far more about radio-controlled airplanes than his wife and three children. He'd labored for forty years at an ice cream cone factory, a salaried employee who never rose above midlevel manager. Loyalty mixed with a false sense of contentment—that had been his father-in-law up to the day that a three-pack-a-day cigarette habit finally stopped his heart.

Until they met, Pam had known little love or security. Miserly with emotion but exacting in devotion, she'd always given far less than she demanded. And pointing out that reality brought only anger. His own mistake with other women, early in their marriage, merely proved her point—that nothing and no one could ever be counted on.

Not mothers, fathers, siblings, or husbands.

All of them failed.

And so had she.

Having a baby out of wedlock and never telling her husband he was not the father. She seemed to still be paying the price of that failure.

He ought to cut her some slack. But it took two to make a bargain, and she wasn't willing—at least not yet—to deal.

The shooter disappeared from the window.

Malone's attention snapped back to the café.

He watched as the man exited the building and headed toward his parked car, climbed in, and left. He abandoned his position, raced through the alley, and spotted Pam.

He crossed the street and jumped into the passenger seat. "Crank it up and get ready."

"Me? Why don't you drive?"

"No time. Here he comes."

He saw the Volvo round the bend in the highway that paralleled the shore and speed past.

"Go," he urged.

And she followed.

GEORGE HADDAD ENTERED HIS LONDON FLAT. THE TRIP TO Bainbridge Hall had generated its usual frustration so he ignored his computer, which signaled that there were unread e-mails, and sat at the kitchen table.

For five years he'd stayed dead. To know, but not to know. To understand, but at the same time to be confused.

He shook his head.

What a dilemma.

He glanced around. The soothing, cleansing magic of the apartment was no more. Clearly it was time. Others must know. He owed that revelation to every soul destroyed in the *nakba,* whose land was stolen, whose property was seized. And he owed it to the Jews.

Everyone had a right to the truth.

The first time months ago had not seemed to work. That was why yesterday, he'd again reached for the phone.

Now, for the third time, he dialed an international call.

MALONE WATCHED THE ROAD AHEAD AS PAM SPED DOWN THE coastal highway, south, toward Copenhagen. The Volvo was half a mile ahead. He'd allowed several cars to pass, which provided a buffer, but cautioned her more than once not to fall too far back.

"I'm not an agent," Pam said, her eyes glued out the windshield. "Never done this before."

"They didn't teach you this in law school?"

"No, Cotton. They taught you this in spy school."

"I wish they'd had a spy school. Unfortunately I had to learn on the job."

The Volvo quickened its pace and he wondered if they'd been spotted. But then he saw that the car was simply passing another. He noticed Pam starting to keep pace. "Don't. If he's watching, that's a trick to find out if he has company. I can see him, so stay where you are."

"I knew that Justice Department education would pay off."

Levity. Rare for her. But he appreciated the effort. He hoped this lead paid off. Gary had to be nearby, and all he'd need was one chance to get the boy out.

They found the outskirts of the capital. Traffic slowed to a crawl. They were four cars back as the Volvo maneuvered through Charlottenlund Slotspark, entered north Copenhagen, and motored south into the city. Just before the royal palace, the Volvo turned west and wound a path deep into a residential neighborhood.

"Careful," he said. "Easy to be spotted here. Stay back."

Pam allowed more room. Malone was familiar with this

part of town. The Rosenborg Slot, where the Danish crown jewels were displayed, stood a few blocks away, the botanical gardens nearby.

"He's headed somewhere specific," he said. "These houses all look alike, so you have to know where you're going."

Two more turns and the Volvo cruised down a tree-lined lane. He told her to stop at the corner and watched as their quarry wheeled into a driveway.

"Pull over to the curb," he said, motioning.

As she parked the car, he found his Beretta and opened the door. "Stay here. And I mean it. This could get rough, and I can't find Gary and look after you, too."

"You think he's there?"

"Good chance."

He hoped she wasn't going to be difficult.

"Okay. I'll wait here."

He started to climb out. She grabbed his arm. Her grip was firm but not hostile. A jolt of emotion surged through him.

He faced her, the fear plain in her eyes.

"If he's there, bring him back."

15

WASHINGTON, DC
7:20 AM

STEPHANIE WAS GLAD LARRY DALEY HAD LEFT. SHE LIKED THE man less each time they were around each other.

"What do you think?" Green asked.

"One thing is clear. Daley has no idea what the Alexandria Link is. He just knows about George Haddad, and he's hoping that the man knows something."

"Why do you say that?"

"If he knew, he wouldn't be wasting time with us."

"He needs Malone to find Haddad."

"But who says he needs Haddad to connect anything? If the classified files were complete, he wouldn't waste time with Haddad. He'd just hire a few brains, figure out whatever it is, and go from there." She shook her head. "Daley is a bullshit artist, and we were just bullshitted. He needs Cotton to find Haddad because he doesn't know squat. He's hoping Haddad has all the answers."

Green sat back in his chair with an undisguised anxiety. She was beginning to think that she'd misjudged this New Englander. He'd stood with her against Daley, even making clear that he'd quit if the White House fired her.

"Politics is a nasty business," Green muttered. "The president is a lame duck. His agenda stalled. Time's running out. He's definitely looking for a legacy, his spot in the history books, and men like Daley see it as their duty to provide one. I agree with you. He's fishing. But how any of this could be useful is beyond me."

"Apparently it's potent enough that the Saudis, and the Israelis, both acted on it five years ago."

"And that's significant. The Israelis aren't prone to capriciousness. Something made them want Haddad dead."

"Cotton's in a mess," she said. "His boy is at risk and he's not going to get a bit of help from us. In fact, officially we're going to sit back and watch, then take advantage of him."

"I think Daley is underestimating his opposition. There's been a lot of planning here."

She agreed. "That's the problem with bureaucrats. They think everything is negotiable."

The cell phone in Stephanie's pocket startled her with its vibration. She'd left word not to be disturbed unless it was vital. She answered the call, listened for a moment, then clicked off.

"I just lost an agent. The man I sent to meet Malone. He was killed at Kronborg Castle."

Green was silent.

Pain built behind her eyes. "Lee Durant had a wife and children."

"Any word from Malone?"

She shook her head. "They haven't heard from him."

"Perhaps you were right earlier. Maybe we should involve other agencies?"

Her throat tightened. "It wouldn't work. This has to be handled another way."

Green sat still, lips pursed, eyes unwavering, as if he knew what had to be done.

"I intend to help Cotton," she said.

"And what could you do? You're not a field agent."

She recalled how Malone had told her the same thing not long ago in France, but she'd handled herself well enough. "I'll get my own help. People I can trust. I have a lot of friends who owe me favors."

"I can help, too."

"I don't want you involved."

"But I am."

"There's nothing you can do," she said.

"You might be surprised."

"And what would Daley do then? We have no idea who his allies are. It's better I do this quietly. You stay out of it."

Green's face registered nothing. "What about the briefing this morning on Capitol Hill?"

"I'll do it. That way Daley should be placated."

"I'll give you whatever cover I can."

A smile bent the edges of her mouth. "You know, this may have been the best few hours we ever spent together."

"I'm sorry that we didn't spend more time like this."

"Me, too," she said. "But I have a friend who needs me."

16

MALONE LEFT THE CAR AND WORKED HIS WAY CLOSER TO THE house where the Volvo sat parked. He could not approach from the front—too many windows, too little cover—so he detoured into a grassy alley adjacent to the house next door and approached from the rear. The dwellings in this part of Copenhagen were like his neighborhood in Atlanta—shady lanes of compact brick residences surrounded by equally compact front and rear yards.

He shielded the Beretta at his side and used the foliage to mask his continued advance. So far he'd seen no one. A shoulder-high hedge divided one yard from the next. He maneuvered to where he could see over the hedge and spotted a rear door into the house where the shooter had gone. Before he could decide on what course to take, the rear door was flung open and two men emerged.

The shooter from Kronborg and another man, short and stumpy with no neck.

The two were talking, and they walked around to the front of the house. He obeyed his instincts and rushed from his hiding place, entering the backyard through an opening in the hedge. He darted straight for the rear door and, with gun ready, slipped inside.

The one-story house was quiet. Two bedrooms, a den, kitchen, and bath. One bedroom door was closed. He quickly surveyed the rooms. Empty. He approached the closed door. His left hand gripped the knob, his right held the gun, finger on the trigger. He slowly twisted, then shoved open the door.

And saw Gary.

The boy was sitting in a chair, beside the window, reading. His son, startled, glanced up from the pages, then his face beamed when he realized who was there.

Malone, too, felt a surge of elation.

"Dad." Then Gary saw the gun and said, "What's going on?"

"I can't explain, but we have to go."

"They said you were in trouble. Are those men who are trying to hurt me and Mom here?"

He nodded as panic swept over him. "They're here. We have to go."

Gary stood from the chair, and Malone couldn't help himself. He hugged his son hard. This child was his—in every way. Screw Pam.

He said, "Stay behind me. Do exactly as I say. Understand?"

"There going to be trouble?"

"I hope not."

He retraced his route to the rear door and peered outside. The yard was empty. He would need only a minute for them to make their escape.

He exited with Gary close at his heels.

The opening in the hedge loomed fifty feet away.

He maneuvered Gary in front of him, since the last he'd seen of the two men they were heading toward the street. Gun ready, he bolted straight for the yard next door. He kept his attention to their flank, allowing Gary to lead the way.

They passed through the opening.

"How predictable."

He whirled and froze.

Standing twenty feet away was No Neck, Pam in his grasp, a sound-suppressed Glock jammed into her neck. The Kronborg Shooter stood off to the side, gun aimed directly at Malone.

"I found your ex wandering this way," No Neck said with a Dutch twang. "I assume you told her to stay in the car?"

His gaze locked on Pam's. Her eyes pleaded with him to forgive her.

"Gary," she said, unable to move.

"Mom."

Malone caught the desperation in both their voices. He repositioned Gary behind him.

"Let's see how you did, Malone. You tracked my man over

there from the castle into town, waited for him to leave, then followed, thinking your boy would be here."

Definitely the voice from the cell phone last night. "Which all turned out to be right."

The other man was unmoved. A sickening feeling invaded Malone's stomach.

He'd been led.

"Pop the magazine out of that Beretta and toss it away."

Malone hesitated, then decided he had no choice. He did as told.

"Now let's trade. I'll give you your ex and you give me the boy."

"What if I say keep the ex?"

The man chuckled. "I'm sure you don't want your son to watch while I blow his mother's brains out, which is exactly what I'll do, because I don't really want her."

Pam's eyes widened at the prospects that her foolishness had spawned.

"Dad, what's going on?" Gary asked.

"Son, you're going to have to go with him—"

"No," Pam yelled. "Don't."

"He'll kill you," Malone made clear.

No Neck's finger lay firmly on the Glock's trigger, and Malone hoped Pam stood still. He stared at Gary. "You have to do this for Mom. But I'll be back for you, I swear. You can count on it." He hugged the boy again. "I love you. Be tough for me. Okay?"

Gary nodded, hesitated an instant, then stepped toward No Neck, who released his grip on Pam. She instantly hugged Gary and started crying.

"You okay?" she asked.

"I'm fine."

"Let me stay with him," she said. "I won't give you any

trouble. Cotton can find whatever it is you want and we'll be good. I promise."

"Shut up," No Neck said.

"I swear to you. I won't be a problem."

He leveled the gun at her forehead. "Take your tight ass over there and shut up."

"Don't push him," Malone said to her.

She gave Gary one more hug, then slowly retreated his way.

No Neck chuckled. "Good choice."

Malone stared his adversary down.

The man's gun suddenly swung right and three sound-suppressed bullets left the barrel and plowed into the Kronborg Shooter. The body teetered, then dropped, spine-first, to the ground.

Pam's hand covered her mouth. "Oh, Jesus."

Malone saw the shocked look on Gary's face. No fifteen-year-old should be forced to watch that.

"He did exactly what I told him to do. But I knew you were following. He didn't. Actually told me he hadn't been followed. I don't have time for idiots. This little exercise was to get all the bravado out of your system. Now go get what I want." No Neck pointed the Glock at Gary's head. "We need to leave without you interfering."

"All the bullets in my gun were tossed away."

He watched Gary. Interestingly, the young face conveyed not a hint of anxiety. No panic. No fear. Just resolve.

No Neck and Gary started to leave.

Malone held the gun at his side, his mind reeling with possibilities. His son was only a few inches from a loaded Glock. He knew that once Gary was gone, he'd have no choice but to deliver the link. He'd avoided that unpleasant choice all day, since doing it would generate a whole host of dilemmas. No Neck had clearly anticipated what he would do from the beginning, knowing they'd all end up right here.

His blood seemed to turn to ice and a disturbing feeling swept through him.

Uncomfortable.

But familiar.

He kept his movements natural. That was the rule. His former profession had been all about chances. Weighing odds. Success had always been a factor of dividing odds into risk. His own hide had many times been on the line, and in three instances risk had overridden odds and he'd ended up in the hospital.

This was different. His son was at stake.

Thank heaven the odds were all in his favor.

No Neck and Gary approached the hedge opening.

"Excuse me," Malone said.

No Neck turned.

Malone fired the Beretta and the bullet found the man's chest. He seemed not to know what had happened—his face a mix of puzzlement and pain. Finally blood seeped from the corners of his mouth and his eyes surrendered.

He fell like a tree under an ax, twitched a moment, then stopped.

Pam rushed to Gary and swept him into her arms.

Malone lowered the gun.

SABRE WATCHED AS COTTON MALONE SHOT HIS LAST OPERA-tive. He was standing in the kitchen of a house that faced the rear of the dwelling where Gary Malone had been held the past three days. When he'd rented that locale, he'd rented this one, too.

He smiled.

Malone was a clever one, and his operative incompetent. Tossing the magazine had emptied the gun of bullets, except for the one already in the chamber. Any good agent, like Malone, always kept a bullet in the chamber. He recalled from his army special forces training the time a recruit had shot himself in the leg after supposedly unloading his weapon—forgetting about the loaded round.

He'd hoped that somehow Malone would get the best of his hired help. That was the idea. And the opportunity came once he'd spotted Pam Malone heading for the house. He'd radioed his minion and told him how to use her carelessness to make the point even clearer to Malone, bribing the man to shoot the other with a pledge of a bonus.

Thankfully, Malone had ensured that the payment would never be made.

Which also meant there was no one left alive to connect Sabre to anything.

Even better, Malone had his son back, which should calm his enemy's most dangerous instincts.

But that didn't mean this endeavor was over.

Not at all.

In fact, only now could it finally begin.

PART TWO

PART
TWO

17

WEDNESDAY, OCTOBER 5
VIENNA, AUSTRIA
1:30 PM

SABRE BRAKED AT THE GATE AND WOUND DOWN THE DRIVER'S-
side window. He displayed no identification, but the guard
immediately waved him through. The sprawling château
stood thirty miles southwest of downtown among forests
known as the Vienna Woods. Three centuries old and built by
aristocracy, its mustard-colored walls of baroque splendor
encased seventy-five spacious rooms, all topped by steep
gables of Alpine slate.

A bright sun poured past the Audi's hazy windshield, and
Sabre noted that the asphalt drive and side parking lots were
all empty. Only the guards at the front gate and a few
groundskeepers tending the walkways disturbed the otherwise tranquil scene.

Apparently this was to be a private discussion.

He parked beneath a porte cochere and climbed out into a
balmy afternoon. Immediately he buttoned his Burberry
jacket and followed a pebbled path to the *schmetterlinghaus,*
an iron-and-glass enclave a hundred yards south of the
main château. Painted an unadorned green, its walls lined
with hundreds of panels of Hungarian glass, the imposing

nineteenth-century structure easily blended into the forested surroundings. Inside, its fortified indigenous soil supported a variety of exotic plants, but the building took its name— *schmetterling*—from the thousands of butterflies roaming free.

He jerked open a rickety wooden door and stepped into a dirt foyer. A leather curtain kept hot, humid air inside.

He pushed through.

Butterflies danced through the air to the accompaniment of soft instrumental music. Bach, if he wasn't mistaken. Many of the plants were in bloom, the tranquil scene a stunning contrast with the stark images of autumn outlined through the moisture-dotted glass.

The building's owner, the Blue Chair, sat among the foliage. He possessed the face of a man who'd worked too much, slept too little, and cared nothing about nutrition. The old man wore a tweed suit atop a cardigan sweater. Which had to be uncomfortable, Sabre thought. Yet, he silently noted, cold-blooded creatures needed lots of warmth.

He slipped off his jacket and approached an empty wooden chair.

"Guten morgen, Herr Sabre."

He sat and acknowledged the greeting. Apparently German would be their language of the day.

"Plants, Dominick. I've never asked, but how much do you know about them?"

"Only that they produce oxygen from carbon dioxide."

The old man smiled. "Wouldn't you say they do so much more? What about color, warmth, beauty?"

He glanced at the transplanted rain forest, watched the butterflies, and listened to the peaceful music. He cared nothing about soothing aesthetics but knew better than to express that opinion, so he simply said, "They have their place."

"You know much about butterflies?"

A china plate smeared with blackened banana rested in the old man's lap. Insects sporting wings of sapphire, crimson, and ivory were eagerly devouring the offering.

"The odor attracts them." The old man gently stroked the wings of one. "Truly beautiful creatures. Flying gems, exploding into the world in a burst of color. Sadly, they live only a few weeks before rejoining the food chain."

Four greenish gold butterflies arrived at the banquet.

"This species is quite rare. *Papilio dardanus*. The mocker swallowtail. I import their chrysalides specially from Africa."

Sabre hated bugs, but he tried to appear interested and waited.

Finally the old man asked, "All went well in Copenhagen?"

"Malone is on his way to find the link."

"Just as you predicted. How did you know?"

"He has no choice. To protect his son, he needs to expose the link so he's no longer vulnerable. A man like that is easy to read."

"He may realize that he was manipulated."

"I'm sure he does, but he genuinely thinks, in the end, he managed to get the upper hand. I doubt he assumes I wanted those men to die."

A crease of amusement invaded the old man's face. "You enjoy this game, don't you?"

"It has some satisfying aspects." He paused before adding, "When played right."

A few more butterflies joined those already on the plate.

"It's actually a lot like these precious creatures," the Blue Chair said. "They gorge themselves, drawn by the lure of easy food." Gnarly fingers plucked one by the wings, the dark spiracle and tiny legs wrenched as the insect tried to break free. "I could easily kill this specimen. How hard would it be?"

The Blue Chair released his hold. Orange and yellow wings sputtered then caught air.

"But I could just as easily let it go." The old man focused on him with eyes full of zest. "Use Malone's instincts to our advantage."

"That's the plan."

"What will you do once the link is found?" the Blue Chair asked.

"Depends."

"Malone will need to be killed."

"I can handle that."

The old man threw him a glance. "He might prove a challenge."

"I'm ready."

"There's a problem."

He'd wondered why he'd been summoned back to Vienna.

"The Israelis are alerted. Seems George Haddad made another call to the West Bank, and Jewish spies within the Palestinian Authority reported his contact to Tel Aviv. They know he's alive, and I assume they know where he is, too."

That *was* a problem.

"The Chairs are aware of this exposure and have ratified the authority I granted you to handle the matter as you see fit."

Which he planned to do anyway.

"As you know, the Israelis have far different motivations than we do. We want the link. They want it gone."

Sabre nodded. "They bombed their own people in that café just to kill Haddad."

"Jews are a problem," the Blue Chair quietly declared. "They've always been difficult. Being different and obstinate breeds unmitigated pride."

Sabre decided to leave that comment alone.

"We intend to help end the Jewish problem."

"I wasn't aware there was a problem."

"Not for us, but for our Arab friends. So you must stay ahead of the Israelis. They cannot be allowed to interfere."

"Then I need to leave."

"Where did Malone go?"

"London."

The Blue Chair went silent, concentrating on the bugs fluttering in his lap. Finally he swiped the butterflies away. "On the way to London, there's a stop you need to make."

"Is there time?"

"No choice. Another contact within the Israeli government has some information that he will only convey, in person, to you, and he wants to be paid."

"Don't they all?"

"He's in Germany. It shouldn't take long. Use one of the company jets. I'm told this man has been sloppy. He's exposed, though he doesn't realize it. Resolve our account with him."

He understood.

"And needless to say, there will be others there, watching. Please make the show memorable. The Israelis need to understand this is a high-stakes affair." The old man shifted in the wooden chair, then angled his stiletto of a nose back down toward the plate. "You're also aware of what occurs this weekend?"

"Of course."

"I need a financial dossier on a certain individual. By Friday. Can it be done?"

He knew the correct answer, though he didn't have time for that, either. "Certainly."

The Blue Chair told him the name he was to investigate, then said, "Have the information delivered here. In the meantime, do what you do best."

18

STEPHANIE DECIDED TO STAY IN THE CAPITAL. THE MAJOR PLAY-
ers were all here, and if she was going to help Malone she
would need to be close to every one of them. She was connected to Atlanta and Magellan Billet headquarters through
her laptop and cell phone and presently had three agents
heading for Denmark. Another two were already in London,
a solo on the way to Washington. Her hotel room, for now,
would be command central.

She'd been waiting for the past twenty minutes, and when
the phone on the desk finally rang, she smiled. One thing
about Thorvaldsen, he was punctual. She lifted the receiver.
"Yes, Henrik."

"So sure it was me?"

"Right on time."

"Lateness is rude."

"I couldn't agree more. What did you learn?"

"Enough to know we have a problem."

Yesterday Thorvaldsen had dispatched a squadron of investigators to backtrack the movements of the two men Malone had shot. Since one of them had killed a federal agent,
she was also able to muster Europol's help.

"Ever heard of *der Orden des Goldenen Vliesses*? The Order of the Golden Fleece?"

"It's a European economic cartel. I'm aware of it."

"I need an Internet connection to your laptop."

"That's classified," she said lightheartedly.

"I assure you, with what I know, I have all the clearances I need."

She told him the routing address. A minute later five photographs materialized on her screen. Three were head shots—two, full-body. The five men were well into their seventies, faces like caricatures, full of dull angles, cold and expressionless, each casting a veneer of sophistication—the aristocratic bearing of men accustomed to having their way.

"The Order of the Golden Fleece was re-formed in the late forties, just after the communist socialization of Austrian industry. It was organized in Vienna, the initial membership restricted to a select group of industrialists and financiers. In the fifties it diversified, adding manufacturing and mining magnates, along with more financiers."

She slid a notepad closer and clicked open a ballpoint pen. "What do you mean, *re*-formed?"

"The name comes from a French medieval order that Philip, the duke of Burgundy, created in 1430. But that group of knights lasted only a few decades. Through the centuries reincarnations appeared, and a social Order of the Golden Fleece still exists in Austria. But it's the economic cartel of the same name that poses a threat."

Her eyes were locked on the screen, her memory absorbing the stern faces.

"An interesting group," Thorvaldsen said. "A strict code of statutes governs the Order's business. Membership is restricted to seventy-one. A Circle of five Chairs governs. What's called the Blue Chair heads both the Circle and the Order. These people wear crimson robes and dangle gold

medallions around their necks. Each medallion is forged
with fire steels and flints emitting tongues of flame encir-
cling a golden fleece. Quite dramatic."

She agreed.

"You need to understand about the five on your screen. The
face at the top left is an Austrian industrialist, Alfred Hermann. He presently occupies the Blue Chair. A billionaire
several times over, he's the owner of European steel factories,
African mines, Far East rubber plantations, and banking concerns worldwide."

Thorvaldsen explained about the other four. One owned a
controlling interest in the VRN Bank that was nationwide in
Austria, Germany, Switzerland, and Holland, along with
pharmaceutical and automobile companies. Another dominated the European securities markets with investment firms
that handled portfolios for many European Union nations. A
third wholly owned two French companies and one Belgian
that, outside the United States, were the world's leading aircraft producers. The last was the self-designated "king of
concrete," his companies the leading producers throughout
Europe, Africa, and the Middle East.

"That's a formidable group," she said.

"To say the least. A distinctive Aryan flavor permeates the
Chairs, and always has—German, Swiss, and Austrian
members dominating. The Chairs are elected from the membership and serve for life. A Shadow is simultaneously chosen who can immediately step in and succeed at death. The
Blue Chair is elected by the Chairs and likewise serves for
life."

"Efficient devils."

"They pride themselves on it. The entire membership
meets twice a year in a formal Assembly, once in late spring,
the other just before winter, on a four-hundred-acre estate
owned by Alfred Hermann outside Vienna. The rest of the

year business is conducted by the Chairs or through standing committees. There's a chancellor, treasurer, and secretary, along with a support staff that work out of Hermann's château. Organization is intentionally streamlined. No unnecessary parliamentary delays."

She jotted notes on the pad.

"The Blue Chair is not allowed a vote, either in the Circle or at Assembly, unless there's a tie. The odd numbers of seventy-one members and five Chairs create the possibility."

She had to admire Thorvaldsen's investigative efforts. "Tell me about the membership."

"The majority are European, but four Americans, two Canadians, three Asians, a Brazilian, and an Australian are among the current seventy-one. Men and women. They went coed decades ago. Turnover is only occasional, but a waiting list ensures that seventy-one will always be maintained."

She was curious. "Why be headquartered in Austria?"

"For the same reason many of us have money there. An express provision in the national constitution forbids violations of bank secrecy. Money is difficult to trace. The Order is well financed. Members are assessed equally based on a projected budget. Last year's topped one hundred fifty million euros."

"And what do they spend that kind of revenue on?"

"What people have sought for centuries—political influence, mainly toward the European Community's efforts to centralize currency and reduce trade barriers. The emergence of Eastern Europe also interests them. Rebuilding the infrastructure of the Czech Republic, Slovakia, Hungary, Romania, and Poland is big business. Through some carefully placed contributions, members have obtained more than their fair share of contracts."

"Still, Henrik, a hundred fifty million euros couldn't be spent on simply securing contracts and bribing politicians."

"You're right. There's a greater purpose to what the group does."

She was getting impatient. "I'm waiting."

"The Middle East. That's their highest priority."

"How in the world do you know all this?"

Silence came from the other end of the phone.

She waited.

"I'm a member."

19

LONDON
12:30 PM

MALONE WALKED WITH PAM DOWN THE RAMP AS THEY DE-planed from their British Airways flight. They'd spent the night at Christiangade, then flown together from Copenhagen to England, Pam on a layover as she made her way back to Georgia, Malone as a final destination. Gary was left with Thorvaldsen. His son knew the Dane from the past two summers he'd spent in Denmark. Until he could determine exactly what was happening, Malone believed Christiangade the safest place for Gary. For added measure, Thorvaldsen hired a cadre of private security to patrol the estate. Pam had not been happy with the decision, and they'd argued. Eventually she understood the wisdom, especially considering what had happened in Atlanta. With the crisis ended, she needed to get back to work. She'd departed quickly with no notice to her firm. Leaving Gary was not what she'd wanted, but finally she conceded that Malone could protect him better than she ever could.

"Hope I still have a job," she said.

"I imagine your billable hours are enough to garner forgiveness. You going to tell them what happened?"

"I'll have to."

"It's okay. Tell them what you need to."

"Why are you keeping on with this?" she said. "Why not let it alone?"

He noticed that she seemed to have slept much of her gloom away. She'd repeatedly apologized for yesterday and he'd brushed it aside. He actually didn't want to talk with her and, thanks to their late booking, they hadn't sat together on the flight. Which was good. There were still things that needed to be said about Gary. Unpleasant things. But now was not the time.

"It's the only way to make sure it doesn't happen again," he said. "If I'm not the only one who knows about the link, then I'm not a target anymore. And by the way, neither are you or Gary."

"What do you plan to do?" Pam asked.

He truly didn't know, so he said, "I'll figure that out when I get there."

They wove a path through the crowded concourse toward the terminal, their silence and thoughtful steps salient signals that they were better off apart. Dormant senses, tuned from twelve years as a Justice Department agent, were once again alert. He'd noticed something on the plane. A man. Sitting three rows ahead on the opposite side of the cabin. A string-bean body, brown as a berry, his cheeks dark with stubble. He'd boarded in Copenhagen, and something about him had grabbed Malone's attention. Nothing during the

flight had been a problem. But even though the man had de-
planed ahead of them, he was now positioned at their rear.

And that seemed a problem.

"You shot that man yesterday without a hint of remorse,"
Pam said. "That's scary, Cotton."

"Gary's safety was at stake."

"That what you used to do?"

"All the time."

"I've seen all the death I want to see."

So had he.

They kept walking. He could tell she was thinking. He'd
always known when her brain was churning.

"I didn't mention it yesterday," she said, "with all that happened, but I have a new man in my life."

He was glad, but wondered why she was telling him.
"Been a long time since we were concerned with each other's
business."

"I know. But he's kind of special." She lifted her arm and
displayed her wrist. "He gave me this watch."

She seemed proud of it, so he indulged her. "A TAG
Heuer. Not bad."

"I thought so, too. Surprised the heck out of me."

"He treat you good?"

She nodded. "I enjoy my time with him."

He didn't know what to say.

"I only mention it to let you know that maybe it's time we
made peace."

They entered the terminal, crowded with people. Time
they parted ways.

"Mind if I come along with you?" she asked. "My plane
to Atlanta doesn't leave for seven hours."

He'd actually been rehearsing his goodbye, intent on keeping it nonchalant. "Not a good idea. I need to do this alone."

He didn't have to say what they were both thinking. *Especially after yesterday.*

She nodded. "I understand. I just thought it'd be a good way to pass the afternoon."

He was curious. "Why would you want to come? Thought you wanted away from all this?"

"I almost got killed over that link, so I'm curious. And besides, what am I going to do in this airport?"

He had to admit she looked great—five years his junior, but she looked even younger. And her countenance was too much like the old Pam, at once helpless, independent, and appealing, for him to be flippant. The features on her freckled face, the blue eyes, sent a rush of memories through his brain, ones that he'd fought hard to repress, especially since August when he'd found out about Gary's parentage.

He and Pam had been married a long time. Shared a life. Good and bad. He was forty-eight years old, divorced more than a year, separated for nearly six.

Maybe it was time he got over it. What happened happened, and he'd been no angel.

But brokering a peace would have to wait, so he simply said, "You get on back to Atlanta and stay out of trouble, okay?"

She smiled. "I could say the same to you."

"That's impossible for me. But I'm sure that new man in your life would like to have you home."

"We still need to talk, Cotton. We've both avoided the subject."

"We will, but after all this. How about a truce till then?"

"Okay."

"I'll let you know how things go, and don't worry about Gary. Henrik will look after him. He'll be well protected. You have the phone number, so check on him whenever."

He threw her a cheerful wave to match his grin, then drifted toward the terminal exits and a taxi. He hadn't brought a bag. Depending on how long he stayed, he'd buy some things later, after he found the link.

But before leaving the building he needed to check one more thing.

At the exit doors he approached an information counter and plucked a city map from its holder. He casually turned and studied it, allowing his gaze to drift from the map to the stream of people flowing through the broad terminal.

He'd expected String Bean to be waiting for him to leave, if indeed he was following.

Instead, his problem tailed Pam.

Now he was concerned.

He tossed the map on the counter and headed across the terminal. Pam entered one of the many cafés, apparently intent on passing the time with a meal or a coffee. String Bean assumed a position in a duty-free shop where he could clearly observe the café.

Interesting. Apparently Malone wasn't the flavor of the day.

He, too, entered the café.

Pam was sitting in a booth, and he walked over. Surprise flooded her face. "What are you doing here?"

"Changed my mind. Why don't you come along?"

"I'd really like that."

"One condition."

"I know. My mouth stays shut."

STEPHANIE ALLOWED THORVALDSEN'S WORDS TO AGAIN PLAY across her mind. Then she calmly asked, "You're a member of the Order of the Golden Fleece?"

"For thirty years. I always thought it nothing more than a

way for people with money and power to mingle with one another. That's what we do most of the time—"

"When you're not paying off politicians or bribing for contracts."

"Come now, Stephanie. You know the way of the world. I don't make the rules. I just play by the ones in place."

"Tell me what you know, Henrik. And please, no bullshit."

"My investigators traced the two dead men from yesterday to Amsterdam. One has a lady friend. She told us that her lover worked regularly for another man. Once she managed to see him, and from her description I believe I've seen him, too."

She waited for more.

"Interestingly, for many years now, at Order functions, I've heard quite a bit about the lost Library of Alexandria. The occupant of the Blue Chair, Alfred Hermann, is obsessed with the subject."

"You know why?"

"He believes there's much we can learn from the ancients."

That she doubted, but she needed to know, "What's the connection between the two dead men and the Order?"

"The man the woman described has been present at Order functions. Not a member. An employee. She didn't hear his name, but her boyfriend once used a term I've heard before, too. *Die Klauen der Adler.*"

She silently translated. The Talons of the Eagle. "You going to tell me more?"

"How about when I'm sure?"

Back in June, when she'd first met Thorvaldsen, he hadn't been all that forthcoming, which had only fueled the already existing friction between them. But since then she'd learned not to underestimate the Dane. "Okay. You said the Order's main interest was the Middle East. What did you mean?"

"I appreciate you not pressing."

"Got to start cooperating with you sometime. Besides, you weren't going to tell me anyway."

Thorvaldsen chuckled. "We're a lot alike."

"Now, that scares me."

"It's not all that bad. But to answer your question about the Middle East, unfortunately the Arab world only respects strength. They also know how to deal, however, and they have much to bargain with, especially oil."

She couldn't argue with that conclusion.

"Who's the Arab's number one enemy?" Thorvaldsen asked. "America? No. Israel. That's the thorn in their side. There it sits. Right in the middle of *their* world. A Jewish state. Partitioned out in 1948 when nearly a million people were, if you believe the Arab line, forcibly displaced. Land Palestinians, Egyptians, Jordanians, Lebanese, and Syrians had claimed for centuries was simply surrendered by the world to the Jews. The *nakba,* the catastrophe, they called it. A fitting name." Thorvaldsen paused. "For both sides."

"And war immediately broke out," Stephanie said. "The first of many."

"Every one of them, thankfully, won by Israel. For the past sixty years the Israelis have clung to *their* land, and all because God told Abraham that it was to be so."

She remembered the passage Brent Green had quoted. *The Lord said to Abram, lift up now your eyes and look from the place where you are northward and southward and eastward and westward, for all the land which you see, to you I will give it, and to your seed forever.*

"God's promise to Abraham is one reason why Palestine was given to the Jews," Henrik said. "Supposedly their ancestral homeland, bequeathed by God Himself. Who's to argue with that?"

"At least one Palestinian scholar I know of."

"Cotton told me about George Haddad and the library."

"He shouldn't have."

"I don't think he gives a damn about rules at the moment, and you're not one of his favorite people right now, either."

She deserved that one.

"My sources in Washington tell me that the White House wants Haddad found. I assume you know that."

She did not answer.

"I wouldn't imagine you'd confirm or deny that one. But there's something happening here, Stephanie. An event of substance. Men of power don't usually waste their time on nonsense."

She agreed.

"You can blow people up. Terrorize them every day. Solves nothing. But when you possess what your enemy either wants, or doesn't want anyone else to have, then you have real power. I know the Order of the Golden Fleece. Leverage. That's what Alfred Hermann and the Order are after."

"And what will they do with it?"

"If it strikes at the heart of Israel, as it may well, then the Arab world would deal to obtain it. Everyone in the Order stands to profit from friendly relations with the Arabs. The price of oil alone is enough to command their attention, but new markets for their goods and services—that's an even greater prize. Who knows? The information might even call into question the Jewish state, which could soothe a multitude of open sores. America's long-standing defense of Israel is costly. How many times has it happened? An Arab nation claims Israel should be destroyed. The United Nations weighs in. The U.S. denounces it. Everyone becomes angry. Swords are rattled. Then concessions and dollars have to be doled out to quell tempers. Imagine, if that was no longer needed, how much more accommodating the world, and America, could be."

Which might be the legacy Larry Daley wanted for the president. But she had to say, "What could possibly be that powerful?"

"I don't know. But you and I a few months ago read an ancient document that fundamentally changed everything. Something of equal power might be present here, too."

He was right, but the reality was, "Cotton needs this information."

"He'll get it, but first we have to learn the whole story."

"And how do you plan to do that?"

"The Order is convening its winter gathering this weekend. I wasn't going, but I am now."

20

LONDON
1:20 PM

MALONE CLIMBED FROM THE TAXI AND STUDIED THE QUIET street. Lots of gabled façades, fluted side posts, and flowery sills. Each of the picturesque Georgian houses seemed a serene abode of antiquity, a place that would naturally harbor bookworms and academics. George Haddad should be right at home.

"This where he lives?" Pam asked.

"I hope so. I haven't heard from him in nearly a year. But this is the address I was given three years ago."

The afternoon was cool and dry. Earlier, he'd read in *The Times* how England was still in the midst of an unusual autumn drought. String Bean had not followed them from Heathrow, but perhaps someone else had taken up the task since the man was clearly in communication with others. Yet no other taxis were in sight. Strange still having Pam with him, but he deserved the feeling of awkwardness. He'd asked for it by insisting she come.

They climbed the stoop and entered the building. He lingered in the foyer, out of sight, watching the street.

But no cars or people appeared.

The bell for the flat on the third floor gave a discreet tinkle. The olive-skinned man who answered the door was short and doughy, with ash-white hair and a square face. Brown eyes came alive when he saw his guest, and Malone noticed an instant of repressed excitement in the broad grin of welcome.

"Cotton. What a surprise. I was just thinking of you the other day."

They warmly shook hands and Malone introduced Pam. Haddad invited them in. Daylight was dimmed by thick lace curtains, and Malone quickly absorbed the décor, which seemed an intentional mismatch—there was a piano, several sideboards, armchairs, lamps adorned with pleated silk shades, and an oak table where a computer was engulfed by books and papers.

Haddad waved his arm as if to embrace the clutter. "My world, Cotton."

The walls were dotted with maps, so many that the sage-green wall covering was barely visible. Malone's gaze raked them, and he noted that they depicted the Holy Land, Arabia, and the Sinai, their time line varying from modern to ancient. Some were photocopies, others originals, all interesting.

"More of my obsession," Haddad said.

After a genial exchange of small talk, Malone decided to get to the point. "Things have changed. That's why I'm here." He explained what had happened the day before.

"Your son is okay?" Haddad asked.

"He's fine. But five years ago I asked no questions because that was part of my job. It's not anymore, so I want to know what's going on."

"You saved my life."

"Which ought to buy me the truth."

Haddad led them into the kitchen, where they sat at an oval table. The tepid air hung heavy with a lingering scent of wine and tobacco. "It's complicated, Cotton. I've only in the past few years understood it myself."

"George, I need to know it all."

An uneasy understanding passed between them. Old friendships could atrophy. People changed. What was once appreciated between two people became uncomfortable. But Malone knew Haddad trusted him, and he wanted to reciprocate. Finally the older man spoke. Malone listened as Haddad told them about 1948 when, as a nineteen-year-old, he'd fought with the Palestinian resistance, trying to stop the Zionist invasion.

"I shot many men," Haddad said. "But there was one I never forgot. He came to see my father. Unfortunately that blessed soul had already killed himself. We captured this man, thinking him a Zionist. I was young, full of hate, no patience, and he spoke nonsense. So I shot him." Haddad's eyes moistened. "He was a Guardian and I killed him, never learning anything." The Palestinian paused. "Then, fifty-some years later, incredibly, another Guardian visited me."

Malone wondered about the significance.

"He appeared at my home, standing in the dark, saying the same thing that the first man said in 1948."

"I'm a Guardian."

Had Haddad heard right? The question formed immediately in his mind. "From the library? Am I to be offered an invitation?"

"How do you know that?"

He told the man what had happened long ago. As he spoke, Haddad tried to assess his guest. He was wiry with coal-black hair, a thick mustache, and sunburned skin that bore the texture of tawny leather. Neat and quietly dressed, with a manner to match. Not unlike the first emissary.

The younger man sat silent and Haddad decided this time he, too, would be patient. Finally the Guardian said, "We've studied your writings and your published research. Your knowledge of the Bible's ancient text is impressive, as is your ability to interpret the original Hebrew. And your arguments on the accepted translations are persuasive."

He appreciated the compliment. Those came few and far between in the West Bank.

"We're an ancient band. Long ago the first Guardians saved much of the Library of Alexandria from destruction. A great effort. From time to time—to those, like yourself, who could benefit—we've offered an invitation."

Many questions formed in his mind, but he asked, "The Guardian I shot said that the war we were fighting back then wasn't necessary. That there are things more powerful than bullets. What did he mean?"

"I wouldn't know. Obviously your father failed to appear at the library, so he never benefited from our knowledge—and we did not benefit from his. Hopefully, you'll not fail."

"What do you mean failed to appear?"

"To have the right to use the library you must prove yourself through the hero's quest." The man produced an envelope. "Interpret these words wisely and I'll see you at the entrance, where it will be my honor to allow you into the library."

He accepted the packet. "I'm an old man. How could I possibly take a long journey?"

"You'll find the strength."

"Why should I?"

"Because in the library you will find answers."

"My mistake," Haddad said, "was telling the Palestinian authorities about that visit. I spoke the truth, though. I couldn't make the journey. When I reported what happened, I thought I was speaking with friends in the West Bank. But Israel's spies heard everything, and the next thing I knew you and I were in that café when it exploded."

Malone recalled the day. One of the scariest in his life. He'd barely managed to extricate them both.

"What were you doing there?" Pam asked him, concern in her voice.

"George and I had known each other for years. We share an interest in books, especially the Bible." He pointed. "This man is one of the world's experts. I've enjoyed picking his brain."

"I never knew you had an interest," Pam said.

"Apparently there was a lot neither one of us knew about the other." He saw that she registered his true meaning, so he let that truth hang and said, "When George sensed trouble and didn't trust the Palestinians, he asked for my help. Stephanie sent me to find out what was happening. Once that bomb went off, George wanted out. Everyone assumed he died in the blast. So I made him disappear."

"Code-named the Alexandria Link," Pam said.

"Someone obviously found out about me," Haddad declared.

Malone nodded. "The computer files were breached. But there's no mention of where you live, just that I'm the only one who knows your whereabouts. That's why they went after Gary."

"And for that I'm truly sorry. I would never want to place your son in jeopardy."

"Then tell me, George, why do people want you dead?"

"At the time the Guardian visited me, I was working on a theory regarding the Old Testament. I'd previously published several papers on the then current state of that holy text, but I was formulating something more."

The lines at the corners of Haddad's eyes deepened, and Malone watched as his friend seemed to struggle with his thoughts.

"Christians tend to focus on the New Testament," Haddad said. "Jews use the Old. I daresay most Christians have little understanding of the Old Testament, beyond thinking that the New is a fulfillment of the Old's prophecies. But the Old Testament is important, and there are many contradictions in that text—ones that could readily call its message into question."

He'd heard Haddad speak on the subject before, but this time he sensed a new urgency.

"Examples abound. Genesis gives two conflicting versions of creation. Two varying genealogies of Adam's offspring are laid out. Then the flood. God tells Noah to bring seven pairs of clean animals and one pair of unclean. In another part of Genesis it's just one pair of each. Noah releases a raven to search for land in one verse, but it's a dove in another. Even the length of the flood is contradicted. Forty days and nights or three hundred seventy? Both are used. Not to mention the dozens of doublets and triplets contained within the narratives, like the differing names used to describe God. One portion cites YHWH, *Yahweh,* another *Elohim.* Wouldn't you think at least God's name could be consistent?"

Malone's memory flashed back a few months to France, where he'd heard similar complaints about the four Gospels of the New Testament.

"Most now agree," Haddad said, "that the Old Testament was composed by a host of writers over an extremely long period of time. A skillful combination of varied sources by scribal compilers. This conclusion is absolutely clear and not new. A twelfth-century Spanish philosopher was one of the first to note that Genesis 12:6—*at that time the Canaanites were in the land*—could not have been written by Moses. And how could Moses have been the author of the Five Books when the last book describes in detail the precise time and circumstances of his death?

"And the many literary asides. Like when ancient placenames are used, then the text notes that those places are still visible *to this day.* This absolutely points to later influences shaping, expanding, and embellishing the text."

Malone said, "And each time one of these redactions occurred, more of the original meaning was lost."

"No doubt. The best estimate is that the Old Testament was composed between 1000 and 586 BCE. Later compositions came around 500 to 400 BCE. Then the text may have been tinkered with as late as 300 BCE. Nobody knows for sure. All we know is that the Old Testament is a patchwork, each segment written under differing historical and political circumstances, expressing differing religious views."

"I appreciate all that," Malone said, thinking again about the New Testament contradictions from France. "Believe me, I do. But none of it is revolutionary. Either folks believe the

Old Testament is the Word of God, or they believe it a collection of ancient tales."

"But what if the words have been altered to the point that the original message is no longer there? What if the Old Testament, as we know it, is not, and never was, the Old Testament from its original time? Now, that could change many things."

"I'm listening."

"That's what I like about you," Haddad said, smiling. "Such a good listener."

Malone could see from Pam's expression that she didn't necessarily agree, but, keeping to her word, she stayed silent.

"You and I have talked about this before," Haddad said. "The Old Testament is fundamentally different from the New. Christians take the text of the New literally, even to the point of it being history. But the stories of the Patriarchs, Exodus, and the conquest of Canaan are not history. They're a creative expression of religious reform that happened in a place called Judah long ago. Granted, there are kernels of truth to the accounts, but they're far more story than fact.

"Cain and Abel is a good example. At the time of that tale there were only four people on earth. Adam, Eve, Cain, and Abel. Yet Genesis 4:17 says *Cain lay with his wife and she became pregnant.* Where did the wife come from? Was it Eve? His mother? Wouldn't that be eye-opening? Then, in recounting Adam's bloodline, Genesis 5 says that Mahalale lived eight hundred ninety-five years, Jared eight hundred years, and Enoch three hundred sixty-five years. And Abraham. He was supposedly a hundred years old when Sarah gave birth to Isaac, and she was ninety."

"No one takes that stuff literally," Pam said.

"Devout Jews would argue to the contrary."

"What are you saying, George?" Malone asked.

"The Old Testament, as we currently know it, is a result of

translations. The Hebrew language of the original text passed out of usage around 500 BCE. So in order to understand the Old Testament, we must either accept the traditional Jewish interpretations or seek guidance from modern dialects that are descendants of that lost Hebrew language. We can't use the former method because the Jewish scholars who originally interpreted the text, between 500 and 900 CE, a thousand or more years after they were first written, didn't even know Old Hebrew, so they based their reconstructions on guesswork. The Old Testament, which many revere as the Word of God, is nothing more than a haphazard translation."

"George, you and I have discussed this before. Scholars have debated the point for centuries. It's nothing new."

Haddad threw him a sly smile. "But I haven't finished explaining."

21

VIENNA, AUSTRIA
2:45 PM

ALFRED HERMANN'S CHÂTEAU OFFERED HIM AN ATMOSPHERE reminiscent of a tomb. Only when the Order's Assembly convened, or the Chairs gathered, was his solitude interrupted.

Neither was the case today.

And he was pleased.

He was ensconced in his private apartment, a series of spacious rooms on the château's second floor, each room flowing naturally through the other in the French style of no corridors. The winter session of the 49th Assembly would open in less than two days' time, and he was pleased that all seventy-one members in the Order of the Golden Fleece would be attending. Even Henrik Thorvaldsen, who at first had said he would not be coming, had now confirmed. The membership hadn't talked collectively since spring, so he knew the discussions over the coming days would be arduous. As Blue Chair, his task was to ensure that the proceedings were productive. The Order's staff was already at work preparing the château's meeting hall—and all would be ready by the time the members arrived for the weekend—but he wasn't worried about the Assembly. Instead his thoughts were on finding the Library of Alexandria. Something he'd dreamed of accomplishing for decades.

He stepped across the room.

The model, which he'd commissioned years ago, consumed the chamber's north corner, a spectacular miniature of what the Library of Alexandria may have looked like at the time of Caesar. He slid a chair close and sat, his eyes absorbing the details, his mind wandering.

Two pillared colonnades dominated. Both, he knew, would have been filled with statues, the floors sheathed in rugs, the walls draped in tapestries. In the many seats lining the corridors, members bickered over the meaning of a word or the cadence of a verse, or engaged in some caustic controversy about a new discovery. Both roofed chambers opened into side rooms where papyri, scrolls, and later codices lay stored in bins, loosely stacked, tagged for indexing, or on shelves. In other rooms copyists labored to produce replicas, which were sold for revenue. Members enjoyed a high salary and exemption from taxes, and were provided dining and lodging. There were lecture halls, laboratories, observatories—even a zoo. Grammarians and poets received the most prestigious posts— physicians, mathematicians, and astronomers the best equipment. The architecture was decidedly Greek, the whole thing resembling an elegant temple.

What a place, he thought.

What a time.

At only two points in human history had knowledge radically expanded on a global scale. Once during the Renaissance, which continued to the present, and the other during the fourth century BCE, when Greece ruled the world.

He thought about the time three hundred years before Christ and the sudden death of Alexander the Great. His generals fought over his grand empire, and eventually the realm was divided into thirds, and the Hellenistic Age, a period of worldwide Greek dominance, began. One of those thirds was claimed by a far-thinking Macedonian, Ptolemy, who declared himself king of Egypt in 304 BCE, founding the Ptolemaic dynasty, capitaled in Alexandria.

The Ptolemies were intellectuals. Ptolemy I was a historian. Ptolemy II a zoologist. Ptolemy III a patron of literature. Ptolemy IV a playwright. Each chose leading scholars and scientists as tutors for his children and encouraged great minds to live in Alexandria.

Ptolemy I founded the museum, a place where learned men could congregate and share their knowledge. To aid their endeavors, he also established the library. By the time of Ptolemy III, in 246 BCE, there were two locations—the main library near the royal palace and another, smaller one headquartered in the sanctuary of the god Serapis, known as the Serapeum.

The Ptolemies were determined book collectors, dispatching agents throughout the known world. Ptolemy II bought Aristotle's entire library. Ptolemy III ordered that all ships in the Alexandria harbor be searched. If books were found, they were copied, the copies returned to the owners, the originals stored in the library. Genres varied from poetry and history to rhetoric, philosophy, religion, medicine, science, and law. Some 43,000 scrolls were eventually housed in the Serapeum, available to the general public, and another 500,000 at the museum, restricted to scholars.

What happened to it all?

One version held that it burned when Julius Caesar fought Ptolemy XIII in 48 BCE. Caesar had ordered the torching of the royal fleet, but the fire spread throughout the city and may have consumed the library. Another version blamed Christians, who supposedly destroyed the main library in 272 CE and the Serapeum in 391, part of their effort to rid the city of all pagan influences. A final account credited Arabs with the library's destruction after they conquered Alexandria in 642. The caliph Omar, when asked about books in the imperial treasury, was quoted as saying, *If what is written agrees with the Book of God, they are not required. If it disagrees, they are not desired. Destroy them.* So for six months scrolls supposedly fueled the baths of Alexandria.

Hermann always winced at that thought—how one of humanity's greatest attempts to collect knowledge might simply have burned.

But what really happened?

Certainly, as Egypt was confronted with growing unrest and foreign aggression, the library became victim to persecution, mob violence, and military occupation, no longer enjoying special privileges.

When had it finally disappeared?

No one knew.

And was the legend true? A group of enthusiasts, it was said, had managed to extract scroll after scroll, copying some, stealing others, methodically preserving knowledge. Chroniclers had hinted at their existence for centuries.

The Guardians.

He liked to imagine what those dedicated enthusiasts may have preserved. Unknown works from Euclid? Plato? Aristotle? Augustine? Along with countless other men who would later be regarded as fathers of their respective fields.

No telling.

And that's what made the search so enticing.

Not to mention George Haddad's theories, which offered Hermann a way to further the Order's purposes. The Political Committee had already determined how the destabilization of Israel could be manipulated for profit. The business plan was both ambitious and feasible. Provided Haddad's research could be proven.

Five years ago Haddad had reported a visit from someone known as a Guardian. Israel's spies had conveyed that information to Tel Aviv. The Jews had overreacted, as always, and immediately tried to kill Haddad. Thankfully the Americans had intervened, and Haddad was still among the living. Hermann was equally thankful that his American political sources were now negotiable, recently confirming those facts and adding more, which was why Sabre had moved on Cotton Malone.

But who knew anything? Perhaps Sabre would learn more from the corrupt Israeli waiting in Germany?

The only certainty was George Haddad.

He had to be found.

22

SABRE STROLLED DOWN THE COBBLESTONED LANE. ROTHEN-burg lay a hundred kilometers south of Würzburg, a walled city encircled by stone ramparts and watchtowers straight out of the Middle Ages. Inside, narrow streets wound tight paths between half-timbered brick-and-stone buildings. Sabre searched for one in particular.

The *Baumeisterhaus* stood just off the market square, within shouting distance of the ancient clock tower. An iron placard announced that the building had been erected in 1596, but for the past century the three-story structure had hosted an inn and restaurant.

He pushed through the front door and was greeted by the sweet smell of yeast bread and apple-cinnamon. A narrow ground-floor dining hall emptied into a two-story inner courtyard, the whitewashed walls dotted with antlers.

One of the Order's contacts waited in an oak booth, a thin puny figure known only as Jonah. Sabre walked over and slid into the booth. The table was draped in a dainty pink cloth. A china cup filled with black coffee rested in front of Jonah, a half-eaten Danish on a nearby plate.

"Strange things are happening," Jonah said in English.

"That's the way of the Middle East."

"Stranger than normal."

This man was attached to the Israeli Home Office, part of the German mission.

"You asked me to watch for anything on George Haddad. Seems he's risen from the dead. Our people are in an uproar."

He feigned ignorance. "What's the source of that revelation?"

"He actually called Palestine in the last few days. He wants to tell them something."

Sabre had met with Jonah three times before. Men like him, who placed euros ahead of loyalty, were useful, but at the same time they demanded caution. Cheaters always cheated. "How about we stop hedging and you tell me what it is you want me to know."

The man savored a sip of his coffee. "Before he disappeared five years ago, Haddad received a visit from someone called the Guardian."

Sabre already knew that, but said nothing.

"He was given some kind of information. A little strange, but it gets even stranger."

He'd never appreciated the sense of drama Jonah liked to invoke.

"Haddad's not the first to have had that experience. I saw a file. There have been three others since 1948 who received similar visits from someone called the Guardian. Israel knew about each, but all those men died within days or weeks of the visit." Jonah paused. "If you recall, Haddad almost died, too."

He began to understand. "Your people are keeping something to themselves?"

"Apparently so."

"Over what period of time have these visits occurred?"

"About every twenty years for the past sixty or so. All

THE ALEXANDRIA LINK 119

were academics, one Israeli and three Arabs, including Haddad. The murders were all conducted by the Mossad."

He needed to know, "And how did you manage to learn that?"

"As I said, the files." Jonah went silent. "A communiqué came a few hours ago. Haddad is living in London."

"I need an address."

Jonah provided it, then said, "Men have been sent. From the assassination squad."

"Why kill Haddad?"

"I asked the ambassador the same question. He's former Mossad and he told me an interesting tale."

"I assume that's why I'm here?"

Jonah tossed him a smile. "I knew you were a smart man."

David Ben-Gurion realized that his political career was over. Ever since his days as a frail child in Poland he'd dreamed about the deliverance of the Jews to their biblical homeland. So he'd fathered the nation of Israel and led it through the tumultuous years of 1948 to 1963, commanding its wars and delivering statesmanship.

Tough duty for a man who'd actually wanted to be an intellectual.

He'd devoured philosophy books, studied the Bible, flirted with Buddhism, even taught himself ancient Greek in order to read Plato in the original. He possessed a relentless curiosity about the natural sciences and detested fiction. Verbal battle, not crafted dialogue, was his preferred mode of communication.

Yet he was no abstract thinker.

Instead he was a tight, craggy man with a halo of silvery hair, a jawbone that projected willpower, and a volcanic temper.

He'd proclaimed Israel's independence in May 1948,

ignoring last-minute admonitions from Washington and overruling doomsday predictions by his closest associates. He recalled how, within hours of his declaration, the military forces of five Arab nations invaded Israel, joining Palestinian militias in an open attempt to destroy the Jews. He'd personally led the army, and 1 percent of the Jewish population had ultimately died, as well as thousands of Arabs. More than half a million Palestinians lost their homes. In the end the Jews prevailed, and many had labeled him a combination of Moses, King David, Garibaldi, and God Almighty.

For fifteen more years he led his nation. But now it was 1965, and he was nearly eighty and tired.

Even worse, he'd been wrong.

He stared at the impressive library. So much knowledge. The man who'd called himself a Guardian had said the quest would be a challenge, but if he managed to succeed, the rewards would be incalculable.

And the envoy had been right.

He'd read once that the measure of an idea was how relative it was not only to its time, but beyond.

His time had produced the modern nation of Israel, but in the process thousands had died—and he feared that many more would perish in the decades ahead. Jews and Arabs seemed destined to fight. He'd thought his goal righteous, his cause just, but no longer.

He'd been wrong.

About everything.

Carefully he again paged through the weighty volume open on the table. Three such tomes had been waiting when he'd arrived. The Guardian who'd visited him six months back had been standing at the entrance, a broad grin on his chapped face.

Never had Ben-Gurion dreamed that such a place of

*learning existed, and he was grateful that his curiosity
had allowed him to amass the courage for the quest.*

*"Where did all this come from?" he'd asked on enter-
ing.*

"The hearts and minds of men and women."

*A riddle but also a truth, and the philosopher within
him understood.*

"Ben-Gurion told that story in 1973, days before he died,"
Jonah said. "Some say he was delirious. Others that his mind
had wandered. But whatever he may have actually learned at
that library, he kept to himself. One fact is clear, though.
Ben-Gurion's politics and philosophy changed dramatically
after 1965. He was less militant, more conciliatory. He
called for concessions to the Arabs. Most attributed that to
advancing age, but the Mossad thought there was more. So
much that Ben-Gurion actually became suspect. That's why
he was never allowed a political comeback. Can you imagine? The father of Israel kept at bay."

"Who's this Guardian?"

Jonah shrugged. "The files are quiet. But for those four
who received visits—somehow the Mossad learned about
each one and acted swiftly. Whoever it is, Israel doesn't want
anyone talking to them."

"So your colleagues plan to eliminate Haddad?"

Jonah nodded. "As we speak."

He'd heard enough, so he slid from the booth.

"What of my payment?" Jonah quickly asked.

He slipped an envelope from his pocket and tossed it on
the table. "That should bring our account current. Let us
know when there's more to tell."

Jonah pocketed the bribe. "You'll be the first."

He watched as his contact stood and headed not for the
front door, but toward an alcove where restrooms were lo-

cated. He decided this was as good an opportunity as any, so he followed.

At the bathroom door, he hesitated.

The restaurant was half filled, ill lit, and noisy, the table occupants self-absorbed, buzzing with talk in several languages.

He entered, locked the door, and quickly surveyed the scene. Two stalls, a sink, and a mirror, amber light from incandescent fixtures. Jonah occupied the first stall, the other was empty. Sabre grabbed a handful of paper towels and waited for the toilet to flush, then withdrew a knife from his pocket.

Jonah stepped from the stall, zipping his pants.

Sabre whirled and plunged the knife into the man's chest, twisting upward, then with his other hand clamped paper towels over the wound. He watched as the Israeli's eyes first filled with shock, then went blank. He kept the towels in place as he withdrew the blade.

Jonah sank to the floor.

He retrieved the envelope from the man's pocket, then swiped the metal on Jonah's trousers. Quickly he grasped the dead man's arms and dragged the bleeding body into the stall, propping the corpse on the toilet.

He then closed the stall door and left.

Outside, Sabre followed a guide who was steering a walking tour to the town's *rathaus*. The older woman pointed to the ancient city hall and spoke about Rothenburg's long history.

He hesitated and listened. Bells clanged for four PM.

"If you'll look up at the clock, watch the two bull's-eye windows to the right and left of the face."

Everyone turned as the panels swung open. A surmounted mechanical man appeared and drained a tankard of wine while another figure looked on. The guide droned about the historical significance. Cameras clicked. Camcorders whined. The event lasted about two minutes. As Sabre strolled away, he caught a glimpse of one tourist, a man, who deftly angled a lens away from the clock tower and focused on his retreat.

He smiled.

Exposure was always a risk when betrayal became a way of life. Luckily, he'd learned all he needed to know from Jonah, which explained why that liability had been permanently suppressed. But the Israelis were now aware of Jonah's contact. The Blue Chair seemed not to care and had specifically instructed him to provide a "good show."

Which he'd done.

For the Israelis and for Alfred Hermann.

23

LONDON
2:30 PM

MALONE WAITED FOR GEORGE HADDAD TO FINISH EXPLAINING. His old friend was hedging.

"I wrote a paper six years ago," Haddad said. "It dealt with a theory I had been working on, one that concerns how the Old Testament was originally translated from Old Hebrew."

Haddad told them about the Septuagint, crafted from the third to the first centuries BCE, the oldest and most complete rendition of the Old Testament into Greek, translated at the Library of Alexandria. Then he described the Codex Sinaiticus, a fourth-century CE manuscript of the Old and New Testaments used by later scholars to confirm other biblical texts, even though no one knew whether it was correct. And the Vulgate, completed about the same time by St. Jerome, the first translation from Hebrew directly to Latin, major revisions to which occurred in the sixteenth, eighteenth, and twentieth centuries.

"Even Martin Luther," Haddad said, "tinkered with the Vulgate, removing parts for his Lutheran faith. The whole meaning of that translation is muddled. A great many minds have altered its message.

"The King James Bible. Many think it presents original words, but it was created in the seventeenth century from a translation of the Vulgate into English. Those translators never saw the original Hebrew, and if they had, it's unlikely they could have understood it. Cotton, the Bible as we know it today is five linguistic removes from the first one ever written. The King James Bible proclaims itself authorized and original. But that does not mean genuine, authentic, or even true."

"Are there any Hebrew Bibles?" Pam asked.

Haddad nodded. "The oldest surviving one is the Aleppo Codex, saved from destruction in Syria in 1948. But that's a tenth-century CE manuscript, produced nearly two thousand years after the original text from who-knows-what."

Malone had seen that manuscript's crisp, cream-colored parchment, with faded brown ink, in Jerusalem's Jewish National Library.

"In my article," Haddad said, "I hypothesized how certain manuscripts could help resolve these questions. We know that the Old Testament was studied by ancient philosophers at the Library of Alexandria. Men who actually understood

Old Hebrew. We also know they wrote about their thoughts. There are references to these works, quotations and passages, in surviving manuscripts, but unfortunately the original texts are gone. Further, there may well be ancient Jewish texts—we know the library accumulated many of those. Mass destruction of Jewish writings became common later in history, especially Old Testaments in Hebrew. The Inquisition alone burned twelve thousand copies of the Talmud. Studying just one of those could prove decisive to resolving any doubts."

"What does it matter?" Pam asked.

"It matters a great deal," Haddad said. "Especially if it's wrong."

"In what way?" Malone asked, becoming impatient.

"Moses parting the Red Sea. The Exodus. Genesis. David and Solomon. Since the eighteenth century archaeologists have dug in the Holy Land with a vengeance—all to prove that the Bible is historical fact. Yet not one shred of physical evidence has been unearthed that confirms anything in the Old Testament. Exodus is a good example. Supposedly thousands of Israelites trekked across the Sinai Peninsula. They camped at locations specifically identified in the Bible, locations that can still be found today. But not a shard of pottery, not a bracelet, not anything has ever been found from that time period to confirm Exodus. This same evidentiary void is present when archaeology has tried to corroborate other biblical events. Don't you think that odd? Wouldn't there be some remnant of at least one incident depicted in the Old Testament still lying in the earth somewhere?"

Malone knew that Haddad, like many people, bought into the Bible only so much as history. That school of thought believed there was some truth there, but not much. Malone, too, possessed doubts. From his own reading he'd come to the conclusion that those who defended the narrative as history formed their conclusions far more from theological than from scientific considerations.

But still, so what?

"George, you've said all this before, and I agree with you. I need to know what's so important that your life is at stake?"

Haddad rose from the table and led them to where the maps adorned the walls. "I've spent the past five years collecting these. It hasn't been easy. I'm ashamed to say, I actually had to steal a few."

"From where?" Pam asked.

"Libraries, mainly. Most don't allow photocopying of rare books. And besides, you lose details in a copy, and it's the details that matter."

Haddad stepped to a map that depicted the modern state of Israel. "When the land was carved out in 1948 and the Zionists given their supposed portion, there was much talk about the Abrahamic covenant. God's word that this region—" Haddad pressed his finger onto the map. "—this precise land, was supposedly Abraham's."

Malone noted the boundaries.

"Being able to understand Old Hebrew has given me some insight. Maybe too much. About thirty years ago I noticed something interesting. But to appreciate that revelation, it's important to appreciate Abraham."

Malone was familiar with the story.

"Genesis," Haddad said, "records an event that profoundly affected world history. It may well be the most important day in all human history."

Malone listened as Haddad spoke of Abram, who traveled from Mesopotamia to Canaan, wandering among the population, faithfully following God's commands. His wife, Sarai, remained barren and eventually suggested that Abram couple with her favorite handmaiden, an Egyptian slave named Hagar, who'd stayed with them since the clan's expulsion from Egypt by the pharaoh.

"The birth of Ishmael," Haddad said, "Abram's first son, from Hagar, becomes critical in the seventh century CE, when a new religion formed in Arabia. Islam. The Koran calls Ishmael *an apostle and a prophet. He was most acceptable in the sight of his Lord.* Abram's name appears in twenty-five of the one hundred fourteen chapters of the Koran. To this day *Ibrahim* and *Isma'il* are common first names for Muslims. The Koran itself commands Muslims to follow the religion of Abraham."

"He was not a Jew nor yet a Christian; but he was true in faith and he joined not gods with God."

"Good, Cotton, I see you've studied your Koran since we last talked."

He smiled. "I gave it a reading or two. Fascinating stuff."

"The Koran makes clear that *Abraham and Isma'il* raised the foundation of the House."

"The Kaaba," Pam said. "Islam's holiest shrine."

Malone was impressed. "When did you learn about Islam?"

"I didn't. But I watch the History Channel."

He caught her grin.

"The Kaaba is in Mecca. Adult Muslims have to make a pilgrimage there. Problem is, when they gather each year so many people come that several hundred are trampled to death. That's in the news all the time."

"The Arabs, particularly Muslim Arabs, trace their heritage to Ishmael," Haddad said.

Malone knew what came next. Thirteen years after the birth of Ishmael, Abram was told by God that he would be father to a multitude of nations. First he was ordered to change his name to *Abraham* and Sarai's to *Sarah*. Then God announced that Sarah would give birth to a son. Neither

Sarah nor Abraham believed God, but within a year Isaac was born.

"The day of that birth may well be the most important day in human history," Haddad said. "Everything changed after that. The Bible and the Koran differ on many points relative to Abram. Each recounts a separate tale. But according to the Bible, the Lord told Abraham that all the land surrounding him, the land of Canaan, would belong to Abraham and his heir, Isaac."

Malone knew the rest. God reappeared to Isaac's son Jacob and repeated the promise of the land, saying that through Jacob would come a people to whom the land of Canaan would everlastingly belong. Jacob was told to change his name to *Israel*. Jacob's twelve sons evolved into separate tribes, held together by the covenant between God and Abraham, and they each established their own families, becoming the twelve tribes of Israel.

"Abraham is the father of all three of the world's main religions," Haddad said. "Islam, Judaism, and Christianity trace their roots to him, though the story of his life differs in each. The entire conflict in the Middle East, which has endured for thousands of years, is simply a debate over which account is correct, which religion has the divine right to the land. The Arabs through Ishmael. The Jews from Isaac. The Christians by Christ."

Malone recalled the Bible and said, *"The Lord had said to Abram: Leave your country, your people and your father's household and go to the land I will show you. I will make you into a great nation and I will bless you. I will make your name great and you will be a blessing. I will bless those who bless you, and whoever curses you I will curse; and all peoples on earth will be blessed through you."*

"You say the words with conviction," Pam said.

"They have meaning," Haddad said. "Jews believe they

are what grant them exclusive ownership of Palestine. I've spent most of my adult life studying the Bible. It's an amazing book. And what separates it from all other epic tales is simple. Nothing mystical or magical. Instead, human responsibility is its focus."

"Do you believe?" Pam asked.

Haddad shook his head. "In religion? No. I've seen its manipulation too clearly. In God? That's another matter. But I've seen His neglect. I was born a Muslim. My father was Muslim, as was his. After the war in 1948, though, something overtook me. That's when the Bible became my passion. I wanted to read it in its original form. To know what it truly meant."

"Why do the Israelis want you dead?" Malone asked.

"They are the descendants of Abraham. The ones God said He would bless—their enemies the ones He would curse. Millions have died through the centuries, thousands over the past fifty years, simply to prove those words. Recently, Cotton, I was embroiled in a debate. A particularly arrogant man in a local pub told me that Israel possessed the absolute right to exist. He gave me six reasons, which hinged separately on archaeology, history, practicality, humanity, defense, and, to him the most important, entitlement." Haddad paused. "Entitlement, Cotton. Biblical entitlement. The Abrahamic covenant. God's land given to the people of Israel, proclaimed in all its glory in the words of Genesis."

Malone waited.

"What if we have it all wrong?" Haddad glared at the map of Israel alongside another map of Saudi Arabia.

"Do go on," a new voice said.

They all turned.

Standing in the front doorway was a short man with glasses and a fading hairline. Beside him was a woman, midthirties, small and compact, dark complexion. Both held

sound-suppressed weapons. Malone immediately registered
the make and model of the guns and knew who these two
worked for.

Israel.

24

WASHINGTON, DC
9:50 AM

STEPHANIE FINISHED HER BREAKFAST AND SIGNALED THE
waiter for the check. She sat in a restaurant near Dupont Circle, not far from her hotel. The entire Magellan Billet had
been mobilized and seven of her twelve lawyers were now
directly assisting her. The murder of Lee Durant had provided them all with motivation, but there were risks associated with her efforts. Other intelligence agencies would
quickly learn what she was doing, which meant Larry Daley
would not be far behind. To hell with them. Malone needed
her, and she wasn't about to let him down. Again.

She paid the bill and signaled a taxi that, fifteen minutes
later, deposited her on 17th Street adjacent to the National
Mall. The day was bright and sunny, and the woman she'd
called two hours ago occupied a shaded bench not far from
the World War II Memorial. She was a leggy blonde, strong-
bodied, with, Stephanie knew, a shrewdness that demanded
she be handled with caution. Stephanie had known Heather

Dixon for nearly a decade. Carrying a married surname from a short-lived relationship, Dixon was an Israeli citizen attached to the Washington mission, part of the Mossad's North American contingent. They'd worked together, and against each other, which was par for the course when it came to the Israelis. Stephanie was hoping today would be a friendly venture.

"Good to see you," she said as she sat.

Dixon was dressed stylishly, as always, in brown-and-gold glen plaid pants, a white oxford shirt, and a black bouclé vest.

"You sounded concerned on the phone."

"I am. I need to know about your government's interest in George Haddad."

The vacuous stare of an intelligence officer faded from Dixon's attractive face. "You've been busy."

"As have your people. Lots of chatter about Haddad the past few days." She was actually at a disadvantage, because Lee Durant had been her contact point with the Israelis, and he hadn't had a chance to report all of what he'd learned.

"What's the American interest?" Dixon asked.

"Five years ago one of my agents almost died because of Haddad."

"And then you hid the Palestinian away. Kept him all to yourself. And didn't bother to tell your ally."

Now they were getting to the meat of the coconut. "And you didn't bother to tell us that you'd tried to blow the man up, along with my agent."

"That, I know nothing about. Way out of the loop. But I do know that Haddad has surfaced, and we want him."

"As do we."

"What's so important on your end?"

She couldn't decide if Dixon was fishing or stalling.

"You tell me, Heather. Why did the Saudis bulldoze entire

villages in west Arabia to the ground five years ago? Why is the Mossad focused on Haddad?"

She bored her gaze into her friend.

"Why did he need to die?"

A CALM FATALISM OVERTOOK MALONE. ONE RULE EVERYONE IN the intelligence business respected—*Don't screw with the Israelis*. Malone had violated that wisdom when he'd allowed Israel to believe Haddad died in the bombed café. Now he knew that they knew. Lee Durant had said the Israelis were hyper, but he'd mentioned nothing about Haddad's secrecy being compromised. Otherwise he would never have allowed Pam to come along.

"You really should lock your door," the intruder declared. "All sorts of people could enter."

"You have a name?" Malone asked.

"Call me Adam. She's Eve."

"Interesting labels for an Israeli assassination squad."

"What do you mean?" Pam asked. "Assassination?"

He faced her. "They've come to finish what they started five years ago." He turned toward Haddad, who showed not the slightest hint of fear. "What is it they want kept quiet?"

"The truth," Haddad said.

"I don't know anything about that," Adam said. "I'm not a politico. Just hired help. My orders are to eliminate. You understand that, Malone. You were once in the business."

Yes, he could relate. Pam, though, appeared to be another story.

"All of you are nuts," she said. "You talk about killing like it's just part of the job."

"Actually," Adam said, "it's my only job."

Malone had learned when he'd first started with the Magellan Billet that survival many times hinged on knowing when to hold and when to fold. As he stared at his old friend, a warrior of long standing, he saw that Haddad knew the time had come for him to choose.

"I'm sorry," Malone whispered.

"Me, too, Cotton. But I made my decision when I placed the calls."

Had he heard right? "Calls?"

"One awhile back, the other two recently. To the West Bank."

"That was foolish, George."

"Perhaps. But I knew you'd come."

"Glad *you* did, 'cause I didn't."

Haddad's gaze tightened. "You taught me a great deal. I recall every lesson, and up until a few days ago I adhered to them strictly. Even those about safeguarding what really matters." The voice had grown dull and toneless.

"You should have called me first."

Haddad shook his head. "I owe this to the Guardian I shot. My debt repaid."

"What a contradiction," Adam said. "A Palestinian with honor."

"And an Israeli who murders," Haddad said. "But we are what we are."

Malone's mind was clicking off possibilities. He had to do something, but Haddad seemed to sense his plotting. "You've done all you can. For now, at least." Haddad motioned. "Look after her."

"Cotton, you can't just let them kill him," Pam whispered, desperation in her voice.

"But he can," Haddad said, a touch of bitterness in his tone. Then the Palestinian glared at Adam. "Might I say a final prayer?"

Adam gestured with the gun. "Who am I to deny such a reasonable request."

Haddad stepped toward one of the wall chests and reached for a drawer. "I have a cushion in here that I kneel upon. May I?"

Adam shrugged.

Haddad slowly opened the drawer and used both hands to withdraw a crimson pillow. The old man then approached one of the windows and Malone watched as the pillow dropped to the floor.

A gun came into view.

Firmly grasped in Haddad's right hand.

STEPHANIE WAITED FOR AN ANSWER TO HER QUESTION.

"Haddad is a threat to the security of Israel," Dixon said. "He was five years ago, and he remains one today."

"Care to explain?"

"Why aren't you asking your own people this?"

She'd hoped to avoid this line of questioning but decided to be honest. "There's a division."

"And where are you among that division?"

"I have a former agent who's in trouble. I intend to help him."

"Cotton Malone. We know. But Malone knew what he was getting into when he hid Haddad."

"His son didn't."

Dixon shrugged. "Several of my friends have died from terrorists."

"A bit sanctimonious, aren't you?"

"I don't think so. The Palestinians leave us little choice in how to deal with them."

"They're doing nothing different from what the Jews did in 1948." She couldn't resist.

Dixon smirked. "If I'd known we were going to have this argument again, I wouldn't have come."

Stephanie knew Dixon didn't want to hear about the terrorism of the late 1940s, which was far more Jewish than Arab in origin. But she wasn't going to cut her friend any slack. "We can talk about the King David Hotel again if you want."

The Jerusalem locale had served as British military and criminal investigative headquarters. After a local Jewish Agency was raided and sensitive documents removed to the hotel, militants retaliated with a bomb in July 1946. Ninety-one dead, forty-five injured, fifteen of the dead were Jews.

"The British were warned," Dixon said. "Not our fault they chose to ignore it."

"What does it matter if they were called?" she said. "It was an act of terrorism—Jew against Brit—a way to press your agenda. The Jews wanted the British and Arabs out of Palestine and they used whatever tactic worked. Just as Palestinians have tried for decades."

Dixon shook her head. "I'm sick of hearing that crap. The *nakba* is a joke. Arabs fled Palestine in the 1940s on their own because they were scared to death. The rich ones panicked; the rest left after Arab leaders asked them to. They all honestly believed we'd be crushed in a few weeks. The ones who left went only a few miles into neighboring Arab states. And nobody, including you, ever talks about all the Jews who were forced from those same Arab states." Dixon shrugged. "It's like, *So what? Who cares about them?* But the poor pitiful Arabs. What a tragedy."

"Take a man's land and he'll fight you forever."

"We didn't *take* anything. We bought the land, and most of it was uncultivated swamp and scrub nobody wanted. And by the way, eighty percent of those Arabs who left were peasants, nomads, or Bedouins. The landowners, the ones who raised so much hell, lived in Beirut, Cairo, and London."

Stephanie had heard that before. "The Israeli party line never changes."

"All the Arabs had to do," Dixon said, "was accept the 1947 UN resolution that called for two states, one Arab, the other Jewish, and everybody would have won. But no. Absolutely not. No compromise. Repatriation was always and still is a condition prerequisite to any discussion, and that's not going to happen. Israel is a reality that will not disappear. It's sickening how everybody feels for the Arabs. They live in camps as refugees because the Arab leadership likes that. If they didn't, they'd do something about it. Instead they use the camps, and the designated living zones, as a way to embarrass the world for what it did in 1948. Yet nobody, including America, ever chastises *them*."

"Right now, Heather, I'm only interested in Cotton Malone's son and George Haddad."

"So is the White House. Our people were told you were interfering in the Haddad matter. Larry Daley says you're a pain in the ass."

"He should know."

"Tel Aviv doesn't want any interference."

Stephanie suddenly regretted her decision to meet with Dixon. But she still needed to ask, "What's so important? Tell me, and I might stay out of it."

Dixon chuckled. "That's a good one. Does anybody ever actually fall for it?"

"I thought it might work here." She'd hoped their friendship meant something. "With us."

Dixon glanced around at the concrete walkways. People strolled the mall, enjoying the day. "This one's serious, Stephanie."

"How bad?"

Dixon's hand slipped around her back and reappeared with a gun.

"This serious."

25

LONDON

MALONE SAW THE GUN IN HADDAD'S HAND AND KNEW THAT his friend had decided this was to be his last stand. No more hiding. Time to face his demons.

Haddad fired first, the bullet thudding into Eve's chest and propelling the younger woman off her feet, a wound gushing blood.

Adam fired and Haddad cried out in agony as the bullet pierced his shirt and blew out his spine, dotting the wall and maps behind him in crimson smears.

Haddad's legs buckled, his mouth gaped open, but not a sound escaped as the old man collapsed to the floor.

Pam screamed, a piercing falsetto.

The air seemed to have escaped from the room. Malone felt himself at the mercy of a bitter heart.

He faced Adam, who lowered his weapon.

"I came to kill him, that's all," Adam said, the geniality in his voice faded. "My government has no trouble with you, Malone, though you did deceive us. But that was your job. So we'll let it slide."

"So kind of you."

"I'm not a murderer, just an assassin."

"What about her?" he asked, pointing at Eve's body.

"Nothing I can do. Just like there's nothing you can do for him. There's a price to be paid for mistakes."

Malone said nothing, though he was half mad with terror and anguish. Surely the shots had been heard and the police called.

The Israeli turned and disappeared.

Footsteps receded down the stairway.

Pam seemed frozen in place, staring in disbelief at Haddad's corpse, the old man's mouth still open in a final protest. They exchanged glances but no words. He could almost understand the Israeli's thinking. He was indeed a paid assassin, employed by a sovereign state, empowered to kill. But the son of a bitch was still a murderer.

George Haddad was dead.

And there was a price to be paid for that, too.

Dark thoughts held him in their thrall. He bent down and retrieved Haddad's gun, then stood and turned for the door.

"Stay here," he told Pam.

"What are you going to do?"

"Kill the son of a bitch."

STEPHANIE WAS MORE PUZZLED THAN FRIGHTENED AT THE sight of a gun. "Apparently, Heather, the rules have changed. I thought we were allies."

"That's the funny thing about U.S.–Israeli relations. Sometimes it's hard to tell which side we're actually on."

"And you apparently feel a certain freedom since the White House called."

"Always nice when the Americans are in conflict."

"Larry Daley wants Haddad for himself. You realize that, don't you? This is a diversion to occupy your time while our agents find him."

"Good luck. Only we and Malone know where."

Stephanie didn't like the sound of that. This needed to end. Since she'd first sat down, the fingers of her right hand had rested on her leg, the tips atop the radio controller nestled inside her loose-fitting slacks. "That depends on whether or not U.S. intelligence has a source within your organization."

"This operation is being held fairly close, so I doubt there'll be any leaks. Besides, Haddad is most likely dead by now. Our agents were sent hours ago."

Stephanie's left hand motioned to the gun while her right stayed steady on her leg. "What's the point of this show?"

"Unfortunately, you've become a problem to your government."

"Gee, I thought my resignation would be enough."

"Not any longer. I believe you were warned to stay out of this, yet you've mobilized the entire Billet. Contrary, of course, to what you were told."

"Larry Daley doesn't give me orders."

"But his boss does."

She quickly realized that if she was now a target, Brent Green might be, too. Killing the attorney general, though, posed more logistical problems than her own death would entail. The White House had apparently concluded that corpses never appeared on the Sunday-morning news shows. Her fingers prepared to depress the panic button. "You here to do Daley's dirty work?"

"Let's just say that our interests are similar. Besides, we like it when the White House owes us."

"Plan to shoot me here?"

"No need. I have some associates willing to do it."

"Your people?"

She shook her head. "Amazingly, Stephanie, you've managed to do what politicians have tried to do for centuries. Get Jews and Arabs to cooperate. The Saudis are working with us on this one. We apparently have a common goal, so all differences have been put aside." Dixon shrugged. "Just this once."

"And that also eliminates the problem of Israel killing an American."

Dixon scrunched her face in mock contemplation. "See the benefits? We find the problem, they eliminate it. Everybody wins."

"Except me."

"You know the rules. Your friend today can be your enemy tomorrow, and vice versa. Israel has few friends in this world, but threats come from all over. We do what we have to."

Stephanie had first faced a gun while searching with Malone for the Knights Templar. She'd witnessed death there, too. Thank goodness she'd thought ahead. "Do what you have to."

Her right index finger activated the signal that would alert her agents, less than a minute away, to come.

All she had to do was stall.

Heather Dixon's eyes suddenly rolled skyward, then closed as her head pitched forward and her body went limp.

The gun thudded to the grass.

Stephanie caught Dixon as she slumped toward her. Then she saw it. A feathered dart protruding from Dixon's neck. She'd seen one before.

Calmly, she turned.

Standing a few feet behind the bench was a woman. Tall, skin the color of a muddy stream, long dark hair. She wore an expensive cashmere jacket atop hip-slung jeans, the tight-fitting ensemble highlighting a lean, shapely form. She held a magnum air pistol in her left hand.

"Appreciate the assist," Stephanie said, trying to mask her surprise.

"That's what I came for."

And Cassiopeia Vitt smiled.

MALONE BOUNDED DOWN THE STAIRS TOWARD THE GROUND floor. Adam would not be easy to kill. Pros never were.

He kept descending two steps at a time and checked the gun's magazine. Seven shots remained. He told himself to be careful. Surely the Israeli would know he'd come after him. Actually, he'd invited the challenge since, before leaving, Adam had not confiscated Haddad's weapon. Pros never left that kind of opportunity. And the line about professional courtesy made no sense. Assassins could not care less about protocol. They were the janitors of the intelligence business. Sent in solely to clean up the mess. Witnesses were part of that mess. So why not clean up everything? Maybe Adam wanted a confrontation? Killing an American agent, retired or otherwise, came with consequences. But if the agent attacked first—that was another matter.

He flushed confusion from his mind as he found the ground floor. His index finger nestled against the trigger, and he readied himself for a fight.

More familiar feelings returned. Ones that, as he'd come to learn a few months ago, were simply part of his psyche. In France he'd actually made peace with those demons when he realized that he was a player and always would be, regardless of retirement. Yesterday at Kronborg Slot, Pam had chided him that he'd needed the rush—that she and Gary had never been enough. He'd resented the insult because it wasn't true. He didn't *need* the rush, but he certainly could *handle* it.

He stepped into October sunlight, which seemed strong after the building's gloom, and calmly descended the front stoop. Adam was fifty feet away, walking on the sidewalk.

Malone followed.

Parked cars lined both sides of the narrow street. From busy avenues at either end of the block came the steady roar of traffic. A few people meandered along the opposite sidewalk.

Talking would be a waste of time.

So he raised his weapon.

But Adam spun.

Malone dove to the pavement.

A bullet whizzed by, pinging off one of the cars. He rolled and clicked off a shot in Adam's direction. The Israeli had wisely abandoned the sidewalk, now using the parked cars as cover.

Malone rolled into the street, between two cars.

He balanced on his knees and peered through the windshield, searching for his target. Adam was holed up ten vehicles ahead. Pedestrians on the far sidewalk scattered.

Then he heard a moan.

He turned and saw Pam lying on the stairs leading into George Haddad's building.

Her left arm a mass of blood.

26

WASHINGTON, DC

STEPHANIE WAS GLAD TO SEE CASSIOPEIA VITT. THE LAST TIME she'd worked with the mysterious Moorish woman, they'd been in the French Pyrénées, embroiled in a different di lemma.

"Lay her down and let's get out of here," Vitt said.

Stephanie stood from the bench and allowed Heather Dixon's head to smack the wooden slats.

"That'll leave a nasty bruise," Vitt said.

"Like I care. She was about to have me killed. You want to tell me why you're here?"

"Henrik thought you might need help. He didn't like the feeling he was getting from his Washington contacts. I was in the neighborhood—New York—so he asked if I could keep an eye on you."

"How'd you find me?"

"Wasn't hard."

For the first time Stephanie was appreciative of Thorvaldsen's secretive ways.

"Remind me to include him on my Christmas card list."

Cassiopeia smiled. "He might like that."

Stephanie motioned at Dixon. "Damn disappointing. I thought she was my friend."

"Hard to come by in your business."

"Cotton is in deep trouble."

"Henrik thinks the same thing. He was hoping you were going to provide help."

"At the moment, I'm a target," she said.

"Which brings us to our other problem."

She did not like the sound of those words.

"Ms. Dixon didn't come alone." Cassiopeia pointed off toward the Washington Monument. "Two men in a car over that knoll. And they don't look Israeli."

"Saudis."

"Now, that's a feat. How did you manage to piss everybody off?"

Two men crested the knoll, headed their way.

"No time to explain," Stephanie said. "Shall we?"

They hustled in the opposite direction, a fifty-yard head start on their pursuers, which meant nothing if the men decided to shoot.

"I assume you planned for this contingency?" she asked Cassiopeia.

"Not entirely. But I can improvise."

MALONE FORGOT ABOUT ADAM AND SCRAMBLED FROM HIS safe position behind the parked car to where Pam lay bleeding. Street dust clung to his clothes. He turned for an instant and caught a glimpse of the Israeli racing away.

"You all right?" he asked her.

Pam's face grimaced in pain, her right hand clamped to her injured left shoulder.

"Hurts," she said in a strangled whisper.

"Let me see."

She shook her head. "Holding it . . . helps."

He reached out and started to peel her hand away. Her eyes went wide with pain and anger. "Don't."

"I have to see."

He didn't have to say what they were both thinking. *Why didn't she stay upstairs?*

She relented, removed her bloody fingers, and he saw what he suspected. The bullet had merely grazed her. A flesh wound. Anything worse would have already been obvious. People shot went into shock. Their bodies shut down.

"Just skimmed you," he said.

Her hand re-vised the wound. "Thanks for the diagnosis."

"I do have some experience at getting shot."

Her eyes softened at that realization.

"We have to go," he said.

Her face scrunched in pain. "I'm bleeding."

"No choice." He helped her to her feet.

"Damn, Cotton."

"I realize it hurts. But if you'd stayed upstairs like I said—"

Sirens wailed in the distance.

"We have to go. But first there's one other thing."

She seemed to recover her composure, determined to keep calm and stay lucid, so he led her into the building.

"Keep a clamp," he told her as they climbed the stairs to Haddad's apartment. "The bleeding should stop. It's not that deep."

Sirens were coming closer.

"What are we doing?" she asked, as they found the third-floor landing.

He recalled what Haddad had said right before the shooting started. *You taught me a great deal. I recall every lesson, and up until a few days ago I adhered to them strictly. Even those about safeguarding what really matters.* When he'd first hid Haddad away, he'd taught the Palestinian to keep his most important things ready to go at a moment's notice. Time to find out if Haddad meant what he'd said.

They entered the apartment.

"Go into the kitchen and find a towel," he said, "while I tend to this."

They had maybe two or three minutes.

He bolted for the bedroom. The tight space wasn't much larger than his own apartment in Copenhagen. Piles of long-neglected books and papers lay stacked on the floor, the bed unmade, the nightstands and dresser loaded like flea-market tables. He noticed more maps on the walls. Israel, past and present. No time to consider them.

He knelt beside the bed and hoped his instincts were right.

Haddad had called the Middle East knowing a confrontation would ensue. When that inevitable conflict arrived, he hadn't shied from the fight but had instead gone on the offensive, knowing he'd lose. But what had his friend said? *I knew you'd come.* Damn foolish. There'd been no need for Haddad to sacrifice himself. Guilt about the man he'd murdered decades ago had apparently swirled through the old man's head for a long time.

I owe this to the Guardian I shot. My debt repaid.

That, Malone *could* understand.

He probed beneath the bed and felt something. He grabbed hold and freed a leather satchel, quickly unbuckling its straps. Inside lay a book, three spiral notebooks, and four folded maps. Of all the information scattered about the apartment this, he hoped, was the most important.

They had to go.

He raced back to the den. Pam emerged from the kitchen with a towel clamped to her arm.

"Cotton?" she said.

He heard the question in her voice. "Not now."

With the satchel in hand he shoved her out the door, but

not before he grabbed a shawl from the back of one of the chairs.

They quickly descended.

"How's the bleeding?" he asked as they found the sidewalk.

"I'll live. Cotton?"

The sirens were no more than a block away. He draped the shawl around her shoulders to shield the injury.

They walked casually.

"Keep the towel on the arm," he said.

A hundred feet and they found a boulevard, plunging into a sea of unknown faces, resisting the temptation to hasten their pace.

He glanced back.

Flashing lights appeared at the far end of the block and stopped before Haddad's house.

"Cotton?"

"I know. Let's just get out of here."

He knew what she wanted. When they'd returned to the apartment he'd noticed, too. No blood on the wall. None on the floor. No suffocating stench of death.

And the bodies of Eve and George Haddad were gone.

27

RHINE VALLEY, GERMANY
5:15 PM

SABRE STARED AT THE TOWERING MOUNDS THAT ENGULFED THE river's edge. Steeply scarped banks lined both sides of the narrow gap. Deciduous forests abounded, the hillsides relieved only by sparse green scrub and gangly grapevines. For nearly seven hundred years the highest elevations had supported fortresses with names like Rheinstein, Sooneck, and Pfalz. Rounding the treacherous turn of the Lorelei, where ships once foundered on rocks and rapids, high atop the river's east bank he spied the rounded keep of Burg Katz. Farther on stood Stolzenfels, the tawny tint of its two-century-old limestone barely discernible. The final marker on his journey appeared a few minutes later.

The unmistakable outline of Marksburg.

He'd left Rothenburg two hours ago and followed the autobahn north, maintaining a constant ninety miles an hour, slowed only on the outskirts of Frankfurt, where he'd caught the beginnings of the afternoon commute. From there, two routes wound north to Cologne: A60 or follow the Rhine on the two-lane N9. He'd decided that the first half of the journey would be here, along the river, but the remainder had to be by autobahn. So he slowly threaded his way out of the ancient valley and followed the blue markers for A60.

An entrance ramp appeared and he sped onto the superhighway. He revved the rented BMW's engine and settled into the far-left lane. A patchwork quilt of hills, woods, and pasture rolled out on either side.

He glanced in the rearview mirror.

His tail, a silver Mercedes, was still there.

Back a respectable distance and shielded by three cars, the Mercedes could easily have gone unnoticed. But he'd been expecting them and they hadn't disappointed, following him ever since he'd left Rothenburg. He wondered if the body in the *Baumeisterhaus* had been found. Killing Jonah had probably saved the Israelis the trouble—betrayal came at an extreme cost in the Middle East—but the Jews had also lost the opportunity to interrogate a traitor, which may have soured their mood.

He loved the way Germans built superhighways—three wide lanes, few curves, sparse exits. Perfect for speed and privacy. A sign informed him that Cologne lay eighty-two kilometers ahead. He knew his position. Just south of Koblenz, fifteen kilometers east of the Rhine, the Mosel River fast approaching.

He switched lanes.

Farther back, beyond the Mercedes, he noticed four more vehicles.

Right on time.

Nine years he'd been searching for the Library of Alexandria, and all on behalf of the Blue Chair. The old man was obsessed with finding whatever was out there, and initially he'd thought the search ridiculous. But as he'd learned more, he'd come to realize that the goal wasn't as far-fetched as he'd first thought. Lately he'd begun to think there might even be something to find. The Israelis were certainly engrossed. Alfred Hermann seemed focused. He'd learned many things. Now it was time to use that knowledge.

For himself.

He'd sensed months ago that this might be his opportunity. He could only hope Cotton Malone was resourceful enough to avoid whatever the Israelis threw at him in London. They'd moved fast. Always did. But from everything he knew, and had witnessed, Malone was an expert, albeit out of practice. He should be able to handle the situation.

The viaduct appeared ahead.

He watched the first of the four sedans pass the silver Mercedes, change lanes, and abruptly position itself in front.

Two more cars quickly paralleled the Mercedes in the left lane.

Another hugged its bumper.

They all raced onto the bridge.

The span stretched more than half a mile, the Mosel River meandering eastward four hundred feet below. Halfway, exactly as Sabre had instructed, the lead car braked and the silver Mercedes reacted, pounding its brakes.

Just as that happened, the two adjacent cars slammed the driver's side and the car following rammed the bumper.

The combination of blows, along with speed, forced the Mercedes rightward, onto the guardrail.

In an instant the car became airborne.

Sabre imagined what was happening.

The torque from its upward acceleration would force the occupants back into their seats. They'd probably fumble for the seat-belt releases, but would never have the chance to release them. And if they did, where would they go? The four-hundred-foot fall would take a few seconds, and the jolt of the car's undercarriage slamming into the river would be like hitting concrete. Nothing would survive. Icy water seeping into the cabin would quickly send the hulk to the muddy bottom, where eventually the current would drag it east toward the even swifter Rhine.

Gone.

The four cars passed and the driver in the rear vehicle tossed him a wave. He returned the gesture. These men had been expensive, short notice and all, but worth every euro.

He kept speeding north toward Cologne.

It would take the Israelis a few days to determine what had happened. A problem was dead in Rothenburg and their field team was missing. He wondered if he'd been identified. Probably not. If they knew his identity, then why waste time taking pictures? No. He was still an unknown commodity.

Confusion reigned. In Israel and, soon, in Austria.

He liked that.

Time to convert that chaos into order.

28

WASHINGTON, DC

STEPHANIE WONDERED WHAT HER NEW COMPANION HAD planned. Cassiopeia Vitt was smart, wealthy, and daring, a woman who could handle herself in difficult situations. Not a bad combination. Provided she'd thought ahead.

"How do we get out of here?" she asked, as they trotted down the mall.

"You have any ideas?"

Actually she did, but she said nothing. "You're the one who appeared out of nowhere."

Cassiopeia smiled. "No need to be a smart-ass."

"We're being herded. I assumed you knew that."

The Lincoln Memorial loomed ahead at the west end of the mall. The Reflecting Pool blocked any retreat southward. To the north, tall trees lined a busy boulevard.

"Contrary to what you and Henrik believe," she said, "I'm not helpless. I have two agents on Constitution Avenue. I had just hit the panic button when you showed up."

"Bad news. Those two men left."

"What do you mean?"

"Right after you sat down with Dixon. They drove off."

The mall ended at the base of the Lincoln Memorial. She looked back. The two pursuers had stopped their advance.

"Apparently we're where they want us."

A taxi roared toward them from the direction of Independence Avenue.

"About time," Cassiopeia said, waving a black handkerchief.

The cab stopped and they leaped inside.

"I called a few minutes ago." Cassiopeia slammed the rear door and said to the driver, "Just drive around. We'll tell you when to let us out."

The cab sped away.

Stephanie plunged a hand into her pocket and found her cell phone. She dialed the number for the agents she'd positioned as backup. Two men were about to be fired.

"You want to tell me why you left me there?" she calmly said into the phone when it was answered.

"We were ordered away," the man said.

"I'm your boss. Who contradicts me?"

"*Your* boss."

Amazing. "Which one?"

"The attorney general. Brent Green himself came and told us to leave."

MALONE TOSSED THE SATCHEL FROM GEORGE HADDAD'S apartment onto the bed. He and Pam were inside a hotel not far from Hyde Park, a familiar place he'd chosen for its congestion because, as he was taught, *Nowhere better to hide in than a crowd.* He also liked the pharmacy next door. There he'd purchased gauze, antiseptic, and bandages.

"I have to work on that shoulder," he said.

"What do you mean? Let's find a hospital."

"I wish it were that simple."

He sat on the bed beside her.

"It's going to be that simple. I want a doctor."

"If you'd stayed upstairs like I told you, nothing would have happened."

"I thought you needed help. You were going to kill that man."

"Don't you get it, Pam? Wasn't watching George die enough? These SOBs are serious. They'll kill you as soon as look at you."

"I came to help," she quietly said.

And he saw something in her eyes he hadn't seen for years. Sincerity. Which raised a whole lot of questions he didn't want to ask. Nor, he was sure, would she want to answer. "Doctors would involve police, which is a problem." He sucked a few deep breaths. He was worn by fatigue and worry. "Pam, there are a lot of players here. The Israelis didn't take Gary—"

"How do you know that?"

"Call it instinct. My gut tells me they didn't do it."

"They sure killed that old man."

"Which was why I hid him away in the first place."

"He called them, Cotton. You heard him. He called knowing they'd come."

"He was doing his penance. Killing comes with consequences. George faced his today." And the thought of his dead friend brought with it a renewed pang of regret. "I need to work on that wound."

He slipped the shawl from around her shoulders and noticed that the towel was sticky with blood. "Did it open back up?"

She nodded. "On the way here."

He peeled the compress away. "Whatever's happening is complicated. George died for a reason—"

"His body was gone, Cotton. Along with the woman's."

"The Israelis apparently cleaned up their mess fast." He carefully examined her arm and saw that the cut was indeed shallow. "Which only goes to prove what I'm saying. There are multiple players. At least two, maybe three, possibly four. Israel is not in the habit of killing American agents. But the people who murdered Lee Durant don't seem to care. It's almost like they're inviting trouble. And *that,* the Israelis never do."

He stood and entered the bathroom. When he returned he popped open a bottle of antiseptic and handed her a fresh towel. "Bite on this."

A puzzled look came to her face. "Why?"

"I need to disinfect that wound and I don't want anyone to hear you scream."

Her eyes went wide. "That stuff hurts?"

"More than you can imagine."

STEPHANIE SWITCHED OFF THE CELL PHONE. *BRENT GREEN HIMself came and told us to leave.* Shock stiffened her spine, but decades in the intelligence business allowed nothing in her countenance to betray her surprise.

She faced Cassiopeia across the cab's rear seat. "I'm afraid, at the moment, you're the only person I can trust."

"You seem disappointed."

"I don't know you."

"That's not true. In France you checked me out."

Cassiopeia was right—she'd been thoroughly vetted, and Stephanie learned that the dark-skinned beauty had been born in Barcelona thirty-seven years ago. Half Muslim, though not noted as devout, Cassiopeia possessed master's degrees in engineering and medieval history. She was the sole shareholder and owner of a multicontinent conglomerate based in Paris and involved in a broad spectrum of international business ventures with assets in the multibillion-dollar range. Her Moorish father had started the company and she'd inherited control, though she was little involved with its everyday operation. She also served as the chairwoman for a Dutch foundation that worked closely with the United Nations on international AIDS relief and world famine, particularly in Africa. Stephanie knew from personal experience that Vitt shied away from little, and she could wield a rifle with the accuracy of a sniper. At times a bit too brassy for her own good, Cassiopeia had been associated with Stephanie's late husband and understood more about Stephanie's personal life than she cared for anyone to know. But she trusted the woman. No question. Thorvaldsen had chosen wisely when he sent her.

"I have a serious problem."

"That much we already know."

"And Cotton is in trouble. It's imperative I contact him."

"Henrik hasn't heard from him. Malone said he'd call when he's ready, and you know him better than anyone."

"How's Gary?"

"Just like his father. Tough. He's safe with Henrik."

"Where's Pam?"

"On her way back to Georgia. She flew with Malone to London and was leaving from there."

"The Israelis are in London, too. Assassination squad."

"Cotton's a big boy. He can handle it. We have to decide what to do about *your* problem."

Stephanie, too, had been thinking about that conundrum. *Brent Green himself came and told us to leave.* Which might explain why the Capitol Police had been scarce. Usually they were everywhere. She glanced out the taxi and saw that they were near Dupont Circle and her hotel. "We need to make sure we're not being followed."

"The Metro might be a better way to go."

She agreed.

"Where are we headed?" Cassiopeia asked.

She spied the air pistol stuffed beneath Cassiopeia's jacket. "You have any more darts that rock people to sleep?"

"Plenty."

"Then I know exactly where we need to go."

29

LONDON
7:30 PM

MALONE WATCHED PAM SLEEP. HE WAS SLOUCHED IN A CHAIR beside the hotel room's window, George Haddad's satchel lying in his lap. He'd been right about the disinfectant: Pam had bitten hard on the towel as he'd doused the wound. Tears had welled in her eyes, but she'd been tough. Not a sound betrayed her agony. Feeling bad for her, he'd bought her a new shirt from the lobby boutique.

He was tired, too, but his "Billet nerves," as he called them, supplied his muscles with boundless energy. He could recall times when days had passed without eating, his body charged with adrenaline, his focus on staying alive and getting the job done. He'd thought that rush a thing of the past. Something he'd never experience again.

And here he was.

Right in the middle.

The past few hours could have been a gruesome nightmare except that, in undreamlike fashion, the events played clear in his mind. His friend George Haddad had been shot right before his eyes. People with agendas were after something. All none of his business any other time. But some of those same people had kidnapped his son and blown up his bookshop. No. This was personal.

He owed them.

And like Haddad, he intended to pay his debts.

But he needed to know more.

Haddad had been cryptic in his comments both before and after the Israelis appeared. Even worse, he'd never finished explaining what he'd noticed years ago—what exactly motivated Israel to kill him. Hoping that the leather satchel lying in his lap contained answers, he unbuckled the clasps and removed a book, three notebooks, and four maps.

The book was an eighteenth-century volume, the cover tooled leather and brittle like sun-dried skin. None of its lettering was legible, so he carefully parted the binding and read the title sheet.

A Hero's Journey by Eusebius Hieronymus Sophronius.

He scanned the pages.

A novel written more than two hundred years ago in an unimaginative and pedantic style. He wondered about its significance and hoped the notebooks would explain.

He thumbed through each one.

The tight script was Haddad's, written in English. He read closer.

. . . the clues left with me by the Guardian have proven troubling. The hero's quest is difficult. I'm afraid I've been the fool. But not the first. Thomas Bainbridge was also a foolish man. In the latter part of the eighteenth century, he apparently was extended an invitation to the library and completed the hero's quest. A condition of the invitation must surely be that the visit stay private. The Guardians have not spent two millennia protecting their cache only to have it revealed by an invitee. But Bainbridge violated that trust and wrote of his experience. In an effort to ease his treachery, he couched his tale as fiction titled not so curiously, A Hero's Journey. *The book was printed in limited copies and hardly noticed. In Bainbridge's day, the world was teeming with fantastic tales (novels regarded with little respect), so the protagonist's journey to some mythical library was viewed with little enthusiasm. I found a copy three years ago, which I stole from a Welsh estate. Reading it offers little insight. Bainbridge, though, could not resist one final violation of the trust the Guardians placed in him. In the years before he died he erected an arbor in the garden of his Oxfordshire mansion. Into the marble he carved the image of a painting and Roman letters. The painting, by Nicolas Poussin, was originally known as* Happiness Subdued by Death *but its more common name today is* The Shepherds of Arcadia II.

Malone knew little of Poussin, though he was familiar with the name. Luckily, in one of the notebooks, Haddad provided some details.

Poussin was a troubled soul, much like Bainbridge. He was born in Normandy in 1594, and the first thirty years of his life were ones of trials and tribulations. He suffered a lack of patrons, unappreciative courtesans, poor health, and debt. Even working on the ceiling in the Grand Gallery at the Louvre left him uninspired. Not until Poussin left France for Italy in 1642 did a change occur. That journey, which normally would have been one of a few weeks, took Poussin nearly six months. Once in Rome, Poussin began to paint with a new style and confidence, one that did not go unnoticed, one that quickly earned him the label of the most celebrated artist in Rome. Many have speculated that somewhere along his journey Poussin was inducted into a great secret. Interestingly, when The Shepherds of Arcadia *was finished, the patron who commissioned the piece, Cardinal Rospigliosi, who later became Pope Clement IX, chose not to hang the work in public, but kept it in his private apartment. Rospigliosi was an artistic man with an interest in the arcane and esoteric. He possessed an outstanding personal library, and historians eventually labeled him "the freethinking pope."*

A clue as to what Poussin may have personally experienced can be found in a letter written six years after The Shepherds of Arcadia *was completed. Its drafter, a priest, the brother of Louis XIV's finance minister, thought what he'd learned from Poussin might be of interest to the French monarchy. I found the letter a few years ago among the archives of the Cossé-Brissac family:*

*He and I discussed certain things, which I shall with
ease be able to explain to you in detail—things which
will give you, through Monsieur Poussin, advantages
which even kings would have great pains to draw from
him, and which, according to him, it is possible that nobody else will discover in the centuries to come. And
what is more, these are things so difficult to discover
that nothing now on this earth can prove of better fortune nor be their equal.*

*Quite a statement—and puzzling, too. But what Bain-
bridge erected in his garden is even more puzzling. After
completing* The Shepherds of Arcadia, *for some inexplic-
able reason, Poussin painted its reverse image in what has
been labeled* The Shepherds of Arcadia II. *This is what
Thomas Bainbridge chose for his marble bas-relief. Not
the original, but its counterpart. Bainbridge was clever,
and for two hundred years his monument, ripe with symbolism, stood in obscurity.*

Malone read on, his mind lost in a maze of possibilities.
Unfortunately, Haddad did not reveal much more. The remainder of the notes dealt with the Old Testament, its translations, and its narrative inconsistencies. Not a word about
what Haddad may have noticed that had generated so much
interest. Nor was there any message from a Guardian. No details of any hero's quest, only a fleeting reference at the end
of one of the notebooks.

*In the drawing room of Bainbridge Hall is more of Bain-
bridge's arrogance. Its title is particularly reflective.* The
Epiphany of St. Jerome. *Fascinating and fitting, as great
quests often begin with an epiphany.*

A bit more flesh to the bones, but still a lot of unanswered questions. And he'd learned that wrestling with questions that possessed no answers was the fastest way to immobilize the brain.

"What are you reading?"

He glanced up. Pam was still lying in the bed, head on the pillow, eyes open.

"What George left."

She slowly sat up, cleared the sleep from her eyes, and checked her watch. "How long have I been out?"

"An hour or so. How's the shoulder?"

"Sore."

"It will be for a few days."

She stretched her legs. "How many times were you shot, Cotton? Three?"

He nodded. "You don't forget any of them."

"Neither did I. If you recall, I took care of you."

She had.

"I loved you," she said. "I know you may not believe that. But I did."

"You should have told me about Gary."

"You hurt me with what you did. I never understood why you had to screw around on me. Why I wasn't enough."

"I was young. Stupid. Full of myself. It was twenty years ago, for God's sake. And after, I was sorry. I tried to be a good husband. I really did."

"How many women were there? You never said."

He wasn't going to lie. "Four. One-night stands, every one of them." Now he wanted to know. "And you?"

"Just one. But I saw him for several months."

That stung. "You loved him?"

"As much as a married woman could love somebody other than her husband."

He saw her point.

"Gary came from that." She seemed to be wrestling with a question mark that kept appearing from her past. "When I look at Gary a part of me is sometimes angry for what I did—God help me—but a part of me is grateful, too. Gary was always there. You came and went."

"I loved you, Pam. I wanted to be your husband. I was really sorry for what I did."

"It wasn't enough," she muttered, eyes to the floor. "I didn't know it at the time, but I came to realize that it would never be enough. That's why we stayed separated five years before we divorced. I wanted our marriage, but then again I didn't."

"You hated me that bad?"

"No. I hated myself, for what *I* did. It's taken me years to come to that realization. Take it from one who knows, a person who hates herself is in a lot of trouble. She just doesn't know it."

"Why didn't you tell me about Gary when it happened?"

"You didn't deserve the truth. At least, that's what I thought. Only in the past year have I realized the mistake. You screwed around, I screwed around, but I got pregnant. You're right. I should have told you way back. But that's maturity talking and, like you said, we were both young and stupid."

She went silent. He did not intrude.

"That's why I stay angry at you, Cotton. Can't cuss myself out. But it's also why I finally told you about Gary. You do realize that I didn't have to say a word and you would have never known a thing? But I wanted to make it right. I wanted to make peace with you—"

"And with yourself."

She slowly nodded. "Most of all." Her voice broke.

"Why'd you come after me at Haddad's? You knew there'd be shooting."

"Let's just say it was another foolish move."

But he knew better. Time to tell her the truth. "You can't go home to Atlanta. A man was following you in the airport. That's why I came back."

Her face was fixed in a brooding stare. "You should have told me."

"Yeah, I should have."

"Why would someone be following me?"

"Getting ready for another opportunity. Maybe a loose end that needed tying up."

He saw she understood his meaning.

"They want to kill me?"

He shrugged. "I have no idea. That's the problem. We're guessing."

She lay back down on the bed, apparently too tired, sore, and bewildered to argue. "What are you going to do? Haddad's dead. The Israelis should go away."

"Which gives us an open-field run to find whatever it is George was looking for. That hero's quest. He left this stuff on purpose. He wanted us to go."

She settled her head on the pillow. "No. He wanted you to go."

He saw her wince in pain. "Let me get you some ice for that shoulder. It'll help."

"I won't argue with you."

He stood, grabbed the empty bucket, and headed for the door.

"I *would* like to know what's worth dying for," she said.

He stopped. "You'd be surprised how little it can be."

"I think I'll call Gary while you're gone," she said. "I want to make sure he's okay."

"Tell him I miss him."

"He's okay there?"

"Henrik will take good care of him. No worries."

"So where are we going to start looking?"

Good question. But then, as he stared across the room at the contents of the satchel, he knew there was only one answer.

30

LONDON
9:00 PM

SABRE STARED OUT THE WINDOW INTO THE NIGHT. HIS OPERA-tive, who'd been waiting at Heathrow Airport for Malone to arrive, had followed the ex-agent to this apartment, which sat on a solid block of gabled buildings that surely coddled neat lives, good order, and careful privacy.

Typical British.

His operative had also heard shots from inside the building and watched a shootout ensue between Malone and an-other man—Malone's ex-wife nicked by one of the bullets. The assailant had then fled, and Malone and his ex-wife had returned inside before leaving with a leather satchel.

That had been hours ago, and he hadn't heard from his op-erative since. Of course he'd been on a flight from Cologne to London most of that time, but still, she should have re-ported something by now.

He was tired, but energized, as his goal crept ever closer.

He'd easily gained entrance to George Haddad's apartment, wondering if Haddad would be there, but no one had been inside. Maps dotted the walls. With his penlight he'd examined the odd assortment, but the locations—the Middle East—were not surprising. Many of the books and sheaves of ill-arranged papers were likewise on the subject of the day.

The Library of Alexandria.

For the past hour he'd studied the material within the pale penumbra of his penlight. He wondered about Haddad's fate. The man whom Cotton Malone had challenged on the street was surely Israeli. Jonah had made clear in Rothenburg that an assassination squad was headed to London. Had Malone interrupted them? Did they finish their task? Or had Haddad fled into hiding? Impossible to know, since his operative had wisely stayed with Malone.

No feeling of triumph surged through him, though he'd managed to locate Haddad exactly according to plan. He could only hope his operative had done her job equally well.

He'd saved it for last, but the computer was next. So he switched on the machine and scanned its screen.

For all his messiness in the apartment Haddad seemed to have been a meticulous electronic organizer.

He opened a few files and scrolled through.

Haddad had researched the Library of Alexandria in great detail. But interestingly he'd also studied the Guardians. Alfred Hermann had told Sabre about them. Jonah had filled in some of the blanks. But one of Haddad's files offered even more.

. . . their origins are unknown, lost due to the absurdity of ancient men who, without impunity, erased human memory.

By the time of the second century, man had mastered the arts of war and torture. In many parts of the world em-

*pires had been formed, which provided laws and a mea-
sure of security. But neither of those concepts protected
people from their own rulers. Religion formed, and priests
became the willing ally of despots. Egypt was one place
where this travesty occurred. But sometime around the
second century, an Egyptian religious order emerged that
worshiped not power but the preservation of knowledge.*

*A crude form of monastery had then begun where men
of like mind and purpose congregated. These places were
intentionally isolated and notoriously avoided. This one
group was fortunate. Its members actually staffed both libraries at Alexandria as clerks and stewards. From these
service posts access to everything was possible, and as the
human race prospered and learned more how to annihilate one another, this group withdrew into itself.*

*Originally they merely copied texts, but eventually they
pilfered. The sheer volume of the library (several hundred
thousand manuscripts) forced decisions, but over the next
three hundred years, as the library fell further out of favor,
stealing texts became easier, particularly since no accurate inventories existed. By the time of the Muslim invasion in the seventh century, the Guardians owned a great
deal of the library at Alexandria. That was when they disappeared, reemerging from time to time, offering invita-
tions to come and learn.*

Sabre kept reading, wondering how George Haddad had
managed to obtain such detailed information. This Palestinian seemed full of surprises.

Movement at the corner of his eye brought his senses
alert. Shadows came alive. A dark form crept closer.

His hands left the keyboard. Unfortunately he carried no
weapon. He whirled, ready for a fight.

A woman materialized into the glow of the computer screen.

His operative.

"That sort of foolishness can get you hurt," he said.

"I'm not in the mood."

He regularly employed her to help all over Britain. She was slender-boned and fine-featured. Today her black hair was brushed tight and caught into a heavy plait.

"Where have you been?" he asked.

"Following Malone. They're in a hotel near Hyde Park."

"What about Haddad?"

She shook her head. "Don't know. I stayed with Malone. He took a chance coming back up here—the police were on the way—and he left with that satchel."

He admired her instincts. "We still need to find the Palestinian."

"He'll come back, if he's not dead already. You look different."

Gone were his gleaming dark locks and shaggy clothes. Instead his hair was short, windblown, and sandy brown. He was neatly dressed in jeans and a canvas shirt beneath a cloth jacket. Before leaving Germany he'd first reported what he'd learned to the Blue Chair, then made the physical change— all part of his carefully conceived plan, most of which Alfred Hermann knew little about.

"You approve?" he asked.

"I liked the other look."

He shrugged. "Maybe next time. What's happening?"

"I have somebody watching the hotel. They'll call if Malone moves."

"Nothing more from the Israelis?"

"Their man tore off from here."

He looked around. Maybe he'd just wait for Haddad to return. That seemed the easiest course. He definitely needed everything off Haddad's computer, but he didn't want to take the machine. Too cumbersome. A copy would be better, and he noticed a flash drive lying among the clutter. He grabbed the gadget and snapped it into an empty USB port.

He checked the drive. Empty.

A few clicks of the mouse and he'd copied all the files from the hard drive.

Then he noticed something else, beyond the monitor.

A tiny red light.

He stared closer through the mess of paper and spotted a pocket tape recorder lying on the table. He lifted the unit and noticed no difference in the coating of dust that frosted the desktop. Which meant the unit had been laid there recently. The tape was spent, but the power remained on.

He flicked REWIND.

His operative stood silent.

He engaged PLAY.

The entire encounter between Malone, Haddad, and eventually the Israelis had been recorded. He listened in amazement to Haddad's murder. The last thing he heard was Cotton Malone's declaration that he intended to *kill the son of a bitch*.

He switched off the machine.

"Haddad's dead?" the woman said. "Killed here? Why isn't this a crime scene?"

"I assume the Israelis cleaned up before the police arrived."

"Now what?"

"We have Malone. Let's see where he leads."

31

MALONE LEFT THE ROOM AND WALKED DOWN THE HALL. HE'D earlier noticed an ice machine, which was surprising. More and more American conveniences seemed to be invading European hotels.

He was angry at himself for placing Pam in danger. But at the time, what choice had there been? He couldn't have left her at Heathrow with a man following. And who was he? Perhaps involved with those who'd taken Gary? That seemed logical. But he still knew precious little.

The Israelis had reacted promptly to Haddad's signal that he was alive. Yet Pam was right. With Haddad dead, their interests were protected, their problem solved. Still, Pam had been the one followed. Not him.

Why?

He found the ice machine and discovered that it wasn't working. Though the compressor churned, no ice filled the bin. Much like America, too, he thought.

He pushed through the stairway door and descended one floor.

There the machine was brimming with ice. He stood in a cubicle off the hall and filled his bucket.

He heard a door to one of the rooms slam shut, then voices. He was still scooping ice when two men passed the alcove, talking excitedly. He turned to leave and caught the facial profile of one of the men, along with his lanky frame and sunburned skin.

String Bean. From Heathrow.

Here, one floor down from where they were staying.

He retreated into the alcove and peered around the doorway, watching as the men entered the elevator.

Heading up.

He bolted for the stairwell door and leaped up the risers. He eased open the door just as the elevator dinged and the two men strolled from the car.

He slipped out the door and carefully peered down the corridor. He watched as one of the men scooped a used room-service tray from the carpet and balanced it on one hand. The other man withdrew a short-barreled revolver. They were headed straight for the room where Pam was waiting.

He cursed himself.

Haddad's gun was on a table in the room. He hadn't brought it with him. Real smart. He'd have to improvise.

The men stopped at the door. The one with the gun knocked, then stepped to one side. The other pretended to be a steward, the tray balanced high on one hand.

Another knock.

Maybe Pam was still on the phone with Gary? Which would give him the moment he needed.

"Room service," he heard the man say.

Unlike American hotels, where peepholes were standard, the British did not usually provide them, and this hotel was no exception. He could only hope Pam would not be foolish enough to turn the knob.

"I have a food order for you," the man said in a raised voice.

A pause.

"A gentleman placed the order."

Damn. She could readily believe he might have ordered while she was sleeping. He had to act. He raised the ice bucket to shield his face and started down the hall.

"The food is for this room," the man was explaining.

He heard locks releasing.

Peering around the raised bucket he saw the armed man notice him. The gun was immediately shielded. Malone used that moment of relaxation to his advantage and slung the ice and bucket into the armed man's face, then planted his right fist into the jaw of the man with the tray. He felt bone crack and the man slammed to the carpet, the tray and its contents scattered.

Ice Man recovered from the initial shock and was raising his gun when Malone pounded two blows to the head and jammed a knee into the chest.

The assailant crumpled downward and lay still.

The room door opened.

Pam stared at him.

"Why would you open that door?" he asked.

"I thought you ordered food."

He grabbed the gun and stuffed it in his belt. "And I wouldn't have told you?" He quickly searched both men but found no identification.

"Who are they?" Pam asked.

"That's the one following you in the airport."

He grabbed String Bean's arms and dragged him into their room. He then gripped the other man's legs and pulled him inside. "You're a stubborn woman." He kicked the door shut.

"I was hungry."

"How's Gary?"

"He's doing well. But I didn't get to say much."

One of the men started moaning. They'd be conscious

soon. He grabbed the leather satchel and Haddad's gun. "Let's go."

"We're leaving?"

"Unless you want to be around when they wake up."

He saw that prospect was not appealing to her.

"You have a gun," she reminded him.

"Which I don't want to use. This isn't the Wild West. We're in a hotel, with people. So let's do the smart thing and leave. There are plenty more hotels in this town."

She grabbed the shawl and gently wrapped her shoulders. They left the room and quickly caught the elevator. Downstairs, they exited into a chilly night. He surveyed his surroundings and concluded it was going to be tough to know if they were being followed. Simply too much to watch. The nearest Tube station was two blocks away, so he headed for it, determined to keep a lookout.

His mind churned.

How had the man from Heathrow found them? Even more troubling, how did the man pretending to be a steward know that he wasn't in the room?

A gentleman placed the order.

He faced Pam as they walked. "Did you tell that guy through the door that you didn't order anything?"

She nodded. "That's when he said you did."

Not entirely correct. He'd said a *gentleman* placed the order.

But still. Lucky guess?

No way.

32

STEPHANIE LED CASSIOPEIA THROUGH THE QUIET NEIGHBOR-HOOD. For the past few hours they'd stayed hidden in the sub-urbs. She'd made one call to Billet headquarters from a pay phone at a Cracker Barrel restaurant and learned that there had been no contact from Malone. Not so from the White House. Larry Daley's office had called three times. She'd told her staff to say that she'd get back to him at her first op-portunity. Aggravating, she knew. But let Daley wonder if the next time he saw her jovial face, it would be live on CNN. That fear should be enough, for now, to keep the deputy na-tional security adviser in check. Heather Dixon and the Is-raelis, though, were another matter.

"Where are we going?" Cassiopeia asked.

"To deal with a problem."

The neighborhood was heavy with beaux arts architecture that had been fashionable, she realized, with the nineteenth-century industrialists who'd first populated the tree-lined av-enues. Colonial row houses and cobblestoned walks only added to the wealthy mien in the night air.

"I'm not one of your agents," Cassiopeia said. "I like to know what I'm getting into."

"You can leave whenever you want."

"Nice try. You're not getting rid of me that easy."

"Then stop asking questions. You quiz Thorvaldsen like this?"

"Why don't you like him? In France you stayed at his throat."

"Look where I am, Cassiopeia. Cotton's in a mess. My own people want me dead. The Israelis and Saudis are both after me. You think it's wise I like anyone?"

"That's not an answer to my question."

No, it wasn't. But she couldn't voice the truth. That through his association with her late husband, Thorvaldsen had come to know her strengths and weaknesses, and near him she felt vulnerable.

"Let's just say that he and I are far too well acquainted with each other."

"Henrik's worried about you. That's why he asked me to come. He sensed trouble."

"And I appreciate that. But it doesn't mean I have to like him."

She spotted the house, another of the many symmetrical brick residences with carvings, a portico, and a mansard roof. Lights burned only in the downstairs windows. She scanned the street.

Still quiet.

"Follow me."

ALFRED HERMANN RARELY SLEPT. HE'D CONDITIONED HIS mind long ago to operate on less than three hours' rest.

He was not old enough to have personally experienced World War II, though he harbored vivid childhood memories of Nazis parading through the streets of Vienna. In the decades after, he'd actively battled the Soviets and challenged their puppet regimes that had dominated Austria. Hermann money dated from the Hapsburgs and had managed to survive two centuries of volatile politics. During the past fifty years the family fortune had grown tenfold, and much of that success could be traced to the Order of the Golden Fleece. To be intimately associated with such a select group from around the world came with advantages that his father and grandfather had never enjoyed. But to be in charge—that provided even greater benefits.

His tenure, though, was coming to an end.

At his death, his daughter would inherit everything. And the thought was not comforting. True, she was like him in some ways. Bold and determined, and she appreciated the past and coveted, with an enthusiasm similar to his own, that most precious of human commodities—knowledge. But she remained unpolished. A work in progress. One he feared might never be completed.

He stared at his daughter who, like him, slept little. He'd named her Margarete, after his mother. She was admiring the model of the Library of Alexandria.

"Can we find it?" she quietly asked.

He stepped close. "I believe Dominick is near."

She appraised him with keen gray eyes. "Sabre is not to be trusted. No American should be."

They'd had this discussion before. "I trust no one."

"Not even me?"

He grinned. They'd had this discussion before, too. "Not even you."

"Sabre has too much freedom."

"Why begrudge him? We give him difficult tasks. You can't do that and expect him to work as we see fit."

"He's a problem—American ingenuity and all that—you just don't know it."

"He's a willful man. He needs purpose. We provide that to him. In return he furthers our goals."

"I've sensed more from him lately. He tries hard to mask his ambition, but it's there. You just have to pay attention."

He thought he'd taunt her. "Perhaps you're attracted to him?"

She scoffed at his question. "That'll never happen. In fact, I'll fire him once you're gone."

He wondered about her assumption that she would inherit all that he owned. "There's no guarantee you'll be Blue Chair. That selection is made among the Chairs."

"I'll be in the Circle. I assure you. It's a simple step from there to where you are."

But he wasn't so sure. He knew of her contacts with the other four Chairs. He'd actually encouraged them as a test. His wealth far surpassed that of the others in age, volume, and scope. Financial institutions he controlled were heavily entangled with many members, including three of the Chairs. Never would any of them want others to know of that vulnerability, and the price of his silence had always been their loyalty. He'd manipulated their weaknesses for decades, but his daughter's attempts had been feeble. So a word of caution was in order. "Once I'm gone, it's true, Dominick will have to deal with you, as you will with him. But don't be so quick. Men like him, with little emotion? No morals? A daring heart? You might find them valuable."

He hoped she was listening but feared, as always, that her ears remained filtered. Her mother had died when she was eight and, in her youth, she'd seemed a product of him—*of the rib,* she liked to say—yet age had not matured that early promise. Her education had started in France, continued in England, and was completed in Austria, her business experience honed in the boardrooms of his many corporations.

But the reports from there had not been encouraging.

"What would you do if you found the library?" she asked.

He concealed his amusement. She apparently did not want to discuss Sabre or herself anymore. "It's beyond imagining what great thoughts are there."

"I heard you speaking yesterday about those. Tell me more."

"Ah, the Piri Reis Map, from 1513, found in Istanbul. I was running on about that. I didn't know you were listening."

"I always listen."

He grinned at the observation. They both knew it wasn't so.

"I was telling the chancellor of how the map had been drawn on a gazelle hide by a Turkish admiral who was once a pirate. Full of incredible detail. The South American coastline is there, though European navigators hadn't yet charted that region. The Antarctic continent is also shown, long before being coated with ice. Only recently, using ground radar, have we been able to determine that shoreline's contour. Yet the 1513 representation is as good as ours. On the face of the map, the cartographer noted that he used charts drawn in the days of Alexander, Lord of the Two Horns. Can you imagine? Perhaps ancient navigators visited Antarctica thousands of years ago, before the ice accumulated, and recorded what they saw."

Hermann's mind swirled with what else may have been lost from the fields of mathematics, astronomy, geometry, meteorology, and medicine.

"Unrecorded knowledge is either forgotten or muddled beyond recognition. Do you know of Democritus? He conceived the notion that all things were made of a finite number of discrete particles. Today we call them atoms, but he was the first to acknowledge their existence and formulate the atomic theory. He wrote seventy books—we know that from other references—yet not one has survived. And centuries passed before other men, in other times, thought of the same thing.

"Almost nothing Pythagoras wrote remains. Manetho recorded Egypt's history. Gone. Galen, the great Roman healer? He wrote five hundred treatises on medicine. Only fragments remain. Aristarchus thought that the sun, not the earth, was the center of the universe. But Copernicus, who lived seventeen centuries later, is the man history credits with that revelation."

He thought of more. Eratosthenes and Strabo, geographers. Archimedes, the physicist and mathematician. Zenodotus and his grammar. Callimachus the poet. Thales, the first philosopher.

All their ideas gone.

"It's always been the same," he said. "Knowledge is the first thing eradicated once power is attained. History has proven that over and over."

"So what is it Israel fears?" she asked.

He knew she'd eventually work him around to that subject.

"Perhaps it's more fear than reality," she noted. "Changing the world is difficult."

"But it can be done. Men—" He paused. "—and women have done it for centuries. And violence has not always brought about the most monumental changes. Often it's been mere words. The Bible fundamentally changed mankind. The Koran likewise. The Magna Carta. The American Constitution. Billions of people govern their lives by those words. Society has been altered by them. It's not so much the wars as the treaties that follow that truly alter the course of history. The Marshall Plan changed the world more expressly than World War II itself. Words are indeed the true weapons of mass destruction."

"You dodged my question," she said in a playful tone, one that reminded him of his long-dead wife.

"What is it Israel fears?" he repeated.

"Why won't you tell me?"

"Perhaps I don't know."

"I doubt it."

He considered telling her everything. But he hadn't survived by being foolish. Loose talk had been the downfall of more than one successful man.

"Let's simply say that the truth is always difficult to accept. For people, for cultures, even for nations."

STEPHANIE LED THE WAY INTO THE REAR YARD AND WAS STARTLED by its manicured appearance. Flowers abounded. Colorful asters, waxbells, goldenrod, pansies, and mums. A terrace formed a peninsula, its flagstones dotted with wrought-iron furniture, more blooms sprouting from decorative pots.

She guided Cassiopeia to the thick trunk of a tall maple, one of three stately trees shading the garden.

She checked her watch: 9:43 PM.

She'd brought them this far through a combination of anger and curiosity, but the next step was where she irrefutably crossed the line.

"Get that air pistol ready," she whispered.

Her cohort slid a dart down the barrel. "I hope you note my blind obedience to this foolishness."

She considered the next move.

Breaking into the house was certainly an option. Cassiopeia possessed the requisite skills. But simply knocking on the door would work, too. She actually liked that approach. Their course, though, was instantly set when the rear door opened and a black form strolled out among the slender pillars supporting a shallow colonnade. The tall man was wearing a bathrobe tied at the waist, his feet sheathed in slippers that scraped off the terrace.

She motioned to the gun, then at the form.

Cassiopeia aimed and fired.

A soft pop, then a swish accompanied the dart's flight.

Its tip found the man, who cried out as his hand reached for his shoulder. He seemed to fiddle with the dart, then gasped as he collapsed.

Stephanie raced over. "Stuff works fast."

"That's the idea. Who is this?"

They stared down at the man.

"Congratulations. You just shot the attorney general of the United States. Now help me drag him into the house."

33

THURSDAY, OCTOBER 6
LONDON
3:15 AM

SABRE STUDIED HIS LAPTOP. FOR THE PAST THREE HOURS HE'D been scanning what he'd downloaded off George Haddad's computer.

And he was astounded.

The information was certainly as much as he would have gleaned from the Palestinian himself, and without the aggravation of forcing the Arab to talk. Haddad had apparently spent years researching the Library of Alexandria, along with the mythical Guardians, assimilating an impressive array of data.

A whole series of files concerned an English earl named Thomas Bainbridge, of whom he'd heard Alfred Hermann speak. According to Haddad, in the latter part of the eighteenth century Bainbridge visited the Library of Alexandria, then wrote a novel about his experience that, according to the notes, contained clues to the library's location.

Had Haddad found a copy?

Was that what Malone had retrieved?

Then there was Bainbridge's ancestral estate west of London. Haddad had apparently visited several times and believed more clues lay there, especially concerning a marble arbor and something called *The Epiphany of St. Jerome*. But no details were offered to explain the significance of either.

Then there was the hero's quest.

An hour ago he'd found a narrative account of what had happened five years back in Haddad's West Bank home. He'd read the notes with interest and now reassembled the events in his mind, his excitement piqued.

"You're saying that the library still exists?" Haddad *asked the Guardian.*

"We've protected it for centuries. Saved what would have been lost through ignorance and greed."

Haddad motioned with the envelope that his guest had handed him. "This hero's quest shows the way?"

The man nodded. "To those who understand, the path will be obvious."

"And if I don't understand?"

"Then we'll never see each other again."

He considered the possibilities and said, "I fear that what I want to learn is better left hidden."

"Why would you say that? Knowledge should never be feared. I'm familiar with your work. I study the Old Testament, too. That's why I was chosen as your Guardian." The younger man's face brightened. *"We have sources you can't even imagine. Original texts. Correspondence. Analyses. From men long ago, who knew far more than you or me. My mastery of Old Hebrew is not on your level. You see, for a Guardian, there are levels of achievement, and the only way to ascend is through accomplishment. Like you, I'm fascinated by Christianity's interpretation of the Old Testament, how it was manipulated. I want to learn more, and you, sir, can teach me."*

"And learning will help you ascend?"

"Proving your theory would be a great accomplishment for us both."

So he opened the envelope.

Sabre scrolled down to what that envelope contained. Haddad had apparently scanned the document into the computer. The words were penned in a sharply angled masculine script, all in Latin. Luckily Haddad had translated the message. Sabre read the hero's quest, the supposed path to the Library of Alexandria.

How strange are the manuscripts, great traveler of the unknown. They appear separately, but seem as one to those who know that the colors of the rainbow become a single white light. How to find that single ray? It is a mystery, but visit the chapel beside the Tejo, in Bethlehem, dedicated to our patron saint. Begin the journey in the shadows and complete it in the light, where a retreating star finds a rose, pierces a wooden cross, and converts silver to gold. Find the place that forms an address with no place, where is found another place. Then, like the shepherds of the

*painter Poussin, puzzled by the enigma, you will be flooded
with the light of inspiration. Reassemble the fourteen stones,
then work with square and compass to find the path. At
noon, sense the presence of the red light, see the endless
coil of the serpent red with anger. But heed the letters.
Danger threatens one who arrives with great speed. If
your course remains true, the route will be sure.*

Sabre shook his head. Riddles. Not his strong point. And
he had not the time to wrestle with them. He'd reviewed
every file from the computer, but Haddad had not deciphered
the message.

And that was a problem.

He was not a historian, a linguist, or a biblical scholar. Alfred Hermann was the supposed expert, but Sabre wondered
how much the Austrian actually knew. Both of them were
opportunists, trying to make the most of a unique situation.

Just for differing reasons.

Hermann was trying to forge a legacy, to stamp his mark
on the Order of the Golden Fleece. Perhaps even to smooth
Margarete's ascendency to power. God knew she needed
help. He knew she'd eliminate him once Hermann was gone.
But if he could preempt her, stay a step ahead, just beyond
her grasp, he just might succeed. He wanted an all-expenses-
paid pass straight to the top. A seat at the table. Bargaining
power to become a full-fledged member of the Order of the
Golden Fleece. If the lost Library of Alexandria contained
what Alfred Hermann had told him it might, then possessing
it was worth more than any family fortune.

His cell phone rang.

The LCD display indicated that it was his operative. About
time. He answered.

"Malone's on the move," she said. "Bloody early. What do
you want me to do?"

"Where did he go?"

"Took a bus to Paddington Station, then a train west."

"Is Oxfordshire on that route?"

"Straight through it."

Apparently Malone was curious, too. "Did you arrange that extra help, like I asked?"

"They're here."

"Wait at Paddington Station. I'm on my way."

He clicked off the phone.

Time to start the next phase.

STEPHANIE TOSSED A TUMBLER OF WATER IN BRENT GREEN'S face. They'd dragged his limp body into the kitchen and fastened him to a chair with packing tape Cassiopeia found in a drawer. The attorney general stirred himself out of unconsciousness, shaking the moisture from his eyes.

"Sleep well?" she asked.

Green was still coming around, so she helped him with another splash.

"That's enough," Green said, lids wide open, his face and bathrobe soaked. "I assume there's a good reason why you've decided to violate so many federal laws." The words came with the speed of molasses and in the tone of a funeral director, both normal for Green. Never had she heard him talk fast or loud.

"You tell me, Brent. Who you working for?"

Green glanced at the bindings that held his wrists and ankles. "And I thought we were making progress in our relationship."

"We were until you betrayed me."

"Stephanie, I've been told for years that you're a loose

cannon, but I always admired those traits in you. I'm beginning, though, to see the other side's complaint."

She came close. "I didn't trust you, but you faced off
against Daley and I thought maybe, just maybe, I was
wrong."

"Do you have any idea what would happen if my security
detail came to check on me? Which, by the way, they do each
night."

"Nice try. You waved them off months ago. Said it wasn't
necessary unless the threat level was elevated, and it's not at
the moment."

"And how do you know that I didn't press my panic button
before I fell to the terrace?"

She removed the transmitter she carried from her pocket.
"I pressed mine, Brent, back on the mall, and you know what
happened? Not a damn thing."

"Might be different here."

She knew that Green, like all senior administrative staff,
carried a panic button. It instantly relayed trouble to either a
nearby security detail or the Secret Service command center.
It could also act as a tracking device.

"I watched your hands," she said. "Both empty. You were
too busy trying to figure out what stung you."

Green's face stiffened, and he stared at Cassiopeia. "You
shot me?"

She gave him a gracious bow. "At your service."

"What's the chemical?"

"Fast-acting agent I found in Morocco. Quick, painless,
short-term."

"I can attest to all those." Green turned back toward
Stephanie. "This must be Cassiopeia Vitt. She knew your
husband, Lars, before he killed himself."

"How in the world do you know that?" She hadn't mentioned what happened to anyone on this side of the Atlantic

Ocean. Only Cassiopeia, Henrik Thorvaldsen, and Malone knew.

"Ask me what you came to ask me," Green said with a quiet resolve.

"Why'd you call off my security detail? You left me bare-ass for the Israelis. Tell me you did it."

"I did."

The admission surprised her. She was too accustomed to lies. "Knowing that the Saudis would try to kill me?"

"I knew that, too."

Anger swelled inside her and she fought the urge to lash out, saying only, "I'm waiting."

"Ms. Vitt," Green said. "Are you available to keep an eye on this woman until this is over?"

"Why do you give a damn?" Stephanie blurted out. "You're not my keeper."

"Somebody has to be. Calling Heather Dixon wasn't smart. You're not thinking."

"Like I need you to tell me that."

"Look at yourself. Here you are, assaulting the chief law enforcement officer of the United States with little or no information. Your enemies, on the other hand, have access to an abundance of intelligence, which they are using to full advantage."

"What in the hell are you babbling about? And you never did answer the question."

"That's true. I didn't. You wanted to know why I called off your security detail. The answer is simple. I was asked to, so I did."

"Who asked you?"

Green's eyes surveyed her with the unruffled look of a Buddha.

"Henrik Thorvaldsen."

34

BAINBRIDGE HALL, ENGLAND
5:20 AM

MALONE ADMIRED THE MARBLE ARBOR IN THE GARDEN.
They'd taken a train twelve miles north from London, then a
taxi from the nearby town station to Bainbridge Hall. He'd
read all of Haddad's notes stashed in the satchel and
skimmed through the novel, trying to make sense of what
was happening, remembering everything he and Haddad had
discussed through the years. But he'd come to the conclusion
that his old friend had taken the most important things with
him to his grave.

Above stretched a velvet sky. A cool draft of night air
chilled him. Manicured grass stretched out from the garden
in a pewter sea, the bushes and shrubs islands of shadow.
Water danced in a nearby fountain. He'd decided on a
predawn visit as the best way to learn anything, and had obtained a flashlight from the hotel concierge.

The grounds were unfenced and, as far as he could see,
not alarmed. The house itself, he assumed, would be another
matter. From what he'd read in Haddad's notes, the estate
was a minor museum, one of hundreds owned by the British
Crown. Several of the mansion's ground-floor rooms were

lit, and he spotted, through uncurtained panes, what appeared to be a cleaning crew.

He turned his attention back to the arbor.

The wind rustled the trees then rose to sweep the clouds. Moonlight vanished, but his eyes were fully accustomed to the eerie pall.

"You plan to tell me what this thing is?" Pam asked. She'd been uncharacteristically quiet on the trip.

He directed the light onto the image etched into the marble. "That's from a painting called *The Shepherds of Arcadia Two*. Thomas Bainbridge went to a lot of trouble to have it carved." He told her what Haddad had written concerning the image, then used the beam to trace the letters beneath.

D   O.V.O.S.V.A.V.V.   M

"What did he say about those?" Pam asked.

"Not a word. Only that this was a message and that there are more inside the house."

"Which certainly explains why we're here at five o'clock in the morning."

He caught her irritation. "I don't like crowds."

Pam brought her eyes close to the arbor. "Wonder why he separated the D and the M like that?"

He had no idea. But there was one thing he did comprehend. The pastoral scene of *The Shepherds of Arcadia II* depicted a woman watching as three shepherds gathered around a stone tomb, each pointing at engraved letters. *ET IN ARCADIA EGO*. He knew the translation.

And in Arcadia I.

An enigmatic inscription that made little sense. But he'd seen those words before. In France. Contained within a sixteenth-century codex describing what the Knights Templar had secretly accomplished in the months before their mass arrest in October 1307.

Et in arcadia ego.

An anagram for *I tego arcana dei.*

I conceal the secrets of God.

He told Pam about the phrase.

"You can't be serious," she said.

He shrugged. "Just telling you what I know."

They needed to explore the house. From a safe distance in the garden, among belts of towering cedars, he studied the ground floor. Lights flicked on and off as the cleaners went about their work. Doors to the rear terrace were propped open with chairs. He watched as a man stepped outside carrying two garbage bags, which he tossed into a pile, then disappeared back inside.

He glanced at his watch: 5:40 AM.

"They're going to have to finish soon," he said. "Once they're gone, we should have a couple of hours before anyone arrives for work. This place doesn't open till ten." He'd learned that from a sign near the main gate.

"No need to say how foolish this is."

"You always wanted to know what I did for a living, and I never could tell you. Top secret, and all that crap. Time to find out."

"I liked it better when I didn't know."

"I don't believe that. I remember how aggravated you'd get."

"At least I didn't have any bullet wounds."

He smiled. "Your rite of passage." Then he motioned her forward. "After you."

SABRE WATCHED AS THE SHADOWY FORMS OF COTTON MALONE and his ex-wife merged with the trees behind Bainbridge

Hall. Malone had come straight to Oxfordshire. Good. Everything hinged on his curiosity. His operative had also done her job. She'd hired the three extra men he'd requested and delivered him a weapon.

He drew a few long breaths and welcomed the brisk night air, then removed the Sig Sauer from his jacket pocket.

Time to meet Cotton Malone.

MALONE APPROACHED THE OPEN REAR DOOR, STAYING TO ONE side, embracing the shadows, and peered inside.

The room beyond was an elaborate parlor. Shimmering light cascaded from the vaulted ceiling, illuminating gilded furniture and paneled walls livened by tapestries and paintings. No one was in sight, but he heard the whine of a floor polisher and the blare of a radio from beyond the archways.

He motioned and they entered.

He knew nothing of the house's geography, but a placard told him he was in the Apollo Room. He recalled what Haddad had written. *In the drawing room of Bainbridge Hall is more of Bainbridge's arrogance. Its title is particularly reflective.* The Epiphany of St. Jerome. *Fascinating and fitting, as great quests often begin with an epiphany.*

So they needed to find the drawing room.

He led Pam to one of the exits that opened into a foyer possessing the majestic lines of a cathedral transept, arches eloquently stacked atop one another. Interesting, the abrupt change in style and architecture. Less light softened the outlines of the furniture into gray shadows. Within one of the arches he spotted a bust.

He crept across the marble floor, careful with his rubber soles, and discovered the likeness of Thomas Bainbridge. The middle-aged face was replete with furrows and curves, the jaw clenched, the nose beaklike, the eyes cold and squinty. From what he'd read in Haddad's notes, Bainbridge was apparently a learned man of science and literature, as well as a collector—acquiring art, books, and sculptures with a calculated judgment. He'd also been an adventurer, traveling to Arabia and the Middle East at a time when both places were as familiar to the West as the moon.

"Cotton," Pam said in a low voice.

He turned. She'd drifted to a table where brochures were stacked. "Layout of the house."

He stepped close and grabbed one from the pile. Quickly he found a room labeled DRAWING. He oriented himself. "That way."

The floor polisher and radio continued to duel upstairs.

They departed the dim foyer and wound their way through wide corridors until they entered a lit hall.

"Wow," Pam said.

He, too, was impressed. The grand space was reminiscent of the vestibule to a Roman emperor's palace. Another startling contrast to the rest of the house.

"This place is like Epcot," he said. "Each room's a different time and country."

A chandelier's rich glow illuminated white marble stairs, lined down the center with a deep maroon runner. The risers led straight up to a peristyle of fluted Ionic columns. Twists and curls of black iron railing linked the pink marble columns. Niches on both floors framed busts and statues as if in a museum gallery. He glanced up. The ceiling would not have been out of place inside St. Paul's Cathedral.

He shook his head.

Nothing about the manor's exterior hinted at such opulence.

"The drawing room is up those stairs," he said.

"I feel like we're going to meet the queen," Pam said.

They followed the elegant runner up the unrailed risers. Paneled double doors at the top opened into a darkened room. He flicked a switch and another chandelier, fashioned from animal tusks, burned bright, displaying a crowded salon, worn and comfortable, the walls hung with velvet the color of pea soup.

"Wouldn't have expected much less," he said, "after that entranceway."

He closed the doors.

"What are we looking for?" Pam asked.

He studied the wall paintings, most portraits of sixteenth- and seventeenth-century figures. No one he recognized. Maple bookcases stood in rows below the portraits. His bibliophile's eye quickly noticed that the volumes were innocuous, only for show, with no historical or literary value. Bronze busts topped the cases. Again, no familiar image.

"The Epiphany of St. Jerome," he said. "Maybe one of those portraits."

Pam rounded the room, studying each image. He counted them. Fourteen. Most were of women, elaborately dressed, or men adorned in wigs and flowing robes common three hundred years ago. Two sofas and four chairs formed a U before a stone hearth. He imagined this was where Thomas Bainbridge may have spent a lot of time.

"None of these," Pam said, "has anything to do with a St. Jerome."

He was puzzled. "George said it was here."

"Maybe so. But it's not now."

35

WASHINGTON, DC

STEPHANIE STARED AT BRENT GREEN AND HER IMPASSIVE EXpression gave way to a look of astonishment. "Thorvaldsen told you to call off my backup? How do you even know the man?"

"I know a great many people." He motioned to his bindings. "Though at the moment I find myself at your mercy."

"Calling off her protection was foolish," Cassiopeia said. "What if I hadn't been there?"

"Henrik said you were, and that you could handle things."

Stephanie worked to control her rage. "It was my ass."

"Which you so foolishly placed on the line."

"I had no idea Dixon was going to attack me."

"Which is my point exactly. You're not thinking." Green again motioned with his head at his bindings. "This is another example of foolishness. Contrary to what you might think, a security detail will check in here shortly. They always do. I may crave my privacy but, unlike you, I'm not reckless."

"What are you doing?" she asked. "Why are you in this? Are you working with Daley? Was all that earlier between you and him just a dog-and-pony show for my benefit?"

"I have neither the time nor the patience for dog-and-pony shows."

Stephanie was not impressed. "I've had my fill of lies. Malone's boy was taken because of me. Cotton is in London right now with an Israeli assassination squad. I can't find him, so I can't warn him. George Haddad's life may be at stake. Then I learn that my boss leaves me bare-ass to the wind, knowing the Saudis want to kill me? What am I supposed to think?"

"That your friend, Henrik Thorvaldsen, thought enough to send you help. That your other friend, me, decided the help needed to work alone. How about that? Make sense?"

She considered his words.

"And one other thing," Green said.

She glared at him.

"This friend particularly cares what happens to you."

MALONE WAS ANNOYED. HE'D COME TO BAINBRIDGE HALL hoping for answers. Haddad's notes had pointed them straight here. Yet nothing.

"Maybe there's another drawing room?" Pam said.

But he checked the brochure and determined that this was the only space so labeled. What was he missing? Then he spotted something. Adjacent to one of the window alcoves, where elaborate stained-glass panes waited for the morning sun, a section of wall shone bare. Portraits filled every other available space. But not there. And the faint outline of a rectangle loomed clear on the wall covering.

He hurried to the bare spot. "One's gone."

"Cotton, I'm not trying to be difficult, but this could have been a wild-goose chase."

He shook his head. "George wanted us here."

He paced the room in thought and realized they couldn't linger. One of the cleaning crew might come this way. Though he carried Haddad's and String Bean's guns, he didn't want to use either.

Pam was examining the tables that backed the two sofas. Books and magazines were decoratively stacked amid sculptures and potted plants. She was studying one of the small bronzes—an older man, his skin wizened, his body muscular, dressed in a waist cloth. The figure was perched on a rock, his bearded face concentrating on a book.

"You need to see this," she said.

He approached and saw what was etched at the statue's base.

ST. JEROME

DOCTOR OF THE CHURCH

He'd been so busy trying to find complicated pieces that the obvious had escaped him. Pam motioned to a book just beneath the sculpture.

"The Epiphany of St. Jerome," she said.

He examined the spine. "Good eye."

She smiled. "I can be useful."

He gripped the heavy bronze and lifted. "So be useful and grab the book."

STEPHANIE WASN'T SURE HOW TO TAKE BRENT GREEN'S REmark. "What do you mean? This *particular* friend?"

"It's a bit difficult to discuss at the moment."

And she spotted something curious in Green's eyes. Anxiety. For five years he had been the administration's bulldog in many a battle with Congress, the press, and special-interest groups. He was a consummate pro. A lawyer who pleaded the administration's case on a national stage. But he was also deeply religious and, to her knowledge, never even a hint of scandal had been attached to his name.

"Let's just say," Green said in a half whisper, "that I wouldn't have wanted the Saudis to kill you."

"Not a great comfort to me at the moment."

"What about his security detail?" Cassiopeia asked. "I have the feeling he's not bluffing on that one."

"Check the front and keep an eye on the street," she said, making clear through her gaze that she wanted a moment alone with Green.

Cassiopeia left the kitchen.

"Okay, Brent. What do you have to say that you couldn't say in front of her?"

"What are you, Stephanie, sixty-one years old?"

"I don't talk about my age."

"Your husband has been dead a dozen years. That has to be tough. I never married, so I wouldn't know what it's like to lose a spouse."

"It's not easy. What does that have to do with anything?"

"I know you and Lars were estranged when he died. It's time you start trusting somebody."

"Gee, tell you what. I'll schedule interviews and everyone, including those trying to kill me, will get a chance to convince me of their trustworthiness."

"Henrik's not trying to kill you. Cassiopeia isn't. Cotton Malone's not." He paused. "I'm not."

"You called off my backup, knowing I was in trouble."

"And what would have happened if I hadn't? Your two agents would have burst onto the scene, gunfire would have ensued, and what would have been solved?"

"I'd have Heather Dixon in custody."

"And by morning she would have been released, after

surely the secretary of state and probably the president him-self intervened. Then you would have been fired and the Saudis would kill you at their leisure. And you know why? Because nobody would have cared."

His words made sense. Damn him.

"You moved too fast and you didn't think it through." Green's eyes had softened, and she saw something else she'd never seen before.

Concern.

"Earlier I offered my help. You refused. Now I'm going to tell you what you don't know. What I didn't tell you then."

She waited.

"I allowed the file on the Alexandria Link to be compro-mised."

MALONE OPENED THE BOOK ABOUT ST. JEROME, A THIN volume, only seventy-three yellowed leaves, with an 1845 printing date. He paged through and absorbed a few details.

Jerome lived from 342 to 420 CE. He was fluent in Latin and Greek and, as a young man, made little effort to check his pleasure-loving instincts. Baptized by the pope in 360, he dedicated himself to God. For the next sixty years he trav-eled, wrote treatises, defended the faith, and became a recog-nized father of the Christian religion. He first translated the New Testament then, toward the end of his life, translated the Old directly from Hebrew into Latin, creating the Vul-gate, which the Council of Trent eleven hundred years later proclaimed the authoritative text of the Catholic Church.

Three words caught Malone's eye.

Eusebius Hieronymus Sophronius.

Jerome's birth name.

He thought of the novel from the leather satchel. *A Hero's Journey* by Eusebius Hieronymus Sophronius.

Apparently Thomas Bainbridge had chosen his pen name with great care.

"Anything?" Pam asked.

"Everything." But his excitement faded, replaced by the chill of an unpleasant realization. "We need to get out of here."

He rushed to the doors, switched off the lights, and eased them open. The marble hall loomed, quiet. The radio continued to play in some far-off room, now a sporting event of some sort, the crowd and commentator loud. The floor polisher was silent.

He led Pam to the top of the stairs.

Three men burst into the hall below, weapons in hand.

One raised and fired.

He shoved Pam to the floor.

The bullet pinged off the stone. He quickly rolled them both behind one of the columns and saw Pam grimace in pain.

"My shoulder," she said.

Three more bullets tried to find them through marble. He palmed Haddad's automatic and readied himself. None of the shots so far had been accompanied by a loud retort—only pops, like pillows fluffing. Sound suppressors. At least he possessed the high ground. From his vantage point he spotted two shooters advancing toward the right side of the lower floor while the other remained to the left. He could not allow the two to take up that position—they'd be able to shoot around the column—so he fired.

The bullet missed but its proximity caused the attackers to hesitate, enough for Malone to adjust his aim and fire a slug into the lead man, who cried out, then thudded to the floor. The other man leaped for cover, but Malone managed one more shot that sent the pursuer scurrying back toward the hall entrance. Blood streamed from the downed man, pooling into a bright red lake on the white marble.

More shots came their way. The air reeked of gunfire.

Five bullets remained in Haddad's gun, but Malone still carried the one he'd taken from String Bean, too. Maybe five more shots. He registered fear in Pam's eyes, but she was remaining calm, considering.

He thought about retreating into the drawing room. The double doors, if barricaded with furniture, might buy them a few minutes to escape through one of the windows. But they were on the second floor, which would surely pose additional obstacles. Regardless, that might be their only play unless the men below wanted to expose themselves and give him a clear shot.

Which wasn't likely.

One of the men scampered to the base of the stairs. The other covered his advance with four shots that snapped off the wall behind them. Malone had to conserve ammunition and could not fire until it really counted.

Then he realized what they were doing.

For him to fire at one, he'd have to expose himself at the column's edge to the other. So he did the unexpected, ignoring the left side and curling himself around the right, sending a bullet into the red carpet runner ahead of the advancing attacker.

The man leaped from the stairway and sought cover.

Pam reached for her shoulder and he spotted blood. Her wound had reopened. Too much jostling. Her blue eyes stared back, full of fear.

Two shots banged through the hall.

Not sound-suppressed. High-caliber.

Then, silence.

"Hello," a male voice called out.

He peered around the column. Standing below was a tall man with grizzled sandy blond hair. He had a broad brow, a short nose, and a round chin. He was squarely built and dressed in jeans and a canvas shirt beneath a leather jacket.

"It looked like you needed help," the man said, gun at his right side.

The two attackers lay on the floor, blood oozing onto the marble. This man was apparently a good shot, too.

Malone retreated back behind the column. "Who are you?"

"A friend."

"Forgive me if I'm skeptical."

"Wouldn't blame you. So stay there and wait for the police. You can explain about these three dead bodies." He heard footsteps, receding. "And by the way, you're welcome."

Something occurred to him. "What about the cleaning crew? Why aren't they rushing in here?"

The footsteps stopped. "They're unconscious, upstairs."

"Your doing?"

"Not mine."

"What's your interest?"

"The same as many who've come here in the middle of the night. I'm looking for the Library of Alexandria."

Malone said nothing.

"Tell you what. I'm staying at the Savoy, room 453. I have some information that I doubt you possess, and you might have some I don't know about. If you'd like to talk, come find me. If not, we'll probably see each other again along the way. Your choice. But together we might be able to speed up the process. It's up to you."

Heels clacked the floor with a solid tread, fading away into the house.

"What the hell was that?" Pam asked.

"His way of introducing himself."

"He killed two men."

"For which I'm grateful."

"Cotton, we've got to get out of here."

"Tell me about it. But first we need to know who those men are."

He fled from the column and rushed down the marble stairs. Pam followed. He searched all three corpses but found no identification.

"Grab the guns," he said, pocketing six spare magazines lifted from the bodies. "These guys came ready for a fight."

"I'm actually getting used to seeing blood," she said.

"I told you it'd get easier."

He thought more about the man. The Savoy. Room 453. His way of saying, *You can trust me.* Pam still clutched the book about St. Jerome, and he carried the leather satchel from Haddad's apartment.

Pam turned to leave.

"Where you going?" he asked.

"I'm hungry. I hope the Savoy has an excellent breakfast."

He grinned.

She caught on quick.

36

WASHINGTON, DC

STEPHANIE WASN'T SURE SHE COULD TAKE MUCH MORE. HER gaze locked onto Brent Green. "Explain yourself."

"We allowed the files to be compromised. There's a traitor among us and we want him. Or her."

"Who's *we*?"

"The Justice Department. It's a top-secret investigation. Only myself and two others know. My two closest deputies, and I'd place my life in their hands."

"Liars couldn't care less about your faith."

"Agreed. But the leak isn't in Justice. It's higher. Outside the department. We dangled bait and it was taken."

She could not believe what she was hearing. "And you risked Gary Malone's life in the process."

"No one could have predicted that. We had no idea anyone, other than the Israelis and the Saudis, gave a damn about George Haddad. The leak we're trying to plug runs straight to them, not anywhere else."

"That you know of." Her thoughts flooded with the Order of the Golden Fleece.

"If I had possessed any clue that Malone's family was in danger, I would never have allowed the tactic to be used. "

She wanted to believe that.

"We actually thought Haddad's whereabouts was a relatively harmless piece of information. Allowing the Israelis to know Haddad was alive didn't seem that risky, especially since there was nothing in the file to indicate where he was hidden."

"Except a trail straight to Cotton."

"And we assumed that, if challenged, Malone would know what to do."

"He's out, Brent," she almost shouted. "He doesn't work for us anymore. We don't place ex-operatives in danger, especially without their knowledge."

"We weighed those risks and decided that to find our leak, they were worth taking. Having the boy kidnapped changed everything. I'm glad Cotton was able to retrieve him."

"That's so wonderful of you. You'll be lucky if he doesn't break your nose."

"This White House is an abomination," Green muttered. "Bunch of righteous, corrupt pricks."

She'd never heard Green speak that way before.

"They expound how Christian they are, how American, but their allegiance is only to themselves—and the dollar. Decision after decision has been made, each one clothed in an American flag, that does nothing but fatten the pockets of major corporations—entities that have contributed heavily to their party cause. It sickens me. I sit in meetings where policy is couched in terms of what's good television, rather than what's good for the nation. I keep silent. Say nothing. Be a team player. But that doesn't mean I'm going to allow this country to be compromised. I took an oath, and unlike many in this administration, mine means something to me."

"So why not expose them for what they are?"

"So far I'm not aware that anyone has broken the law. Disgusting, immoral, greedy? I've seen those, but they're not illegal. I assure you, if anyone, the president included, had crossed the line, I would have acted. But no one has gone that far."

"Except the leak."

"Which is precisely why I'm so interested—a dam has to be cracked before it'll break."

She wasn't fooled. "Let's face it, Brent, you like being the chief law enforcement officer, and you wouldn't last long if you went after one of them and failed."

Green appraised her, worry in his eyes. "I like you remaining alive more."

She brushed away his concern. "Did you find the leak?"

"I believe we—"

Cassiopeia rushed back into the kitchen. "We've got company. Two men just wheeled to the curb. Suits and earpieces. Secret Service."

"My detail," Green said. "Coming to check for the night."

"We need to go," Cassiopeia made clear.

"No," Green said. "Cut me loose and I'll handle them."

Cassiopeia headed for the back door.

Stephanie made a decision, the kind she'd made a hundred thousand times. And even though she'd clearly chosen horribly throughout the day, like her daddy used to say, *Right, wrong, doesn't matter. Just do something.*

"Wait."

Stephanie stepped to the counter and searched a couple of drawers, finding a knife. "We're cutting him loose." She approached Green and said, "I hope I know what I'm doing."

SABRE HUSTLED THROUGH THE OXFORDSHIRE WOODS TO where he'd left his car. Dawn was coming to the English countryside. Mist shrouded the fields around him, the cool air damp. He was pleased with his first encounter with Cotton Malone. Just enough to whet the American's curiosity, while satisfying any paranoia. Killing the men he'd hired to attack Malone had seemed a perfect introduction. He would have shot all three if Malone hadn't taken down the one.

Surely Malone had searched the bodies after he left, but Sabre had made certain that not one of the men carried identification. His instructions had been for them to confront Malone and pin him down. But once Malone eliminated the first of their number, the game had changed. He wasn't surprised. Malone had proven in Copenhagen that he knew how to handle himself.

Thank heaven for the tape recorder in Haddad's apartment. That, combined with the information from the computer, had schooled him enough so he could entice Malone into his confidence. All he had to do now was return to the Savoy and wait.

Malone would come.

He emerged from the forest and spotted his car. Another vehicle was parked behind it and he saw his operative pacing.

"You son of a bitch," she screamed. "You killed those men."

"And the problem?"

"I hired them. How many others you think I can employ if it's known we bloody well kill our own?"

"Who would know that? Besides you and me."

"You asshole. I watched from outside. You shot them from behind. They never saw it coming. That's what you intended all along."

He reached his car. "You always were bright."

"Screw you, Dominick. Those men were friends of mine."

Now he was curious. "You sleep with any of them?"

"None of your damn business."

He shrugged. "You're right."

"I'm through with you. No more. Get yourself another helper." She stormed toward her car.

"Don't think so," he called out.

She whirled to face him, expecting a rebuke. They'd argued before. But this time he shot her in the face.

Nothing and no one was going to interfere. Too much effort had gone into what he'd planned. He was about to double-cross one of the most powerful economic cartels on the planet. Failure would come with dire consequences. So he wasn't going to fail. There would be no trails left to him.

He opened the car door and slid inside.

Only Cotton Malone remained to be handled.

STEPHANIE STOOD IN THE KITCHEN, CASSIOPEIA BESIDE HER, and listened as Brent Green answered the front door and spoke with the two Secret Service agents. Either she'd guessed right or they'd shortly be arrested.

"This is foolishness," Cassiopeia whispered.

"It's my foolishness, and I didn't ask you or Henrik to get involved."

"You're a stubborn bitch."

"Look who's talking. You could have left. I'd say you're a bit stubborn yourself."

She listened as Green small-talked about the night weather and how he'd spilled a tumbler of water on his robe. She'd freed Green from the chair and watched in amusement as he'd peeled tape from his wrists and ankles. What the late-night comedians would have given to see him wince as the hair on his arms and legs came away with each tug. But the New Englander had promptly smoothed his wet hair and emerged from the kitchen.

She heard again what Green had said with genuine conviction.

This friend particularly cares what happens to you.

"He sells us out and we're through," Cassiopeia whispered.

"He won't."

"What makes you so sure?"

"Twenty years of mistakes."

Green finally told the agents good night. She eased open the swinging door and watched as Green gathered a parting glimpse through the louvers. He turned toward her and said, "Satisfied?"

She walked through the dining room. Cassiopeia followed.

"Okay, Brent. What now?"

"Together we're going to save your hide and at the same time plug the leak."

"And by the way, you never mentioned who it is."

"No. I didn't. Because I don't know."

"I thought you said you'd identified the person?"

"What I started to say was that I believe we might have the problem identified."

"I'm waiting."

"You're not going to like this."

"Try me."

"At the moment, the Israelis' main conduit is Pam Malone."

PART
THREE

37

7:40 AM

HENRIK THORVALDSEN HATED TO FLY, WHICH WAS WHY NONE of his companies owned planes. To relieve some of his discomfort, he always sat in first class and flew early in the morning. The larger seats, amenities, and time of day eased his phobia. Gary Malone, on the other hand, seemed to love the experience. The boy had eaten all of the breakfast the flight attendant served, plus most of Henrik's.

"We'll be landing soon," he said to Gary.

"This is great. Any other time I'd be home in school. Now I'm in Austria."

He and Gary had grown close over the past two years. When he'd visited Malone for summer vacation, Gary had stayed many a night at Christiangade. Father and son liked to sail the forty-foot ketch tied to the estate's dock, bought long ago for trips across the Øresund to Norway and Sweden, but now hardly used. Thorvaldsen's own son, Cai, had loved the water. He missed the boy terribly. Dead now almost two years. Gunned down in Mexico City for no reason he'd ever been able to learn. Malone had been there on assignment and had done what he could, which eventually led them to know each other. But he'd not forgotten what happened there. He'd eventually discover the truth about his son's death. Debts like that never went unpaid. Spending time with Gary, though, brought him a measure of the joy life had cruelly denied him.

"I'm glad you could come," he said. "I didn't want to leave you at the estate."

"I've never been to Austria."

"A lovely place. Dense forests. Snowy mountains. Alpine lakes. Spectacular scenery."

He'd watched closely all yesterday and it seemed Gary was dealing well with his ordeal, especially considering he'd watched as two men were shot to death. When Malone and Pam left for England, Gary had understood why they needed to go. His mother had to return to her job and his father needed to discover why Gary was at risk. Christiangade was a familiar place and Gary had eagerly stayed. But yesterday, after talking to Stephanie, Thorvaldsen knew what had to be done.

"This meeting you have to attend," Gary said. "Is it important?"

"It could be. I'll have to appear at several sessions, but we'll find things for you to do while I'm there."

"What about Dad? He know we're doing this? I didn't tell Mom."

Pam Malone had telephoned a few hours before and spoken briefly with Gary. But she'd hung up before Thorvaldsen had been able to talk with her. "I'm sure one of them will call back and Jesper will let them know where we are."

He was taking a chance bringing Gary with him, but he'd decided it was the smart play. If Alfred Hermann was behind the original kidnapping, which Thorvaldsen firmly believed was the case, then having Gary at the Assembly, surrounded by influential men and women from around the world, each with their supporting cast of staff and security, seemed the safest course. He wondered about the kidnapping. From the little he'd been told about Dominick Sabre, the American was a professional, not prone to employing such sloppy help as the three Dutchmen who'd botched Gary's abduction. Something wasn't right. Malone was good, he'd give him that, but things had unfolded with uncanny precision. Had the entire thing been staged simply for Malone's benefit? A way to spur him forward? If so, that meant Gary was truly no longer in any danger.

"Remember what we talked about," he said to Gary. "Careful with your words. Lots of listening."

"I got it."

He smiled. "Excellent."

Now he could only hope he'd read Alfred Hermann correctly.

38

VIENNA
8:00 AM

HERMANN SHOVED HIS BREAKFAST ASIDE. HE DETESTED EATing, particularly amid a crowd, but he loved the château's dining hall. He'd personally chosen its design and neo-Gothic décor, the window casements and ceiling coffers bearing the coats of arms of illustrious Crusaders, the walls sheathed in canvases that depicted the Christian capture of Jerusalem.

Breakfast was spectacular, as usual, and a cadre of white-jacketed stewards attended to his guests. His daughter sat at the opposite end of the long table, the remainder of the twelve seats filled by a select group of Order members—the Political Committee—who'd arrived yesterday to attend the weekend Assembly.

"I hope everyone is enjoying themselves," Margarete said to the assemblage. Crowds were what she handled best.

Hermann noticed her frowning at his untouched plate, but she said nothing about it. Hers would be a private rebuke—as if an appetite, in and of itself, brought a long life and good health. If only it were that easy.

Several of the committee members rattled on about the château and its exquisite furnishings, noting some of the changes he'd made since the previous spring. Even though these were men and women of wealth, together they were not worth even a quarter of the Hermann fortune. Each, though, was useful in some way. So he thanked them for noticing and waited. Finally he said, "I'm interested in what the Political Committee plans to tell the Assembly on Concept 1223."

That initiative, adopted three years ago at the spring Assembly, involved a complex plan for the destabilization of Israel and Saudi Arabia. He'd embraced the concept, which was why he'd cultivated sources within the Israeli and American governments—sources that had unexpectedly led him to George Haddad.

"Before we do that," the chairman of the committee said, "can you tell us whether your labors are bearing fruit? Our plans will have to be altered if you're not successful."

He nodded. "Events are unfolding. And quickly. But if I succeed, has a market for the information been secured?"

Another committee member nodded. "We've made inquiries with Jordan, Syria, Egypt, and Yemen. All are interested, at least in arranging talks."

He was pleased. He'd learned that an Arab state's enthusiasm—whether for goods, services, or terror—increased in direct proportion to its neighbor's interest.

"It's risky ignoring the Saudis," another said. "They have ties to many of our members. Retaliation could be costly."

"Your negotiators," he said, "will have to ensure that they stay calm until it's to *our* advantage to deal with them."

"Isn't it time you tell us exactly what's involved?" one of the committee members asked.

"No," he said. "Not yet."

"You're involving us deeply in something that, quite frankly, Alfred, I have questions about."

"What is it you question?"

"What could possibly be so enticing to Jordan, Syria, Egypt, and Yemen to the exclusion of Saudi Arabia?"

"The elimination of Israel."

Silence gripped the room.

"Granted, that's a common goal for all those nations, but it's also impossible. That state is here to stay."

"That's what was said about the Soviet Union. Yet when its purpose was seriously challenged, then exposed for the fraud that it was, look what occurred. Dissolution in a matter of days."

"And you can make that happen?" asked another.

"I wouldn't be wasting our time if I didn't think it possible." One of the other members, a friend of long standing, seemed frustrated with his obliqueness, so he decided to be a bit conciliatory. "Let me offer this. What if the validity of the Old Testament were called into question?"

A few of the guests shrugged. One asked, "So what?"

"It could fundamentally shift the Middle Eastern debate," Hermann said. "The Jews are intent on upholding the correctness of their Torah. The Word of God and all that. Nobody has ever seriously challenged them. There's been talk, speculation, but if the Torah was proven wrong, imagine what that does to Jewish credibility. Think how that could incite other Middle Eastern states."

He meant what he'd said. No oppressor had ever been able to defeat the Jews. Many had tried. The Assyrians. Babylonians. Romans. Turks. The Inquisition. Even Martin Luther loathed them. But the so-called children of God had stubbornly refused to surrender. Hitler might have been the worst. And yet, in his wake, the world merely granted them their biblical homeland.

"What do you have against Israel?" one of the committee members asked. "I've questioned from the beginning why we're wasting time on this."

The woman had indeed dissented, joined by two others. They were clearly in the minority, and relatively harmless, so he'd allowed their discourse simply as a way to add a semblance of democracy to the process.

"This is about far more than Israel." He saw he held their collective attention, even his daughter's. "Played correctly, we may be able to destabilize both Israel and Saudi Arabia. On this, the one is linked to the other. If we can create the appropriate amount of turmoil in both states, control it, then properly time its release, we may be able to irrevocably topple both governments." He faced the Political Committee chairman. "Have you discussed how our members can exploit that process once we set it into motion?"

The older man nodded. He'd been a friend for decades and was near the top of the list for a place in the Circle. "The scenario we envision is based on the Palestinians, Jordanians, Syrians, and Egyptians all wanting whatever we provide—"

"That's not going to happen," said one of the men, another of the dissenters.

"And who would have thought the world would displace nearly a million Arabs and grant the Jews a homeland?" Hermann made clear. "Many in the Middle East said that would not happen, either." His words came out sharp, so he laced what he was about to say with a tone of compromise. "At the very least we can bring down that silly wall the Israelis have erected to guard their borders and challenge every ancient claim they've ever made. Zionist arrogance would suffer, perhaps enough to galvanize the surrounding Arab states into unified action. And I haven't even mentioned Iran, which would love nothing more than to totally obliterate Israel. This will be a blessing for them."

"What could do all that?"

"Knowledge."

"You can't be serious. All this is based on us *learning* something?"

He hadn't expected this frank discussion, but this was his moment. The committee huddled around his dining room table was charged by Order statutes with formulating the collective's political policy, which was closely intertwined with initiatives from the Economic Committee because, for the Order, politics and profit were synonymous. The Economic Committee had established a goal of increasing revenues for those members desiring to heavily invest in the Middle East by at least 30 percent. A study had been undertaken, an initial euro investment determined, potential profits estimated under current economic and political conditions, then several scenarios envisioned. In the end a 30 percent goal was deemed achievable. But markets in the Middle East were limited at best. The entire region could explode over the most minuscule occurrence. Every day brought another possibility for disaster. So consistency was what the Political Committee sought. Traditional methods—bribes and threats—were not effective with people who routinely strapped explosives to their chests. The men who controlled decisions in places such as Jordan, Syria, Kuwait, Egypt, and Saudi Arabia were far too wealthy, far too guarded, and far too fanatical. Instead the Order had come to understand that a new form of currency needed to be found—one Hermann believed he would soon possess.

"Knowledge is far more powerful than any weapon," he said in a hushed whisper.

"All depends on the knowledge," one of the members declared.

He agreed. "Success will hinge on us being able to disseminate what we learn to the right buyers for the right price at the right time."

"I know you, Alfred," one of the older men said. "You've planned this thoroughly."

He grinned. "Things are finally progressing. The Americans are now interested, and that opens a whole new avenue of possibilities."

"What of the Americans?" Margarete asked, impatience in her voice.

Her question annoyed him. She needed to learn not to reveal what she didn't know. "It seems there are some in power within the United States who want to humble Israel, too. They see a benefit to American foreign policy."

"How is any of this possible?" one of the committee members asked. "Arabs and Arabs, along with Arabs and Jews, have been warring for thousands of years. What's so damn frightening?"

He'd established a lofty goal for both himself and the Order, but a voice inside him said that his diligence was about to be rewarded. So he stared down the men and women seated before him and declared, "I should know the answer to that question before the weekend ends."

39

WASHINGTON, DC
3:30 AM

STEPHANIE SAT IN THE CHAIR, EXHAUSTED. BRENT GREEN faced her from the sofa. He was actually slouching, which she'd never seen him do before. Cassiopeia had fallen asleep upstairs. At least one of them would be rested. She certainly wouldn't. It seemed like forty-eight days instead of forty-eight hours since she'd last been here, not trusting Green, leery of what he had to say, angry at herself for placing Malone's son in jeopardy. And though Gary Malone was now safe, the same doubts about Brent Green swirled through her mind, especially considering what he'd told her a few hours ago.

The Israelis' main conduit is Pam Malone.

She cradled a Diet Dr Pepper that she'd found in Green's refrigerator. She motioned with the can. "You actually drink these?"

He nodded. "Taste just like the original, but no sugar. Seemed like a good concept to me."

She smiled. "You're a strange fellow, Brent."

"I'm just a private man who keeps what he likes to himself."

She was heartsore and mind-weary, wrestling a deep anxiety that wanted to jar her attention away from Green. They'd intentionally left all the lights off to convey to any watchful eyes that the house's occupant was down for the night.

"You thinking about Malone?" he asked through the dark.

"He's in trouble."

"Nothing you can do until he calls in."

She shook her head. "Not good enough."

"You have an agent in London. What are the chances of finding Cotton?"

Not likely. London was a big city, and who knew if Malone was there? He could have left for anywhere in Britain. But she didn't want to think about impossibilities, so she asked, "How long have you known about Pam?"

"Not long."

She resented being kept out of the loop and decided that to get something she was going to have to give. "There's another player in your game."

"I'm listening." Green's tone indicated that his interest was piqued. Finally she knew something he didn't.

She told him what Thorvaldsen had said about the Order of the Golden Fleece.

"Henrik never said a word about that to me."

"Gee, that's a shocker." She downed another swallow of her soft drink. "He tells only what he wants you to know."

"Did they kidnap Malone's son?"

"They're at the top of my list."

"That explains things," Green said. "The Israelis have been unusually cautious throughout this entire operation. We dangled the link, hoping their contact here would take the bait. For several years, privately, their diplomats have made inquiries concerning George Haddad. We didn't fool them entirely when Malone hid him away. They sifted through the remains of that ruined café, but the bomb did a thorough job.

Yet even after we tossed the link out there for them to notice, the Israelis played everything close."

"Tell me something I don't know."

"Malone's son being taken baffled us. That's why I delayed our meeting when you first called with the news."

"And I thought it was simply because you didn't like me."

"You do take patience to endure, but I've learned to adapt."

She grinned.

Green reached for a crystal dish on the coffee table that contained salted nuts. She was hungry, too, so she grabbed a handful.

"We knew Israel wasn't the culprit in Gary Malone's abduction," Green said. "And we were curious why they stayed so quiet when it happened." He paused. "Then, after you called me, I was told about Pam Malone."

She was listening.

"She became involved with a man about three months ago. A successful lawyer with an Atlanta firm, a senior partner, but also a Jewish patriot. Huge supporter of Israel. Homeland Security believes that he's helped finance one of the more militant factions in the Israeli government."

She knew American money had long fueled Israeli politics. "I had no idea you were that involved with things on a daily basis."

"Again, Stephanie, I'm many things you don't realize. I have a public image, which is demanded. But when I took this job I didn't intend to be a talking head. I'm the chief law enforcement officer of this country, and I do my job."

She noticed that he hadn't eaten any of his nuts. Instead, with his right palm open flat, the dark form of his left hand was picking through them.

"What are you doing?" she asked.

"Finding halves."

"Why?"

"More salt on those."

"Excuse me?"

"If you have a whole peanut, the middle isn't salted. But if the nut is split and salted, then there's twice the salt."

"You're not serious."

He plucked a nut and tossed it into his mouth.

"Why does half a nut have more salt than a whole?"

"Aren't you paying attention?" he asked in an amused tone. "Two salted halves, joined, have more salt than a single whole." He tossed another into his mouth.

She couldn't decide if he was serious or just aggravating her, but he continued to search for halves. "What do you do with the whole ones?"

"Save them to the end. I only eat them as a last resort. But I'll trade you a whole for a half."

She liked this Brent Green. A touch of playfulness. A dry sense of humor. Suddenly she felt protective of him. "You want those arrogant fools in the White House just as bad as I do. You've heard the talk about you. They call you the Right Reverend Green. They withhold things. They use you only to further their image."

"I'd like to think I'm not that petty."

"What's petty about sticking it up their ass? If anybody needs it, they do. The president included."

"I agree." He brushed peanut debris from his hands and kept chewing. She was indeed starting to appreciate the man sitting across from her.

"Tell me more about Pam," she said.

"She and the lawyer have dated for about three months. We know he's connected to Heather Dixon. They've met several times."

She was perplexed. "I'm missing something. How would the Israelis assume Pam would be involved with any of this?

She and Malone have been estranged for a long time. They hardly speak. And you said yourself you don't think they kidnapped Gary."

"The Israelis had to know something we didn't. They anticipated all this, knew it would happen, and knew that Pam Malone would connect with Cotton. It's the only thing that makes sense. She was intentionally cultivated. Now tell me about this Order of the Golden Fleece. I think the Israelis knew they were involved, too, and that the boy, at some point, would be taken. Maybe they were planning to do it themselves?"

"Pam's a spy?"

"The extent of her involvement is a mystery. And unfortunately the lawyer in Atlanta she was dating died the day before yesterday." Green paused. "Shot in a parking garage."

Nothing new. The Middle East routinely ate its own.

"What do you know about him?" she asked.

"We were looking at his participation in a money-for-arms deal. Tel Aviv publicly says it's trying to stop those, but privately they encourage the practice. I'm told the lawyer made all the moves on Pam. Spent a lot of time with her. Gave her gifts. That sort of thing. For someone who wants people to think she's tough, Pam Malone is simply lonely and vulnerable."

She caught something in his tone. "That describe you, too?"

Green did not immediately answer, and she wondered if she'd crossed his emotional line. Finally he said in low whisper, "More than you know."

She wanted to explore that path and was about to make an attempt when footsteps pounded down the stairway. Cassiopeia's outline appeared in the doorway.

"We have company. A car just pulled up to the curb."

Green stood. "I saw no headlights."

"It came dark."

Stephanie was concerned. "Thought you were asleep."

"Somebody has to watch out for you two."

The phone rang.

No one moved.

Another ring.

Green stepped through the darkness, found the cordless receiver, and answered. Stephanie noticed that his tone feigned sleep.

A few moments of silence.

"Then by all means, come in. I'll be down in a moment."

Green clicked off the unit.

"Larry Daley. He's outside and wants to see me."

"That's not good," Stephanie said.

"Maybe not. But get out of sight and let's see what the devil wants."

40

MALONE LOVED THE SAVOY. HE'D STAYED THERE A FEW TIMES on the U.S. and British governments' dimes. One thing about the Magellan Billet—the perks had been as plentiful as the risks. He hadn't visited in several years, but he was glad to see that the late-Victorian hotel still projected its grand mixture of opulence and naughtiness. A night in a room facing the Thames, he knew, cost more than most people in the world earned in a year. Which meant their savior apparently liked to travel in style.

They'd quickly departed Bainbridge Hall, stealing the cleaning crew's van, which he'd parked a few miles from the train station. There they'd caught the 6:30 train back to London. All had been quiet at Paddington Station, and he'd avoided taxis, taking the Tube to the Savoy.

Pam's shoulder seemed okay. The bleeding from Bainbridge Hall had stopped. Inside the hotel he found a house phone and asked to be connected to room 453.

"You move fast," said the voice on the other end of the line.

"What do you want?"

"At the moment, I'm hungry. So breakfast is my main priority."

Malone caught the message. "Come on down."

"How about the café in ten minutes? They have a lovely buffet."

"We'll be waiting."

The man who appeared at their table was the same one from two hours ago, only now sporting olive chinos and a tan twill shirt. His clean-shaven, handsome face brimmed with goodwill and civility.

"Name's McCollum. James McCollum. People call me Jimmy."

Malone was too tired and suspicious to be friendly, but he stood. The handshake was firm and confident. The other man's eyes, the color of jade, stared back, eager. Pam stayed seated. Malone introduced himself and her, then came straight to the point. "What were you doing at Bainbridge Hall?"

"You could at least thank me for saving your life. I didn't have to do that."

"Just happen to be in the neighborhood?"

The man's thin lips curled into a grin. "You always like this? No foreplay, just right to it?"

"You're dodging my question."

McCollum slid out a chair and sat. "I'm starving. How about we get some food and I'll tell you all about it?"

Malone did not move. "How about you answer my question."

"Okay, in the interest of goodwill. I'm a treasure hunter on the trail of the Library of Alexandria. I've been searching for whatever remains of it for more than a decade. I was at Bainbridge Hall because of those three men. They killed a woman four days ago, a damn good source, so I stayed on their trail hoping to learn who they're working for. Instead they led me to you."

"You said back at the estate you have information I don't. What makes you think that?"

McCollum shoved back his chair and stood. "I said I might have some information you don't. Look, I don't have the time or patience for this. I've been at that estate before. You're not the first to go there. Each one of you amateurs knows a kernel of truth mixed with a lot of fantasy. I'm willing to bargain with some of what I know to learn the tiny shred that you may know. That's all, Malone. Nothing more sinister."

"So you shot two men in the head to prove your point?" Pam asked, and Malone spotted the look of a skeptical lawyer.

McCollum locked his gaze on Pam. "I shot those men to save your life." Then he glanced around at their surroundings. "I love this place. Did you know that the first martini was actually poured in the American Bar at the Savoy? Hemingway, Fitzgerald, Gershwin—they all drank there. Lots of history."

"You like history?" Pam asked.

"An occupational necessity."

"You going somewhere?" Malone asked.

McCollum stood rigid, his manner calm and unruffled, though Malone had deliberately tried to shake him. "You're way too suspicious for me. Go ahead. Take the hero's quest. Hope you succeed."

This man was knowledgeable. "How do you know about that?"

"Like I said, I've been on this trail awhile. How long have you been at it? My guess? You're a rookie. Worse, you're a rookie with an attitude. I've met a ton of people just like you. They think they know it all. Truth is, they don't know spit. That library has stayed hidden for fifteen hundred years for a reason." McCollum paused. "You know, Malone, you're like the jackass standing in some wonderful knee-high grass with his head cocked over the fence eating weeds. Nice to meet you. I'm going to go sit at that table over there and have breakfast."

McCollum negotiated his way across the half-empty café.

"What do you think?" he asked Pam.

"Arrogant. But you can't hold that against him."

He smiled. "He knows something, and we're not going to find out a thing sitting here."

She stood. "I agree. So let's go eat with our new friend."

SABRE SAT AT THE TABLE AND WAITED. IF HE'D CALCULATED correctly, they would be coming over shortly. There's no way Malone could resist. His knowledge had to be limited to what George Haddad had managed to tell him—which, from the tape he'd heard, wasn't much. What Malone retrieved from Haddad's apartment before fleeing may have filled in gaps, but he was betting that the most vital questions remained unanswered.

Which was also a problem for him.

He was forcing himself to interact. Something different. He was accustomed to the silence of his own thoughts—intimate company came rarely, confined to the occasional woman who provided sex. He hired most. Professionals, like him, doing their job, saying at night what he wanted to hear, then leaving in the morning. The harsh realities of physical danger and intellectual tension, at least for him, neutered rather than stimulated sex. Grave consequences sapped the brain. Occasionally he slept with the hired help. But as with the Brit he'd shot earlier, that sometimes came with annoying side effects. Instead of romance, he craved solitude.

He'd played this particular role before, with others, when he'd needed to secure their confidence. The words and actions, the way he walked and carried himself, the swaggering voice all came from one of his mother's many boyfriends. This one had been a beat cop in Chicago, where they'd lived when he was twelve. He remembered how the man had tried to impress her with unabashed confidence. He recalled a White Sox game and a trip to the lakefront. He later learned that, like most of his mother's lovers, the cop had shown only enough interest to impress his mother. Once they got what they really wanted, which usually was measured in nights in his mother's bed, the attention stopped. He came to hate all her suitors. Not one of them was there when he buried her. She died alone and broke.

And he wasn't going to repeat her fate.

He stood and headed for the buffet line.

He loved the Savoy, rooms furnished with expensive antiques and serviced by Old World valets. The kind of luxury

Alfred Hermann and the rest of the Order of the Golden Fleece routinely enjoyed. He wanted that privilege, too. On his terms. Not theirs. But to alter reality he needed Cotton Malone, and he wondered if some of what he sought lay inside the leather satchel Malone toted. So far he'd managed to stay one step ahead of his adversary, and out of the corner of his eye he was pleased to see that he still retained that advantage.

Malone and his ex-wife were making their way through the rapidly filling tables.

"All right, McCollum," Malone said as he approached. "We're here."

"You buying?"

"Sure. The least I can do."

He forced a chuckle. "I just hope that's not the *most* you can do."

WASHINGTON, DC

STEPHANIE AND CASSIOPEIA RETREATED INTO THE KITCHEN AS Brent Green answered his front door. They resumed their positions near the swinging door and listened as Green ushered Daley into the dining room and the two men sat at the table.

"Brent," Daley said, "we have some issues to discuss."

"We've always had those, Larry."

"We have a serious problem. And I use the plural *we* because I came to help *you* solve it."

"I was hoping that it was important, considering the time. So why don't you tell me what *our* problem is?"

"Three bodies were found a short while ago at an estate west of London. Two with bullets to the head, the other to the chest. Another body, a woman, was found a few miles away. Bullet to the head. Same caliber gun delivered the head shots. A cleaning van was stolen from the estate. The crew had been knocked unconscious. It was driven into a nearby town and left. A man and a woman were seen leaving the van, then taking a train to London. Surveillance video from Paddington Station confirmed that Cotton Malone and his ex-wife came off that train."

Stephanie knew where this was leading.

"I assume," Green said, "you're implying Malone killed those four people."

"Sure looks that way."

"Apparently, Larry, you've never prosecuted a murder."

"And you have?"

"Six, actually. When I was an assistant state's attorney. You have no idea if Malone shot those people."

"Maybe not, Brent. But I have enough to excite the hell out of the British. I'll leave the details for them to work out."

Stephanie realized that this could pose a problem for Cotton, and she saw in Cassiopeia's eyes that her friend agreed.

"The Brits have identified Malone. The only reason they haven't gone after him is that they've asked us what he's doing there. They want to know if it's official. You don't by any chance know the answer?"

Silence hung in the air, and she imagined the look of granite on Green's face. Stonewalling was what he did best.

"That's beyond my jurisdiction. And who's to say Malone is doing anything there that concerns us?"

"I guess I just look stupid."

"Not always."

"Cute, Brent. Humor. Something new for you. But as I was saying, Malone is there for a reason and four people are dead because of him, regardless of whether he pulled the trigger. And my guess is that it involves the Alexandria Link."

"More leaps in logic. That how the White House sets policy?"

"I wouldn't involve the White House. You're not high on their favorite-people list at the moment."

"If the president doesn't want me to serve any longer, he can certainly do something about that."

"I'm not sure your resignation is enough."

Stephanie realized Daley was finally coming to the purpose of this visit.

"What do you have in mind?" Green asked.

"Here's the thing. The president's poll numbers aren't that good. True, we have three years left and then our two terms are gone, but we'd like to go out on top. Who wouldn't? And nothing spikes polling numbers like a good rally around the flag, and nothing makes for a better rally than a terrorist act."

"For once, you're correct."

"Where's Stephanie?"

"How would I know?"

"You tell me. A day or two ago you were willing to resign in support of her. I tell her not to involve the Billet in this affair, and she promptly mobilizes the whole damn agency. She do that with your approval?"

"I'm not her keeper."

"The president fired her. She's been relieved."

"Without consulting me?"

"He consulted himself, and that's enough. She's out."

"And who will be in charge of the Magellan Billet?"

"How about a little story? It's not mine. It comes from one of my favorite books, *Hardball,* by Chris Matthews. Not on the same side of the political aisle as me, but still a smart guy. He tells of how former senator Bill Bradley was at a dinner given in his honor. Bradley wanted another pat of butter and couldn't get the waiter carrying the tray to come his way. Finally he went over to the guy and told him that he apparently didn't know who he was. 'I'm Bill Bradley. Rhodes scholar, professional basketball player, U.S. senator, and I'd like some more butter.' The waiter wasn't impressed and simply said that Bradley apparently didn't know who *he* was. So the waiter told him. 'I'm the guy in charge of the butter.' You see, Brent, power is what you hold. So, for now, I'm the guy in charge of the Magellan Billet."

"Weren't you a corporate lobbyist before working at the White House? Before that, a political consultant? What qualifies you to manage the Justice Department's most sensitive intelligence division?"

"The fact that the president values my opinion."

"And that you'll kiss his ass whenever he bends over."

"I didn't come here to argue qualifications. The decision has been made. So where's Stephanie?"

"I assume she's at her hotel."

"I've issued a warrant for her arrest."

"And who at Justice assisted with that?"

"White House counsel handled the particulars. She's broken quite a few laws."

"Care to tell me which ones?"

"How about assault on a foreign national? I have a member of the Israeli mission swearing Stephanie tried to kill her. The woman has a nasty bump on her head to prove it."

"You plan to prosecute?"

"I plan to haul her sorry ass off somewhere where there aren't any reporters."

"From which she will not return."

More silence.

"Shit happens, Brent."

"That include me?"

"Actually, it does. Seems the Israelis don't like you and they won't say why. Maybe it's all that Christian conservatism junk you like to preach." Daley paused. "Or maybe it's just that you're an asshole. I don't know."

"Interesting, the respect you have for my office."

"I have respect for the people who placed *me* in office, as you should. Let's be clear. We could use a good terrorist strike, and no one I know of will shed many tears if you're the victim. Nothing but a win–win for us. Three birds with one stone and all that shit. You're gone. Israel is happy, for once. Our poll numbers climb. Everyone looks to the president for leadership. Life is good."

"So you came here to threaten the attorney general of the United States?"

"Now, why would you say such a thing? I came to *pass along* the threat. It's only right you know, so that appropriate security precautions can be taken. Stephanie, too. For some reason the Israelis are pissed at her. But of course you know nothing of her whereabouts, so we can't warn her. Too bad. You, though, are another matter. Consider yourself advised."

"I assume the Israelis themselves would not be involved in any killing?"

"Of course not. It's not a terrorist state. But they're a resourceful bunch and can farm the project out. They have ties to, shall we say, unsavory elements. That's why you're being advised."

Stephanie heard someone stand.

"All part of the job, Brent."

"And if I'm a good boy and toe the line those *unsavory elements* will lose interest in me."

"Can't really say. But it's possible. Why don't you try it and let's see?"

The room went silent longer than was comfortable. Stephanie imagined two lions facing each other.

"Is the president's legacy worth all this?" Green asked.

"That what you think this is about? No way. This is about *my* legacy. What *I* can deliver. And that kind of political capital is worth more than gold."

She heard soles slap hardwood, heading away from the kitchen.

"Larry," Green said, his voice rising.

The steps stopped.

"I'm not afraid of you."

"You should be."

"Take your best shot. Then I'm going to take mine."

"Yeah, right. Brent, after I take mine you'll be back in Vermont six feet down in a box."

"Don't be so sure."

Daley chuckled. "The funny thing about all this is that my two biggest pains in the ass may well bring this administration out of the toilet. Talk about working with what you have."

"We might surprise you."

"You keep thinking that. Have a blessed day."

A door opened, then closed.

"He's gone," Green said.

Stephanie stepped from the kitchen and said, "Guess you can't tell me what to do anymore."

She registered fatigue in his gray eyes. She was tired, too.

"You finally managed to get yourself fired."

"Which is the least of our concerns," Cassiopeia made clear.

"There's a traitor in this government," Green said. "And I plan to find him."

"I assure you, Mr. Attorney General," Cassiopeia said, "you've never dealt with those *unsavory elements*. Daley's right. The Israelis won't be doing any of the dirty work themselves. They hire that out. And the people they employ are a problem."

"Then we're all going to have to be careful."

Stephanie almost smiled. Brent Green possessed more courage than she'd imagined. But there was something else. She'd detected it earlier and now she was sure. "You have a plan, don't you?"

"Oh, yes. I'm not without resources."

42

VIENNA, AUSTRIA
10:50 AM

ALFRED HERMANN BID HIS GOODBYES TO THE POLITICAL Committee and excused himself from the dining room. He'd been told that his special guest had finally arrived.

He navigated the ground-floor corridors and entered the château's spacious foyer just as Henrik Thorvaldsen shuffled in from outside. He slipped a smile onto his face and said in English, "Henrik. So wonderful to see you."

Thorvaldsen also smiled as he spotted his host. "Alfred. I wasn't going to come, but I decided I simply had to visit with everyone."

Hermann approached and shook hands. Forty years he'd known Thorvaldsen and the Dane had changed little. The stiff, crooked spine had always been there, bent at a grotesque angle like a piece of hammered tin. He'd always admired Thorvaldsen's disciplined emotions, which stayed studied, mannered, as if he were running through a memorized program. And that required talent. But Thorvaldsen was a Jew. Not devout or overt, but still Hebrew. Even worse, he was Cotton Malone's close friend, and Hermann was convinced that Thorvaldsen had not come to the Assembly to socialize.

"I'm glad you're here," Hermann said. "I have much to talk to you about."

They often spent time together at the Assembly. Thorvaldsen was one of the few members whose fortune could compete with the Hermanns'. He was deeply connected to most European governments, and his billions of euros spoke for themselves.

A twinkle appeared in the Dane's eyes. "I'm anxious to hear it all."

"And who is this?" Hermann asked, motioning to the young lad standing beside Thorvaldsen.

"Gary Malone. He's with me for a few weeks while his father is away and I decided to bring him."

Fascinating. Thorvaldsen was testing him. "Wonderful. There are a few other young people who have come with members. I'll see to it that they are all properly entertained."

"As I knew you would."

Stewards entered with luggage. Hermann motioned and the bags were hauled to the second floor. He'd already designated which bedchamber Thorvaldsen would occupy.

"Come, Henrik. To my study while your belongings are situated. Margarete is anxious to see you."

"But I have Gary."

"Bring him. It'll be fine."

MALONE ATE HIS BREAKFAST AND TRIED TO ASSESS JIMMY McCollum, though he seriously wondered whether that was the man's real name.

"You going to tell me what your interest in all this is?" McCollum asked. "The Library of Alexandria isn't exactly the Holy Grail. Others have looked, but they're usually fanatics or kooks. You don't look like either."

"Neither do you," Pam said. "What's your interest?"

"What happened to your shoulder?"

"Who said anything did?"

McCollum scooped a forkful of eggs into his mouth. "You've been cradling it like it's broken."

"Maybe it is."

"Okay, you're not going to tell me." McCollum faced Malone. "Lot of mistrust here for a person who saved both your asses."

"She asked a good question. What's your interest in the library?"

"Let's just say that if I were to find something, there are people who would reward my efforts in a great many ways. Personally, I think it's a waste of time. But I do have to wonder why men are killing each other. Somebody knows something."

Malone decided to cast a little bait into the water. "The hero's quest you mentioned. I know about it. Clues that lead the way to the library." He paused. "Supposedly."

"Oh, they do. Believe me. Others have been. I've never met or talked to one of them, but I've heard about the experience. The hero's quest is real, as are the Guardians."

Another key word. This man was well informed. Malone turned his attention back to an English muffin, which he lathered with plum jam. "What can we do for each other?"

"How about you tell me why you went to Bainbridge Hall?"

"The Epiphany of St. Jerome."

"Now, that's a new one. Care to explain?"

"Where you from?" Malone suddenly asked.

McCollum chuckled. "You still sizing me up? Okay, I'll play along. Born in the great state of Kentucky. Louisville. And before you ask, no college. Army. Special forces."

"Like, if I check I'm going to find a recruit named Jimmy McCollum? Time for you to get real."

"Hate to tell you, but I have a passport and a birth certificate and you'll find my name there. Did my stint. Honorable discharge. But does all that really matter? Seems the only thing that counts is here and now."

"What are you after?" Malone asked.

"I'm hoping there's plenty there when this library is found, though I still don't know your interest."

"This quest might prove a challenge."

"Now, that's the first thing you've said that makes sense."

"I mean, there are others who might be looking, too."

"Tell me something I don't know."

"How about the Israelis?"

He caught a moment of puzzlement in McCollum's lively eyes, then clarity returned, along with a smile. "I do love a challenge."

Time to reel him in. "We have *The Epiphany of St. Jerome.*"

"Lot of good that'll do if you don't know its significance." Malone agreed.

"I have the hero's quest," McCollum said.

That revelation grabbed Malone's attention, especially

since George Haddad had not left them the details of that journey.

"What I want to know," McCollum said, "is do you have Thomas Bainbridge's novel?"

Pam was still eating, working on some fruit and yogurt. She certainly knew the first rule of lawyering—never reveal what you know—but he decided that to receive he was going to have to give. "I do." Then to tantalize his listener, he added, "And more."

McCollum scrunched his face in admiration. "I knew I'd chosen well when I decided to save your hide."

HERMANN WATCHED AS THORVALDSEN AND HIS YOUNG WARD left his study. Margarete stood beside him. They'd had a pleasant thirty-minute visit.

"Your thoughts?" he asked his daughter.

"Henrik was his usual self. Taking in far more than he gives."

"That's his nature, as it is mine." *And it should be yours, too,* he thought. "Sense anything?"

She shook her head.

"Nothing about the boy?" he asked.

"He seemed well mannered."

He decided to tell her some of what she did not know. "Henrik is peripherally involved with an initiative the Circle is presently pursuing. It's critical to what we discussed at breakfast."

"The Library of Alexandria?"

He nodded. "One of his close associates, a man named Cotton Malone, is part of what's happening."

"Sabre running the operation?"

"Quite well. Everything is going as planned."

"The boy is named Malone. He part of it, too?"

"Cotton Malone's son."

Her face showed surprise. "Why is he here?"

"Actually, that was smart on Henrik's part. With members present, we'll all be on our best behavior. This could be the safest place for them both. Of course, accidents sometimes happen."

"You'd hurt the boy?"

He stared hard. "I'll do what's necessary to protect our interests. As you should be willing to do."

She said nothing and he allowed her a moment. Finally she said, "Do we need an accident to happen?"

He was glad she was beginning to appreciate the gravity. "Depends on what our dear friend Henrik has in mind."

"HOW'D YOU GET THAT NAME?" MCCOLLUM ASKED. "COTTON."

"Actually it's quite—," Pam began.

Malone cut her off. "Long story. We can discuss it another time. Right now, I want to know about the hero's quest."

"You always that touchy about your name?"

"What I'm touchy about is wasted time."

McCollum was finishing a plate of fruit. He noticed that the man ate healthy. Oatmeal, strawberries, eggs, juice.

"Okay, Malone. I have the quest. I retrieved it from an invitee who died before going."

"Your doing?"

"Not this time. Natural causes. I found him and I stole the quest. Don't ask me who, because I'm not telling. But I have the clues."

"And do you know if they're real?"

McCollum chuckled. "In my business you never know that until you get there. But I'll take my chances."

"What do you really need?" Pam asked. She'd stayed un-characteristically quiet during breakfast. "Obviously you know more than we do. Why waste your time with us?"

"To be honest, I have a problem. For the past few weeks I've wrestled with the quest. It's a riddle. One I can't solve. I thought you two might be of some help. In return, I'm willing to share what I know."

"And you're willing to shoot two men in the head," Malone said.

"They would have done the same to you. Which, by the way, ought to give you pause. Who'd want to do that?"

An excellent question, Malone thought. No one had followed them from London, of that he was sure. It made no sense that killers would be waiting for them at Bainbridge Hall. He'd only decided to visit there a few hours ago.

"This quest," McCollum said, "has a lot more to it than I first thought. Now you tell me the Jews are also involved."

"A friend of mine was killed yesterday, which should end Israel's interest."

"This friend know anything about the library?"

"It's what got him killed."

"He's not the first."

He needed to know something. "I assume you'd want to peddle the found manuscripts to dealers?"

McCollum shrugged. "I want to profit for my trouble. That bother you?"

"If the manuscripts still exist, they would need to be preserved and studied."

"I'm not greedy, Malone. Surely somewhere in the find would be a few scraps I could sell for my trouble." McCollum paused. "Along with credit for the find, of course. That would be worth something all by itself."

"Fame and fortune," Pam said.

"The time-immemorial reward," McCollum said. "They both have their satisfying aspects."

He'd heard enough. "Tell us the clues."

McCollum sat before them, aloof as a deity, mischievous as a demon. This one bore watching. He killed far too easily. But if he possessed the hero's quest, then he might be their only path forward.

McCollum reached into his pocket and produced a slip of paper. "That's how it starts off."

Malone accepted the note-sized sheet and read.

How strange are the manuscripts, great traveler of the unknown. They appear separately, but seem as one to those who know that the colors of the rainbow become a single white light. How to find that single ray? It is a mystery, but visit the chapel beside the Tejo, in Bethlehem, dedicated to our patron saint.

"Where's the rest?" he asked.

McCollum chuckled. "Figure this part out, then we'll see. One step at a time."

Malone stood.

"Where you going?" McCollum asked.

"To earn my keep."

43

STEPHANIE HAD FACED MANY THINGS, BUT NEVER ARREST. Larry Daley was upping the ante.

"We need to strike at Daley now," she made clear.

She, Green, and Cassiopeia were standing in Green's kitchen, coffee brewing on the counter. The aroma reminded her that she was hungry.

"What do you have in mind?" Cassiopeia asked.

Not once in twelve years had she compromised the Billet's security. She took her oath to heart. But an abyss of doubt made her unsure of what to do next. She finally decided there was but one option and said, "We were investigating Daley."

A new earnestness swept over Green's face. "Explain."

"I wanted to know what made the man tick, so I assigned an agent to find out. She worked him, off and on, for nearly a year. I learned a lot."

"You continue to amaze me, Stephanie. Do you know what would have happened if he'd found out?"

"Guess I would have been fired, so what does it matter now?"

"He's trying to kill you. Perhaps he does know."

"I doubt it. She was good. But Daley is up to his eyeballs in trouble. You said earlier that you never found any violations of law. I did. Lots of them. Campaign finance, bribery, fraud. Daley's the pipeline for what people of means need from the White House, people who don't want their names on disclosure forms."

"Why didn't you move on him?"

"I was planning to—then this leak occurred. It had to wait."

"And now that he's in charge of the Magellan Billet, will he find out what you did?" Cassiopeia asked.

She shook her head. "I have all the information locked away, and the agent who handled the investigation transferred from the Billet months ago. No one other than she and I knew."

Green poured coffee into two mugs. "What do you want to do?"

"Since I have my friend here, who possesses a multitude of skills, I thought we'd finish the investigation."

"I don't like the sound of that," Cassiopeia said.

Green motioned. "You ladies add what you like to your coffee."

"None for you?" Stephanie asked.

"Never drink it."

"Then why do you have a coffeemaker?"

"I do have guests." He paused. "Occasionally."

Green's solidity, his masculine dependability, yielded for an instant to a boyish sincerity, and she liked it.

"Anyone I know?" she asked.

Green smiled.

"You're full of surprises," she said.

"A lot like somebody else we all know," Cassiopeia said, sipping her coffee.

Green nodded, seeming to like the change of topic. "Henrik is a fascinating man. Always a step ahead. But what about you, Stephanie? What do you mean about finishing the investigation?"

She savored the steaming brew and allowed a sip to warm her throat. "We need to pay a visit to his house."

"Why?" Cassiopeia asked. "Even if we manage to get inside, his computer is surely secured by a password."

She smiled. "Not a problem."

Green scanned her with an air of curiosity, then he could no longer conceal his astonishment. "You don't need a password, do you?"

She shook her head and said, "Time to nail that SOB."

MALONE ENTERED THE SAVOY'S BUSINESS CENTER. THE SPAcious facility was fully equipped with computers, faxes, and copiers. He told the attendant what he needed and was quickly ushered to a terminal, the charge applied to McCollum's room.

He started to sit, but Pam cut him off.

"May I?" she asked.

He decided to allow her the honor. On the walk over from the café he'd seen that she knew what he intended to do.

"Why not? Have at it."

He handed her the sheet with the beginning of the quest then faced McCollum. "You said you acquired this recently?"

"No. I didn't mention a time. Nice try, Malone."

"I need to know. It's important. In the last few months?"

Their benefactor hesitated, then nodded.

Malone had been thinking. "From what I know, the Guardians have been inviting people to the library for centuries. So the clues have to change. They'd adapt the quest to its time. I'm betting they even adapt it to the invitee. Why not? Make it personal. They go to a lot of trouble for everything else. Why not this?"

McCollum nodded. "Makes sense."

Pam was pounding the keyboard.

"The first part," Malone said. "*How strange are the manuscripts, great traveler of the unknown. They appear separately, but seem as one to those who know that the colors of the rainbow become a single white light. How to find that single ray?* That's bullshit. Just a way of saying there's a lot of information. But the next part, *It is a mystery, but visit the chapel beside the Tejo, in Bethlehem, dedicated to our patron saint.* That's where we start."

"Got it," Pam said.

He smiled. She was ahead of him, and he liked that.

"I did a search on Tejo and Bethlehem."

"Isn't that too easy?" McCollum asked.

"The Guardians can't be oblivious to the world. The Internet exists, so why wouldn't they assume an invitee would use it?"

He stared at the screen. The website Pam had found was for Portugal, a travel and tourism page that dealt with local attractions in and around Lisbon.

"Belém," Pam said. "Just outside downtown. Where the River Tejo meets the sea. *Belém* is Portuguese for 'Bethlehem.' "

He read about the point of land southwest of central Lisbon. The spot where Portuguese caravels had long ago set out for the Western world. Da Gama to India, Magellan to circumnavigate the globe, Dias to round the Cape of Good Hope. Belém eventually flourished thanks to the riches—mainly spices—that poured into the country from the New World. The Portuguese king built a summer palace there, and wealthy citizens flocked to surround it. Once a separate municipality, now it was a magnet for tourists who came to enjoy its shops, cafés, and museums.

"Henry the Navigator is connected to the locale," Pam said.

"Let's find out," he said, "about *a chapel dedicated to our patron saint.*"

A few clicks of the mouse and Pam pointed at the screen. "Way ahead of you."

A monstrous building of weathered stone filled the screen. Elaborate spires reached for a cloudy sky. The look combined Gothic and Renaissance architecture with obvious Moorish influences. Bold images dotted the stone façade.

"The Monastery of Santa Maria de Belém," he noted from the screen.

Pam scrolled down, and he read that it was one of Portugal's best-known monuments, often referred to as the Jerónimos Monastery. Many of the country's greatest figures, including its kings and queens, were entombed there.

"Why did this show up?" he asked Pam.

She clicked on a link.

"I typed in several key words and the search engine pointed straight here. In 1498, when da Gama returned from his voyage after discovering the route to India, the Portuguese king granted funds for the building of the monastery. The Order of St. Jerome took possession of the site in 1500, and the foundation stone was laid on January 6, 1501."

He knew the significance of that date from his childhood. His mother had been Catholic and they'd attended church regularly, especially after his father died. January 6. The Feast of the Epiphany.

What had Haddad written in his journal?

Great quests often begin with an epiphany.

"The main chapel at the monastery," Pam said, "was even-

tually dedicated to St. Jerome. Cotton, you remember what
Haddad said about him."

He did. An early church father who, in the fourth century,
translated many scriptural texts into Latin, including the Old
Testament.

"There's a link to more on Jerome," she said, and the
screen changed with another click of the mouse.

They all three read. Malone saw it first. "He's the patron
saint of libraries. Looks like this quest starts in Lisbon."

"Not bad, Malone."

"We earn our keep?"

"Like I said, I'm lousy with puzzles. You two seem good
at them. But the rest is tougher."

He grinned. "How about we take a stab at it together and
see where it leads?"

44

Vienna
1:00 PM

THORVALDSEN STEPPED FROM THE BATHROOM AND WATCHED
Gary unpack. Other than what he'd been wearing when he
was kidnapped a few days ago, the boy had no clothes. So
yesterday Jesper had made a trip into Copenhagen and purchased a few things.

"This house is old, isn't it?" Gary asked.

"Built many generations ago, like Christiangade."

"Lots of old stuff in Europe. Not like back home."

He grinned. "We have been around a bit longer."

"Great room."

He, too, thought the accommodations interesting. On the second floor. Near their host. A first for him. A dainty chamber with feminine furnishings that surely once belonged to a woman of taste.

"Do you like history?" he asked.

Gary shrugged. "Not until the past two summers. It's a lot more interesting here, when you see it."

He decided it was time to tell the boy their situation. "What did you think of our host and his daughter?"

"Not all that friendly. But they seem to like you."

"I've known Alfred a long time, but I'm afraid he's plotting something."

Gary sat on the bed.

"I think he may have been behind your abduction."

He watched as the boy began to realize their predicament. "You sure?"

He shook his head. "That's why we're here. To find out."

"I want to know, too. Those men upset my mother, and I don't like that."

"You afraid?"

"You wouldn't have brought me if I was in danger."

He liked the answer. This lad was smart. "You watched two men die. Few fifteen-year-olds can claim that. You okay?"

"The one Dad shot deserved what he got. He tried to take me away. Dad did what he had to. What are you going to do?"

"I'm not sure. But a lot of people will be here over the next few days. Powerful people. From them, I should be able to learn what we need to know."

"This like a club or something?"

"You could say that. People with similar interests who come together to discuss those interests."

On the bedside table his cell phone jangled. He stepped across and spied the number. Jesper. He pushed TALK.

"A call has come through. From Tel Aviv."

"Then by all means let's hear it."

A few seconds later, after the connection was established, he heard a deep baritone voice say, "Henrik, what have you started?"

"Whatever do you mean?"

"Don't play coy. When you called yesterday I was suspicious, but now I'm downright paranoid."

He'd placed a call yesterday to the Israeli prime minister's office. Since he donated millions to Jewish causes and financed a multitude of Israeli politicians, including the current prime minister, his call had not been ignored. He'd asked one simple question—what's Israel's interest in George Haddad? He'd purposely not talked directly with the prime minister, directing his inquiry through his chief of staff, who was now, he noticed, uneasy. So he asked, "Did you find an answer to my question?"

"The Mossad told us to mind our own business."

"Is that how they speak to those in charge?"

"It is when they want us to mind our own business."

"So you have no answer?"

"I didn't say that. They want George Haddad dead and they want Cotton Malone stopped. Seems Malone and his ex-wife are presently on their way to Lisbon, and that's after four people were killed last night west of London at a museum. Interestingly, the Brits know Malone was involved in those killings, but didn't move on him. They let him walk right out of the country. Our side thinks that's because the

Americans green-lighted what he did. They think America is back in our business—where it concerns George Haddad."

"How do your employees know any of that?"

"They have a direct line to Malone. They know exactly where and what he's doing. In addition, they've been anticipating this for some time."

"Seems like everyone is busy there."

"To say the least. The prime minister and I value your friendship. You're a patron of this nation. That's why you're getting this call. The Mossad is going to take Malone out. Agents are on the way to Lisbon. If you can warn him, do it."

"I wish that were so, but I have no way."

"Then may God look after him. He's going to need it."

The line clicked dead.

He pushed END.

"Problem?" Gary said.

He grabbed his composure. "Just a minor matter with one of my companies. I still have a business to run, you know."

The boy seemed to accept the explanation. "You said we were here for some kind of club, but you never told me what that has to do with me."

"Actually, that's an excellent question. Let me answer it as we walk. Come, I'll show you the estate."

ALFRED HERMANN HEARD THE DOOR TO HENRIK THORVALD-sen's room close. The listening device installed in the bedchamber had worked perfectly. Margarete sat across from him as he switched off the speaker.

"That Dane is a problem," she said.

Took her long enough to realize it. Clearly Thorvaldsen was here to probe, but he wondered about the phone call. His old friend had said little to indicate its nature, and he doubted that it had anything to do with business.

"Is he right?" Margarete said. "Did you take that boy?"

He'd allowed her to listen for a reason, so he nodded. "Part of our plan. But we also allowed him to be saved. At the moment Dominick is cultivating the seeds we planted."

"The library?"

He nodded. "We think we have the trail."

"And you plan to entrust Sabre with that information?"

"He's our emissary."

She shook her head in disgust. "Father, he's a greedy opportunist. I've told you that for years."

His patience ran out. "I didn't allow you to learn what's happening so that we could argue. I need your help."

He saw that she'd caught the tension in his voice.

"Of course. I didn't mean to overstep."

"Margarete, the world is a complicated place. You have to use the resources available. Focus. Help me deal with what is before us, and let Dominick worry about his part."

She sucked a deep breath and slowly exhaled through clenched teeth, a habit she routinely employed when nervous. "What do you want me to do?"

"Wander the grounds. Casually run into Henrik. He thinks himself safe here. Make him feel that way."

45

STEPHANIE DID NOT LIKE HER NEW APPEARANCE. HER SILVER-blond hair was now a light auburn, the result of a quick coloring by Cassiopeia. Different makeup, new clothes, and a pair of clear eyeglasses completed the alteration. Not perfect, but enough to help her hide in public.

"I haven't worn Geraldine wool trousers in a long time," she said to Cassiopeia.

"I paid a lot for them, so take care."

She grinned. "As if you can't afford it."

A crew-neck blouse and navy jacket rounded out the outfit. They were sitting in the rear of a cab, trudging through late-morning traffic.

"I hardly recognize you," Cassiopeia said.

"You saying I dress like an old woman?"

"Your wardrobe could use a little updating."

"Maybe if I survive all this, you can take me shopping."

An amused light gathered in Cassiopeia's eyes. Stephanie liked this woman. Her confidence could be infectious.

They were headed to Larry Daley's house. He lived in Cleveland Park, a beautiful residential neighborhood not far from the National Cathedral. Once the summer refuge for

Washingtonians seeking escape from the city heat, now it harbored quirky shops, trendy cafés, and a popular art deco theater.

She told the driver to stop three blocks away from the address and paid the fare. They walked the remainder of the way.

"Daley's an arrogant ass," Stephanie said. "Thinks no one's watching him. But he keeps records. Stupid as hell, if you ask me, but he does it."

"How did you get close to him?"

"He's a womanizer. I simply provided him an opportunity."

"Pillow talk?"

"The worst kind."

The house was another of the former Victorian retreats. She'd at first wondered how Daley could afford the surely astronomical mortgage, but learned that it was a rental. A sticker in a ground-floor window announced that the property was alarmed. It was the middle of the day, and Daley would be at the White House, where he stayed for at least eighteen hours. The conservative press loved to extol his work ethic, but Stephanie wasn't fooled. He just didn't want to be out of the loop, not for a moment.

"Make you a deal," she said.

Cassiopeia's face melted into a cunning grin. "You want me to break in?"

"Then I'll handle the alarm."

SABRE WAS ADJUSTING TO THE PERSONALITY OF JIMMY MC-Collum. The name itself was another matter. He hadn't used it in a long time but thought it prudent, given that Malone might well check him out. If so, he would appear in army records. There was a birth certificate, Social Security card, and little more, because he'd changed his name once he moved to Europe. *Dominick Sabre* added a note of confidence and mystique. The men who'd hired him knew little but his name, so it was important that the label convey the right allure. He'd come across it in a German cemetery, an aristocrat who died in the 1800s.

Now he was Jimmy McCollum again.

His mother named him James, after her father, whom he'd called Big Daddy—one of the few males in his life who'd shown him respect. He never knew his own father, nor did he believe that his mother actually knew which one of her lovers could be blamed. Though she'd been a good mother and treated him with kindness, she'd been a dismal woman, drifting from man to man, marrying three times, and squandering her money. He left home when he was eighteen to join the army. She'd wanted him to go to college, but academics didn't interest him. Instead, like his mother, opportunity was what drew him.

Unlike her, though, he'd managed to seize every one that had come his way.

The army. Special forces. Europe. The Chairs.

For sixteen years he'd labored for others, doing their bidding, accepting their tokens, satisfied with their meager praise.

Now it was time to labor for himself.

Risky? Certainly.

But the Circle respected power, admired cleverness, and negotiated only with strength. He wanted a membership. Perhaps even a Chair. Even more, if the lost Library of Alexandria contained what Alfred Hermann believed, he might well be able to affect the world.

That meant Power.

In his hands.

He had to find the library.

And the man sitting across the aisle on the TAP flight from London to Lisbon was going to lead the way.

Cotton Malone and his ex-wife had solved the first part of the hero's quest in only a few minutes. He was confident they could decipher the rest and, once that was done, he'd eliminate them both.

But he wasn't stupid. Malone would certainly be wary.

He'd just have to be unpredictable.

STEPHANIE WATCHED AS CASSIOPEIA TRIPPED THE LOCK ON THE back door to Larry Daley's house.

"Less than a minute," she said. "Not bad. They teach you that at Oxford?"

"Actually, I did learn to pick my first lock there. A liquor cabinet, if I recall."

She opened the door and listened.

Beeps dinged from an adjacent hall. Stephanie raced to the keypad and punched in a four-digit code, hoping the fool hadn't altered the sequence.

The beeping stopped and the indicator light changed from red to green.

"How did you know?"

"My girl watched him enter it."

Cassiopeia shook her head. "Is he an idiot?"

"It's called thinking with the wrong head. He thought she was there only to please him."

She studied the sunlit interior. A modern décor. Lots of black, silver, white, and gray. Abstract art dotted the walls. No meaning anywhere. No feeling. How fitting.

"What are we after?" Cassiopeia asked.

"This way."

She followed a short hall to an alcove that, she knew, served as an office. Her agent had reported that Daley downloaded everything onto password-secured flash drives, never keeping any data on either his laptop or White House computer. The call girl her agent had hired to seduce Daley spotted that idiosyncrasy one evening while Daley worked on the computer and she worked on him.

She told Cassiopeia what she knew. "Unfortunately, she didn't actually see his hiding place."

"Too busy?"

She smiled. "We all have our jobs. And don't knock it. Call girls are some of the most productive sources."

"And you say I'm twisted."

"We need to find his hiding place."

Cassiopeia plopped down into a wooden desk chair that accepted her meager weight with squeaks and groans. "Has to be in easy reach."

Stephanie inventoried the alcove. The desk supported a blotter, a pen-and-pencil holder, and pictures of Daley with the president and vice president, along with a reading lamp. A narrow set of floor-to-ceiling shelves consumed two of the walls. The whole alcove was about six feet square. The floor, like the rest of the house, was hardwood.

Not many hiding places.

The books on the shelves drew her attention. Daley seemed to love political treatises. There weren't many—a hundred or so. Paperbacks and hardcovers mixed, many of the bindings veined with cracks, indicating that the pages had been read. She shook her head. "A connoisseur of modern politics, and he reads all sides."

"Why do you have such an attitude toward him?"

"Just always felt like I need to take a shower after being around him. Not to mention he tried to fire me from day one." She paused. "And finally succeeded."

A key scraped in the front-door lock.

Stephanie's head whirled. She stared back down the hall toward the front of the house.

The door opened and she heard Larry Daley's voice. Then she heard another person. Female.

Heather Dixon.

She motioned and they darted down the hall into one of the bedrooms.

"Let me get the alarm," Daley said.

A few seconds of silence.

"That's strange," Daley said.

"Problem?"

Stephanie immediately knew. She'd neglected to reset the system after they'd entered.

"I'm sure I set that alarm before I left," Daley said.

A few moments of silence, then she heard the *click* of a bullet being chambered.

"Let's take a look around," Dixon said.

46

LISBON
3:30 PM

MALONE STARED AT THE MONASTERY OF SANTA MARIA DE Belém. He, Pam, and Jimmy McCollum had flown from

London to Lisbon, then taken a cab from the airport to the waterfront.

Lisbon sat perched on a broad switchback of hills that overlooked the sealike Tejo estuary, a place of wide symmetrical boulevards and handsome tree-filled squares. One of the world's grandest suspension bridges spanned the mighty river and led to a towering statue of Christ, arms outstretched, which embraced the city from the eastern shore. Malone had visited many times and was always reminded of San Francisco, both in physical makeup and in the city's propensity for earthquakes. Several had left their mark.

All countries possessed splendid things. Egypt, the pyramids. Italy, St. Peter's. England, Westminster. France, Versailles. Listening to the cabdriver on the ride from the airport, he knew that, for Portugal, national pride came from the abbey that sprawled out before him. Its white limestone façade stretched longer than a football field, aged like old ivory, and combined Moorish, Byzantine, and French Gothic in an exuberance of decorations that seemed to breathe life into the towering walls.

People crowded everywhere. A camera-toting parade streamed in and out from the entrances. Across a busy boulevard and train tracks that fronted the impressive south façade, tourist buses waited in an angled line, like ships moored in a harbor. A sign informed visitors of how the abbey was first erected in 1500 to satisfy a promise made by King Manuel I to the Virgin Mary and was built on the site of an old mariners' hospice first constructed by Prince Henry the Navigator. Columbus, da Gama, and Magellan had all prayed here before their journeys. Through the centuries the massive structure had served as a religious house, a retirement home, and an orphanage. Now it was a World Heritage Site, restored to much of its former glory.

"The church and abbey are dedicated to St. Jerome," he

heard one of the tour guides say to a crowd in Italian. "Symbolic in that both Jerome and this monastery represented new points of departure for Christianity. Ships left here to discover the New World and bring them Christ. Jerome translated the ancient Bible into Latin, so more could discover its wonder." He could tell that McCollum understood the woman, too.

"Italian one of your languages?" he asked.

"I know enough."

"A man of many talents."

"Whatever's necessary."

He caught the surly attitude. "So what's next in this quest?"

McCollum produced another slip of paper upon which was written some of the first excerpt and more of the cryptic phrases.

It is a mystery, but visit the chapel beside the Tejo, in Bethlehem, dedicated to our patron saint. Begin the journey in the shadows and complete it in the light, where a retreating star finds a rose, pierces a wooden cross, and converts silver to gold. Find the place that forms an address with no place, where is found another place. Then, like the shepherds of the painter Poussin, puzzled by the enigma, you will be flooded with the light of inspiration.

He handed the sheet to Pam and said, "Okay. Let's take a visit and see what's there."

They followed a thick swarm of tourists to the entrance. A sign indicated that admission to the church was free, but a ticket was required for the rest of the buildings.

Inside the church, in what was identified as the lower choir, the groined ceiling loomed low and produced an imposing gloom. To his left stood the cenotaph of Vasco da

Gama. Simple and solemn, it abounded with nautical symbols. Another tomb, of the poet Luis de Camões, rested to his right along with a baptismal font. Bare walls in both niches added to both the austerity and the grandeur. People crowded the alcoves. Cameras flashed. Tour guides droned on about the significance of the dead.

Malone strolled into the nave and the initial dimness of the lower choir gave way to a bright wonder. Six slender columns, each a profusion of ornamentation twined with carved flowers, stretched skyward. The late-afternoon sun poured through a series of stained-glass windows. Rays and shadows chased one another across the limestone walls, gray with age. The vaulted roof resembled a sheaf of ribs, the columns like canopy supports, the mesh holding in place like a ship's rigging. Malone felt the presence of Saracens who once ruled Lisbon, and noticed Byzantine fancies. A thousand details multiplied around him without repetition.

Remarkable.

Even more remarkable, he thought, given that ancient masons possessed the nerve to build something so massive upon Lisbon's quivering ground.

Wooden pews that once accommodated monks now held only the inquisitive. A low murmur of voices echoed across the nave, periodically overshadowed by a calm voice through a public address system that requested silence in a variety of languages. Malone located the source of the admonition. A priest before a microphone, at the people's altar, in the center of the cross-shaped interior. Nobody seemed to pay the warning any heed—especially not the tour guides, who continued on with their paid discourses.

"This place is magnificent," Pam said.

He agreed. "The sign out front said it closes at five. We need tickets to the rest."

"I'll go get them," McCollum said. "But doesn't the clue lead us only here, to the church?"

"I have no idea. To be sure, let's have a look at whatever else there is."

McCollum made his way back through the clot of people to the portico.

"What do you think?" Pam asked, still holding the sheet of paper.

"About him or the quest?"

"Both are a problem."

He smiled. She was right. But as for the quest, "Some of it now makes sense. *Begin the journey in the shadows and complete it in the light.* The entrance does that nicely. Like a basement back there, then it opens into a bright attic."

The priest again quietly admonished the crowd to stay silent and everyone again ignored him.

"He has a tough job," Pam said.

"Like the kid taking names when the teacher leaves the room."

"Okay, Mr. Genius," she said. "What about *where a retreating star finds a rose, pierces a wooden cross, and converts silver to gold. Find the place that forms an address with no place, where is found another place.*"

He was already thinking about that and his attention was drawn forward, to the chancel, where a rectangular floor plan led to a concave wall backdropping the high altar, all topped with a combination of hemispherical dome, barrel vault, and stone-coffered ceiling. Ionic and Corinthian pillars rose symmetrically on three sides of the chancel, framing vaulted stone chambers that displayed elaborate royal tombs. Five paintings wrapped the concave wall, everything drawing the eye to the majestic baroque sacrarium that stood in the center, elevated, above the high altar.

He wove his way around loitering tourists to the far side of the people's altar. Velvet ropes blocked any entrance to the chancel. A placard informed him that the sacrarium, made entirely of silver, had been crafted by goldsmith João de Sousa between 1674 and 1678. Even from fifty feet away the ornate repository, full of detail, appeared magnificent.

He turned and stared back through the nave, past the pillars and pews, to the lower choir, where they'd entered.

Then he saw it. In the upper choir, past a thick stone balustrade, fifty feet above the church floor. High in the farthest exterior wall, a huge eye glared down at him. The circular window stretched ten feet or more in diameter. Mullions and traceries radiated from its center. Roof ribs wound a twisting path back toward it and seemed to dissolve into its shadowless radiance, bright as a stage lamp and suffusing the church's interior.

A common adornment to many medieval churches. Named after its fanciful shape.

Rose window.

Facing due west. Late in the day. Blazing like the sun.

But there was more.

At the center of the upper choir's balustrade stood a large cross. He stepped forward and noticed that the cross fit perfectly into the round of the window, the brilliant rays flooding past it into the nave.

Where a retreating star finds a rose, pierces a wooden cross, and converts silver to gold.

Seems they'd found the place.

47

VIENNA
4:30 PM

THORVALDSEN ADMIRED ALFRED HERMANN'S SPECTACLE OF
flowers, water, and marble, the enormous garden an obvious
labor of several generations. Shady walks wound out from
the château to grassy glades, the brick paths lined with statues, bas-reliefs, and fountains. Every so often French influences yielded to a clear taste for Italy.

"Who are the people who own this place?" Gary asked.

"The Hermanns are a family of long standing in Austria,
just as my family is in Denmark. Quite wealthy and powerful."

"Is he your friend?"

An interesting question, considering his suspicions. "Up
until a few days ago, I believed that to be the case. But now
I'm not so sure."

He was pleased with the boy's inquisitiveness. He knew
about Gary's parentage. When he'd returned from taking
Gary back home after their summer visit, Malone had told
him what Pam had revealed. Thorvaldsen had feigned ignorance when he'd first seen her a few nights ago, though he'd
instantly known her identity. Her presence in his house, with
Malone, signaled trouble, which was why he'd stationed Jes-

per outside the study door. Pam Malone was high-strung. Luckily she'd calmed down. She should have been back in Georgia by now. Instead, the caller from Tel Aviv had said, *Seems Malone and his ex-wife are presently on their way to Lisbon.*

What was happening? Why go there? And where was the Talons of the Eagle?

"We've come here," he said to Gary, "to help your father."

"Dad never said anything about us leaving. He told me to stay put and be careful."

"But he also said for you to do as I say."

"So when he yells at me, I expect you to take the blame."

He grinned. "With pleasure."

"You ever seen a person shot?"

He knew Tuesday's memory had to be troubling, no matter how brave the lad wanted to be. "Several times."

"Dad shot the man dead. But you know what? I didn't care."

He shook his head at the bravado. "Careful, Gary. Don't ever become accustomed to killing. No matter how much someone may deserve it."

"I didn't mean it that way. It's only, he was a bad man. He threatened to kill Mom."

They passed a marble column surmounted by a statue of Diana. A breeze caressed the trees and trembled shadows cast out on the undulating turf. "Your father did what he had to do. He didn't like it. He just did it."

"And I would have, too."

Genetics be damned. Gary was Malone's son. And though the boy was but fifteen, his indignation could certainly be aroused—just like his father's—especially if a loved one was threatened. Gary knew his parents had traveled to London, but he didn't know his mother was still involved. He deserved the truth.

"Your mother and father are on their way to Lisbon."

"That's what the call in the room was about?"

He nodded and smiled at the decisive manner in which the boy handled news.

"Why is Mom still with him? She didn't say a word about staying when she called last night. They don't get along."

"I have no idea. We'll have to wait until one of them calls again." But he desperately wanted to know the answer to that question, too.

Ahead, he spotted their destination. A circular pavilion of colored marble topped by gilded iron. Its open balustrade overlooked a crystalline lake, the silvery surface quiet in the shade.

They entered and he approached a railing.

Massive vases packed with aromatic flowers dotted the interior. As always, Hermann had made sure the estate was a showpiece.

"Somebody's coming," Gary said.

He did not look back. He didn't have to. He saw her in his mind. Short, dumpy, exhaling loudly as she walked. He kept his gaze toward the lake and enjoyed the sweet smell of grass, flowers, and experience.

"Is she coming fast?"

"How did you know it's a woman?"

"You'll learn, Gary, that you cannot win a fight if your enemy is not, in some ways, predictable."

"It's Mr. Hermann's daughter."

He continued to admire the lake, watching a family of ducks paddle toward shore. "Say nothing to her about anything. Listen, but speak little. That's how you discover what you need to know."

He heard soles slapping the pavilion's stone flooring and turned as Margarete marched close.

"They told me in the house that you'd come here," she

said. "And I remembered this was one of your favorite places."

He smiled at her evident satisfaction. "It has privacy. So far from the château. The trees provide tranquility. I do like this spot. A favorite of your mother's, if I recall."

"Father built it specially for her. She spent her last day alive here."

"You miss her?"

"She died when I was young. So we were never close. But Father misses her."

"You don't miss your mother?" Gary asked.

Though the boy had violated what he'd been cautioned, Thorvaldsen didn't mind the inquiry. He was actually curious, too.

"Of course I miss her. It's simply that we were not close— as mother and daughter."

"You seem to have acquired an interest in the family businesses and the Order."

He watched as thoughts dialed into her mind. She'd inherited more of her father's rugged Austrian looks than her mother's Prussian beauty. Not a particularly attractive woman—dark-haired, brown eyes, with a thin, high nose. But who was he to judge, considering his crooked spine, bushy hair, and weathered skin? He wondered about suitors, but decided this woman would never give herself to anyone. She was a taker.

"I'm the only Hermann left." And she added a smile that was surely intended to be comforting, but instead flashed with annoyance.

"Does that mean you will inherit all this?"

"Of course. Why wouldn't I?"

He shrugged. "I have no idea what your father thinks. I have found, though, that there are no guarantees in this world."

He saw that she did not like his implications. He gave her no time to react and asked, "Why did your father try to harm this boy?"

His sudden inquiry inspired a baffled look. She clearly wasn't a master of the stoic, either—not like her father.

"I have no idea what you're talking about."

He wondered. Maybe Hermann had kept his plans from her.

"Then you have no idea what *die Klauen der Adler* is doing?"

"He's not my responsib—" She caught herself.

"Not to worry, my dear. I know of him. I only wondered if you did."

"That man is a problem."

Now he knew she was not a part of anything. Too much information flowed far too freely. "I wholeheartedly agree. But as you say, neither of us has any responsibility for him. Only the Circle."

"I was unaware the members knew of him."

"There are many things I'm aware of. In particular, what your father is doing. That, too, is a problem. "

She seemed to catch the conviction in his tone. Her chubby face flashed a nervous smile. "Remember where you are, Henrik. This is Hermann land. We command what happens here. So you shouldn't concern yourself."

"That's an interesting observation. One I'll try not to forget."

"I think, perhaps, you and Father need to finish this conversation."

She turned to leave, and as she did he raised an arm in a quick gesture.

From thick cypresses, heavy with age, three men materialized, dressed in camouflage fatigues. They trotted forward and arrived just as Margarete stepped from the pavilion.

Two of the men grabbed her.

One clamped a hand over her mouth.

She resisted.

"Henrik," Gary said. "What's Jesper doing here?"

The third man was his chamberlain, who'd flown in earlier and infiltrated the estate. From other visits, Thorvaldsen knew—contrary to Margarete's boast—that the heaviest security was confined to the house. The remaining hundreds of acres were neither fenced nor patrolled.

"Stand still," he said to her.

She stopped struggling.

"You're going with these gentlemen."

Her head shook violently.

He'd expected her to be difficult. So he nodded and the hand over her mouth was replaced with a cloth, one he knew contained enough anesthetic to induce a deep sleep. Only a few seconds were required for the vapors to work. Her body went limp.

"What are you doing?" Gary asked. "Why are you hurting her?"

"I'm not. But I assure you, they would have hurt you if your father had not acted." He faced Jesper. "Keep her safe, as we discussed."

His employee nodded. One of the men draped Margarete's stout body over his shoulder, and all three retreated into the trees.

"You knew she'd come out here?" Gary asked.

"As I said, it's good to know your enemy."

"Why are you taking her?"

He liked lessons and missed teaching Cai. "You don't drive a car without insurance. What we're about to do has risks, as well. She's our insurance."

48

WASHINGTON, DC

STEPHANIE FROZE. HEATHER DIXON WAS ARMED AND ON guard. Cassiopeia's eyes raked the bedroom, and she knew that her cohort was looking for anything that could be used as a weapon.

"What is it?" she heard Daley ask Dixon.

"Your alarm is off. That means somebody's here."

"Big leap in logic, wouldn't you say?"

"Did you arm the panel before you left?"

A moment of silence passed. Stephanie knew they were trapped.

"I don't know," Daley said. "I may have forgotten. Wouldn't be the first time."

"Why don't I take a look just to be sure?"

"Because I don't have time for you to play soldier, and that gun in your hand is getting me hot. You're some kind of sexy."

"A flatterer today. That'll get you everything."

More silence, then a protest with a half-smothered moan.

"Easy on my head. That knot hurts."

"You okay?" Daley asked.

A zipper released.

"Toss that gun down," Daley said.

Footsteps thumped up the stairway.

She stared at Cassiopeia and whispered, "I don't believe this."

"At least we know where both of them are."

Good point, but little comfort. "I've got to check this out."

Cassiopeia clamped a hand onto her arm. "Leave them be."

Contrary to the past twelve hours where she'd made, at best, questionable decisions, she was thinking clearly now. She knew what needed to be done.

She crept from the bedroom and entered the den. A stairway just beyond led up, the front door to her right. She heard murmured voices, laughter, and the sound of the floorboards being challenged.

"What the hell's going on?" Stephanie wondered out loud.

"Didn't your investigation find this?"

She shook her head. "Not a word. Must be recent."

Cassiopeia disappeared back down the hall. She lingered a moment and spotted the same revolver Heather Dixon had drawn on her yesterday, lying in one of the chairs.

She grabbed the gun and left the den.

MALONE STARED AT THE ROSE WINDOW AND CHECKED HIS watch: 4:40 PM. This late in the year, the sun would start to set sometime in the next ninety minutes.

"This building is oriented on an east–west axis," he said to Pam. "That window is there to catch the evening sun. We need to go up there."

He spotted a doorway where an arrow indicated the upper choir. He walked over and found, nestled against the church's north wall, a wide stone stairway with a barrel-vaulted ceiling that made it look more like a tunnel.

He followed a crowd up.

At the top they entered the choir.

Two rows of high-backed wooden benches faced each other, ornamented with festoons and arabesques. Above them hung baroque paintings of various apostles. The aisle between the benches led to the church's west wall and the rose window thirty feet above.

He stared up.

Dust motes floated in the sheets of bright sunlight. He turned and studied the cross rising at the far end of the upper choir. He and Pam approached the balustrade and he admired the dramatic realism of the carved image of Christ. A placard at its base informed in two languages

CRISTO NA CRUZ

CHRIST ON THE CROSS

C. 1550

ESCULTURA EM MADEIRA POLICROMA

POLYCHROMED WOODEN SCULPTURE

"Where a retreating star finds a rose, pierces a wooden cross," Pam said. "This is it."

He agreed. But he was thinking about the next words.

And converts silver to gold.

He glanced back at the blazing rose window and followed the dusty rays as they passed the cross and entered the nave. Below, the light cleaved a trench on the checkerboard floor down a center aisle that bisected the pews. People milled about and didn't seem to notice. The light continued east to the people's altar and threw a faint glowing line onto its red carpet.

McCollum appeared from the lower choir and walked down the center aisle toward the front of the church.

"He's going to be wondering where we are," Pam said.

"He's not going anywhere. He seems to need us."

McCollum stopped between the last of the six columns and looked around, then turned and spotted them. Malone held up his palm and motioned for him to wait there, then displayed his index finger, signaling they'd be down in a minute.

He'd told McCollum the truth. He was pretty good with puzzles. This one had, at first, proved confusing, but now, staring down into a mass of carvings, ribs, and arches, a harmony of lines and interweaving stones that time, nature, and neglect had barely altered, he knew the solution.

His gaze followed the rays of the setting sun as they crossed into the chancel, bisected the high altar, and found the silver sacrarium.

Which glinted gold.

He hadn't noticed the phenomenon when they'd been down close. Or perhaps the retreating sun had not as yet properly angled itself. But the transformation was now clear.

Silver to gold.

He saw that Pam noticed, too.

"That's amazing," she said. "How the light does that."

The rose window was clearly positioned so the setting sun would, at least for a few minutes, find the sacrarium. Apparently the silver receptacle had been placed with great deliberation, one of the six paintings surrounding it removed, the symmetry that medieval builders cherished disturbed.

He thought of the final part of the quest.

Find the place that forms an address with no place, where is found another place.

And he headed for the stairs.

At ground level he approached the velvet ropes that still blocked access into the chancel. He noticed the interplay of black, white, and red marble, which lent an atmosphere of nobility—only fitting, because the chancel served as a royal family mausoleum.

The sacrarium stood thirty feet away.

Close inspection of it was not a part of the visitors' experience. The priest at the people's altar announced over the public address system that the church and monastery would close in five minutes. Many of the tours were already departing, and more people started for the exit.

He'd noticed earlier that there was some sort of image etched on the sacrarium's door, behind which would have once been stored the blessed sacrament. Perhaps it still held the Host. Though a World Heritage Site, more tourist attraction than church, the nave was surely used for special observances. Similar to St. Paul's and Westminster. Which would explain why people were kept at a distance from what was clearly the building's centerpiece.

McCollum came close. "I have tickets."

He pointed to the sacrarium. "I need a closer look at that, without all these witnesses."

"Could be tough. I assume everyone is going to be hustled out of here in the next few minutes."

"You don't strike me as a man who bows to authority."

"Neither do you."

He thought about Avignon and what he and Stephanie had done there on a rainy June night.

"Then let's find a place to hide till everyone leaves."

STEPHANIE TIPTOED BACK INTO THE ALCOVE. SHE NEEDED TO find Daley's hiding place before things climaxed upstairs. She hoped neither Dixon nor Daley was in a rush, though Daley had sounded hurried.

Cassiopeia was already quietly searching.

"The report said he never left this desk with the flash drives. He used them on his laptop, but didn't leave with them. He'd always tell her to head on to the bedroom and he'd be right along." Her words were more breath than voice.

"We're really pushing it staying here."

She stopped and listened. "Sounds like they're still busy."

Cassiopeia eased open the desk drawers, testing for hiding places. But Stephanie doubted that she'd find anything. Too obvious. Her gaze again scanned the bookshelves and her eyes stopped at one of the political treatises, a thin, taupe-colored volume with blue lettering.

Hardball by Chris Matthews.

She recalled the story Daley had shared with Green when he'd boasted about his newfound authority with the Magellan Billet.

What was it he'd said?

Power is what you hold.

She reached for the book, opened it, and discovered that the last third of the pages had been glued together; a cavity about a quarter inch deep had been hollowed out. Nestled inside were five flash drives, each labeled with a Roman numeral.

"How did you know?" Cassiopeia whispered.

"I'm actually frightened that I did. I'm beginning to think like the idiot."

Cassiopeia started for the rear of the house, toward the back door, but Stephanie grabbed her arm and motioned for the front. Confusion stared back at her—an expression that questioned, *Why ask for trouble?*

They stepped into the den, then the foyer.

An alarm keypad adjacent to the front door indicated that the system was still idle. She held Dixon's gun.

"Larry," she called out.

Silence.

"Larry. Could I have a moment?"

Footsteps thumped across the upper floor and Daley appeared in the bedroom doorway, pants on, bare-chested.

"Love the hair, Stephanie. New look? And the clothes. Catchy."

"Just for you."

"What are you doing here?"

She flashed the book. "Came for your stash."

Alarm flooded Daley's boyish face.

"That's right. Time for you to sweat. And Heather?" Her voice rose. "I'm disappointed in your choice of lovers."

Dixon paraded naked from the bedroom, sporting not even a hint of shame. "You're dead."

Stephanie shrugged. "That remains to be seen. At the moment I have *your* gun." She displayed the weapon.

"What are you going to do?" Daley asked.

"Haven't decided yet." But she wanted to know, "You two been at this long?"

"It's not your concern," Dixon said.

"Just curious. I interrupted only to let you know that now there's more to this game than just *my* hide."

"You apparently know quite a bit," Daley said. "Who's your friend?"

"Cassiopeia Vitt," Dixon answered.

"I'm flattered you know me."

"I owe you for the dart in the neck."

"No need to thank me."

"Back to bed for you two," Stephanie said.

"I don't think so." Dixon started down the stairs, but Stephanie aimed the automatic. "Don't push me, Heather. I'm recently unemployed and have a warrant out for my arrest."

The Israeli stopped, perhaps sensing that this was not the time to challenge.

"The bedroom," Stephanie said.

Dixon hesitated.

"Now."

Dixon retreated to the top of the stairs. Stephanie gathered up the Israeli's clothes, including her shoes. "You wouldn't dare risk public exposure," she said to Daley, "coming after us. But she might. This will at least slow her down."

And they left.

VIENNA
6:40 PM

THORVALDSEN DONNED THE CRIMSON VESTMENT. ALL MEMbers were required to wear their robe during Assembly. The first session would begin at seven, and he wasn't looking forward to it. Too much talk, usually, and little action. He'd never needed a cooperative to accomplish his goals. But he enjoyed the fellowship that came after the gatherings.

Gary was sitting in one of the upholstered chairs.

"How do I look?" he asked in a jovial tone.

"Like a king."

The regal robes were ankle-length, made of velvet and richly embroidered in gold thread with the Order's motto, *JE L'AY EMPRINS.* I have dared. The ensemble dated from the fifteenth century and the original Order of the Golden Fleece.

He reached for the neck chain. Solid gold with a black enameled flint forming fire steels. An ornate golden fleece hung from its center.

"This is presented to each member when inducted. Our symbol."

"Looks expensive."

"It is."

"This really important to you?"

He shrugged. "It's something I enjoy. But it's not like a religion."

"Dad told me you're Jewish."

He nodded.

"I don't know much about Jews. Only that millions were killed in World War II. It's not something I really understand."

"You're not alone. Gentiles have wrestled with our existence for centuries."

"Why do people hate Jews?"

He'd many times pondered that question—along with the philosophers, theologians, and politicians who'd debated it for centuries. "It started for us with Abraham. Ninety-nine years old when God visited him and made a covenant, creating a Chosen People, the ones to inherit the land of Canaan. But unfortunately, that honor came with responsibility."

He could see the boy was interested.

"Have you ever read the Bible?"

Gary shook his head.

"You should. A great book. On the one hand, God granted to the Israelites a blessing. To become the Chosen People. But it was their response to that blessing that ultimately determined their fate."

"What happened?"

"The Old Testament says they rebelled, burned incense, credited idols for their good fortune, walked according to the dictates of their own hearts. So God scattered them among the Gentiles as punishment."

"That why people hate them?"

He finished fastening his mantle. "Hard to say. But Jews have faced persecution ever since that time."

"God sounds like He has a temper."

"The God of the Old Testament is far different from the one in the New."

"I'm not sure I like that one."

"You're not alone." He paused. "Jews were the first to insist that man is responsible for his own acts. Not the gods' fault life went bad. *Your* fault. And that made us different. Christians took it further. Man brought his exile from Eden on himself, but because God loved man He redeemed us with the blood of His son. The Jewish God is angry. Justice is His aim. The Christian God is one of mercy. Huge difference."

"God should be kind, shouldn't He?"

He smiled, then looked around the elegant room. Time to bring things to a head. "Tell me what you think about what happened in the pavilion?"

"I'm not sure Mr. Hermann will appreciate you taking his daughter."

"Just as your parents didn't appreciate what happened to you. The difference is, she's a grown woman and you're a teenager."

"Why is all this happening?"

"I imagine we'll know that soon."

The bedchamber door suddenly swung open and Alfred Hermann stormed inside. He, too, sported a regal robe with a gold medallion, his mantle adorned with a blue silk.

"You have my daughter?" Hermann said, face full of fury.

Thorvaldsen stood rigid. "I do."

"And you obviously know this room is wired for sound."

"That didn't require much intelligence."

He could see the tension building. Hermann was in un-charted territory.

"Henrik, I will not tolerate this."

"What do you plan to do? Recall the Talons of the Eagle to deal with me?"

Hermann hesitated. "That's what you want, isn't it?"

Thorvaldsen stepped close. "You crossed the line when you kidnapped this young man." He pointed at Gary.

"Where is Margarete?"

"Safe."

"You don't have the stomach to hurt her."

"I have the stomach to do whatever is needed. You should know that about me."

Hermann's intense gaze gripped him like a hook. He'd al-ways thought the Austrian's bony face more fitting for a farmer than an aristocrat. "I thought we were friends."

"I did, too. But apparently that meant nothing when you took this young man from his mother and destroyed his fa-ther's bookshop."

The Assembly's first session was about to begin, which was why he'd timed his revelation with care. Hermann, as Blue Chair, must at all times exhibit discipline and confi-dence. Never could he allow the members to know of his personal predicaments.

Nor could he be late.

"We must go," Hermann finally said. "This is not over, Henrik."

"I agree. For you, it's only beginning."

50

"WOULDN'T YOU SAY YOU PUSHED DALEY TO THE MAX?"
Green asked Stephanie.

She and Cassiopeia were riding in Green's limousine, the
rear compartment soundproofed from the front seat by a
sheet of Plexiglas. Green had picked them up downtown
after they'd left Daley's house.

"He wouldn't have come after us. Heather might have
been able to wear his clothes, but not his shoes. I doubt she'd
be chasing us barefoot and unarmed."

Green did not seemed convinced. "I assume there's a purpose for letting Daley know you were there?"

"I'd be interested to hear that one, too," Cassiopeia added.
"We could have been out without him ever knowing."

"And I'd still be in the crosshairs. This way he has to be
careful. I have something he wants. And if nothing else,
Daley's a dealer."

Green pointed at the copy of *Hardball*. "What's so vital?"

Stephanie reached for the laptop she'd told Green to bring.
She slid one of the flash drives into an empty port and typed
AUNT B'S into the space for a password.

"Your girl learn that, too?" Cassiopeia asked.

She nodded. "An eatery out in Maryland. Daley goes there a lot on weekends. Country-style food. One of his favorites. Struck me as odd—I considered Daley a five-star-restaurant connoisseur."

The screen displayed a list of files, each labeled with one-word identifiers.

"Congress," she said.

She clicked on one.

"I learned that Daley is a master of dates and times. When he squeezes a member for a vote, he has precise information about every cash contribution ever sent that member's way. It's odd, because he never funnels money directly. Instead lobbyists who like the idea that they're currying favor with the White House do the dirty work. That led me to think he keeps records. Nobody's memory is that good." She pointed at the screen. "Here's an example." She counted. "Fourteen payments to this guy totaling a hundred eighty-seven thousand dollars over a six-year period. Here's the date, place, and time of each payment." She shook her head. "Nothing frightens a politician more than details."

"We're talking bribes?" Green asked.

She nodded. "Cash payments. Pocket money. Not enough to draw attention, but enough to keep the lines of communication open. Simple and sweet, but it's the kind of political capital Daley accumulates. The kind this White House uses. They've managed to pass some pretty sweet legislation."

Green stared at the screen. "Must be a hundred or more House members."

"He's effective. I'll give him that. The money is spread around. Both sides of the aisle."

She clicked another file, which displayed a list of senators. Thirty or so. "He also has a cadre of federal judges. They get into financial trouble, just like everybody else, and he has people right there to help out. I found one in Michigan who talked. He was on the verge of bankruptcy until one of his friends appeared with money. His conscience finally got to him, especially after Daley wanted him to rule a particular way. Seems a lawyer in a case before him was a big party contributor and needed a little guarantee on victory."

"Federal courts are a hotbed of corruption," Green muttered. "I've said that for years. Give somebody a lifetime appointment and you're asking for trouble. Too much power, too little oversight."

She grabbed another of the flash drives. "One of these is enough to indict several of those turkey buzzards."

"Such an eloquent description."

"It's the black robes. They look just like buzzards, perched on a limb, waiting to pick a carcass clean."

"Such little respect for our judiciary," he said with a grin.

"Respect is earned."

"Might I interject something," Cassiopeia said. "Why don't we just go public? Draw attention. Not the way I usually handle things, but it seems like it would work here."

Green shook his head. "As you noted earlier, I don't know much about the Israelis. And you don't understand the PR machine of this administration. It's a master of spin. They'd cloud the issue to the point of obscurity, and we'd lose Daley and the traitor."

"He's right," Stephanie said. "That won't work. We have to do this ourselves."

Traffic stopped the car and Green's cell phone rang a soft chime. He reached into his suit pocket and removed the unit, studying the LCD. "This should prove interesting." He pressed two buttons and talked into the speakerphone. "I've been waiting for your call."

"Bet you have," Daley said.

"Seems I might not make it to that box in Vermont after all."

"That's the thing about chess, Brent. Every move is an adventure. Okay, I'll give you credit, yours was a good one."

"You have to give Stephanie credit for that."

"I'm sure she's there, so well done, Stephanie."

"Anytime, Larry."

"This changes little," Daley made clear. "Those elements I mentioned are still agitated."

"You need to calm them down," Stephanie said.

"Do you want to talk?" Daley asked.

Stephanie started to speak, but Green held up his hand. "And the benefit of that?"

"Could be great. There's a lot at stake."

She couldn't resist. "More than your ass?"

"Much more."

"You lied when you said you knew nothing about the Alexandria Link, didn't you?" Green asked.

"*Lie* is such a harsh word. More that I concealed facts in the interest of national security. That the price I'm going to have to pay?"

"I think it's reasonable, considering."

Stephanie knew Daley would realize they could disseminate his secrets at will. Both she and Green possessed contacts in the media, ones that would love to dirty this administration.

"All right." Resignation filled Daley's tone. "How do you want to do this?"

Stephanie knew the answer. "Public. Lots of people."

"That's not a good idea."

"It's the only way we're going to do it."

The speaker was quiet for a moment before Daley said, "Tell me where and when."

51

MALONE AWOKE, SITTING PROPPED AGAINST A ROUGH STONE
wall.

"It's after seven thirty," Pam whispered in his ear.

"How long was I out?"

"An hour."

He could not see her face. Total darkness engulfed them.
He recalled their situation. "Everything okay up there?" he
said quietly to McCollum.

"Nice and quiet."

They'd left the church just before five and hustled to the
upper choir, where another doorway led out into the cloister.
Visitors had been slow in leaving, taking advantage of the late-
afternoon sun for a few last photos of the opulent Moorish-
style decorations. The upper gallery had offered no safe
refuges, but running along the church's north wall at ground
level they'd found eleven wooden doors. A placard explained
that the compact spaces had once served as confessionals.

Though the doors to ten confessionals had been locked,
McCollum had managed to open one thanks to a hole drilled
beneath the locking bolt. Apparently the lock was faulty, and
the hole was how the staff gained entrance. McCollum had

used an impressive knife from his pocket to slide the bolt, re-locking it after they'd entered. Malone had not known the man was armed. No way he'd carried the knife on the airplane, but McCollum had checked a small bag at the London airport, now stored in a locker at the Lisbon airport. Malone, too, had stored the satchel from Haddad's apartment in a Lisbon locker. McCollum's not mentioning the knife only raised Malone's level of suspicion.

Inside the confessional, a screened iron grate opened into another dark cubbyhole. A door in the second chamber led into the church, allowing the penitent to enter. The screen separated the two so that penance could be administered.

Malone had grown up Catholic and recalled a similar arrangement, though simpler in construction, at his church. He'd never understood why he couldn't see the priest who was absolving him of sin. When he'd asked, the nuns who'd taught him had simply said separation was required. He came to learn that the Catholic Church was big on what to do, but didn't particularly like to explain why. Which partly explained why he no longer practiced the religion.

He glanced at the luminous dial of Pam's TAG watch. Nearly eight PM. Early, but the site had now been closed three hours.

"Any movement outside?" he asked McCollum softly.

"Not a sound."

"Let's do it," he whispered through the dark. "No use sitting here any longer."

He heard McCollum's knife again snap into place, then the scraping of metal on metal.

The confessional's door creaked open.

He came to his feet but had to crouch against the low ceiling.

McCollum swung the door inward. They stepped out into the lower gallery, the cool night air welcome after three hours in what amounted to a closet. Across the open cloister, in the upper and lower galleries, incandescent fixtures burned softly, the elaborate tracery between the arches more shadow than detail. Malone stepped into the nearest arch and stared up at the night sky. The gloom of the shadowy cloister seemed accented by a starless night.

He headed straight for the stairway that led to the upper choir. He hoped the door that opened into the church—the one he'd earlier used to find the choir from the nave— remained unlocked.

He was glad to discover that it stood open.

The nave was cemetery-quiet.

Light from the exterior floods that bathed the outer façade backlit the stained-glass windows. A handful of weak bulbs broke the thick darkness only in the lower choir.

"This place is different at night," Pam said.

He agreed, and his guard was up.

He headed straight for the chancel and hopped over the velvet ropes. At the high altar, he climbed five risers and stood before the sacrarium.

He turned and focused back toward the upper choir at the far end.

The pale gray iris of the rose window stared back at him, no longer alive with the sun.

McCollum seemed to have anticipated what he'd need and appeared beside him holding a candle and matches. "Offering rack, back near the baptismal font. I saw it earlier."

He grabbed the candle and McCollum lit the wick. He brought the dim glow close to the sacrarium and studied the image molded into the door.

Mary sat with the infant in her lap, Joseph behind her, all three crowned by halos. Three bearded men, one kneeling before the child, paid homage. Three other men—one strangely wearing what appeared to be a military helmet—

gazed on. Above the scene, with clouds parted, a five-pointed star shone down.

"It's the Nativity," Pam said from behind him.

He agreed. "Sure looks like it. The three Magi following the star, coming to praise the newborn king."

He recalled the quest and what they should be looking for here, where silver turned to gold. *Find the place that forms an address with no place, where is found another place.*

A challenging riddle.

"We need to get out of here, but we also need a picture of this. Since none of us has a camera, any ideas?"

"After I bought the tickets," McCollum said, "I walked upstairs. There's a gift shop. Full of books and postcards. Bound to be a picture there."

"Good thought," he said. "Lead the way."

SABRE CLIMBED THE STAIRS TO THE UPPER GALLERY, PLEASED that he'd made the right choice. When Alfred Hermann had tasked him with finding the library, his ultimate plan had quickly formed in his mind, and the Israeli surveillance team's elimination in Germany had cemented his course.

Hermann would never have sanctioned deliberately provoking the Jews, and it would have been impossible to explain why those murders had been necessary, which was simply to throw the other side off balance for the few days he'd need to accomplish his goal.

If it were even possible.

But it just might be.

He would never have deciphered the hero's quest alone, and involving anyone other than Malone would have done nothing except escalate his chances of exposure. Making Malone his supposed ally was the only viable course.

Risky, but the move had proven productive. Half the quest seemed solved.

He crested the stairs and entered the upper gallery, turning left and walking straight for a set of glass doors, out of place in this medieval setting. His cell phone, stuffed inside his trouser pocket, had already silently recorded four calls from Alfred Hermann. He'd debated whether to make contact and soothe the old man's anxiety, but decided that would be foolish. Too many questions—and he could provide few answers. He'd long studied the Order, especially Alfred Hermann, and believed he understood their strengths and weaknesses.

Above all, the members were dealers.

And before the Israelis or the Saudis or the Americans could be squeezed, the Order of the Golden Fleece was going to have to deal with him.

And he would not come cheap.

MALONE FOLLOWED PAM AND McCOLLUM INTO THE RIB-vaulted upper gallery, admiring the workmanship. From the bits and pieces he'd heard from the tour guides earlier, the Jeronymite Order, which took possession of the monastery in 1500, was a closed group devoted to prayer, contemplation, and reformist thinking. They'd possessed no direct evangelical or pastoral mission. Instead they'd focused on living an exemplary Christian life through divine worship—much like their patron saint, Jerome himself, whom he'd read about in the book from Bainbridge Hall.

They stopped before glass doors custom-fit into one of the elaborate arches. Beyond was the gift shop.

"Couldn't be alarmed," McCollum said. "What's to steal? Souvenirs?"

The doors were thick sheets of glass adorned with black metal hinges and chrome handles.

"They open outward," Malone said. "We can't kick 'em in. That glass is half an inch thick."

"Why don't you see if they're locked?" Pam said.

He grasped one of the handles and pulled.

The door swung open.

"I can see why your clients value your opinion."

"Why would they lock them?" she said. "This place is a fortress. And he's right, what is there to steal? The doors themselves are worth more than the merchandise."

He smiled at her logic. Some of her surly attitude had returned, but he was glad. Kept him sharp.

They stepped inside. The dark, musty space reminded him of the confessional. So he swung the door out ninety degrees and locked it into position, as it would be when visitors milled in and out all day.

A quick survey told him that the shop was about twenty feet square, with three tall display cases abutting one wall, book racks on the other two, and a counter and a cash register lining the fourth. A freestanding counter loaded with books filled the center.

"We need light," he said.

McCollum approached another pair of glass doors that led out to a blackened stairway. A set of three switches poked from the wall.

"We're inside the monastery," Malone said. "The light's not going to be visible outside the walls. Still, on and off quick and let's see what happens."

McCollum flicked one of the switches. Four tiny halogen floods that illuminated the glass cases sprang to life. Their light was directed in tight beams downward. More than enough illumination.

"That'll do," he said. "Now let's find something with pictures."

Atop the center counter lay a stack of hardcover volumes in Portuguese and English, all titled *Jerónimos Abbey of Santa Maria.* Glossy pages, lots of text. Photos, too. Two thinner books stacked beside them were more pictures than words. He thumbed through the first stack, while Pam scanned the other. McCollum examined the other shelves. Three-quarters of the way through one of the books, Malone found a section on the chancel and a color image of the sacrarium's silver door.

He walked the book over to the light. The photograph was close up and detailed. "This is it."

He read more about the sacrarium, trying to see if any of the information would be useful, and learned that it was crafted of wood sheathed in silver. Its placement in the chancel required that the central painting of the lower row be removed, which subsequently disappeared. The image of that lost painting had been carved on the sacrarium's door, completing the iconographic cycle of the paintings—all of which dealt with the Epiphany. The door showed Gaspar, one of the wise men, worshiping the newborn child. The book noted that the Epiphany was regarded as the submission of the secular to the divine, the three wise men symbolic of the world as it was then known—Europe, Asia, Africa.

Then he found an interesting passage.

A strange phenomenon is reported to occur at certain times of the year, when the sun's rays penetrate the church in an extraordinary way. For twenty days before the spring equinox, and for thirty days after the autumnal equinox, the sun's golden rays, from the hour of Vespers until sunset, entering from the west and covering a distance of 450 paces, pass in a straight line through the choir and the church to the sacrarium, turning its silver into gold. One of Belém's parish priests, a devoted student of the history, observed long ago that, "The sun seems to be asking its Creator for leave of absence from such an illustrious duty for a few hours of the night, promising to return again and shine at dawn."

He read them the paragraph, then said, "The Guardians are apparently well versed."

"And have good timing," Pam said. "It's two weeks since the autumnal equinox."

He tore the picture from the book and thought about the remainder of the clue. *"Find the place that forms an address with no place, where is found another place. That's next. And tougher."*

"Cotton, surely you've already seen the connection."

He had and was pleased that her mind was working, too.

"Where a retreating star finds a rose, pierces a wooden cross, and converts silver to gold. Find the place." She motioned at the photo from the book. "The sacrarium door. Bethlehem. The Nativity. This is Belém. Remember what we read this morning in London. Portuguese for 'Bethlehem.' And what did Haddad write? Great journeys often start with an epiphany."

"I think you're going to make it to Final Jeopardy," he said.

Glass shattered in the distance.

"That came from inside the cloister," McCollum said.

Malone darted for the light switch and killed the halogens. Darkness again engulfed them and his eyes needed a moment to adjust.

Another crash.

He crept to the open door and identified the sound's direction. Catty-corner across the cloister, on the far side, lower level.

He saw movement in the semi-darkness and spotted three men emerging from another set of glass doors.

Each carried a weapon.

The three fanned out into the lower gallery.

52

WASHINGTON, DC
2:45 PM

STEPHANIE HANDED THE ATTENDANT HER TICKET AND ENTERED the National Air and Space Museum. Green had not come with them, because the attorney general's presence in such a public place would not have gone unnoticed. Stephanie had chosen the locale for the building's many transparent walls, reputation as the world's most visited museum, abundance of security staff, and metal detectors. She doubted Daley would, at this point, invoke anything official that might lead to uncomfortable questions, but he could bring Heather Dixon and her new Arab associates.

They pushed through the crowds and glanced around at the museum's three-block-long interior composed of steel, marble, and glass. Ceilings soared at nearly a hundred feet, creating a hangarlike effect, and displayed a history of flight from the Wright Brothers' flier, to Lindbergh's *Spirit of St. Louis,* to the *Apollo 11* moon ship.

"Lots of people," Cassiopeia muttered.

They passed an IMAX theater with a thick line of patrons and entered the busy Space Hall. Daley stood near a full-sized, spiderlike Lunar Module, displayed as it would have appeared on the moon, with an astronaut balanced on its landing leg ladder.

Daley looked calm, considering. Not a hair on his head had escaped its usual brilliantine hold.

"Got your clothes back on," she said as they approached.

"I underestimated you, Stephanie. My mistake. I won't make it again."

"You leave all your escorts at home?" She knew Daley rarely went anywhere without bodyguards.

"All but one."

He motioned and she and Cassiopeia turned. Heather Dixon appeared from the far side of the Skylab exhibit.

"Deal's off, Larry," she said.

"You want to know about the Alexandria Link? She's the one to fill in the gaps."

Dixon strolled through the crowd toward them. A group of noisy children congealed at the Lunar Module, hugging the wooden railing that wrapped the display. Daley led them closer to a narrow walk on its rear side that paralleled a glass wall, the museum's busy cafeteria beyond.

"You're still dead," Dixon said to her.

"I didn't come here to be threatened."

"And I'm only here because my government ordered me."

"First things first," Daley said.

Dixon brought out an electronic device about the size of a cell phone and switched it on. After a few seconds, she shook her head. "They're not wired."

Stephanie knew how the device worked. Billet agents routinely used them. She grabbed the detector and pointed it at Dixon and Daley.

Negative, too.

She tossed it back to Dixon. "Okay, since we're alone, talk."

"You're a bitch," Dixon said.

"Great. Now could you get to the point of this drama?"

"Here it is, short and sweet," Daley said. "Thirty years ago George Haddad was reading a copy of a Saudi Arabian gazette, published in Riyadh, studying place-names in west Arabia, translating them into Old Hebrew. Why he was doing that, I have no idea. Sounds like watching paint dry. But he began to notice that some of the locations were biblical."

"Old Hebrew," Cassiopeia said, "is a tough language. No vowels. Hard to interpret and loaded with ambiguities. You have to know what you're doing."

"An expert?" Dixon asked.

"Hardly."

"Haddad *is* an expert," Daley said, "and here's the problem. These biblical place-names he noticed were concentrated in a strip about four hundred miles long and one hundred wide, in the western portion of Saudi Arabia."

"Asir?" Cassiopeia asked. "Where Mecca is?"

Daley nodded. "Haddad spent years looking at other locales but could find no similar concentration of Old Hebrew biblical place-names anywhere else in the world, and that included Palestine itself."

Stephanie realized that the Old Testament was a record of ancient Jews. So if the place-names in modern-day west Arabia, translated into Old Hebrew, were actually biblical locations, that could have enormous political implications. "Are you saying there were no Jews in the Holy Land?"

"Of course not," Dixon said. "We were there. All he's saying is that Haddad believed that the Old Testament was a record of the Jewish experience in west Arabia. Before they traveled north to what we know as Palestine."

"The Bible came from Arabia?" Stephanie asked.

"That's one way of putting it," Daley said. "Haddad's conclusions were confirmed when he started matching geography. For more than a century archaeologists have tried to find, in Palestine, sites that match biblical descriptions. But nothing fits. Haddad discovered that if you match locales in west Arabia, translated into Old Hebrew, with biblical geography, location after location matches."

Stephanie was still skeptical. "Why has no one noticed this before? Haddad's surely not the only person who can understand Old Hebrew."

"Others have noticed," Dixon said. "Three, between 1948 and 2002."

Stephanie caught the finality of Dixon's tone. "But your government took care of them? That's why Haddad had to be killed?"

Dixon did not answer.

Cassiopeia broke the moment. "This all goes back to the conflicting claims, doesn't it? God made a covenant with Abraham and gave him the Holy Land. Genesis says the covenant passed through Abraham's son Isaac to the Jews."

"It's been assumed for centuries," Daley said, "that the land God identified for Abraham lay in what we know as Palestine. But what if that wasn't the case? What if, instead, the land God identified was somewhere else? Somewhere far from Palestine. In west Arabia."

Cassiopeia chuckled. "You're nuts. The Old Testament has its roots there? In the heart of Islam? The land of the Jews, what God promised them, contains Mecca? A few years ago factions of Islam rioted worldwide over a cartoon of Muhammad. Can you imagine what they would do with this?"

Daley seemed unmoved. "Which is why the Saudis and the Israelis wanted Haddad dead. He said proof of his theory was to be found within the lost Library of Alexandria. And he was told that this was the case by someone called a Guardian."

"As were those other three individuals," Dixon said. "Each one visited by an emissary called a Guardian, who offered a way to find the library."

"What kind of proof could there possibly be?" Stephanie asked.

Daley seemed impatient. "Haddad told the Palestinian authorities five years ago that he believed ancient documents could be used to verify his conclusions. Just an Old Testament, written before the time of Christ, in its original Hebrew could prove decisive. None older than the tenth century exist today. Haddad knew from other writings that have survived that there were biblical texts in the Library of Alexandria. Finding one may be the only way to prove anything, since the Saudis will not allow archaeological research in Asir."

Stephanie remembered what Green told her early Tuesday morning. "That's why they bulldozed those villages. They were afraid. They didn't want anything found. Nothing that might be associated with the Jewish Bible."

"And it's why they now want you dead," Dixon said. "You're interfering in their business. No chances are going to be taken."

Stephanie stared out into the Space Hall. Rockets on display reached for the ceiling. Excited schoolchildren wove their way through the exhibits. She glared at Dixon. "Your government believes all this?"

"That's why those three men were killed. It's why Haddad was targeted."

She pointed at Daley. "He's not a friend of Israel. He'd want to use whatever he found to bring your government to its knees."

Dixon laughed. "Stephanie, you're losing it."

"There's no question that's his motive."

"You have no idea of my motives," Daley said, his indignation rising.

"I know you're a liar."

Daley stared back at her with uncertainty. He almost seemed confused, which surprised her, so she asked, "What's really going on, Larry?"

"More than you can possibly realize."

53

LISBON
8:45 PM

MALONE RETREATED INTO THE GIFT SHOP BUT KEPT HIS ATTENTION on the three armed men, who were advancing in trained movements across the lower gallery. Pros. Great.

He used one of the glass cases adjacent to the open door as a shield, Pam beside him, and continued to peer out into the cloister. McCollum was crouched behind the center table.

"They're down and we're up. Should buy us a few minutes. The church and galleries are big. It'll take time to search. Those locked?" he asked McCollum, motioning to the other set of glass doors leading out of the shop.

"Afraid so. They lead down and out. So they must lock them as a precaution."

He didn't like their position. "We need to get out of here."

"Cotton," Pam said, and he turned his attention back out into the upper gallery. One of the men had emerged from the stairway leading down and started advancing toward the gift shop.

McCollum slipped up behind him and whispered, "Take her over to the register and get behind the counter."

Anyone who could shoot two men in the head and then enjoy his breakfast warranted some respect. So he decided not to argue. He grasped Pam's arm and led her to the far side of the counter.

He saw McCollum palm the knife.

The three glass display cases nestled beside one another with a gap between wide enough to accommodate McCollum. Darkness would shield him, at least until it was too late for his prey to react.

The armed man drew closer.

STEPHANIE WAS LOSING PATIENCE WITH LARRY DALEY. "WHAT do you mean *more than I can possibly realize*?"

"There are some within the administration who want to prove Haddad's theory," Daley said.

She recalled what Daley had said to Brent Green when he thought they were alone. "Including you."

"That's not true."

She wasn't buying it. "Get real, Larry. You're only here because I have the dirt on you."

Daley seemed unfazed. "Time for a reality check, Stephanie. Our media people will spin whatever you do into a tale of fabricated evidence by an out-of-control employee trying to save her job. Sure, there may be some embarrassment, questions from the press, but you don't have enough to take me or anyone else down. I didn't give a dime to anyone. And those lobbyists? It's a swearing contest. A battle you'll lose."

"Maybe. But you'd be radioactive. Your career over."

Daley shrugged. "Occupational hazard."

Cassiopeia was studying the exhibit hall and Stephanie sensed she was anxious. So she said to Daley, "Get to the point."

"The point," Dixon said, "is that we want all this to go away. But somebody within *your* government won't let it die."

"That's right. Him." And she pointed at Daley.

Cassiopeia drifted toward the Lunar Module exhibit and the flurry of teenagers crowded around its base.

"Stephanie," Daley said, "you blamed me for the Alexandria Link being leaked. But you don't know your friends from your enemies. You hate this administration. You think the president is an idiot. But there are others who are far worse. Dangerous people."

"No," she said. "They're all fanatics. Party loyalists who've shot off their mouths for years. Now they're in a position to do something."

"And for the moment, Israel is at the top of their agenda."

"Skip the riddles, Larry. Tell me what you want me to know."

"The vice president is behind this."

Had she heard right? "Get real."

"He's connected to the Saudis. They've financed him for a long time. He's been around. A few terms in Congress, three years as treasury secretary, now the second seat. He wants the top job, makes no secret, and the party faithful have promised him the nomination. He has friends who need good relations with the Saudis, and those friends will be the ones supplying him with money. He and the president disagree on the Middle East. He's tight with the Saudi royal family, but keeps that quiet. Publicly he's climbed their asses a few times. But he made sure the Saudis knew about the Alexandria Link. His token for their goodwill."

What she was hearing rang contrary to what Brent Green had said, since the attorney general himself had taken the blame for the leak.

Cassiopeia returned.

"What is it?" Stephanie asked her.

"Finish this."

"Problem?"

"Bad feeling."

"Too much intrigue in your life," Dixon said to Cassiopeia.

"Too much lying in yours."

Stephanie faced Daley, her thoughts arguing. "I thought you said a few minutes ago that some in the administration *want* to prove Haddad's theory. Now you say the vice president fed it to the Saudis. They'd want it to go away. Which is it?"

"Stephanie, what you took from my house would finish me. I work in the shadows. Always have. But somebody has to do it. Do you want to get me, or do you want who's really behind all this?"

Not an answer to her question. "I want all of you."

"That's not possible. For once, would you listen? You can smack on a log all day long with a hatchet and you might cut through. But slam a wedge down its center and the thing splits every time."

"You're just trying to save your hide."

"Tell her," Daley said to Dixon.

"There's a division in your government. You're still our friend, but there are some who want to change that."

Stephanie wasn't impressed. "That's always the case. Two sides to everything."

"This is different," Dixon said. "More is happening. And Malone is in Portugal."

That grabbed her attention.

"The Mossad plans to deal with him there."

Daley ran a hand through his hair. "Stephanie, two factions are at work. One Arab, one Jew. They both want the same thing and, for once, they want it for the same reason. The vice president is linked to the Arabs—"

An alarm echoed through the cavernous museum, then a flat voice announced through a public address system that the building must be immediately cleared.

Stephanie grabbed Daley.

"It's not me," he quickly said.

SABRE STOOD ROCK-STILL. HE NEEDED THE MAN WITH THE GUN to enter the gift shop.

He would.

He'd have to.

Sabre wondered where the other two had gone. His answer came with movement beyond the set of locked glass doors.

Interesting.

These three obviously knew the geography, and they also knew that the gift shop was their destination.

Had they seen the lights?

The two gunmen to his left tested the doors and found they were locked. The forms then backed away and fired at the glass.

No retorts. Just thumps. Like a hammer to a nail. Metal smacked into the glass, thudded, but did not shatter it.

Bulletproof.

The third gunman in the upper gallery rushed inside the open doorway, his gun leading the way. Sabre waited for the instant of indecision, when his target had to assess his situation, then lunged forward, slamming the man's gun with his foot as he brought the knife around and slashed the man's throat. He gave the man no time to realize his fate, plunging the blade into the nape of his neck.

A few gargled gasps and the man collapsed to the floor.

More thuds dotted the locked glass doors. A couple of kicks loosened nothing. Then he heard footsteps as the two attackers retreated down the stairway.

He grabbed the dead man's gun.

THE ALARM CONTINUED TO BLARE. HUNDREDS OF PATRONS rushed toward the museum entrances. Daley was still in Stephanie's grasp.

"The vice president has allies," he said. "He can't do this alone."

She was listening.

"Stephanie. Brent Green is working with him. He's not your friend." Her eyes locked on Heather Dixon, who said, "He's telling the truth. Who else knew you were coming here? If we wanted you dead, this would not have been the meeting place."

She'd thought herself in control, but now she wasn't so sure. Green was indeed the only other person who knew they were there—if Dixon and Daley were telling the truth.

She released Daley, who said, "Green's in league with the VP. Has been for a while. He's been promised the second seat on the ticket. Brent could never hope to win an election. This is his one shot at moving up."

An announcement again ordered that the building must be cleared. A security guard exited the cafeteria and told them they'd have to leave.

"What's happening?" Daley asked him.

"Just a precaution. We need to clear the building."

Through the far glass walls, Stephanie saw people streaming away from the road and trees that separated the museum from the grassy mall.

Some precaution.

They hustled back toward the main entrances. People continued to flood out the doors. Lots of chatter and concerned faces. Most of them were teenagers and families, the talk about what could possibly be happening.

"Let's find another way," Cassiopeia said. "At least be a little unpredictable."

She agreed. They walked off. Daley and Dixon stood rigid, as if trying to make them believe.

"Stephanie," Daley called out.

She turned.

"I'm the only friend you've got. Find me when you realize that."

She did not seize on his words, though she hated the feeling of uncertainty that coursed through her.

"We have to go," Cassiopeia said.

They rushed through more galleries brimming with shiny aircraft, past a gift shop rapidly losing patrons. Cassiopeia seemed intent on using one of the emergency exits—a good play, since the alarms were already activated.

Ahead, from behind a display case loaded with miniature planes, a man appeared. Tall, dressed in a dark business suit. He raised his right palm. Stephanie spotted a thin wire corkscrewing from his left ear.

She and Cassiopeia stopped and turned. Two more men, similarly dressed and equipped, stood behind them. She registered their look and manner.

Secret Service.

The first man spoke into a lapel mike, and the building's alarm went silent.

"Can we do this easy, Ms. Nelle?"

"Why should I?"

The man stepped closer. "Because the president of the United States wants to talk to you."

54

MALONE ROUNDED THE COUNTER AND CROUCHED WHERE Mc-Collum was searching the dead man's pockets. He'd watched the so-called treasure hunter kill their attacker with expert precision.

"Those two are rounding back through the church and headed here," he said.

"I understand," McCollum said. "Here's a couple of spare magazines. And another gun. Any clue who they are?"

"Israeli. Have to be."

"Thought you said they were out of the picture."

"And I thought you said you were an amateur. Lot of skill you just showed."

"You do what you have to when your ass is on the line."

Malone noticed something else clipped to the dead man's waist. He unsnapped the metal unit.

A transceiver locator. He'd used one many times to follow an electronically tagged target. He activated the video screen and saw that it was tracking something in silent mode. A flashing indicator showed the target was nearby.

"We need to go," Pam said.

"That's going to be a problem," Malone said. "The only way out is through that gallery. But the other two gunmen must be near the stairs by now. We need another way down."

He pocketed the locator unit. Weapons in hand, they slipped out of the gift shop.

The two gunmen burst from an archway ninety feet away and started firing.

Sounds like popping balloons snapped through the cloister.

Malone dove to the gallery floor, taking Pam with him. The corners were not ninety degrees, but flared, making the cloister octagonal. He used the angle for cover.

"Head that way," McCollum said. "I'll keep them busy."

A continuous stone bench lined the outer perimeter, connecting the arches and forming an elaborate balustrade. Crouching down, he and Pam scampered away from the gift shop, where McCollum was firing at the two gunmen.

Bullets pinged off the stone wall ten feet to his left, some behind, others leading. He realized what was happening. Their shadows, cast from the incandescent fixtures that dimly illuminated the gallery, were betraying their presence. He grabbed Pam, stopped their advance, and hugged the floor. He aimed and, with three bullets, obliterated the lights ahead.

Darkness now sheathed them.

McCollum had stopped firing.

So had the gunmen.

He motioned and they hustled ahead, still crouched, using the arches, tracery, and stone bench for protection.

They came to the end of the gallery.

To their right, the inside wall of the next gallery stretched. No doors. At the far end was another unbroken wall. To his immediate left rose a set of glass doors, one swung open, inviting guests inside. A placard identified the room as the refectory. Perhaps there might be a way down inside?

He motioned and they entered.

Three thuds pounded the glass as bullets slammed against its exterior. None penetrated. More bulletproof material. Thank heaven for whoever selected the doors.

"Cotton, we've got a problem," Pam said.

He stared into the refectory.

Through the darkness, broken only by the scattered rays seeping in from the windows, he saw a spacious rectangle topped by a ribbed ceiling, similar to that of the church. A low stone cornice encircled the room, below which ran a colorful tile mosaic. No doors led out. The windows were ten feet overhead with no way to get to them.

He spied only two openings.

One was at the far end, and he trotted the fifty-foot length and saw that it may have once been a fireplace but was now only a decorative niche.

Sealed.

The other opening was smaller, maybe four by five feet, recessed three feet into the outer wall. The refectory was once the abbey's dining hall, so this may have been where food was prepared before serving.

Pam was right. They had a problem.

"Climb in there," he told her.

She didn't argue and wiggled her body up onto a stone shelf above an empty basin. "I must be out of my mind to be here."

"A little late to be noticing that."

He kept his eyes on the doors leading out to the upper

gallery. A shadow grew in the dim light. He saw that Pam was safely inside and climbed in after her, atop the basin, pressing his spine against the shelf as far into the niche as possible.

"What are you going to do?" she asked in his ear.

"What I have to."

SABRE HAD SEEN THE MEN DIVIDE. ONE CHASED AFTER MA-lone; the other slipped into the archway that led back down to the church. He decided the high ground would be better, so he carefully inched his way to the same doorway, hoping it led to the upper choir, where Malone and his ex-wife had stood earlier.

He liked the hunt, especially when the prey offered a challenge. He wondered about the identity of these men. Were they Israelis, as Malone thought? Made sense. He knew from Jonah that an assassination squad had been dispatched to London, but George Haddad had already been handled. He'd heard that encounter on the tape, confirmed by Malone. So what were Israelis doing here? After him? Unlikely. But who else?

He found the doorway and slipped inside.

To his left dropped the stairway to the church. Through the blackness he heard footsteps below.

He entered the choir, stopping where the balustrade met the outer stone wall and carefully looking below. Windows high in the church's south façade glowed with ambient light. The blackened figure of a man, gun in hand, crept down the aisle formed from the end of the pews to the church's north wall, keeping to the shadows, trying to make his way to the lower choir.

He ticked off two shots.

The suppressed bangs popped through the cavernous nave. One found the mark and the man cried out, reeled, then staggered against a pew. He readjusted his aim, made only moderately difficult by the dimness, and with two more shots sank the man to the floor.

Not bad.

He released the gun's magazine and replaced it with a fresh one from his pocket.

He turned to leave. Time to find Malone.

A gun appeared in his face.

"Drop the weapon," the voice said in English.

He hesitated and tried to find a face to the voice, but the blackness revealed only a shadow. Then he realized the man wore a hood. The chilly prick of another gun barrel nipped his neck.

Two problems.

"One more time," the first man said. "Drop the weapon."

No choice. The gun clattered to the floor.

The pistol in his face lowered. Then something whirled through the air and slammed into the side of his skull. Before any semblance of pain registered in his brain, the world around him went silent.

55

MALONE GRIPPED THE AUTOMATIC AND WAITED. HE RISKED ONE glance around the niche where he and Pam were hiding.

The shadow continued to expand as the gunman drew closer.

He wondered if his attacker knew there was no exit. He assumed the man did not. Why else would he be advancing? Simply wait out in the gallery. But he'd learned long ago that many people who killed for a living were plagued with impatience. Do the job and get out. Waiting only increased the chances of failure.

Pam was breathing hard and he couldn't blame her. He, too, was fighting a quick heart. He told himself to calm down. *Think. Be ready.*

The shadow now stretched across the refectory's wall.

The man burst inside, gun pointed.

His initial view would be of a dark, empty chamber devoid of furnishings. The niche at the far end should immediately grab his attention, then the second break in the wall. But Malone did not wait for all that comprehension to register. He rolled out of his hiding place and fired.

The bullet whizzed past his target and ricocheted off the wall. The gunman seemed stunned for an instant, but quickly recovered and swung his gun toward Malone, then apparently realized that he was exposed.

This was going to be a duel.

Malone fired again and his bullet found the man's thigh.

A cry of agony, but the attacker did not go down.

Malone planted a third bullet in the gunman's chest. He teetered, then dropped spine-first to the floor.

"You're a tough man to kill, Malone," a male voice said from beyond the doorway.

He registered the voice. Adam, from Haddad's apartment. Now he knew. Israelis. But how had they found him?

He heard footsteps. Running away.

He hesitated, then rushed to the doorway, intent on finishing what he'd started in London.

He stopped and peered out.

"Over here, Malone," Adam called out.

He stared across the open cloister, diagonally to the far side where Adam stood beneath one of the arches. The face was unmistakable.

"You're a good shot, but not this good. It's just you and me now."

He saw Adam disappear into the doorway that led down to the church.

"Pam, stay put," he said. "Defy me this time and you can deal with the gunmen yourself."

He bolted from the refectory and raced down the gallery. Where was McCollum? Two gunmen were definitely down. He'd seen only three earlier. Had Adam killed McCollum? *Just you and me.* That's what the Israeli had said.

He decided that following Adam down into the church would be foolish. Do the unexpected. So he hopped onto one of the benches that lined the outer edge of the gallery and stared below. The ornamentation and tracery decorating the cloister were both impressive and substantial. He stuffed the gun in his belt and swung his body out, gripping the top of the stone bench and allowing his feet to find a projecting gargoyle disguising a drain. Balancing, he bent down, gripped the stone, and pivoted himself to a ledge that extended from one of the arch supports. From there it was six feet to the grass of the cloister garden.

Adam suddenly appeared from the church, in the far gallery, running down its length.

Malone gripped the gun and fired, the bullet missing but definitely attracting his quarry's attention.

Adam disappeared downward, using for cover the same waist-high benches that Malone had.

The Israeli appeared and clicked off a shot.

Malone dove between two tracery supports into the lower gallery and hit the floor tiles hard. The breath left him. His forty-eight-year-old body could only take so much, regardless of what he'd once done on a daily basis. He scampered back to the bench and carefully stared across the cloister.

Adam was running again.

He sprang to his feet and bolted left, rounding a corner and heading straight toward Adam. His target disappeared into another set of glass doors, custom-fit within two elaborate arches and framed by statues.

He made his way to them and stopped outside.

A sign identified the dark space beyond as the chapter house where the monks had once congregated for meetings. Opening the glass door would be foolish. Not enough light to see much on the other side; only windows, two, their definition clear.

He decided to use what he knew.

So he swung open one glass door and kept his body behind the other, which should protect him from any shots.

None came.

A huge tomb filled the center of the towering rectangle.

He searched with his gaze. Nothing. His eyes were drawn to the windows. The right set were shattered, glass strewn across the floor, a rope disappearing upward, being pulled from the outside.

Adam was gone.

Footsteps slapped off stone, and he saw Pam and McCollum running toward him. He stepped out into the gallery and asked McCollum, "What happened to you?"

"Got slammed across the head. Two of them. Up in the choir. I took one out in the church, then they got me."

"Why are you still breathing?"

"I don't know, Malone. Why don't you ask them?"

He did the math. Three down. Two more supposedly accosted McCollum. Five? Yet he'd only seen three.

He leveled the gun he was holding at McCollum. "Those guys break in here, come after us, try to kill me and Pam, but you they whack on the head and leave. A bit much, wouldn't you say?"

"What's the point, Malone?"

He fished the locator from his pocket. "They work for you. Here to take us out so you didn't have to."

"I assure you, if I wanted you dead you would be."

"They came straight upstairs to that gift shop. Circled it like buzzards. They knew the geography." He held up the locator. "And they were tracking us. I killed one upstairs and was damn close to getting the third. Then he just leaves? Strangest assassination squad I've ever seen."

He flicked on the unit and pointed it at McCollum. He changed the setting from mute and a soft pinging indicated that the receiver had found its target.

"They were tracking you. This will tell us for sure."

"Go for it, Malone. Do what you have to."

Pam had been standing to the side, silent, and he said to her, "Thought I told you to stay up there."

"I did until he came. And, Cotton, he does have a nasty bump on the side of his head."

He wasn't impressed. "He's tough enough to take a shot delivered for our benefit by his hired help."

He aimed the locator at McCollum, but the rhythmic pulse of the beep stayed constant.

"Satisfied?" McCollum asked.

He swung the unit left and right, but the beeping remained unchanged. McCollum was not the source. Pam walked past, studying the inside of the chapter house.

The beeping changed.

McCollum noticed, too.

Malone kept his gun aimed, which told McCollum to stay put. He pointed the unit Pam's way and the pulse intensified.

She heard it, too, and turned toward him.

He lowered the gun and took two steps closer, still swinging the unit. The pulse weakened, weakened again, then solidified when pointed straight at her.

A look of astonishment came to her face, and she asked, "What is it?"

"They were tracking you. That's how they found George. You." Anger surged through him. He tossed the locator down, stuffed the gun in his pocket, and started to pat her down.

"What in the hell are you doing?" she yelled.

She was clearly nervous, but he didn't spare her feelings.

"Pam, if I have to strip you naked and search every cavity, I'm going to find what's on you. So tell me where it is."

Her mind seemed to reel with incomprehension. "Where's what?"

"Whatever that locator is tracking."

"The watch," McCollum said.

He turned. The other man was pointing at Pam's wrist.

"Has to be. Has a power source and it's plenty big to accommodate a pinger."

He grabbed Pam's wrist and unclasped the watch, which
he wrenched free and sent sliding across the gallery floor. He
yanked up the locator and pointed. A solid beat signified that
the watch was indeed the target. He pointed the unit back at
Pam and the pulse subsided.

"Oh, my God," she muttered. "I got that old man killed."

56

MALONE ENTERED THE BUSINESS CENTER FOR THE RITZ FOUR
Seasons. They'd left the monastery through the main entrance. Since the doors could be opened from the inside, the
portal had offered the quickest way out.

They'd then rounded the building and discovered where
Adam and his compatriots had entered. The chapter house's
elegant windows, adorned with old stone tracery, were the
only panes not barred. They stood six feet off the ground and
faced a darkened side street. Two bushy trees had offered excellent cover for the break-in.

They'd then walked a few blocks east into Belém's business district and caught a trolley into Lisbon's center. From
there they'd taken a cab north a few miles to the hotel. No
one said anything on the trip. Malone remained in a quandary. Where he'd thought McCollum was the threat, the dan-

ger turned out to be much closer. But he'd ended any further hunting by tossing the watch into a row of box hedges that lined the cloister garden.

He needed to think.

So they entered one of the business center's conference rooms and closed the door. A phone and a computer waited on the table, along with pens and paper. He liked that about the Four Seasons. Tell 'em what you want and you get it.

"Cotton," Pam said immediately. "That watch was a gift. I told you that. From the man I've been seeing."

He did recall her saying that in London. A TAG. Expensive. He'd been impressed. "Who is he?"

"A lawyer for another firm. Senior partner."

"How long you two been an item?" It came out as if he cared, but he didn't.

"A few months. Come on. How could he have possibly known any of this would happen? He gave me that watch weeks ago."

He wanted to believe her. But wives of agents had been compromised before. He reached for the phone and dialed Atlanta and the Magellan Billet. He told the voice on the other end who he was and what he wanted. He was instructed to hold. Two minutes later a male voice said in his ear, "Cotton, this is Brent Green. Your call has been sent to me."

"I need to talk with Stephanie."

"She's unavailable. Quite a lot is happening here. You'll have to deal with me."

"What's the attorney general doing in the middle of Billet business? You usually stay way back from that."

"It's complicated, Cotton. Stephanie has been relieved of her duties, and we're both in the midst of a battle."

He wasn't surprised. "And it all relates to what I'm doing here."

"Precisely. There are people within this administration who placed your son at risk."

"Who?"

"We're not sure. That's what Stephanie is trying to find out. Can you tell me what's happening there?"

"We're having a ball. Just one party after another. Lisbon's a blast."

"Any reason why you have to be sarcastic?"

"I can think of a ton of them. But I need you to do something. Check out a man named James McCollum. He says he was army, special forces." He gave Green a quick physical description. "I need to know if he's real, and his background." As he made the request he stared straight at McCollum, but the man never flinched. "What's happening with Stephanie?"

"That would take too long. But we need to know what you're doing. That could help her."

"I never knew you cared that much."

"I fail to see why everyone thinks I dislike the woman. Actually, she has a great many strong points. But at the moment she's in trouble. I haven't heard from her, or Ms. Vitt, in several hours."

"Cassiopeia is there?"

"With Stephanie. Your friend Henrik Thorvaldsen sent her."

Green was right. There was a lot happening there. "I also have an issue with my ex-wife. Seems the Israelis have been tracking her."

"We're aware of that. A man she was seeing in Atlanta was an Israeli sympathizer. The Mossad asked him to give her a few things. A watch, a locket, a cocktail ring. All were GPS-active. We assume the idea was that she'd wear one of them at some time or another."

"That means the Israelis knew a move was coming on my son, so they got ready to take advantage of it."

"That's a safe conclusion. Is the Alexandria Link still intact?"

"Didn't know you knew anything about that."

"I do now."

"The Israelis permanently took care of that yesterday and almost got us a little while ago." Now he really needed to think. "I have to go. You have a number where I can dial direct?" Green gave it to him. "Sit tight. I'll be back to you shortly."

"Cotton," Green said. "That lawyer your ex-wife was seeing. He's dead. Shot a few days ago. The Mossad cleaned up their trail."

He registered the message.

"I'd keep her close," Green said. "She's a loose end, too."

"Or something more."

"Either way, she's a problem."

He hung up. Pam stared at him. "Your lover's dead. Israel took care of him. He was working with them."

Shock twisted her face. He could not have cared less. That man had been part of placing Gary at risk. "It's what happens when you pet a rattlesnake. I wondered how we were tracked to the hotel in London. There's no way we were followed from Haddad's apartment."

He saw how upset she was, but there was no time for her feelings. Worrying over impossibilities could get you killed. He faced McCollum. "You heard me. I'm checking you out."

"Through with the theatrics? Remember, I still have the rest of the quest and we don't know where to go from here."

"Who says?" He found the photo from the book in the gift shop and unfolded it. "*Find the place that forms an address with no place, where is found another place.* Okay, we found the place where silver is turned to gold. This. The Nativity.

Bethlehem. Belém. What has an address but no place?" He pointed to the computer. "Lots of addresses and no places associated with a single one. Web addresses."

He sat before the machine.

"The Guardians had to have a way to control the clues. They don't seem the type to just throw something out there and leave it. Once an invitee, or a stranger, made it this far, they'd need a way to stop the quest if they wanted to. What better way than to have the final clues on a website they control."

He typed BETHLEHEM.COM, but was routed to a commercial site loaded with junk. He tried BETHLEHEM.NET and found more of the same. Then, on BETHLEHEM.ORG, the screen turned white and a question appeared in black letters.

WHAT IS IT YOU SEEK?

The cursor flashed below the inquiry above a black line, ready for the answer. He typed in THE LIBRARY OF ALEXANDRIA. The screen flickered, then changed.

NOTHING MORE?

He typed what he thought they wanted to hear.

KNOWLEDGE.

The screen changed again.

28° 41.41N
33° 38.44E

Malone knew what those numbers represented. *Find the place that forms an address with no place, where is found another place.* "It's the other place."

"GPS coordinates," McCollum said.

He agreed, but he needed to ground-site them, so he found a website and entered the numbers.

A few seconds later a map appeared.

He immediately recognized the shape—an inverted isosceles triangle, a wedge cleaving Africa from Asia, home to a unique combination of mountains and deserts surrounded by the narrow Gulf of Suez to the west, the even narrower Gulf of Aqaba on the east, and the Red Sea to the south.

The Sinai.

The GPS coordinates identified a site in the extreme southern region, in the mountains, near the apex of the inverted triangle.

"Looks like we found the place."

"And how do you plan to get there?" McCollum asked. "That's Egyptian territory, patrolled by the United Nations, close to Israel."

Malone reached for the phone. "I don't think it's going to be a problem."

PART
FOUR

57

Vienna
10:30 PM

THORVALDSEN SAT IN THE CHÂTEAU'S GRAND HALL, WATCHING the Order of the Golden Fleece's winter Assembly unfold. He, like the other members, filled a gilded antique chair. They were aligned in rows of eight, the Circle facing them, Alfred Hermann's center chair draped in a blue silk. Everyone seemed anxious to talk, and the discussion had quickly gravitated to the Middle East and what the Political Committee had proposed the previous spring. At that time the plans had been merely tentative. Things were now different. And not everyone agreed.

In fact, there was more dissent than Alfred Hermann had apparently expected. The Blue Chair had already twice interjected himself into the debate, which was a rarity. Usually, Thorvaldsen knew, Hermann remained silent.

"Displacing the Jews is impossible and ridiculous," one of the members said from the floor. Thorvaldsen knew the man, a Norwegian heavy into North Atlantic fishing. "Chronicles makes clear that God chose Jerusalem and sanctified the Temple there. I know my Bible. First Kings says God gave Solomon one tribe, so David would have a lamp before Him in Jerusalem. The city He chose for Himself. The reestablishment of modern Israel was not an accident. Many believe it came by heavenly inspiration."

Several other members echoed the observation with Bible passages of their own from Chronicles and Psalms.

"And what if all that you quote is false?"

The inquiry came from the front of the hall. The Blue Chair stood. "Do you recall when the modern state of Israel was created?"

No one answered his question.

"May 14, 1948. Four thirty-two PM. David Ben-Gurion stood in the Tel Aviv Museum and said that *by virtue of the natural and historic right of the Jewish people* the state of Israel was established."

"The prophet Isaiah made clear that *a nation shall be born in a day,*" one of the members said. "God kept his promise. The Abrahamic covenant. The land of the Jews was returned."

"And how do we know of this covenant?" Hermann asked. "Only one source. The Old Testament. Many of you have today called on its text. Ben-Gurion spoke of the *natural and historic right of the Jewish people.* He, too, was referring to the Old Testament. It's the only existing evidence that mentions these divine revelations—but its authenticity is seriously in doubt."

Thorvaldsen's gaze swept the room.

"If I were to have a deed to each one of your estates, documents that were decades old, translated from your respective languages by people long dead who could not even speak your language, would not each one of you question its authenticity? Would you not want more proof than an unverified and unauthenticated translation?" Hermann paused. "Yet we have accepted the Old Testament, without question, as the absolute Word of God. Its text eventually molded the New Testament. Its words still have geopolitical consequences."

The gathering seemed to be waiting for Hermann to make his point.

"Seven years ago a man named George Haddad, a Palestinian biblical scholar, penned a paper published by Beirut University. In it he postulated that the Old Testament, as translated, was wrong."

"Quite a premise," a member said. The heavyset woman stood. "I take the Word of God more seriously than you."

Hermann seemed amused. "Really? What do you know of this Word of God? You know its history? Its author? Its translator? Those words were written thousands of years ago by unknown scribes in Old Hebrew, a language dead now for more than two thousand years. What do you know of Old Hebrew?"

The woman said nothing.

Hermann nodded. "Your lack of knowledge is understandable. It was a highly inflected language in which the import of words was conveyed by their context rather than their spelling. The same word could, and did, have several distinct meanings, depending on how it was used. Not until centuries after the Old Testament was first written did Jewish scholars translate those words into the Hebrew of the time, and yet those scholars could not even speak Old Hebrew. They simply guessed at the meaning or, even worse, changed the meaning. Then centuries passed, and more scholars, this time Christian, translated the words again. They, too, could not speak Old Hebrew, so they, too, guessed. With all due respect to your beliefs, we have no idea as to the Word of God."

"You have no faith," the woman declared.

"On this I do not, since it does not involve God. This is the work of man."

"What did Haddad argue?" another man asked, his tone suggesting that he was interested.

"Correctly, he postulated that when the *stories* of the covenant made by God to Abraham were first told, Jews already inhabited their Promised Land—what is now Palestine. Of course, this was many, many centuries after the actual promise was supposedly made. According to the biblical premise, the Promised Land was said to extend from the river of Egypt to the great River Euphrates. Many place-names are given. But when Haddad matched the biblical place-names, translated back into Old Hebrew, with actual locations, he discovered something extraordinary." Hermann paused, seemingly pleased with himself. "The Promised Land of Moses and the land of Abraham were both located in western Saudi Arabia, in the region of Asir."

"Where Mecca sits?" came a question from the floor.

Hermann nodded. Thorvaldsen saw that many of the members immediately grasped the significance.

"That's impossible," one member said.

"Actually," Hermann said, "I can show you."

He motioned, and a viewing screen unwound from a ceiling-mounted holder. A projector came to life. A map of western Saudi Arabia, the Red Sea snaking a jagged shoreline from north to south, appeared. A scale meter showed that the area was roughly four hundred kilometers long and three hundred wide. Mountainous regions spread east over a hundred kilometers from the shore, then flattened to the fringes of the central Arabian desert.

"I knew there'd be skeptics among you." Hermann smiled as nervous laughter rippled through the Assembly. "This is modern-day Asir."

He signaled and the screen changed.

LAND OF ASIR

"Projecting the boundaries of the biblical Promised Land onto the map, utilizing locations George Haddad precisely identified, the dotted line delineates the land of Abraham, the solid line the land of Moses. The biblical locations, translated back into Old Hebrew, match rivers, towns, and mountains of this region perfectly. Many even still retain their Old Hebrew designations—adapted, of course, to Arabic. Ask yourself, why has no paleographic or archaeological evidence ever been found to substantiate biblical locations in Palestine? The answer is simple. Those locations are not there. They lie hundreds of miles to the south, in Saudi Arabia."

"And why has no one ever noticed this before?"

Thorvaldsen appreciated the question, as he'd been thinking the same thing.

"There are only half a dozen or so scholars alive who can effectively understand Old Hebrew. None of them, besides Haddad, apparently was curious enough to investigate. But to be certain, I hired one of those experts three years ago to confirm Haddad's findings. And he did. Down to the last detail."

"Can we speak with your expert?" a member quickly asked.

"Unfortunately, he was elderly and passed away last year."

More likely the man was helped into the grave, Thorvaldsen thought. The last thing Hermann needed was a second scholar claiming a spectacular biblical coup.

"But I have a detailed written report that can be studied. It's quite compelling."

Another image appeared on the screen. A second illustration of the Asir region.

"Here's one example to demonstrate Haddad's point. In Judges 18, the Israelite tribe of Dan established a settlement in a town called Laish, in a region of the same name. The Bible says that this town was close to another called Zidon. Near Zidon lay the fortified city of Zor. Christian historians in the fourth century CE supposedly identified Dan with a village at the headwaters of the Jordan River. In 1838 a team searched and found a mound, which they announced as the remnants of the biblical Dan. That site is now the accepted location of Dan. There's even a modern Israeli settlement, actually called Dan, that flourishes there today."

Thorvaldsen noticed that Hermann seemed to be enjoying himself, as if he'd prepared for this moment a long time. But he wondered if perhaps his unanticipated move on Margarete may have accelerated his host's timetable.

"Archaeologists have explored the mound for the past forty years. Not one piece of evidence has been found to confirm the biblical identity of that site as Dan." Hermann motioned, and the screen changed again. Names appeared on the second map of Asir.

"This is what Haddad discovered. The biblical Dan can easily be identified with a west Arabian village called al-Danadinah, which is located in a coastal region called al-Lith, the principal town of which is also called al-Lith. Translated, that name is identical with the biblical word *Laish*. Also, to this day, a village called Zidon lies nearby. Even closer to al-Danadinah stands al-Sur, which, translated, is Zor."

Thorvaldsen had to admit that the geographic coincidences were intriguing. He removed his rimless glasses and fingered the bridge of his nose, massaging the pinched groove, trying to think.

"And there are more topographical correlations. In 2 Samuel 24:6, the town of Dan was close to a land called Tahtim. No

THE SEARCH FOR A BIBLE LAND

place known as Tahtim survives anywhere in Palestine. But
in west Arabia, the village of al-Danadinah stands near a
coastal ridge called Jabal Tahyatayn, which is an Arabic
form of *Tahtim*. That cannot be an accident. Haddad wrote
that if archaeologists dug in this area, there would be evidence to support the presence of an ancient Jewish settlement. But that has never occurred. The Saudis absolutely
forbid digging. In fact, five years ago, when faced with a
possible threat from Haddad's academic conclusions, the
Saudis destroyed villages in this area, contaminating the
sites, making it nearly impossible for any definitive archaeological evidence ever to be found."

Thorvaldsen noticed that as the Assembly grew more at-
tentive, Hermann became more confident.

"There's more. Throughout the Old Testament, Jordan is

noted by the Hebrew *yarden*. But nowhere is that term ever described as a river. The word actually means 'to descend, a fall in the land.' Yet translation after translation describes the Jordan as a river, its crossing a momentous event. The Palestinian Jordan River is no great waterway. The inhabitants of both banks have waded across it for centuries. But here" he pointed to mountains that cut across the map—"is the great West Arabian Escarpment. Impossible to cross except where the ranges fold, and even there it's difficult. Every instance where the Old Testament speaks of Jordan, the geography and the story match what's on the ground here, in Arabia."

"The Jordan is a mountain range?"

"No other translation from the Old Hebrew makes any sense."

He studied the faces staring back at him and said, "Place-names are handed down as sacred tradition. Old names survive in folk memory and usually reassert themselves. Haddad found that particularly true in Asir."

"Have there not been discoveries that link Palestine with the Bible?"

"There have been discoveries. But none of the inscriptions unearthed so far proves anything. The Moabite Stele found in 1868 speaks of wars fought between Moab and Israel, as mentioned in Kings. Another artifact found in the Jordan Valley in 1993 says the same. But neither say that Israel was located in Palestine. Assyrian and Babylonian records tell of conquests in Israel, but none says where that Israel was located. Kings says the armies of Israel, Judah, and Edom marched seven days in waterless desert. But the rift valley of Palestine, which is commonly regarded as that desert, is no more than one day long and contains plenty of water."

Now Hermann's words came freely, as if he'd held the truths inside far too long.

"Not one remnant of the first Solomon's Temple remains.

Nothing has ever been found, though Kings says he used *great stones, costly stones, hewed stones*. Would not a block have survived?"

He came to the point.

"What's happened is that scholars have allowed their preconceptions to color their interpretations. They wanted Palestine to be the land of the ancient Jews from the Old Testament, so the end governed the means. Reality is far different. Archaeology has indeed proven one thing—that the Palestine of the Old Testament consisted of a people living in hamlets or small towns, mainly scrub farmers, with only fragments of high culture. A rustic society, not the highly astute Israelites of the post-Solomon era. That *is* a scientific fact."

"What does the Psalm say?" a member asked. *"Truth shall spring out of the earth."*

"What do you want to do?" someone asked.

Hermann clearly appreciated the inquiry. "Regardless of the Saudis' refusal to allow any archaeological research, Haddad believed there is proof of his theory that still exists. We are presently trying to locate that proof. If his theory can be substantiated—at least enough to call into question the validity of the Old Testament promises—think of the consequences. Not only Israel, but Saudi Arabia, too, would be destabilized. And we've all been frustrated by that government's corruption. Imagine what the radical Muslims there would do. Their most sacred spot is actually the biblical Jewish homeland? This would be similar to the Temple Mount in Jerusalem, where all three major religions claim a home. That site has bred chaos for thousands of years. The chaos in west Arabia would be equally incalculable."

Thorvaldsen had sat silent long enough. He stood. "You can't believe that these revelations, even if proven, would have such far-reaching effects. What else is there that so interested the Political Committee?"

Hermann stared at him with a contempt that only the two of them understood. The Circle had acted on Cotton Malone, taking his son. Now he'd acted on Hermann. Of course the Blue Chair would never reveal that weakness. Thorvaldsen had wisely played his trump card here, at the Assembly, where Hermann must be careful. But something told him that the Austrian still held one card.

And the smile that curled on the old man's thin lips caused Thorvaldsen to pause.

"That's right, Henrik. There is another aspect. One that will bring the Christians into the fight, as well."

58

VIENNA
10:50 PM

ALFRED HERMANN CLOSED THE DOOR TO HIS PRIVATE APART-ment and removed his robe and neck chain. Their combined weight taxed his tired limbs. He laid the garments across his bed, pleased with the Assembly. After three hours, the members had finally begun to understand. The Order's plan was both grandiose and ingenious. Now he needed to back up his explanation that the proof would be forthcoming.

But he was beginning to grow concerned.

He hadn't heard from Sabre in far too long.

Anxiety twisted his stomach. An unfamiliar feeling. To regain momentum, he'd accelerated his timetable. This might well be his last grand endeavor as Blue Chair—his tenure was drawing to a close. The Order of the Golden Fleece was about opportunity and success. Many a government had been altered, a few even toppled, so that the collective could thrive. What he'd concocted might well bring a few more to their knees, perhaps even the Americans themselves if he played his hand with skill.

He'd known Thorvaldsen might be a problem, which was why he'd ordered Sabre to prepare a financial dossier. Sitting in the *schmetterlinghaus* the day before, watching Sabre dutifully agree to the task, he'd never believed Thorvaldsen would be so aggressive. They'd been long-standing acquaintances. Not necessarily close friends, but certainly compatriots. Somehow, though, the Dane had quickly linked what happened in Copenhagen to him and the Order.

He hadn't expected that a trail existed.

Which made him wonder about Sabre.

How careless had the man been?

Or was it intentional?

Margarete's warnings about Sabre rang through his mind. *Too much freedom. Too much trust.* Why hadn't his acolyte called? The last he knew, Sabre was on his way to London, by way of Rothenburg, to find George Haddad. He'd tried calling several times, but had been unsuccessful. He needed Sabre. Here. Now.

A light rap on the door.

He stepped across and turned the knob.

"Time we talk more," Thorvaldsen said to him.

He agreed.

Thorvaldsen stepped inside and closed the door. "You can't be serious with all this, Alfred. Do you have any idea what your planning could spawn?"

"You're speaking like a Jew, Henrik. That's your flaw.

Blinded by God's supposed promises. Your so-called entitlement."

"I'm speaking as a human being. Who knows if the Old Testament is correct? I certainly have no idea. But the Islamic world will not tolerate any suggestion that its holiest earth was soiled by Judaism. They will react violently."

"The Saudis," he said, "will be given a chance to bargain before any information is released. That's our way. You know that. The violence will be their fault, not ours. Our aim is purely profit. The Political Committee believes a great many economic concessions can be obtained that will benefit our members. And I agree."

"This is insanity," Thorvaldsen declared.

"And what do you plan to do?"

"Whatever I have to."

"You don't have the backbone for this fight, Henrik."

"I might surprise you."

Hermann wondered, so he decided to lay down a challenge. "Perhaps you ought to be more concerned about your own situation. I've checked your financial status. I never realized how tenuous the glassworks business can be. Your Adelgade Glasvaerker is dependent on a variety of volatile factors for success."

"And you think you can affect those?"

"I'm fairly confident I can cause trouble."

"My net worth easily matches yours."

He smiled. "But you value reputation. Unthinkable that one of your companies be perceived as a failure."

"You're welcome to try, Alfred."

He realized that they each possessed billions of euros, most accumulated by ancestors, each of them now a faithful steward. And neither a fool.

"Remember," Thorvaldsen said. "I have your daughter."

He shrugged. "And I have you and the boy."

"Really? You willing to risk her life?"

Hermann had not, as yet, decided on the answer to that question, so he asked, "Is this about Israel? I know you fancy yourself a patriot."

"And I know you're a bigot."

A bolt of anger rocked him. "You've never spoken to me like this before."

"I've always known how you felt, Alfred. Your anti-Semitism is obvious. You try to shield it—after all, there are several Jews in the Order—but it's clear."

Time to end all pretense. "Your religion is a problem. Always has been."

Thorvaldsen shrugged. "No more so than Christianity. We just gave up our warring ways and watched while Christians killed more than enough in the name of the risen Lord."

"I'm not a religious man. You know that, Henrik. This is about politics and profit. And those Jews in the Order? That's what they care about, too. Not one voiced any opposition in the Assembly. Israel is an impediment to progress. Zionists are terrified of the truth."

"What did you mean about the Christians also being involved?"

"If the Library of Alexandria is found, there are texts that could well expose the entire Bible for the fraud that it is."

Thorvaldsen did not seem convinced. "You might find that result a bit difficult to obtain."

"I assure you, Henrik. I've thought this through completely."

"Where is the Talons of the Eagle?"

He threw the Dane a look of approval. "Well done. But he's outside your control."

"But not yours."

He decided to make his point. "You cannot win this. You have my daughter, but that won't stop me."

"Perhaps I need to make myself clear. My family endured the Nazi occupation of Denmark. Many of them were killed and we killed many Germans. I've faced challenge after challenge. I personally care nothing for Margarete. She's an arrogant, spoiled, unintelligent woman. My friend Cotton Malone, his son, and my adopted homeland are my concern. If I need to kill her, then I shall."

Hermann had worried about threats from outside, but the most immediate concern had now arisen from within. This man needed placating. At least for a short while.

"I can show you something."

"You need to stop this."

"There's more at stake here than simply furthering our business interests."

"Then show me."

"I'll have it arranged."

59

MARYLAND
4:50 PM

STEPHANIE SAT IN THE REAR SEAT OF A SUBURBAN, CASSIOPEIA beside her. They motored through the main gate without stopping, the SUV whizzing past armed guards. They'd driven north from Washington into the rugged Maryland countryside. She'd immediately known their destination.

Camp David. The presidential weekend retreat.

Past more guards and another checkpoint, the vehicle stopped before an elegant log cabin engulfed by trees and wrapped in a covered porch. They climbed out into a cool afternoon. The Secret Service agent from the museum waved, and the front door opened.

President Robert Edward Daniels Jr. stepped from the cabin.

She knew the president never used his birth name. Long ago he'd adopted the tag *Danny*. A gregarious soul with a booming baritone voice, Danny Daniels was blessed with a God-given ability to win elections. He'd served as a three-term governor and a one-term senator before claiming the presidency. His reelection last year to a second term had come easily.

"Stephanie, great of you to come," Daniels said as he hopped down the porch steps. The president was dressed in jeans, a twill shirt, and boots.

She gathered her courage and stepped forward. "Did I have a choice?"

"Not really. But it's still good you came. Been having some trouble, I'm told."

Daniels added a cool chuckle, but she was not in the mood—not even from the leader of the free world. "Thanks to your people."

He held up his hands in mock surrender. "Now, that remains to be seen. You haven't even heard what I have to say. And the new look? The hair and clothes? I like it."

Without giving her a chance to reply, he turned to Cassiopeia.

"You must be Ms. Vitt. I've heard a lot about you. Fascinating life you have. And that castle you're reconstructing in France? I'd love to see it."

"You should come. I'll show you."

"I'm told you're building it just like they did six hundred years ago. Amazing."

Stephanie realized Daniels was sending her a message. They were here, and he was informed, so lighten up.

Okay. Time to see where this was headed.

"Contrary to what you think, Stephanie," Daniels said, "I'm not an idiot."

They were sitting on the front porch of the cabin, each in a high-backed wooden rocker. Daniels worked his with vigor, the floorboards straining from his thick six-foot-three-inch frame.

"I don't think I ever called you an idiot," she said.

"My daddy used to tell my mama that he never called her a bitch to her face." He threw her a glare. "Which was true, too."

She said nothing.

"I went to a lot of trouble to have you flushed from that museum. That's one of my favorite places. I love airplanes and space. Studied everything about them when I was younger. Great thing about being president. You can go watch a launch whenever you want." The president crossed his legs and leaned back in the rocker. "I have a problem, Stephanie. A serious one."

"That makes two of us. I'm unemployed and, according to your deputy national security adviser, under arrest. And didn't *you* fire me?"

"I did. Larry asked me to, and I agreed. But it needed to be done, so you could be here now."

Cassiopeia sat forward. "I wondered. But now I know. You're working with the Israelis, aren't you? I've been trying to piece it together. Now it makes sense. They came to you."

"I'm told your father was one of the smartest men in

Spain. Built a financial empire from nothing. One you now run."

"Not my strong point."

"But I hear you're an excellent shot, brave as hell, with a genius IQ."

"And at the moment I find myself in the middle of a political mess."

Daniels's eyes crinkled with amusement. "A mess. That's exactly what we have. And you're right, Israel did contact me. They're irritated with Cotton Malone."

Stephanie knew Daniels was partial to Malone. Two years before, Malone had been involved with a murder trial in Mexico City—the victim a DEA supervisor, Daniels's college roommate, murdered execution-style. She'd sent Malone to ensure a conviction, but during a lunch break he'd found himself in a cross fire that resulted in the death of the Mexican prosecutor and Henrik Thorvaldsen's son. Malone shot the assailants and came home with a bullet in his shoulder, but got the conviction. When he'd wanted to resign early in return for what he'd done, Daniels had personally allowed him out of his navy commission.

"What about you, sir?" she asked. "Irritated with Malone, too?"

"*Sir*? Now that's a first. I've noticed the few times we've been together, you never use that word."

"Didn't realize you were paying such close attention."

"Stephanie, I pay real close attention to a great many things. For example, just a short while ago Cotton Malone called the Magellan Billet. Of course, you've been busy, so the call was routed to Brent Green, on the attorney general's personal order."

"Thought Daley was in charge?"

"I did, too. Why'd Green do that?"

"How do you know he did?" Cassiopeia asked.

"His phones are tapped."

Had Stephanie heard right? "You have his phones bugged?"

"Damn right. Him and a few others. And, yes, one of those is Larry Daley."

Ripples of uncertainty spread through her and she forced her mind to concentrate. This puzzle apparently came with a lot of pieces.

"Stephanie, I've worked my whole life to get here. It's a position where one person can really do something. And I've done all right. Unemployment is at its lowest in thirty years. Inflation is nonexistent. Interest rates are modest. I even pushed through a tax cut two years ago."

"With Larry Daley yanking Congress's chain. Hard to lose." She could not resist. This man may be president, but at the moment her bullshit-tolerance level was well below zero.

Daniels rocked in silence, staring out into the dense woods. "You remember *Rocky III*."

She did not answer.

"I loved those movies. Rocky was always pounded to the breaking point, then that great music played, trumpets and all. He'd see everything clearly, grab a second wind, and beat the crap out of the other guy."

She listened with amusement.

"In *Rocky III* he finds out that Mickey, his trainer, was arranging easy fights. Sure wins. Just so Rocky could keep his title and wouldn't get hurt. Stallone played that great. He wants to fight Mr. T, but Mickey says no, he'll kill you. Rocky gets furious when he realizes he may not be as good as he thought he was. Of course, Mickey dies and Rocky finally KOs Mr. T."

The president's words carried a tone of respect.

"Daley is my Mickey," he said in a near whisper. "He fixed my fights. I'm like Rocky. I don't like it."

"And you didn't know?" she asked.

He shook his head with an odd mixture of annoyance and curiosity. "I was working on nailing him myself when I discovered that you were investigating. Using a call girl? Imaginative. My people weren't as creative. I have to say, when I was told, my opinion of you changed that day."

She needed to know, "How did you know I was doing it?"

"My guys love wiretaps and video. So they listened and watched. We knew about the flash drives. And we also knew his hiding place. So we were just waiting."

"That investigation was months ago. Why didn't you move on him?"

"Why didn't you?"

The answer was obvious. "I can't fire him. You can."

Daniels planted both feet on the deck and balanced on the rocker's edge. "Scandal is a tough thing, Stephanie. There's nobody in this country who's going to believe that I didn't know what Daley was doing. I had to take him out, but with no fingerprints."

"So Daley needed to do it to himself," Cassiopeia said.

Daniels faced her. "That was the preferable way. But Larry specializes in survival. And I have to say, he's good at it."

"What's he got on you?" Stephanie asked.

Her audacity seemed to please rather than anger him. "Other than those compromising pictures of me with a goat, not all that much."

She grinned. "It had to be asked."

"Yes, it did. I see what they say about you, Stephanie. Aggravating you can be. How about we return to my question, which neither of you seems to think is important. Why did Brent Green want to talk directly with Cotton?"

She recalled what Daley said in the museum. "Daley told me Brent is bucking to be the next vice president."

"Which brings us to the purpose of this gathering." Daniels leaned back and started rocking again. "I like to play the good ol' boy. Part of my Tennessee hill country upbringing. It's one reason I love Camp David so much. Reminds me of home. But now it's time to be president. Somebody accessed our secured files and managed a look at the Alexandria Link. Then they leaked that information to two foreign governments, both of which are now in an uproar. The Israelis are really pissed. Yes, publicly it sounds like we're at each other's throats. But privately, I like those folks. Nobody, and I mean nobody, is going to screw with Israel on my watch. Unfortunately, I have some in this administration who think otherwise."

She wanted to ask who, but decided to let him talk.

"Something has been placed in motion, which all started when Cotton Malone's boy was taken. Luckily, with Malone, these folks have no idea who they're dealing with. He'll give 'em fits. Which gives us an opportunity to flesh things out. One of my uncles used to say, *Want to kill snakes? Simple. Set fire to the underbrush and wait for them to slither out. Then you can whack their heads off.* That's what we're going to do here."

Cassiopeia shook her head. "Like I said, what you have, Mr. President, is a mess. I've only been involved for a day or two, but I have no idea who's telling the truth."

"Including me?"

Cassiopeia's emerald eyes tightened. "Including you."

"That's good. You should be suspicious." His voice rang with sincerity. "But I need your help. That's why I fired you, Stephanie. You needed freedom of movement. Now you have it."

"To do what?"

"Find my traitor."

60

THORVALDSEN LED GARY FROM THE CHÂTEAU'S SECOND FLOOR
down to ground level. He'd heard nothing more from Alfred
Hermann since their brief conversation earlier. Gary had
spent the evening with a few of the other guests. Two members had brought their teenage children, and Hermann had
arranged for them to dine in the greenhouse at the rear of the
mansion.

"That was neat," Gary said. "Butterflies land right on your
plate."

Thorvaldsen had visited the *schmetterlinghaus* several
times and also found it fascinating. He'd even thought of
adding one to Christiangade.

"They're remarkable creatures that require great care."

"Place was like a tropical forest."

Neither one of them could sleep. Gary was apparently
a night person, too. So they made their way into Hermann's
library.

Thorvaldsen had heard earlier that the Blue Chair intended to meet with the Economic Committee. Those discussions should go on for a while, which would give him time to
read and prepare. Tomorrow's Assembly would be one of de-

cision. Debate needed to be to the point and accurate. Everyone would leave on Sunday. The Assembly was never a prolonged affair. Staff and committees narrowed issues to only the ones that required a collective vote. These were then presented, discussed, and resolved—the Order's course set for the coming months until spring.

So he needed to be ready.

The cavernous library was two stories tall and encased in shiny walnut paneling. A black marble fireplace flanked by baroque figurines and a French tapestry dominated one wall. Built-in shelves sheathed the remaining three top-to-bottom, the room crowned with a dramatic ceiling painting that made it appear open to the sky.

A spiral staircase corkscrewed a path to the upper shelves. He clung to a slick iron rail and slowly climbed the narrow risers.

"What are we doing here?" Gary asked when they reached the top.

"I want to read something."

He knew of the podium in Hermann's library, upon which was displayed a magnificent Bible. Hermann had boasted that the edition was one of the earliest printed. Thorvaldsen approached the ancient tome and admired its elaborate cover.

"The Bible was the first book created when printing was finally perfected in the fifteenth century. Gutenberg produced many Bibles. This is one. As I told you earlier, you should read it."

Gary stared at the book and Thorvaldsen knew the lad could not appreciate the significance. So he said, "These words changed the course of human history. They altered humankind's social development and forged political systems. This and the Koran may be the two most important books on the planet."

"How can words be that important?"

"It's not simply words, Gary. It's what we do with them. After Gutenberg began mass printing, books quickly spread. They weren't cheap, but by 1500 they were common. More access to information meant more dissent, more informed discussion, more widespread criticism of authority. Information changed the world. Made it a different place." He motioned at the Bible. "And this book changed everything."

He carefully opened the front cover.

"What language is that?" Gary asked.

"Latin." He scanned the index.

"You can read it?"

He smiled at the incredulous tone. "I was taught as a child." He tapped the boy's chest. "You ought to learn, too."

"What would I do if I did?"

"For one thing, you could read this Bible."

He motioned at the index. "Thirty-nine books. Jews revere the first five. Genesis, Exodus, Leviticus, Numbers, and Deuteronomy. They tell the tale of the ancient people of Israel from the creation of the world, through the Great Flood, the Exodus from Egypt, the wanderings in the desert, to the giving of the Law to Moses at Sinai. Quite an epic."

He knew that to Jews those writings meant a great deal. As did the next division, prophets—Joshua, Judges, Samuel, and Kings—which recounted the story of the Israelites from their crossing the River Jordan, to the conquest of Canaan, the rise and fall of their many kingdoms, and their defeat at the hands of the Assyrians and Babylonians.

"These books," he said to Gary, "supposedly tell us how history unfolded for the people of Israel thousands of years before Christ. They were a people whose destiny was tied directly to God and the promises He made."

"But that was a long time ago?"

He nodded. "Four thousand years in the past. Yet Arabs

and Jews have warred with one another ever since trying to prove them true."

He slowly paged through to Genesis and found the passage he'd come to study. *"The Lord said to Abram, lift up now your eyes and look from the place where you are northward and southward and eastward and westward, for all the land which you see, to you I will give it, and to your seed forever."* He paused. "Those words have cost millions their lives."

He silently read again the six most important words.

"What is it?" Gary asked.

He stared at the boy. How many times had Cai asked him the same thing? His son not only had practiced their faith, but had learned Latin and read the Bible, too. He'd been a good man. But another victim of senseless violence.

"The truth is important," he said, more to himself than Gary.

From the place where you are.

"Have you heard from Dad?" Gary asked.

He gazed at the boy and shook his head. "Not a word. He's off looking for something quite like what surrounds us. A library. One that may hold the key to understanding these biblical words."

A commotion below caught his attention. The library's door opened, and voices could be heard. One he recognized—Alfred Hermann.

He motioned, and they retreated to where the upper shelves were broken by a window alcove. The downstairs was dimly lit by an odd assortment of lamps, the upper balcony by recessed ceiling fixtures. He signaled for Gary to be silent. The boy nodded.

He listened.

The other man was speaking English.

An American.

"This is important, Alfred. Actually, it's beyond important. It's vital."

"I'm aware of your situation," Hermann said. "But it's no more vital than ours."

"Malone is on his way to the Sinai. You said that would be okay."

"And it will. Can I pour you some cognac?"

"You trying to calm me down?"

"I'm *trying* to pour you some cognac."

He motioned for Gary to stay put while he crept from the alcove, risking a quick glance beyond the ornate iron railing. Alfred Hermann stood below, pouring from a decanter. Standing beside him was a younger man, maybe early fifties, dressed in a dark suit. His head was crowned by a thick fleece of blond hair. The face was clean-shaven, energetic, cherubic—perfect for a portrait painter or an actor.

Which wasn't far from the mark.

Thorvaldsen knew this man.

The vice president of the United States.

61

CAMP DAVID, MARYLAND

STEPHANIE REGISTERED THE PRESIDENT'S WORDS. "WHAT DO you mean *your* traitor?"

Daniels threw her a troubled look. "Someone in this gov-

ernment is messing with me. They're advancing their own
policies, furthering their own goals, thinking I'm either too
lazy, too pathetic, or too dumb to know. Now, it doesn't take
a genius to figure out the ringleader. My so-called loyal vice
president. He's an ambitious sucker."

"Mr. President—" she said.

"Now, that's a first, too. *Mr. President.* Maybe we're
making some progress in our relationship."

"I've had my reservations about you and this administration."

"That's the problem with career bureaucrats. Us politi
cians come and go. But you people stay, and stay, and stay.
Which means you have lots to compare with. Unfortunately
for me, Stephanie, you're turning out to be right on this one.
I'm surrounded by traitors. My vice president wants this job
so bad he can't stand it. And to get it, he's willing to make a
deal with the devil." Daniels paused, and she did not interrupt his thoughts. "The Order of the Golden Fleece."

Had she heard right?

"He's there. Right now. Meeting with its head. A man
named Alfred Hermann."

She had seriously underestimated Danny Daniels. Just as
she had Brent Green. Both men were quite informed. Cassiopeia rocked in her chair, but Stephanie could see she was
listening closely. She'd told Cassiopeia about the Order.

"My father was a member," Cassiopeia said.

That had not been mentioned earlier when they'd talked.

"For many years he and Henrik attended together. I chose
not to continue the membership after his death."

"Good move," Daniels said. "That group has been linked
to a number of global instabilities. And they're good. No fingerprints anywhere. Of course, the key players usually end
up dead. Like any good gang, they have an enforcement arm.
A man called the Talons of the Eagle. Typical Europeans. A

hired gun with a grand title. They're the ones who took Malone's boy."

"And you're just now telling us?"

"Yes, Stephanie, I am. One of the prerogatives of being the head of the free world is I can pretty much do what I damn well please." He threw her a dissecting glance. "There's a lot going on here. Happening fast. From several angles. I've done the best I can under the circumstances."

She drew him back to the point. "What's the vice president doing with the Blue Chair?"

"Blue Chair? Good to see you're informed, too. I was hoping you were. The VP is selling his soul. That Order is after, of all things, the Library of Alexandria. They're looking for proof of a theory, and though I thought the whole thing bizarre, apparently there's more to it."

"What do the Israelis say?" Cassiopeia asked.

"They don't want anything found. Period. Leave it alone. Seems the Order has been squeezing the Saudi royal house for decades and now they've decided to just swirl everything up. Get the Jews and Arabs all riled. Not a bad play, actually. We've been known to do the same thing. But this will escalate. Fanatics are impossible to predict, whether they be Arab, Israeli—" He paused. "—or American."

"What do you want me to do?" Stephanie asked.

"Let me tell you something else you don't know. Cotton made a second call back to Green. He needed a favor. So Green approved a military airlift for Malone, his ex-wife, and a third man to, if you can believe it, the Sinai. They're in transit now. Our guess is that this third man is the Order's hired gun. Malone also requested an ID check from Green— which, by the way, the attorney general ignored. No inquiries at all. So *we* checked. The name Cotton gave was James Mc-Collum. The description doesn't match, but there was a guy by that name who's ex-army, special forces, now a freelance mercenary. Seems to have the right résumé to work for the Order, wouldn't you say?"

"How did he get connected with Malone?" Cassiopeia said.

Daniels shook his head. "Don't know, but I'm glad Cotton's the one with him. Unfortunately, there's nothing we can do to help."

"We could radio that transport," Cassiopeia said.

The president shook his head. "No way. We can't let anyone know we're in the loop. I want *my* traitors. And to get them we have to remain silent."

"And the finalists are," she said, "Larry Daley and Brent Green."

Daniels cocked his head. "The winner of that contest gets an all-expense-paid trip straight to federal prison. After I personally kick his ass."

His habit of command seemed to return.

"You two are all I have to find out the answer to the question of the day. I can't involve any other agency for obvious reasons. I allowed all this to stay in motion so you'd have an opportunity. Stephanie, I knew you were on to Daley, but thankfully you didn't act on him. Now *we* need to find the truth."

"You actually think the attorney general is involved?" Cassiopeia asked.

"I have no idea. Brent plays that holier-than-thou act to perfection, and maybe he is a God-fearing Bible-toting Christian. But he's also a man who doesn't want to leave a position of power and influence to go be 'of counsel' window dressing at some Washington law firm. That's why he stayed for the second term. Hell, everyone else jumped ship—polished up their résumés with all that juicy government experience and cashed in their contacts. Not Brent."

She felt she needed to say, "He told me that he leaked the Alexandria Link, looking for the traitor himself."

"Hell, maybe he did. I don't know. What I do know is that my deputy national security adviser has been bribing Congress. My vice president is plotting with one of the richest men in the world. And two nations in the Middle East, which normally despise each other, are currently working together to stop a fifteen-hundred-year-old library from being found. That about sum it up, Stephanie?"

"Yes, Mr. President. We get the picture."

"Then find my traitor."

"How do you suggest we do that?"

He smiled at the decisive nature of her question.

"I've given that a lot of thought. Let's have something to eat, then the two of you get some sleep. Both of you look beat. You can rest here in safety."

"This can't wait till morning," she said.

"Has to. You know what makes good grits? Not boiling. It's the simmering in the pot, with the lid on and the heat down low. That's what turns rough cornmeal into heaven. Now we're going to let this simmer for a few hours, then I'll tell you what I have in mind."

62

VIENNA

THORVALDSEN RETREATED TOWARD THE WINDOW ALCOVE BUT kept his ears trained on the conversation below. That the American vice president was here, at Hermann's château, raised a host of new possibilities. He quickly glanced at Gary and brought a finger to his lips, signaling for continued quiet.

Glasses clinked below.

"To our friendship," Hermann said.

"That's what I like about you, Alfred. Loyalty. It's in short supply these days."

"Perhaps your superior might feel the same way."

The other man chuckled. "Daniels is a fool. He has a simplistic view of life and the world."

"And would you say that you're loyal?"

"Absolutely. I've suffered through five years of Danny Daniels. Did exactly what he wanted. Smiled. Defended him. Took some heat for him. But I can't take it anymore. Americans can't take it anymore."

"I hope that time wasn't wasted."

"I've spent the years building coalitions. Making friends. Appeasing enemies. I have everything I need—"

"Except money."

"I wouldn't say that. I have ample commitments to get things rolling. My Arab friends are being quite generous."

"The Order, too, is appreciative of those who show it support. Your president has not been friendly to world business. He seems to like tariffs, trade restrictions, open banking."

"Which is a whole other problem. I assure you, there are many in Washington who feel differently from Daniels."

Sounds from below indicated that the two men were sitting down. Thorvaldsen crept close to the railing. Hermann sat in a chair, the vice president on one of the settees. Both men held drinks.

"Israel is trying to find out what's happening," the vice president said. "They know the link is exposed."

"I've been informed," Hermann said. "I have an associate, as we speak, dealing with that."

"My chief of staff told me that an Israeli surveillance team is missing in Germany and one of their Foreign Office officials was found dead in Rothenburg, suspected of selling information. An assassination squad has been sent to London. Strangely, Tel Aviv actually wanted us to know that."

"Again, my friend, I'm aware."

"Then you surely know that one of our former agents, Cotton Malone, is on his way to the Sinai with, of all people, his ex-wife and another man."

Silence came in response.

"We were curious," the vice president said. "So the other man's fingerprints were obtained from a railing he touched while boarding the military plane in Lisbon. He's an American. James McCollum. You know him?"

"His alias is Dominick Sabre. He works for us."

"And because you're my friend, Alfred, I'm going to respectfully say that you're full of shit. I saw it in your eyes. You didn't know your man was headed to the Sinai."

Another pause.

"He's not required to keep me informed. Results are all that matter."

"So tell me. What's he doing with Cotton Malone, and is he going to find that library?"

"You said the Sinai. They're certainly in a location for that to be possible. Near enough to Alexandria to make transport of the manuscripts in ancient times possible, but also isolated. Trade routes existed there before and after the time of Christ. Pharaohs mined the land for copper and turquoise. Egypt knew the Sinai well."

"You know your history."

"Knowledge is a good thing. Especially here."

"Alfred, this is not some intellectual exercise, I'm trying to fundamentally change American foreign policy. Daniels and I have fought over this. Now I can do something about it. It's time we show the Arabs the same consideration we've always given Israel. And like you with the hired help, I, too, am only interested in results. You and your cohorts want to profit. I want to be in charge."

"And we want you to have the job."

"Then tell me, Alfred. When does the president of the United States die?"

Spindly fingers tickled Thorvaldsen's crooked spine as the vice president's words sank in.

"You seem to be warming to the idea," Hermann said.

"You've convinced me."

"And it's arranged," Hermann said. "Daniels's unannounced trip to Kabul will come to a spectacular end."

"Once he's in the air," the vice president said, "I'll have everything confirmed through the means we discussed. As of now, he leaves next Thursday. Only four people know. Him, me, and our chiefs of staff. Even the Afghan president doesn't know he's coming. He'll be told right before they land. The whole thing is a PR stunt by the White House communications people. Prop up the poll numbers with a rousing trip to the troops."

"The missiles are already there," Hermann said. "The deal was made with one of bin Laden's main deputies. He was most appreciative. This will be their first significant strike at America in several years. We've dealt with these devils before, always at arm's length and with caution, but successfully."

"I still have my concerns. Arabs killing Daniels. But my friends in Arabia tell me most of them are sick of bin Laden, too. They'd love to take him out. His antics make changing world opinion infinitely more difficult. They just can't link up with us so long as it's 'Israel's way or no way.' But with Daniels gone and a change in policy made clear, they'll join with us in getting bin Laden."

"My Political Committee thinks the Arabs will be more than negotiable."

"They know about this?" the vice president asked, surprise in his voice.

"Of course not. They simply explore scenarios—with a change in American foreign policy being one. We've long wanted that to happen."

"Now, Alfred, you know what's on my mind?"

Hermann chuckled. "There's no trail. The emissaries used to negotiate the deal with bin Laden will be sent to Allah next week. That associate you mentioned will handle the matter personally. Nothing will link anybody."

"Lot of trust you place in that man," the vice president said.

"He's never disappointed us."

"It's imperative he doesn't start now. I'll be in Chicago the day Daniels leaves. The White House announces nothing. It's like the president is in Washington, working, and the next thing you know he's on the news in Afghanistan. Then they hide me until he gets back. Standard post-9/11 procedure."

"What will you do after the plane is brought down?" Hermann asked.

"Take the oath and govern for the next three years. Then I'll run, get four more, and walk away."

"I want you to understand that if we are successful in locating the lost library, then what *we* have planned will immediately start."

"Damn right. Sooner the better. I need Israel and the Arabs kept off base. I'll stroke them—you'll smack them. The Saudis will have to deal. They can't afford for their country to implode. And I want oil prices down just as badly as you do. A few dollars a barrel changes our GNP by billions. I'll be mobilizing America to retaliate for Daniels's death. No one will fight me on that one. The whole world will join us. The Arabs will be dangling, begging for friends. That's when they'll climb aboard and we all win."

"My Political Committee believes there could be widespread destabilization."

"Who cares? My poll numbers will be through the roof. Nothing energizes Americans more than a rally around the flag. And I plan to lead one for the next seven years. Arabs are dealers. They'll see that the time for cooperation has come, especially if it hurts Israel."

"You seem to have thought this through."

"I've thought of little else the past few months. I've tried to get Daniels to shift, but he won't bend when it comes to Israel. That damn nation the size of some American counties will be the ruin of all of us. And I don't plan to let that happen."

"The next time we meet," Hermann said, "you'll be president of the United States."

"Alfred, besides the terrorists who'll actually do it, you

and I are the only two people on this planet that know what's coming. I made sure of that."

"As have I."

"So let's make it happen and both enjoy the reward."

63

HERMANN TRIED TO GAUGE THE MAN SITTING ACROSS FROM him. He was indeed the vice president of the United States, but he was no different from the myriad of other politicos he'd bought and sold from around the world, men and women eager for power and lacking in conscience. The Americans liked to portray themselves as above that type of reproach, but ambition was irresistible to anyone who'd tasted its potential. The man here, in his library, on the night of the winter Assembly, was no exception. He talked of lofty political goals and shifts in foreign policy, but he'd been willing from the start to betray his country, his president, and himself.

Thank heaven.

The Order of the Golden Fleece thrived off the moral deficiencies of others.

"Alfred," the vice president was saying. "Level with me. Is it really possible there's evidence Israel has no biblical claim to the Holy Land?"

"Of course. The Old Testament was a major source of study at the Library of Alexandria. The emerging New Testament, toward the end of the library's existence, also was analyzed in detail. We know that from surviving manuscripts. It's reasonable to assume that both texts and analyses of the Bible, in its original Old Hebrew, still exist."

He recalled what Sabre had reported from Rothenburg. Three others had been killed by Israel. Each visited by a Guardian. Each involved in Old Testament study. Haddad himself had received an invitation. Why else had he been extended such an honor? And why had Israel moved to kill the Palestinian?

There had to be a link.

"I was in England recently," the vice president said, "and was shown the Sinai Bible. They told me it was from the fourth century, one of the earliest Old Testaments still around. Written in Greek."

"There's a perfect example," he said. "Do you know the story?"

"Bits and pieces."

Hermann told his guest about a German scholar, Tischendorf, who in 1844 was touring the East in search of old manuscripts. He visited the monastery of St. Catherine, in the Sinai, and noticed a basket filled with forty-three old pages written in ancient Greek. The monks told him they were to be burned for fuel, as others had been. Tischendorf determined that the pages were from the Bible, and the monks allowed him to keep them. Fifteen years later he returned to St. Catherine's on behalf of the Russian tsar. He was shown the remainder of the biblical pages and managed to return them to Russia. Eventually, after the revolution, the communists sold the manuscript to the British, who display it to this day.

"The Sinai Bible," Hermann said, "is one of the earliest surviving manuscripts. Some have speculated Constantine himself commissioned its preparation. But remember, it's written in Greek, so it was translated from Hebrew by someone utterly unknown to us, from an original manuscript that is equally unknown. So what does it really tell us?"

"That the monks at St. Catherine's are still ticked off, more than a hundred years later, that their Bible was never returned. For decades they've petitioned the United States to intervene with the British. That's why I went to see the thing. I wanted to know what all the fuss was about."

"I applaud Tischendorf for taking it. Those monks would have either burned it or just let it decay. Unfortunately much of our knowledge has met a similar fate. We can only hope that the Guardians have been more careful."

"You really believe this stuff, don't you?"

He debated whether he should say more. Things were progressing rapidly, and this man, who would soon be president, needed to understand the situation.

He stood.

"Let me show you something."

THORVALDSEN BECAME INSTANTLY CONCERNED AS ALFRED Hermann rose from his chair and tabled his drink. He risked another peek below and saw the Austrian leading the vice president across the hardwood floor toward the spiral staircase. He quickly surveyed the upper catwalk and saw that there was no other way down. More window alcoves broke the shelves on the remaining three walls, but there'd be no way he and Gary could seek refuge within any of them.

They'd be spotted in an instant.

Hermann and the vice president bypassed the stairway, however, and stopped before a glass case.

HERMANN MOTIONED AT THE LIGHTED CASE. INSIDE RESTED AN ancient codex, its wooden cover pitted, as if attacked by insects.

"It's a fourth-century manuscript, too. A treatise on early church teachings, written by Augustine himself. My father bought it decades ago. It carries no historical significance—copies of it exist—but it looks impressive."

He reached beneath the podium and depressed a button disguised as one of the stainless-steel screws. From an axis at one corner, he swung the top third of the case away from the remainder. Inside the bottom two-thirds rested nine sheets of brittle papyrus.

"These, on the other hand, are quite precious. My father also bought them, decades ago, from the same person who sold him the codex. Some were written by Eusebius Hieronymus Sophronius, who lived in the fourth and fifth centuries. A great church father. He translated the Bible from Hebrew into Latin, creating a work known as the Vulgate that ultimately became definitive. History calls him by another name. Jerome."

"You're a strange man, Alfred. The oddest things excite you. How could those wrinkly old sheets have any bearing today?"

"I assure you, these have great relevance. Enough to perhaps change our thinking. Some of these were also written by Augustine. These are letters between Jerome and Augustine." He saw that the American still was not impressed.

"They had mail in those days?"

"A crude form. Travelers heading in the right direction would take messages back and forth. Some of our best records from that time are correspondence."

"Now, that is interesting."

Hermann came to the point. "Have you ever wondered how the Bible came to be?"

"Not particularly."

"What if it was all a lie?"

"It's a matter of faith, Alfred. What does it matter?"

"It matters a great deal. What if the early church fathers—men like Jerome and Augustine who shaped the course of religious thinking—decided to change things? Remember their time. Four hundred years *after* Christ, long *after* Constantine sanctioned the new Christian religion, at a time when the church was emerging and eliminating philosophies contrary to its teachings. The New Testament was just then coming into being. Various Gospels assimilated and arranged into a unified message. Mainly that God was gentle and forgiving, and that Christ had come. But then there was the Old Testament. What the Jews used. Christians wanted it to be part of their religion, too. Luckily for those early church fathers, Old Testament texts were few, and all were written in Old Hebrew."

"But you said this Jerome translated the Bible into Latin."

"Exactly my point." He reached into the case and lifted out one of the tanned sheets. "These are written in Greek, the language of Jerome's time." Beneath the parchments lay typed pages. He lifted them out. "I had the letters translated. By three different experts to be sure of the work. I want to read you something, then I think you'll see what I'm referring to."

I am aware what ability is requisite to persuade the proud how great is the virtue of humility, which raises us, not by human arrogance, but by divine grace. Our task is to assure the human spirit is lifted and that the message is clear through the words of Christ. Your wisdom, offered when I began this task, has proven correct. This work that I labor over will form the first interpretation of the ancient Scriptures into a language that even the most uneducated could understand. For there to be a connection between the old and the new seems logical. For these Scriptures to be in conflict seems self-defeating and would only elevate the Jewish philosophy to a superior position, since it has existed much longer than our faith. Since we last communicated, I have struggled through more of the ancient text. The progress is made difficult by so many double meanings. Once more I seek your guidance on a critical point. Jerusalem is the sacred city of the old text. The word yeruwshalayim *is used often to identify the location, yet I have noticed that nowhere in the old text is* iyr yeruwshalayim *ever used, which clearly means "city of Jerusalem." Let me demonstrate the problem. From the Hebrew, in Kings, Yahweh says to Solomon, "Jerusalem, the city/capital that I have chosen in it." Further on, Yahweh states, "so that the city in Jerusalem recalling the memory of David before me—the city where I have chosen to establish my name—may be preserved." My brother, can you see the dilemma? The ancient text speaks of Jerusalem not as a city but as a territory. Always it is the "city in Jerusalem," not Jerusalem itself. Samuel actually speaks of it as a region where the Hebrew says "the king and his men set out for Jerusalem against the Jebusites who inhabited the region." I have struggled with the translation, hoping for some error to be discovered, but it is consistent throughout the Hebrew usage. The word* yeruwshalayim, *Jerusalem, always refers to a place comprising a number of cities, not to a single city by that name.*

Hermann stopped reading and stared up at the vice president. "Jerome wrote this to Augustine while he was translating the Old Testament from Hebrew to Latin. Let me read you what Augustine, at one point, wrote to Jerome."

He found another of the translations.

My learned brother, your work seems both arduous and glorious. How amazing it must be to reveal what scribes gone for so long have recorded and all with the divine guidance of our most glorious God. You are certainly aware of the struggles that we all endure in this most dangerous of times. The pagan gods are dying away. The message of Christ is growing. His words of peace, mercy, and love ring true. Many are discovering our new message simply because it is becoming available. Which makes your effort to bring to life the old words that much more important. Your letters clearly explained the problem you are facing. Yet the future of this church, of our God, rests with us. To adapt the message of the old with that of the new is not a sin. As you have said, the words possess many double meanings, so who is to say which is right? Certainly not you or I. You asked for guidance, so I shall give it. Make the old words true to the new. For if the old be different from the new, we surely will be at risk of confusing the faithful and fueling the fires of discontent, which our many enemies keep burning. Yours is a great task. To be able for all to read the old words will mean much. No longer will scholars and rabbis possess control over so important a text. So my brother, work hard and be well knowing that you are doing the work of the Lord.

"You're saying they intentionally changed the Old Testament?" the vice president asked.

"Of course they did. Just this reference to Jerusalem is a good example. Jerome's translation, which is still accepted as correct today, denotes Jerusalem as a city. Jerome's Kings reads, *Jerusalem, the city that I have chosen.* That's absolutely contrary to what Jerome himself wrote in the letter. *Jerusalem, the city/capital that I have chosen in it.* Huge difference, wouldn't you say? And this description of Jerusalem is used throughout Jerome's translation. The Jerusalem of the Old Testament became the city in Palestine because Jerome made it so."

"This is crazy, Alfred. Nobody's going to buy any of it."

"It's not necessary that anyone *buy it.* Once the proof is found, there will be no denying."

"Like what?"

"An Old Testament manuscript penned before Christ should be definitive. Then we can read the words without the Christian filter."

"I wish you luck."

"Tell you what. I'll leave the governing of America to you and you leave this to me."

THORVALDSEN WATCHED AS HERMANN REPLACED THE SHEETS into the display case and closed the compartment. The two men lingered for a few minutes, then left the library. The hour was late, but he wasn't sleepy.

"They're going to kill the president," Gary said nervously.

"I know. Come, we need to leave."

They descended the spiral staircase.

Lamps still burned in the library. He recalled how Hermann liked to boast that there were some twenty-five thousand books, many first editions dating back hundreds of years.

He led Gary to the case containing the codex. The boy hadn't seen what he had. He reached beneath and searched for a switch, but felt nothing. Bending down would be difficult. One of the handicaps of a crooked spine.

"What are you looking for?" Gary asked.

"There's a way to open this case. Have a look and see if there's a button underneath."

Gary dropped to his knees and searched.

"I doubt if it will be obvious." He alternated his attention from the case to the door, hoping no one came inside. "Anything?"

A click, and the case separated slightly about one-third of the way down its length.

Gary stood. "One of the screws. Pretty neat. Unless you poke it, you'd never know."

"Good job."

He revealed the hidden compartment and saw the stiff sheets of papyrus with writing from edge to edge. He counted. Nine. He stared around at the bookshelves and spied some oversized atlases. He pointed, "Bring me one of those large books."

Gary retrieved a volume. Carefully he slid the papyri and translations into the pages to both conceal and protect them.

He reclosed the case.

"What are those?" Gary asked.

"What we came for, I hope."

64

FRIDAY, OCTOBER 7
9:15 AM

MALONE LEANED BACK AGAINST THE BULKHEAD IN THE CAVernous C130H transport. Brent Green had worked fast, hitching them a ride on an air force supply flight out of England bound for Afghanistan. A stop in Lisbon at the Montijo Air Base, supposedly for a minor repair, had allowed them to board with little fanfare. A change of clothes had awaited them; Malone, Pam, and McCollum now sported army combat uniforms in varying shades of beige, green, and brown, along with desert boots and parachutes. Pam had been apprehensive about the chute, but accepted his explanation that it was standard equipment.

The flight time from Lisbon to the Sinai was eight hours and he'd managed a little sleep. He recalled with no affection other flights on other transports, and the pall of oily jet fuel that hung in the air brought back memories of when he was younger. Staying away far more than being home. Making mistakes that hurt him even now.

Pam had clearly not liked the first three hours of the flight. Understandable, given that comfort was the least of the air force's concerns. But finally she'd settled down and fallen asleep.

McCollum was another matter.

He'd seemed right at home, donning his parachute with expert precision. Perhaps he *was* ex–special forces. Malone hadn't heard from Green as to McCollum's background. But whatever was learned would soon be of little consequence. They were about to be out of touch, in the middle of nowhere.

He stared out the window.

Dusty, barren soil stretched in every direction, an irregular tableland, tilting ever upward as the Sinai Peninsula narrowed and erupted into craggy brown, gray, and red granite mountains. The Burning Bush and the theophany of Jehovah all supposedly occurred down there. The great and terrible wilderness of Exodus. Monks and hermits for centuries had chosen it as their refuge, as if being alone brought them closer to heaven. Perhaps it did. He was curiously reminded of Sartre's *Huis Clos* vision.

Hell is other people.

He turned from the window and watched McCollum leave the loadmaster and walk toward him, taking a seat on the aluminum frame that stretched across the bulkhead. Pam lay ten feet away, on the opposite side, still sleeping. Malone was eating one of the meals ready to eat—beefsteak with mushrooms—and drinking bottled water.

"You eat?" he asked McCollum.

"While you were sleeping. Chicken fajitas. Not bad. I remember MREs all too well."

"You do look at home."

"Been here, done this."

They'd both removed their earplugs, which provided only minor insulation from the constant drone of the engines. The aircraft was loaded with pallets of vehicle parts destined for Afghanistan. Malone imagined that there were many similar flights each week. Where once supply routes depended on horses, wagons, and trucks, now the sky and sea offered the fastest and safest routes.

"You look like you've been here, too," McCollum said.

"Does bring back some things."

He was watching his words. Didn't matter that McCollum had helped get them out of Belém in one piece. He remained an unknown. And he killed with expert precision and no remorse. His redeeming quality? He held the hero's quest.

"You've got some pretty good connections," McCollum said. "The attorney general himself arranged this?"

"I do have friends."

"You're either CIA, military intelligence, or something along that line."

"None of the above. I'm actually retired."

McCollum chuckled. "You keep that story. I like it. Retired. Right. You're up to your eyeballs in something."

He finished the meal and noticed the loadmaster eyeing him. He recalled that they could get touchy as to how MREs were trashed. The man motioned and Malone understood. The container at the far end of the bench.

The loadmaster then flashed his open palm four times.

Twenty minutes.

He nodded.

65

VIENNA
8:30 AM

THORVALDSEN SAT INSIDE THE *SCHMETTERLINGHAUS* AND opened the atlas. He and Gary had awoken an hour ago, showered, and eaten a light breakfast. He'd come to the butterfly house not only to avoid the electronic listening devices, but to await the inevitable as well. Only a matter of time before Hermann discovered the theft.

Morning was free time for the members, as the next gathering of the Assembly was not scheduled until late afternoon. He'd kept the parchments inside the atlas beneath his bed all night. Now he was anxious to learn more. Though he could read Latin, his Greek was minimal, and his knowledge of Old Greek, which surely would be the language of

Jerome and Augustine, was nonexistent. He was thankful that Hermann had commissioned the translations.

Gary sat across from him in another chair. "You said last night these may be what we came for."

He decided the boy deserved the truth. "You were kidnapped so as to force your father to find something he hid away years ago. I think that and these papers are linked."

"What are they?"

"Letters between two learned men. Augustine and Jerome. They lived in the fourth and fifth centuries and helped formulate the Christian religion."

"History. I'm starting to like it and all, but there's so much to it."

Henrik smiled. "And the problem today is we have so few documents from that time. Wars, politics, time, and abuse have devastated the record. But here are writings straight from the minds of two learned men."

He knew something about both. Augustine was born in Africa to a Christian mother and a pagan father. Eventually, as an adult, he converted to Christianity and recorded his youthful excesses in *The Confessions,* a book Thorvaldsen knew was still required reading at most universities. He became the bishop of Hippo, an intellectual leader of African Catholicism, and a powerful advocate for orthodoxy; he was credited with formulating much of the church's early thinking.

Jerome, too, was born to a pagan family and misspent his youth. He was also learned and came to be regarded as the most intellectual of all the church fathers. He lived as a hermit and devoted thirty years of his life to translating the Bible. Ever since, he'd been associated with libraries, so much so that he became their patron saint.

From the little that Thorvaldsen had overheard last night, these two men, who lived in differing parts of the ancient world, apparently communicated with each other during a time when Jerome was fashioning his lifework. Hermann had made his point to the vice president about biblical manipulation, but he needed to understand the situation fully. So he found the translation pages and started perusing them, reading the English passages out loud.

My learned brother Augustine, there was a time when I believed the Septuagint to be a wondrous work. I read that text in the library at Alexandria. To hear the thoughts of those scribes, as they recounted the troubles of the Israelites, brought to life the faith that had long filled my soul. But this joy has now been replaced with confusion. In my work to convert the old text it is clear that great liberties were taken in the Septuagint. Passage after passage is not correct. Jerusalem is not a single place, but a region that contains many places. That most sacred of rivers the Jordan is not a river, but a mountain escarpment. As to the names of places, most are wrong. The Greek translation does not conform to the Hebrew. It is as if the entire message was altered, not through ignorance, but by design.

Jerome, my friend, yours is a difficult task, made even more so by our great mission. What you have discovered has not gone unnoticed. I, too, have spent a great deal of time in the library at Alexandria. Many of us have perused the manuscripts. I read an account from Herodotus, who visited Palestine in the fifth century before our Lord. He found the area under Persian rule inhabited by Syrians. He noticed no Israelite or Jewish presence. No Jerusalem or Judah. I found that remarkable considering the old text mentions that was the time when the Jewish Temple was being rebuilt in Jerusalem and Judah enjoyed the status of a great province. If these had existed, the learned Greek

would have noticed, as he carries the reputation of an ar-
dent observer. I found that the first known identification of
ancient Israel with what we call Palestine comes from the
Roman, Strabo. His Histories *is a thorough account, and I*
was privileged to read it in the library. Strabo's work was
completed twenty-three years after our Lord was born, so
he wrote at a time when Christ actually lived. He notes
that the name Judea *was first applied to Palestine during*
Greek rule, the Greek word for a Jewish country being
Ioudaia. *That was only a century before the birth of our*
Lord. So sometime between the visits of Herodotus and
Strabo, some four hundred years apart, the Jews of Pales-
tine established a presence. Strabo himself wrote of a
large body of Israelites who fled from a land to the south
and settled in Palestine. He was not clear as to which
land, but he reasoned that, given the proximity of Egypt
and its easy access, the Exodus must have occurred from
there to Palestine. But nothing proves that conclusion.
Strabo noted that the source of his tale was the Jews of
Alexandria, among whom he spent much time. He was flu-
ent in Hebrew and noted in his Histories *that he, too,*
found errors in the Septuagint. He wrote that the scholars
at the library of Alexandria, who translated the old text
into Greek, simply connected the old text to what they
learned from the Jews at that time. Strabo wrote that the
Jews of Alexandria had forgotten their past and seemed
comfortable creating one.

My learned brother Augustine, I have read the writings of
Flavius Josephus, a Jew who wrote with great authority.
He lived a century after our Lord was born. He clearly
identifies Palestine with the land in the old text, noting
that the region is the only place he knew where a Jewish
political entity existed. Of a more recent time, Eusebius of

Caesarea, on behalf of our most exalted emperor Constantine, has designated names from the old text to sites in Palestine. I have read his work On the Names of Places in Holy Scripture. *But after studying a copy of the old text in Hebrew, it is clear that Eusebius's work is flawed. He seems to have loosely applied meanings to place-names and in some cases simply guessed, yet this work carries a great importance. Pious and credulous pilgrims use it as their guide.*

Jerome, my friend, we must execute this task with great diligence. Our religion is but forming, and there are threats from all sides. What you are attempting is critical to our existence. To have the old text translated into Latin will allow those words to be read by many. I urge you not to alter what those who created the Septuagint started. Our Lord Christ lived in Palestine. For the message we are formulating with the newer testament, we must present one voice. I recognize what you have said: that the old text seems not a record of the Israelites in what we call Palestine. Why should that matter? Our goal is much different from that of those who created the Septuagint. Our newer testament must be a fulfillment of the old. Only in this way will the meaning of our message be elevated to a status greater than the old. To link the old with the new will demonstrate how vital our Lord Christ was and how important His message is. The errors that you note in the Septuagint need not be corrected. As you have written, the Jews who aided those translators had forgotten their past. They knew nothing of their existence from long ago, only what was happening around them at the time. So in your translations, the Palestine that we know should remain the Palestine of both testaments. This is our task, dear brother,

*our mission. The future of our religion, of our Lord Christ,
is with us and He inspires us to do His will.*

Thorvaldsen stopped reading.

Here were two church fathers, perhaps the most brilliant
of all, laboring with how to manipulate the translation of the
Old Testament into Latin. Jerome was clearly privy to a manuscript written in the original Hebrew and had noted errors
in its previous translation into Greek. Augustine knew of
Herodotus and Strabo—the former recognized as the father
of history, the latter of geography. One a Greek, the other
Roman. Men who lived centuries apart and fundamentally
changed the world. Strabo's *Geography* still existed and was
regarded as one of the most precious of ancient texts, reveal-
ing much about that world and its time, but his *Histories* was
gone.

No copy existed.

Yet Augustine had read it.

In the Library of Alexandria.

"What does all that mean?" Gary asked.

"A great deal."

If the early church had falsified the translation of the Old
Testament, adapting its words to fit its purposes, that could
have catastrophic implications.

Hermann was right. The Christians would certainly join
the fight.

His mind raced with what the Blue Chair was planning.
He knew from conversations they'd had through the years
that Hermann was not a believer. He regarded religion as a
political tool and faith as a crutch for the weak. He'd take
great pleasure in watching the three major religions struggle
with the implications that the Old Testament they'd always
known was in fact something altogether different.

The pages Thorvaldsen held were precious. They formed

part of Hermann's proof. But the Blue Chair would need more. Which was why the Library of Alexandria was so important. If it still existed, it might be the only repository that could shed light on the issue. That was Malone's problem, however, given that he was apparently now on his way to the Sinai.

He wished his friend well.

Then there was the president of the United States. His death was planned for next Thursday.

That was Thorvaldsen's problem.

He fished his cell phone from a pocket and dialed.

66

SINAI PENINSULA

MALONE ROUSED PAM. SHE SAT UP FROM THE NYLON SEAT AND removed the earplugs.

"We're here," he said.

She shook sleep from her brain and perked up. "We're landing?"

"We're here," he said again over the engine roar.

"How long have I been out?"

"A few hours."

She stood from the bench, her parachute still strapped to her back. The C130 bumped and ground its way through the morning air. "How long till we land?"

"We're getting out of here shortly. Did you eat?"

She shook her head. "No way. My stomach was in my throat. But it's finally calmed down."

"Drink some water." He motioned at the holder.

She opened the bottle and gulped a few swallows. "This thing is like riding in a boxcar."

He smiled. "Good way of putting it."

"You used to fly on these?"

"All the time."

"Your job was tough."

That was the first time he'd ever heard a concession about his former profession. "I asked for it."

"I'm only beginning to understand. I'm still freaked out about that bugged watch. Stupid me actually thought the man liked me."

"Maybe he did."

"Right. He used me, Cotton."

The admission seemed to hurt. "Using people is part of this business." He paused, then added, "Not a part I ever liked."

She drank more water. "I used you, Cotton."

She was right. She had.

"I should have told you about Gary. But I didn't. So who am I to judge anybody?"

Now was not the time to have this discussion. But he saw that she was bothered by all that had happened. "Don't sweat it. Let's finish this. Then we'll talk about it."

"I'm not sweating it. Just wanted you to know how I felt."

That was a first, too.

At the rear of the plane, an annoying whining accompanied the rear ramp opening. A gust of air rushed into the cargo area.

"What's happening?" she asked.

"They have some chores. Remember, we're just along for

the ride. Walk back that way and stop where the loadmaster is standing."

"Why?"

"Because they asked us to. I'm coming with you."

"How's our friend?" she asked.

"Nosy. We both need to keep an eye on him."

He watched as she headed aft. He then crossed to the opposite bulkhead and said to McCollum, "Time to go."

He'd noticed McCollum had watched their talk.

"She know?"

"Not yet."

"A bit cruel, wouldn't you say?"

"Not if you knew her."

McCollum shook his head. "Remind me not to get on your bad side."

"Actually, that's real good advice."

He saw that his message had struck home. "Sure thing, Malone. I'm just the guy who saved your hide."

"Which is why you're here."

"So generous of you, considering I have the quest."

He gathered up the rigger sack in which he'd stuffed what George Haddad had left for him and the book on St. Jerome. They'd retrieved them from the airport before leaving Lisbon. He clipped the bundle to his chest. "And here's what I've got. So we're even."

McCollum clipped a pack to his chest, too. Supplies they might need. Water, rations, GPS locator. According to the map, a village lay about three miles from where they were headed. If nothing was found they could walk there and find a way twenty miles south to where there was an airport, near Moses Mountain and the St. Catherine's monastery, both popular tourist attractions.

They donned goggles and helmets, then walked aft.

"What are they doing?" Pam asked as he came close.

He had to admit, she looked good in fatigues. "They have a parachute operation to perform."

"With this cargo? They dropping it out somewhere?"

The plane's airspeed slowed to 120 knots, if he remembered correctly, and the nose tipped upward.

He slid a Kevlar helmet onto Pam's head and quickly snapped the neck strap.

"What are you doing?" Confusion flooded her voice.

He adjusted a pair of goggles over her eyes and said, "The rear ramp is down. We all have to do this. Safety precaution."

He checked her harnesses and made sure all four straps were buckled into the quick-release clamp. He'd already made sure his were fine. He hooked both him and Pam to the static line.

He saw that McCollum was already connected.

"How can we land with that ramp open," she yelled.

He faced her. "We're not."

He saw the instant of comprehension. "You can't be serious. You don't expect me to—"

"It'll open automatically. Just hang on and enjoy the ride. This chute is a slow one. Designed for first-timers. When you hit the ground it'll be like a three- or four-foot fall."

"Cotton, you're frickin' insane. My shoulder still hurts. There's no way—"

The loadmaster signaled that they'd arrived near the GPS coordinates he'd provided. No time to argue. He simply lifted her from behind and shoved her forward.

She tried to wrestle free. "Cotton, please. I can't. Please."

He tossed her off the ramp.

Her scream faded fast.

He knew what she was experiencing. The first fifteen feet were pure free fall, like being weightless, as the static line played itself out. Her heart would feel like it was pounding at the back of her throat. Actually, quite a rush. Then she'd feel a tug as the static line released the parachute from the pack, and he watched as Pam's streamed out into the morning sky.

Her body jerked as the chute grabbed air.

Less than five seconds and she was floating to the ground.

"She's going to be pissed," McCollum said in his ear.

He kept his eyes on her descent.

"Yeah. But I always wanted to do that."

67

SABRE HELD ON TO THE RISERS AND ENJOYED THE DRIFT toward the ground. The morning air and the newfangled parachute were making for a slow descent. Malone had told him about the canopies, far different from the ones he recalled from back when you fell like a stone and hoped you didn't break a leg.

He and Malone had followed Pam out of the transport, which had quickly disappeared into the eastern sky. Whether they made it to ground safely was not the crew's concern. Their job was done.

He stared down at the unsparing environment.

A vast, flat plain of sand and stone stretched in all directions. He'd heard Alfred Hermann speak of the southern Sinai. Supposedly the holiest desert on the planet. A harbinger of civilization. The link between Africa and Asia. But battle-scarred. The most besieged territory in the world. Syrians, Hittites, Assyrians, Persians, Greeks, Romans, Crusaders, Turks, the French, the English, Egyptians, and the Israelis had all invaded. He'd listened many times as Hermann rambled on about the region's importance. Now he was about to experience it firsthand.

He was maybe a thousand feet from the ground. Pam Malone floated below him, Malone above. The quiet rang in his ears—a stark contrast with the plane's unabated noise. He remembered the silence from other times he'd jumped. Engine roar fading to a deep nothing. Only the wind could disturb the tranquility, but none stirred today.

A quarter mile east the barren landscape gave way to bleak granite mounds, each with no character, just a heedless jumble of peaks and crags. Was the Library of Alexandria out there? Certainly all signs pointed to that being the case.

He continued to float downward.

Near the base of one of the jagged mounds, maybe a quarter mile away, he spotted the squat of a building. He adjusted the steering lines, angling his trajectory closer to where Pam Malone was about to land. A clear stretch of desert floor. No boulders. Good.

He glanced up and saw Malone follow his lead.

That one might prove more difficult to kill than he'd first thought. But at least he was armed. He'd kept the gun from the monastery, as had Malone, along with spare magazines. When he'd awoken in the church, after being knocked unconscious, his gun was still there. Which he'd found curious.

What had been the point of that attack?

Who cared?

At least he was ready.

MALONE YANKED THE LINES AND DIRECTED HIS DESCENT. THE jumpmaster at the air base in Lisbon had told him that the new chutes were different, and he was right. Slow, smooth ride. They hadn't been wild about Pam—a novice who wasn't even going to know she was jumping until it was too late—but since the command to cooperate had come straight from the Pentagon, no one argued.

"Damn you, Cotton," he heard Pam scream. "Damn you to hell."

He glanced below.

She was five hundred feet from the ground.

"Just let your legs buckle when you hit," he called out. "You're doing fine. The chute will do the work."

"Screw you," she yelled back.

"We used to do that. Didn't work out. Get ready."

He watched as she hit and skidded into the earth, the chute collapsing behind her. He saw McCollum release his rigger sack, which unraveled before him, then find the ground, staying on his feet.

Malone tightened his steering lines and slowed his descent to nearly a stall. He released his rigger sack and felt his boots scrape the sand.

He, too, finished standing up.

Been awhile since he'd last jumped, but he was glad to know that he could still do it. He released his harness and wiggled free of the straps.

McCollum was doing the same.

Pam still lay on the ground. He walked over, knowing what was coming.

She sprang to her feet. "You sorry son of a bitch. You threw me out of that damn plane." She was trying to lunge for him but she hadn't released her harness, the billowing chute acting like an anchor, restricting her movements.

He stayed just out of reach.

"Are you out of your mind?" she yelled. "You never said a frickin' word about jumping out of a plane."

"How did you think we were going to get here?" he calmly asked.

"Ever heard of landing?"

"This is Egyptian territory. Bad enough we had to jump in daylight. But even I thought a night jump cruel."

Rage filled her blue eyes, an intensity he'd actually never seen before.

"We had to get here so the Israelis didn't know. Landing would have been impossible. I'm hoping they're still following that watch of yours, which leads nowhere."

"You're a moron, Cotton. An absolute frickin' moron. You threw me out of that plane."

"I did, didn't I."

She started to fumble with her harness, trying to release her body from the chute's hold.

"Pam, are you going to calm down?"

She continued to search for the release clamp, then stopped.

"We had to get here," he said. "That transport was perfect. We just jumped out along the way; nobody's the wiser. This is pretty barren territory, less than three people per square mile. It's doubtful we were seen. Like I said before. You always wanted to know what I did. Okay. Here it is."

"You should have left me in Portugal."

"Not a good idea. The Israelis might consider you a loose end. You're better off disappearing with us."

"No. You don't trust me. So I'm better off here where you can watch me."

"That thought did occur to me, too."

She was silent for a moment, as if comprehension was dawning. "All right, Cotton," she said in a surprisingly calm tone. "You've made your point. We're here. In one piece. Now could you get me out of this thing?"

He stepped close and unsnapped the harness.

She raised her arms and allowed the pack to hit the ground. Then she popped her right knee into his crotch.

Electrifying pain soared through his spine and found his brain. His legs trembled and he crumpled to the ground.

The breath left him.

Been awhile since he'd been racked.

He folded himself into the fetal position and waited for the misery to subside.

"Hope that was good for you, too," she said, walking away.

68

VIENNA
9:28 AM

HERMANN ENTERED HIS LIBRARY AND SHUT THE DOOR. HE hadn't slept well, but there was little he could do until Thorvaldsen made a mistake. When that happened he'd be ready. Sabre might be gone, but Hermann still employed a cadre of men who would do precisely what he wanted. His chief of the guard, an Italian, had made it clear on more than one occasion that he'd like Sabre's position. Never had he seriously considered the request, but with the Talons of the Eagle away, he was in need of assistance, so he'd told the man to stand by.

He was going to try diplomacy first. That was always preferable. Perhaps he could reason with Thorvaldsen once the Dane saw that demonstrating to the world the Old Testament had been manipulated could be an effective political tool—if managed properly. Many times throughout history, chaos and confusion had been translated into profit. Anything that jostled the Middle East affected oil prices. Knowing that was coming would be invaluable. Controlling its extent, unimaginable. Order members stood to reap enormous profits.

And their newfound ally in the White House would benefit, too.

But to accomplish all this he needed Sabre.

What was he doing in the Sinai?

And with Cotton Malone.

Both seemed to him good signs. Sabre's plan had been to entice Malone to go after the Alexandria Link. After that, success depended on Malone. Either they would learn what they could and then eliminate Malone, or partner up and see where he led. Apparently, Sabre had chosen the latter.

For several years he'd thought about what would happen once he was gone, as he knew that Margarete would be the ruin of the family. Even worse, she was oblivious to her incompetence. He'd tried to teach her, but every effort failed. Truth be known, he liked the fact that Thorvaldsen had taken her. Maybe he could be rid of the problem? But he doubted it. The Dane was not a murderer, no matter how much bravado he liked to portray.

He'd actually come to like Sabre. The man showed promise. He listened well and acted swiftly, but never haphazardly. He'd often thought Sabre might make an excellent successor. No more Hermanns were left. And he must ensure that the fortune endured.

But why had Sabre not checked in?

Was something more happening?

He flushed his doubts away and concentrated on the immediate concern. The Assembly would meet again later. He'd tantalized the members yesterday with the plan. Today he'd drive the point home.

He stepped over to a folio built into the lower portion of a bookcase. Inside, he kept the map he'd commissioned three years ago. The same scholar he'd retained to confirm Haddad's theory about the Old Testament had also mapped his findings. He'd been told how site after biblical site fit perfectly with the geography of Asir.

But he'd wanted to see for himself.

Comparing scriptural landmarks to Hebrew place-names, both in the Old Testament and on the ground, his expert had located biblical places such as Gilgal, Zidon, al-Lith, Dan, Hebron, Beersheba, and the City of David.

He removed the map.

Its image was already loaded on the computer in the meeting hall. The members would soon see what he'd long admired.

Even the question of Jerusalem's twenty-six gates, identified in Chronicles, Kings, Zechariah, and Nehemiah, had
been solved. A walled city would have had no more than four
gates, one leading in each direction. So twenty-six was questionable from the start. But the Hebrew word used throughout the Old Testament for "gate" was *shaar*. That word, like
so many, possessed a double meaning, one of which was
"passage or mountain col." Interestingly, there were twenty-
six identified openings through the mountain escarpment
that separated the identified Jerusalem territory from Judah.
He recalled his own amazement when that reality had been
explained. The King's Gate, Prison Gate, Fountain Gate, Valley Gate, and all the others so descriptively labeled in the
Old Testament could be linked with near-perfect accuracy—
through their proximity to still-existing villages—to mountain passes through the Jordan escarpment located in Asir.

Nothing even remotely close existed in Palestine.

The proof seemed incontrovertible.

The events of the Old Testament had not occurred in
Palestine. Instead they'd all happened hundreds of miles to
the south in Arabia. And Jerome and Augustine knew that,
yet deliberately allowed the errors of the Septuagint not only
to remain, but in fact to flourish, further altering the Old Testament so the passages would seem an indisputable prophecy
for the Gospels of their New Testament. The Jews were not
to enjoy a monopoly on God's Word. For their new religion
to thrive, the Christians needed a connection, too.

So they manufactured one.

Simply finding a Hebrew Bible from before the time of
Christ could prove decisive, but a copy of Strabo's *Histories*
could likewise answer many questions. If the library still existed, he could only hope that one or both would have been
preserved.

He stepped over to the glass case that he'd shown the vice

president last night. The American had been unimpressed, but who cared? America's new president would see the havoc they would wreak. Still, he hoped Thorvaldsen would be more impressed seeing them. He reached beneath and pressed the release button. He swung the case open and thought, for a moment, that his eyes were deceiving him.

Empty.

The letters and translations were gone. How? Not the vice president. Hermann had watched his motorcade leave the estate. No one else knew of the hiding place.

Only one possible explanation.

Thorvaldsen.

Anger sent him darting to his desk. He lifted the phone and called for his chief of the guard. Then he opened a desk drawer and removed his gun.

Margarete be damned.

SINAI PENINSULA

MALONE'S LEGS REMAINED WOBBLY, AND HIS CROTCH ACHED. Pam had said little since their encounter, and McCollum had wisely stayed out of the fight. But Malone couldn't complain. He'd asked for it and she'd delivered.

He stared in every direction at the desolate serenity. The sun had risen quickly, and the air was heating like an oven.

He'd retrieved the GPS unit from his pack and determined that the precise coordinates—28° 41.41N, 33° 38.44E—lay less than a mile away.

"Okay, McCollum. What now?"

The other man slipped a piece of paper from his pocket and read out loud: *"Then, like the shepherds of the painter Poussin, puzzled by the enigma, you will be flooded with the light of inspiration. Reassemble the fourteen stones, then work with square and compass to find the path. At noon, sense the presence of the red light, see the endless coil of the serpent red with anger. But heed the letters. Danger threatens one who arrives with great speed. If your course remains true, the route will be sure.*

"That's all there is to the quest," McCollum concluded.

Malone rolled the cryptic words through his mind.

Pam plopped to the ground and drank some water. "That arbor in England had a Poussin image. What was it? A tomb of some sort with writing on it? Apparently Thomas Bainbridge left a few clues, too."

He was already thinking the same thing.

"You see that building on the way down?" Malone asked McCollum. "West, maybe a quarter mile. It's where the coordinates point."

"Seems the path is clear."

He shouldered his rucksack. Pam stood. He asked her, "You done proving points?"

She shrugged. "Throw me out of another airplane and see what happens."

"You two always like this?" McCollum asked.

He started walking. "Only when we're together."

Malone approached the building he'd seen from the air. Not much to it. Low, squatty, with a tattered tile roof, its foundations crumbling as if being reclaimed by the earth.

The exterior walls stood equal in height and length, broken only by two windows, devoid of anything, about ten feet up. The front door was a decaying slab of thick cedar, hanging askew from black iron hinges.

He kicked it open.

Only a lizard greeted them as it sought refuge across the dirt floor.

"Cotton."

He turned. Pam was motioning to another outcropping. He stepped toward it, each footfall crunching the parched sand.

"Looks like the tomb in that carving at Bainbridge Hall," she said.

Good point. And he studied the four-block-high rectangle with a rounded stone top. He examined the sides for carvings, particularly the lettering *Et in arcadia ego.* Nothing there. Which wasn't surprising, because the desert would have long ago erased any vestiges.

"We're at the right coordinates and this thing does look like the same tomb from the arbor."

He recalled the hero's quest. *Then, like the shepherds of the painter Poussin, puzzled by the enigma, you will be flooded with the light of inspiration.*

He leaned against the tattered stones.

"What now, Malone?" McCollum asked.

Hillocks rose to their north, steadily climbing into barren mountains where black crags cleaved deep paths. The sky burned with a growing glow as the sun crept higher toward midday.

He rolled more of the quest over in his mind.

Reassemble the fourteen stones, then work with square and compass to find the path. At noon, sense the presence of the red light, see the endless coil of the serpent red with anger.

Everything at Belém had been fairly obvious—a mixture of history and technology, which seemed the Guardians' trademark. After all, the idea was for the invitee to succeed. This part was a challenge.

But not impossible.

He surveyed the dilapidated building and makeshift tomb.

Then he saw them and counted.

Fourteen.

SABRE WONDERED IF HE SHOULD SIMPLY KILL THEM BOTH NOW. Was he close enough to figure the rest out himself? Malone had brought him this far and, exactly as he'd hoped, tapped into his resources to get them from England to Portugal to here.

But he told himself to be patient.

He would never have deciphered the quest himself, much less this quickly. By now the Blue Chair was surely looking for him. The Assembly was in session, so he hoped that would provide a diversion until tomorrow. But he knew how much Hermann wanted to know if this trail seemed promising. He also knew what else the old man was planning and how critical his participation would be over the next week. Three emissaries had been used to negotiate with bin Laden. He'd visit all three, killing two but preserving one.

That person and the library would be his bargaining chips.

But all that assumed there was something here to find.

If not, he'd kill Malone and his ex-wife and hope he could lie his way out of trouble.

MALONE STARED AT ONE SIDE OF THE DILAPIDATED BUILDING. Ten feet up loomed one of the bare openings. He walked around to the other side and spied the other portal at a similar height.

He came back to where McCollum and Pam stood and said, "I think I've figured it out. The building's square, as are those two openings."

"Use square and compass," Pam said.

He pointed. "Those two openings are the key."

"What do you mean?" McCollum said. "Going to be kind of tough to get up there."

"Not really. Look around." Boulders and rocks littered the sand. "Notice anything about the rocks?"

Pam stepped over to one and squatted down. He watched as she caressed the sides. "Square. About a foot even all around?"

"I'd say that's right. Remember the clue. *Reassemble the fourteen stones, then work with square and compass to find the path.* There are fourteen of those things scattered about."

Pam stood. "Obviously, this quest has a physical part. Not just anyone could reassemble these stones. I assume they'll provide the boost up to the window?"

He dropped his pack.

So did McCollum, who said, "One way to find out."

Twenty minutes were needed to gather the fourteen square stones and assemble them into a flat-topped pyramid, six on the bottom, then five, capped by three. If needed, one of the three could be stacked on the remaining two for more height, but Malone estimated the pile was more than tall enough.

He stepped up and balanced himself atop.

McCollum and Pam made sure the tower remained stable.

He gazed through the square opening in the crumbling wall. Through the opposite square, twenty feet away, he spotted mountains half a mile in the distance. *At noon, sense the presence of the red light, see the endless coil of the serpent red with anger.*

The shrinking building with the battered roof had been deliberately oriented east to west.

This wasn't a dwelling. No. Like the rose window in Belém, also oriented east to west, it was a compass.

Work with square and compass to find the path.

He checked his watch.

In an hour, he'd do just that.

70

MARYLAND
7:30 AM

STEPHANIE DROVE THE SUBURBAN THAT PRESIDENT DANIELS had supplied them. He'd also provided two Secret Service revolvers and spare magazines. She wasn't quite sure what they were headed into, but apparently he wanted them prepared.

"You realize this truck is probably electronically tagged," Cassiopeia said.

"We can only hope."

"And you realize that this whole thing is nuts. We don't have any idea who to trust, including the president of the United States."

"No question. We're pawns on the chessboard. But a pawn can take the king, if properly positioned."

"Stephanie, we're bait."

She agreed, but said nothing.

They cruised into a small town about thirty miles north of Washington, one of countless bedroom communities that encircled the capital. Following the directions given to her, she recognized the name of the glass-fronted restaurant nestled beneath a canopy of leafy trees.

Aunt B's.

One of Larry Daley's favorite haunts.

She parked and they stepped inside, greeted by the pungent smell of apple-bacon and fried potatoes. A steaming buffet line was being attacked by eager diners. They bypassed the cashier and spotted Daley sitting alone.

"Get some food," he said. "On me." A plate heaped with eggs, grits, and a fried pork chop sat before him.

As agreed, Cassiopeia moved to another table where she could watch the room. Stephanie sat with Daley. "No thanks." She noticed a colorful sign near the buffet line that showed two oversized pink pigs surrounded by the slogan GET YOUR FAT BACK AT AUNT B'S. She pointed. "That why you eat here? To get your fat back."

"I like the place. Reminds me of my mother's cooking. I know you find this hard to believe, but I am a person."

"Why aren't you running the Billet? You're in charge now."

"It's being handled. We have a more pressing problem."

"Like saving your ass."

He sliced his pork chop. "These things are great. You should eat something. You need a little fat back, Stephanie."

"So nice of you to notice my trim figure. Where's your girlfriend?"

"I have no idea. I assume she was sleeping with me to see what she could learn. Which was nothing. I was doing the same thing. Again contrary to what you think, I'm not a complete idiot."

Per Daniels's suggestion, she'd called Daley two hours before and requested the meeting. He'd eagerly agreed. What bothered her was why Daniels, if he actually wanted her to talk to Daley, had interrupted the encounter at the museum. But she simply added that quandary to the growing list. "We didn't finish our conversation."

"Time for a reality check, Stephanie. The stuff you have on me? Keep it. Use it. I don't care. If I go down, so does the president. Truth be told, I wanted you to find it."

She found that hard to believe.

"I knew all about your investigation. That whore you sent my way? I'm not that weak. Do you think that's the first time a woman has tried to learn things on me? I knew you were digging. So I made it easy for you to find what you wanted. But you took your time."

"Nice try, Larry. But that dog doesn't hunt here."

He worked on a combination of eggs and grits. "I know you're not going to believe any of this. But for once could you forget you hate my guts and just listen?"

That's why she'd come.

"I've been doing some snooping. Lot of crap swirling. Strange stuff. I'm not privy to the inner circle, but I'm close enough to cop a feel. When I found out you were looking at me, I figured you'd move on me at some point—and when you did, we could deal."

"Why didn't you just ask for my help?"

"Get real. You can't stand to be in the same room with me. You're going to help me? I figured once you peeped into the window and saw what was happening, then you'd be a lot more receptive. Like you are right now."

"You still bribing Congress?"

"Yeah. Me and about a thousand other lobbyists. Hell, it should be an Olympic sport."

She glanced at Cassiopeia and saw nothing that triggered

alarm. Families and older couples populated the many tables.

"Forget all that. It's the least of our concerns," Daley said.

"I didn't know *we* had any concerns."

"Much more is happening." He gulped a few swallows of orange juice. "Damn, they load this stuff with sugar. But it's good."

"If you eat like this all the time, how do you stay so thin?"

"Stress. Best diet in the world." He tabled the glass. "There's a conspiracy going on, Stephanie."

"To do what?"

"Change the president."

This was new.

"It's the only thing that makes sense." He shoved the plate aside. "The vice president is in Europe attending an economic summit. But I've been told that he left his hotel last night late and went to meet with a man named Alfred Hermann. Supposedly a courtesy visit. But the VP is not a courteous man. He does things for a reason. He's met with Hermann before. I checked."

"And discovered that Hermann heads an organization called the Order of the Golden Fleece."

A look of amazement flooded Daley's face. "I knew you'd be a help. So you already know about it."

"What I want to know is why any of that is important."

"This group cultivates political influence, and they have reach all over the world. Hermann and the VP have been friends awhile. I've heard talk about him and the Order, but the VP keeps his thoughts fairly close. I know he wants to be president. He's gearing up to run, but I think he may be looking for a shortcut."

Daniels had said nothing about this subject.

"You still have those flash drives you took from my house?"

She nodded.

"On one are some digital recordings of telephone conversations. Only a few, but damn interesting. They're with the VP's chief of staff—a true asshole if ever there was one. He funneled the Alexandria Link directly to Alfred Hermann."

"And how did you manage to learn that?"

"I was there."

She kept her face blank.

"Right there with him. So I documented the whole encounter. We met Hermann in New York five months ago. Gave him everything. That's when I brought Dixon in."

That was new, too.

"Yeah. I went to her and told her what was happening with the link. I also told her about the meeting with Hermann."

"That wasn't real bright."

"Seemed so at the time. The Israelis were the only ally I could muster. But they thought the whole thing to Hermann was some kind of backchannel to cause them problems. All I got was Dixon as my babysitter." He swallowed more juice. "Which wasn't all bad."

"Now I'm getting sick."

Daley shook his head. "It was about a month later when the VP's chief of staff and I were alone. Asshole that he is, he still likes to brag. That's what usually gets guys like that in trouble. We'd had a few drinks and he made some comments. By then I was suspicious, so I kept a pocket recorder on me. I got some good stuff that night."

Cassiopeia stood from her table and walked toward the glass wall. Outside, cars came and went in the shaded parking lot.

"He talked about the Twenty-fifth Amendment. How he'd been studying it, learning details. He asked me what I knew about it, which wasn't much. I acted disinterested and drunk, though I was neither."

She knew what the Twenty-fifth Amendment to the Constitution said.

In case of the removal of the President from office or of his death or resignation, the Vice President shall become President.

71

SINAI PENINSULA

MALONE CHECKED HIS WATCH: 11:58 AM. HE'D ALREADY glanced through the two openings once and seen nothing. Pam and McCollum stood below him as he balanced atop the fourteen stones.

Noon arrived and a carillon of bells pealed in the distance.

"That's eerie," Pam said. "Out here in the middle of nowhere."

He agreed. "Sounds a ways off." *Like from heaven,* he thought.

The sun blazed overhead. His body and fatigues were damp with perspiration.

He stared back through the openings.

Point after point, stretching down the backbone of the ridge, came into view. What may have been hermit caves dotted the rock wall like black eyes. Then he noticed something. A stony trail etched up one of the mounds. A camel track? He'd checked in Lisbon before they left and learned that the mountains of this region concealed fertile hollows the local Bedouins called *farsh*. Usually that meant a water source and drew whatever few inhabitants the land enjoyed. St. Catherine's monastery to the south, near Moses Mountain, occupied a *farsh*. He'd assumed more surrounded him.

He watched as shadows disappeared and the color of the granite mountains transformed from pewter to beet red. The twisting course of the path up the hillside, now maroon, assumed the shape of a serpent. The two openings framed the view like a painting.

See the endless coil of the serpent red with anger.

"Anything?" Pam asked him.

"Everything."

STEPHANIE GLARED AT LARRY DALEY. "YOU'RE TELLING ME that the vice president is planning to murder the president?"

"That's exactly what I think is happening."

"And how are you the only one on the planet who's noticed this?"

"I don't know, Stephanie. Maybe I'm just a smart guy. But I know something is happening."

She needed to learn more. That's why Daniels had sent her.

"Larry, you're just trying to save your ass."

"Stephanie, you're like the fellow who's searching for a lost quarter beneath a streetlight. A guy comes along and asks what's he doing. He says, 'I'm looking for my lost quarter.' Guy says, 'Where did you lose it?' The fellow points off in the distance and says, 'Over there.' The guy's puzzled, so he asks, 'Why are you looking here?' And the man says, 'Because this is where the light is.' That's you, Stephanie. Quit looking where the light is and look where you need to."

"Then give me something concrete."

"Wish I could. It's just the little things that all add up. Meetings the VP has avoided that a candidate would not. Pissing off people whom he's going to need. Unconcerned with the party. Nothing overt. Little things that a political junkie like me would notice. There's only a few of us on the inside who would even be privy to these things. These men keep things close."

"Is Brent Green one of those men?"

"I have no idea. Brent's a strange one. The outsider to everyone. I tried to push him yesterday. Threatened him. But he didn't rattle. I wanted to see how he'd react. Then when you appeared in my house and found that book, I knew *you* had to be my ally."

"You may have chosen wrong, Larry. I don't believe a word you say. Killing a president is not easy."

"I don't know about that. Every presidential assassin, whether actual or would-be, was either deranged, loony, or lucky. Imagine what professionals could do."

He had a point there.

"Where are those flash drives?" he asked.

"I have them."

"I hope so, because if anyone else does we're in trouble. They'll know I'm onto them. Me recording those conversations with the VP's chief of staff would be impossible to explain. I need those back, Stephanie."

"Not going to happen. I have a suggestion, Larry. Why don't you just turn yourself in, confess to bribing Congress, and ask for federal protection? Then you can spout all this bullshit to anyone who'll listen."

He sat back in his chair. "You know, I thought for once you and I might have a civil conversation. But no, you want to be a smug-ass. I did what I had to, Stephanie, because that's what the president wanted."

Now she was interested.

"He knew what you were doing with Congress?"

"How else do you think my stock rose so fast in the White House? He wanted things passed and I made sure that happened. This president has been successful in Congress, which also explains how he easily managed a second term."

"You have proof of his involvement?"

"Like I taped Daniels? No. Just reality, Stephanie. Somebody has to make things happen. It's the way of the world. I'm Daniels's guy. I know it, and he knows it."

She glanced over at Cassiopeia and recalled what the other woman had said on the way over. They truly did not know who to trust, including the president.

Daley stood from the table and tossed down a couple of dollars for the tip. "The other day you and Green thought this was all about Daniels's legacy. I told you what you wanted to hear to rock you to sleep." Daley shook his head. "This is about Daniels continuing to breathe. You're a waste of time. I'll handle this another way."

MALONE LED THE WAY UP THE GAUNT ESCARPMENT. EAGLES and buzzards patrolled overhead. The golden sunlight penetrated his brain and suffused his sweaty body. A light wash of rock littered the trail, the parched topsoil a loamy deposit of sand and silt.

He followed the serpentine path to the top, where three massive boulders had long ago toppled and created a tunnel across the crown. Fine dust, sounding like water splashing, rained off the stones. Despite the sun, the corridor was cool. He welcomed the shade. The other side loomed thirty feet away.

Ahead, he suddenly spotted a flash of red.

"You see that?" he asked.

"Yeah," Pam said.

They stopped and watched as it happened again.

Then he realized what was occurring. The noonday sun, as it found gaps between the three fallen stones, played itself off the red granite and colored the tunnel crimson.

Interesting phenomenon.

See the endless coil of the serpent red with anger.

"Apparently," he said, "there's lots of angry red serpents around here."

Halfway through he noticed words etched into the granite. He stopped and read the Latin, translating out loud.

"Draw not nigh hither: put off thy shoes from thy feet, for the place whereon thou standest is holy ground." He knew the passage. "From Exodus. What God said to Moses from the Burning Bush."

"Is this where that happened?" Pam asked.

"No one knows. The mountain about twenty miles south of here, Jebel Musa, is accepted by all three religions as the place. But who knows?"

At the tunnel's end a sudden blaze of warmth embraced him, and he stared out into a curving *farsh* dotted with cypress trees. Soft white clouds chased one another, like tumbleweeds, across the clear sky. His eyes slit lizardlike against the glare.

Pressed against the face of the far mound, tucked into an angle of stupendous cliffs, arose walls and buildings that strained against one another as if they were part of the rock. Their colors—yellow, brown, and white—merged like camouflage. Watchtowers seemed to be floating. Slim green cones of cypresses added contrast to burnt-orange roof tiles. No real logic prevailed as to size and shape. The assemblage reminded Malone of the anarchic charm of a hillside Italian fishing village.

"A monastery?" Pam asked him.

"The map indicated that there are three in this region. None is a great secret."

A path of boulder steps led the way down. The risers descended steeply, grouped three together between sloping stretches of smooth rock. At the bottom another path traversed the *farsh,* past a small lake nestled among the cypresses, and zigzagged up to the monastery's entrance.

"This is the place."

STEPHANIE WATCHED AS DALEY LEFT THE RESTAURANT. CAS-siopeia came over, sat at the table, and asked, "Anything useful?"

"He says that Daniels knew everything he was doing."

"What else could he say?"

"Daley never mentioned that we were at Camp David last night."

"Nobody saw us but those agents and Daniels."

Which was right. They'd slept in the cabin alone with two agents outside. Food had been in the oven waiting when they'd awoken. Daniels himself had called and told them to arrange the meeting with Daley. So Daley either didn't know or refused to say.

"Why would the president want us to meet with him, knowing Daley might contradict what he's told us?" she asked, more to herself than Cassiopeia.

"Add that question to the list."

She watched through the front glass as Daley trudged through the gravelly parking lot toward his Land Rover. She'd never liked the man. When she'd finally confirmed that he was dirty, nothing had pleased her more.

Now she wasn't so sure.

Daley found his car at the far side of the lot and climbed inside.

They needed to leave, too. Time to find Brent Green and see what he'd learned. Daniels had not mentioned them talking with Green, but she thought it best.

Particularly now.

An explosion rocked the building.

Her initial shock was replaced with an awareness that the restaurant was intact. Loud voices and a few screams subsided as others, too, began to realize that the building was still there.

Everything was fine.

Except outside.

She stared through the glass and saw Larry Daley's Land Rover being consumed by flames.

72

SINAI PENINSULA

MALONE APPROACHED THE METAL-CLAD WOODEN GATE. SUN-baked walls of red granite, their foundations resting on giant buttresses, sloped to a terraced foothold where cypress, orange, lemon, and olive trees stood guard. Grapevines protected the base. A warm wind kicked up sand.

No sign of anyone.

Above the gate, Malone spotted more Latin, this time Psalm 118, and he read the pronouncement.

THIS GATE OF THE LORD,
INTO WHICH THE RIGHTEOUS SHALL ENTER

"What do we do?" Pam asked. He'd noticed that the hostility of the terrain matched her rapidly deteriorating temperament.

"I assume that's what the rope is for," he said, motioning.

High above the gate, an iron bell rested inside an open tower. He walked over and yanked. The bell clanged several times. He was about to ring again when high up in the gate a window opened and a bearded young man sporting a straw hat leaned out.

"How may I assist you?" he asked in English.

"We're here to visit the library," McCollum said.

"This is but a monastery, a place of solitude. We have no library."

Malone had wondered how the Guardians ensured that someone who appeared at the gate was an invitee. It could take a great deal of time to make the journey, and at no point in the quest had any constraints been imposed. So there must be a final challenge. One not stated in the quest.

"We're invitees and have completed the quest," he called out. "We seek entrance to the library."

The door to the portal closed.

"That was rude," Pam said.

Malone wiped the sweat from his brow. "They're not just going to swing open the gates to anyone who shows up."

The portal opened again and the young man asked, "Your name?"

McCollum was about to speak, but Malone grabbed his arm. "Let me," he whispered. He stared up and said, "George Haddad."

"Who are those with you?"

"My associates."

The eyes that stared back were fixed, as if trying to deter-mine if he was a man to be trusted.

"A question, if I may?"

"By all means."

"Your route to here. Tell me."

"First to Belém and the Jerónimos Monastery, then to Bethlehem.org, and finally here."

The window closed.

Malone heard bars being removed from behind the gate, then the stout wooden panels inched open and the bearded young man strolled out. He wore baggy pants, tapered at the calf, a russet-colored cloak tucked into his waistband, and a rope belt. His feet were protected by sandals.

He stopped before Malone and bowed. "Welcome, George Haddad. You have completed your quest. Would you like to visit the library?"

"I would."

The young man smiled. "Then enter and find what you seek."

They followed him, single-file, through the gates into a dark corridor lined with towering stone that blocked the sun. Thirty paces, then around a right angle, and they again found daylight inside the walls, a flourishing space of greenery with cypress trees, palms, grapevines, flowers—even a pea-cock paraded about.

What sounded like a flute cast a soothing melody. Malone spotted the source, a musician perched on one of the bal-conies supported by thick wooden brackets. The buildings were crowded together, each one different in size and com-position. He spotted courtyards, staircases, iron railings, vaulted arches, pointed roofs, and narrow walkways. A miniature aqueduct channeled water from one end to the other. Everything seemed to have sprung up by chance. He was reminded of a medieval village.

They followed Straw Hat.

Other than the flute player, Malone had seen no one, though the complex was clean and orderly. Sunbeams battled with curtains in the windows, but he spotted no movement beyond the panes. Terraced vegetable beds loaded with tomatoes stood hearty. One thing caught his attention. Solar panels discreetly fastened to the roofs and a number of dish antennae, each hidden behind either wooden or stone awnings that seemed to be parts of the buildings—like Disney World, Malone thought, where necessities went unnoticed in plain sight.

Straw Hat stopped before a wooden door and opened its lock with an oversized brass key. They entered a refectory, the cavernous dining hall decorated with religious murals of Moses. The air smelled of sausage and sour cabbage. Ceiling boards alternated between chocolate and butter yellow, interrupted by a diamond-shaped panel of powder blue dotted with gold stars.

"Your journey was surely long," Straw Hat said. "We have food and drink."

On one of the tables lay a tray of sand-brown loaves and bowls of tomatoes, onions, and oil. Dates were piled in another bowl. Still another held three huge pomegranates. A kettle emitted steam and he smelled tea.

"That's kind of you," Malone said.

"Real kind," McCollum added. "But we'd like to see the library."

The bony face betrayed the young man's testiness, but only for an instant. "We prefer you to eat and rest. Also, you may want to clean yourselves before entering."

McCollum stepped forward. "We've completed your quest. We'd like to see the library."

"Actually, Mr. Haddad has completed his quest and has earned entry. There was no invitation extended to you or the woman." Straw Hat faced Malone. "By involving these two, your invitation would normally be voided."

"Then why am I here?"

"An exception has been made."

"How do you know who I am?"

"You knew the route of your quest."

Straw Hat offered no more and left the dining hall, closing the door behind him.

They stood in silence.

Finally Pam said, "I'm hungry."

Malone was, too. He laid his rucksack on the table. "Then let's accept their hospitality."

73

MARYLAND

STEPHANIE AND CASSIOPEIA RUSHED FROM THE RESTAURANT. Nothing could be done for Larry Daley. His vehicle was a charred mass, still burning. The explosion had been confined to the car, doing little damage to any of the other vehicles.

A targeted strike.

"We need to go," Cassiopeia said.

She agreed.

They hustled to the Suburban and jumped in, Stephanie behind the wheel. She inserted the key, but hesitated and asked, "What do you think?"

"Unless the president wired this car with a bomb, we're okay. No one went near it while we were in there."

She turned the key. The engine roared to life. She drove away just as a police car rounded a corner and wheeled into the parking lot.

"What did he tell you?" Cassiopeia asked.

She summarized the conversation. "I thought he was full of crap. Conspiracies to kill Daniels. But now—"

An ambulance raced past them in the other lane.

"No need for them to be in a hurry," she said. "He never knew what hit him."

"A bit dramatic," Cassiopeia said. "There are a lot quieter ways to kill him."

"Unless you want attention drawn to the fact. The deputy national security adviser being car-bombed? It's going to be a big deal."

She was driving slowly, keeping well below the speed limit, working her way out of town and back to the highway. She stopped at an intersection and turned south.

"Where to now?" Cassiopeia asked.

"We need to find Green."

Five miles and a car appeared in her rearview mirror, closing fast. She expected it to pass and speed down the nearly empty two-lane highway. Instead the gray Ford coupe eased up close to the Suburban's bumper. She spotted two figures in the front seats.

"We've got company."

They were moving at sixty miles an hour, the road twisty through wooded countryside. Only a few farmhouses disturbed the fields and forest.

A gun appeared out of the front passenger-side window. A pop and the bullet pinged off the rear windshield but did not shatter the glass.

"God bless the Secret Service," she said. "Bulletproof."

"But the tires aren't."

Cassiopeia was right. She increased their speed and the Ford kept pace. She yanked the wheel left and swerved into the oncoming lane, slowing, allowing the Ford to pass. As it did, the man fired into the side of the Suburban, but the shots ricocheted off.

"We've got armor plating, too," Cassiopeia said.

"Gotta love a tank. Any idea who they are?"

"The one shooting chased us on the mall the other day. So I'd say the Saudis have found us."

"They must have been on Daley and we turned up."

"Lucky us."

She whipped the Suburban back into the southbound lane, now tailing the Ford. Cassiopeia lowered her window and shattered the lead car's rear window with two shots. The Ford tried a similar maneuver, changing road sides, but had to return to the southbound lane to avoid an approaching truck. Cassiopeia took advantage of the moment and sent another bullet into the rear window.

The passenger in the Ford aimed his gun out the rear, but Cassiopeia discouraged him from firing with another shot.

"We have more problems," Stephanie said. "Behind us. Another car."

The other vehicle sat tight on their rear bumper. Two men inside, as well. She kept speeding forward—to stop would place them at the mercy of four armed men.

Cassiopeia seemed to assess the situation and made a decision. "I'm going to take out the tires on the one ahead of us. Then we'll see about the one behind."

A pop came from outside, then a bang.

Stephanie felt the right rear of the SUV swerve and instantly realized what had happened. Their own tire had been shot. She pounded the brake and kept the vehicle under control.

Another pop and the left rear jolted.

She knew that ordinary rounds did not explode tires. But they were losing air and she had only a couple of minutes before they'd be riding on rims. She kept the car planing, which should buy them another mile or so.

Cassiopeia handed her a gun and changed the magazine in her weapon. They could initially use the Suburban's defenses to shield them. After that, it would be a shootout, and the early hour and rural location offered far too much privacy to their attackers.

The rear end settled to the road and a loud *clunk* told her the trip was over.

She stopped the Suburban and gripped the gun.

The lead Ford skidded onto the shoulder.

The vehicle behind them did the same.

Armed men rolled from both cars.

MALONE FINISHED OFF THE POMEGRANATE, ONE OF HIS FA-vorite fruits, and swallowed another cup of the bitter tea. They'd been left alone about forty-five minutes, though he could not shake the feeling that they were being watched. He spied the surroundings carefully, trying to decide if the room was wired for video. The tables all stood empty, as did a sideboard against one wall. He imagined a mild clatter of plates, the polite scraping of forks, and chatter in several languages that surely accompanied every meal. A door at the far end stood closed, one he assumed led to the kitchen. The refectory itself was cool—thanks, he reasoned, to thick stone walls.

The exterior door opened and Straw Hat entered.

Malone noticed that every action by the young man

seemed conducted in the manner of a servant, as if he contemplated only one thought at a time.

"Mr. Haddad, are you ready to enter the library?"

Malone nodded. "Belly's full and I'm all rested."

"Then we can go."

McCollum sprang from his chair. Malone had been waiting to see what he'd do. "Mind if we visit a bathroom first?"

Straw Hat nodded at the request. "I can take you. But then you're to return here. Mr. Haddad is the invitee."

McCollum waved the proviso off. "Fine. Just take me to the bathroom."

Straw Hat asked, "Mr. Haddad, do you require use of the facilities?"

Malone shook his head. "You a Guardian?"

"I am."

He studied Straw Hat's young face. The skin was extraordinarily smooth, the cheekbones high, his oval eyes casting an Oriental appearance. "How can you handle this place with so few people? We only saw one coming in."

"There's never been a problem."

"What about intruders?" McCollum asked.

"Mr. Haddad is a learned man. We have nothing to fear."

Malone let it go. "Take him to the bathroom. We'll wait here."

The Guardian turned to Pam.

"I'm fine," she said.

"We shall return shortly."

STEPHANIE BRACED HERSELF FOR A FIGHT. SOMEBODY HAD killed Larry Daley and now they wanted her. She was angry that Cassiopeia had been drawn into the fray, but that was a choice her friend had freely made. And she saw no fear, no regret, just determination in Cassiopeia's eyes.

The four men advanced on the Suburban.

"You take the two in front," Cassiopeia said. "I'll deal with the two behind."

She nodded.

They both prepared to open their doors and fire. Made more sense than just sitting and allowing the men to attack at will. Perhaps a moment of surprise might give them an advantage. She'd use the door and window as a shield for as long as she could.

A thumping sound grew in intensity and the car began to vibrate.

Stephanie saw the two in front scatter as a rush of wind swept over the vehicle and a helicopter glided into view.

Then a car appeared and squealed to a stop.

She heard a rapid bang of gunfire.

The bodies of the two gunmen in front twirled like tops. She glanced in the rearview mirror. The rear car was trying to leave. One of the gunmen lay dead on the highway.

The car wheeled around.

The helicopter hung fifty feet in the air.

A side door opened and a man with a rifle appeared. The helicopter paralleled the escaping car and she saw, but could not hear, shots. The car veered sharply left and crashed into a tree.

The two men in front lay bleeding on the pavement.

She opened the Suburban's door.

"Everyone okay there?" a male voice said.

She turned to see the Secret Service agent from the museum standing by the other parked car.

"Yeah. We're all right."

Her cell phone was ringing from inside the Suburban. She grabbed the unit and answered.

"Thought you might need some help," Daniels said.

SABRE FOLLOWED THE GUARDIAN OUTSIDE AND THROUGH THE warren of quiet buildings. The sun cast long shadows past the rooflines and across the uneven street. A ghost town, he thought. Dead, yet alive.

He was taken to another building where, inside, he found a bathroom floored in lead. A tin container suspended from the ceiling fed the toilet with water. He decided the time was now, so he brought out the gun from the monastery, stepped from the toilet, and jammed the barrel into the younger man's face.

"To the library."

"You're not the invitee."

He made clear, "How about this? I shoot you in the head and find it myself."

The other man seemed more puzzled than frightened.

"Follow me."

74

VIENNA

HERMANN QUICKLY LEARNED THAT THORVALDSEN HAD walked to the *schmetterlinghaus*. His chief of the guard, a burly man with deep olive skin and an eager personality, followed him as he headed that way, too. He did not want to attract attention, so he kept his gait measured, smiling and casually greeting members who milled about in the rose garden near the house.

He liked where Thorvaldsen had gone. The building was far enough away that he could deal with his problem in privacy.

And that was exactly what he needed.

THROUGH THE PLANTS AND GLASS WALLS, THORVALDSEN SAW his host coming. He noticed the determined stride and purposeful manner. He also recognized the chief of the guard.

"Gary, Mr. Hermann is on his way. I want you to retreat to the far side and stay among the plants. He'll likely be in an ill humor and I have to deal with him. I don't want you involved until I call for you. Can you do that for me?"

The boy nodded.

"Off with you, and stay quiet."

The boy scampered down a path that cleaved a trail through the transplanted rain forest and disappeared into the foliage.

HERMANN STOPPED OUTSIDE. "WAIT HERE," HE SAID TO THE chief of the guard. "I don't want to be disturbed. Make sure."

He then swung open the wooden door and pushed through the leather curtain. Butterflies flew in silent zigzags across the warm air. Their musical accompaniment had not, as yet, been switched on. Thorvaldsen sat in one of the chairs he and Sabre had occupied a couple of days ago. He immediately saw the letters and removed the gun from his pocket.

"You have my property," he said in a firm tone.

"That I do. And you apparently want it back."

"This is no longer amusing, Henrik."

"I have your daughter."

"I've decided I can live without her."

"I'm sure you can. I wonder if she realizes."

"At least I still possess an heir."

The jab cut deep. "You feel better saying that?"

"Much. But as you aptly noted, Margarete will likely be the ruin of this family once I'm gone."

"Perhaps she takes after her mother? As I recall, she was an emotional woman, too."

"In many ways. But I will not have Margarete standing in the way of our success. If you intend to harm her, do it. I want my property back."

Thorvaldsen motioned with the letters. "I assume you've read these?"

"Many times."

"You've always spoken decisively when it comes to the Bible. Your criticisms were pointed and, I have to say, well reasoned." Thorvaldsen paused. "I've been thinking. There are two billion Christians, a little more than a billion Muslims, and about fifteen million Jews. And the words on these pages will anger them all."

"That's the flaw of religion. No respect for truth. None of them cares what's real, only what they can pass off as reality."

Thorvaldsen shrugged. "The Christians will have to face the fact that their Bible, both New and Old, is manufactured. The Jews will learn that the Old Testament is a record of their ancestors from a place other than Palestine. And Muslims will come to know that their sacred ground, the holiest of places, was originally a Jewish homeland."

"I don't have time for this, Henrik. Give me the letters, then my chief of the guard will escort you from the estate."

"And how will that be explained to the members?"

"You've been called back to Denmark. Business emergency." He glanced around. "Where's Malone's son?"

Thorvaldsen shrugged. "Entertaining himself somewhere on the estate. I told him to stay out of trouble."

"You should have taken that advice yourself. I know of your ties to Israel, and I assume you've already informed them of what we're planning. But as I'm sure you've been told, they know we're after the Library of Alexandria, just as they are. They've tried to stop us but have so far been unsuccessful. By now it's too late."

"You have a lot of faith in your employee. He might disappoint you."

Hermann could not voice his own uncertainty. Instead he boldly declared, "Never."

MALONE STOOD FROM THE TABLE AND WITHDREW HIS GUN from the rucksack.

"I was wondering how long you were going to sit here," Pam said.

"Long enough to know that our friend isn't coming back."

He shouldered the pack and opened the outside door. No hum of voices. No click of hooves. No flute. The compound seemed at once sacred and eerie.

Bells pealed, signaling three PM.

He led the way through a variety of buildings, each with the tint and texture of dead leaves. A tower, the color of putty, stood solemnly, topped by a convex roof. The street's unevenness revealed its age. The only sign of habitation came from clothes—underwear, socks, trousers—hanging to dry from a balcony.

Around a corner he spotted McCollum and Straw Hat, a hundred feet away, traversing a small square with a fountain. The monastery obviously had access to a well, as water didn't seem a problem. Neither did power, considering the number of solar panels and satellite dishes.

McCollum held a gun to Straw Hat's head.

"Good to know we were right about our partner," he whispered.

"Guess he wants a first look."

"Now, that is downright rude. Shall we?"

SADRE KEPT HIS GUN LEVELED AT THE BACK OF THE GUAR-dian's head. They passed more buildings and headed deeper into the complex, near a point where the human-made met the natural.

He loathed the unholy calm.

An unassuming church washed primrose yellow nestled close to the rock face. Inside, the vaulted nave was naturally lit and crowded with icons, triptychs, and frescoes. A forest of silver and gold chandeliers hung above a richly detailed mosaic floor. The opulence stood in stark contrast with the simple exterior.

"This isn't a library," he said.

A man appeared at the altar. He, too, was olive-skinned, but short with ash-white hair. And older. Maybe seventies.

"Welcome," the man said. "I'm the Librarian."

"You in charge?"

"I have that honor."

"I want to see the library."

"To do that, you must release the man you're holding."

Sabre shoved the Guardian away. "All right." He leveled the gun at the Librarian. "You take me."

"Certainly."

MALONE AND PAM ENTERED THE CHURCH. TWO ROWS OF monolithic granite columns, painted white, their capitals gilded, displayed medallions of Old Testament prophets and New Testament apostles. Frescoes on the walls showed Moses receiving the Law and confronting the Burning Bush. Reliquaries, patens, chalices, and crosses rested in glass-fronted cupboards.

No sign of McCollum or Straw Hat.

To Malone's right, in an alcove, he spotted two bronzed cages. One held hundreds of sandstone-colored skulls, piled upon one another in a ghastly hillock. The other housed a hideous assortment of bones in an anatomical jumble.

"Guardians?" Pam asked.

"Has to be."

Something else about the sunlit nave caught his attention. No pews. He wondered if this was an Orthodox church. Hard to tell from the decoration, which seemed an eclectic mixture of many religions.

He crossed the mosaic floor to the opposite alcove.

Inside, perched on a stone shelf, backdropped by a bright stained-glass window, was a full skeleton dressed in embroidered purple robes and a cowl, propped in a sitting position, head slightly atilt, as if questioning. The finger bones, still clinging to bits of dried flesh and nails, clutched a staff and a rosary. Three words were chiseled into the granite below.

CVSTOS RERVM PRVDENTIA

"Prudence is the guardian of things," he said, translating, but his Greek was good enough to know that the first word could also be read as "wisdom." Either way, the message seemed clear.

What sounded like a door opening then closing echoed from beyond an iconostasis at the front of the church. Clutching the gun, he crept forward and stepped through the doorway in the center of the elaborately decorated panel.

A single door waited on the far side.

He came close.

The panels were cedar, and upon them were inscribed the words from Psalm 118. THIS GATE OF THE LORD, INTO WHICH THE RIGHTEOUS SHALL ENTER.

He grasped the rope handle and pulled. The door opened with a cacophony of moans. But he noticed something else. The ancient panel was equipped with a modern addition—an electronic dead bolt fit to the opposite side. A wire snaked a path to the hinge, then disappeared into a hole drilled into the stone.

Pam saw it, too.

"This is weird," she said.

He agreed.

Then he stared beyond the doorway and his confusion multiplied.

75

MARYLAND

STEPHANIE LEAPED FROM THE CHOPPER THAT HAD DEPOSITED her and Cassiopeia back at Camp David. Daniels waited for them on the landing pad. Stephanie marched straight for him as the helicopter rose back into the morning sky and disappeared across the treetops.

"You may be the president of the United States," she said in a sharp tone, "but you're a sorry son of a bitch. You sent us in there knowing we'd be attacked."

Daniels looked incredulous. "How would I have known that?"

"And a helicopter with a marksman happened to be in the neighborhood?" Cassiopeia asked.

The president motioned. "Let's take a walk."

They strolled down a wide path. Three Secret Service agents followed twenty yards behind.

"Tell me what happened," Daniels said.

Stephanie calmed down, recapped the morning, and finished by saying, "He thought somebody is plotting to kill you." Weird referring to Daley in the past tense.

"He's right."

They stopped.

"I've had enough," she said. "I don't work for you anymore, but you've got me operating in total darkness. How do you expect me to do this?"

"I'm sure you'd like your job back, wouldn't you?"

She did not immediately answer and her silence conveyed, to her annoyance, that she did. She'd conceived of and started the Magellan Billet, heading it for its entire existence. Whatever was happening had, at first, not involved her, but now men she neither liked nor admired were using her. So she answered the president honestly. "Not if I have to kiss your ass." She paused. "Or place Cassiopeia in any more danger."

Daniels seemed unfazed. "Come with me."

They walked in silence through the woods to another of the cabins. Inside, the president grabbed a portable CD player.

"Listen to this."

"Brent, I cannot explain everything, except to say that last evening I overheard a conversation between your vice president and Alfred Hermann. The Order or, more specifically, Hermann is planning to kill your president."

"You hear details?" Green asked.

"Daniels is taking an unannounced visit to Afghanistan next week. Hermann has contracted bin Laden's people and supplied the missiles needed to destroy the plane."

"This is a serious accusation, Henrik."

"Which I'm not in the habit of making. I heard it myself, as did Cotton Malone's boy. Can you inform the president? Just cancel the trip. That'll solve the immediate problem."

"Certainly. What's happening there, Henrik?"

"More than I can explain. I'll be in touch."

"That was taped over five hours ago," Daniels explained. "No call has come from my trusted attorney general. You would think he could have at least tried. Like I'm hard to find."

She wanted to know, "Who killed Daley?"

"Larry, God rest his soul, pushed the envelope. Obviously he was a busy man. He knew something was happening and he chose to Lone Ranger it. That was his mistake. The people who have those flash drives? They're the ones who killed Larry."

She and Cassiopeia stared at each other. Finally she said, "Green."

"Looks like we've found a winner for the who's-a-traitor contest."

"Then have him arrested," she said.

Daniels shook his head. "We need more. Article Three, Section Three, of the Constitution is real clear. Treason against the United States is giving aid and comfort to the enemy. The people who want me dead are our enemy. But no one can be convicted of treason except on the testimony of two witnesses to the same overt act. We need more."

"I guess you could take that flight to Afghanistan and, after your plane is blown from the sky, we'll have our overt act. Cassiopeia and I can be the two witnesses."

"That's a good one, Stephanie. Okay. You were bait. But I had your back covered."

"So nice of you."

"You can't flush birds from the bushes without a good dog. And shooting before that happens is a waste of pellets."

She understood. She'd ordered the same thing herself, many times.

"What do you want us to do?"

The resignation in her voice rang clear.

"See Brent Green."

MALONE STARED AT A PUZZLING SIGHT. THE DOOR FROM THE church opened into what was the face of the mountain. Ahead lay a rectangular hall about fifty feet wide and that much deep. Dimly lit with silver sconces, the granite walls shone mirror-smooth, the floor another handsome mosaic, the ceiling decorated with borders and arabesques of red and brown. On the opposite side of the room stood six rows of gray-and-black-marbled pillars bound with primrose bands. Seven doorways opened between the pillars, each a dark maw. Above each portal was a Roman letter—V S O V O D A. Above the lettering was another biblical passage. From Revelation. In Latin.

He translated out loud.

"Weep not: behold the lion of the tribe of Judah hath prevailed to open the book and loosen the seven seals thereof."

He heard footsteps echoing from beyond the doorways. From which one was impossible to say.

"McCollum's in there," Pam said. "But where?"

He walked to one of the doorways and entered. Inside, a tunnel penetrated the rock, more low-wattage sconces every twenty feet. He glanced into the adjacent opening, which also led into the mountain, only through a different tunnel.

"This is interesting. Another test. Seven possible ways to go." He dropped the pack from his shoulders. "What happened to the days when you just got a library card?"

"Probably went the same place as leaving a plane only when it lands."

He grinned. "You actually did good on that jump."

"Don't remind me."

He stared at the seven doorways.

"You knew McCollum would act, didn't you? That's why you let him go with that Guardian."

"He didn't come for the intellectual experience. And he's no treasure hunter. That man's a pro."

"Just like that lawyer I dated was more than a lawyer."

"The Israelis played you. Don't feel bad. They played me, too."

"You think this was all a setup?"

He shook his head. "More manipulation. We got Gary back too easy. What if I was meant to kill those kidnappers? Then when I went after George, they'd simply follow. Of course you were there and the Israelis were tracking. So they made sure I took you with me by spooking me in the airport and in the hotel. All makes sense. That way the Israelis kill George and they're done. Whoever kidnapped Gary links up with us to find this. Which means the kidnappers have a far different agenda from the Israelis."

"You think McCollum took Gary?"

"Him, or at least whoever he works for."

"So what do we do?"

He fished the spare magazines for his gun from the pack and stuffed them into his fatigues. "Go after him."

"Which door?"

"You answered that yourself in Lisbon when you said Thomas Bainbridge left clues. I read his novel on the plane. Nothing there even remotely close to what we've experienced. His lost library is found in southern Egypt. No hero's quest. Nothing. But that arbor in his garden—that's another matter. I wondered about the last part of the quest McCollum gave us. It would make no sense to just walk in once you get here."

"Unless you've got a gun to someone's head."

"True. But something's wrong." He motioned at the door-ways. "With this type of safeguard, they could easily lead an intruder astray. And where is everybody? This place is de-serted."

He again read the letters above the doors.

V S O V O D A.

And he knew.

"You used to get on me all the time, wondering what good an eidetic memory is."

"No. I wondered why you couldn't remember my birthday or our anniversary."

He grinned. "This time it pays to have good recall. Remember the last part of the quest. *Heed the letters.* The arbor. At Bainbridge Hall. The Roman letters."

He saw them perfectly in his mind.

D OVOSVAVV M.

"Remember, you asked why the D and the M were spaced apart from the other eight." He pointed at the doorways. "Now we know. One gets you in. The other, I assume, gets you out. It's the middle part I'm unsure of, but we're about to find out."

VIENNA

THORVALDSEN ASSESSED HIS SITUATION. HE NEEDED TO BEST Hermann, and he'd brought the gun beneath his sweater for that precise purpose. He still held the letters of St. Augustine and St. Jerome. But Hermann held a weapon, too.

"Why did you kidnap Gary Malone?" he asked.

"I don't have any intention of being questioned."

"Why not humor me for a moment, since I'll soon be leaving?"

"So his father would do what we needed done. And it worked. Malone led us straight to the library."

He recalled what the vice president had surmised the night before and decided to press the point. "And you know that?"

"I always know, Henrik. That's the difference between us. It's why I head this organization."

"The members have no idea what you're planning. They only think they understand." He was fishing to see if anything more might be offered. He'd sent Gary to hide for two reasons. One, so there would be no possibility that what they'd overheard last night would be revealed. That would place them both in absolute jeopardy. Two, he knew Hermann would come armed and he needed to deal with the threat alone.

"They place their trust in the Circle," Hermann was saying. "And we have never disappointed them."

He motioned with the sheets. "Are these what you planned to show me?"

Hermann nodded. "I was hoping that once you saw the fallacy of the Bible, its inherent flaws, you'd understand that we're merely telling the world what it should have been told fifteen hundred years ago."

"Is the world ready?"

"I don't care to debate this, Henrik." He thrust his arm forward and leveled the gun. "What I want to know is, how did you learn of those letters?"

"Like you, Alfred, I always know."

The gun stayed aimed. "I will shoot you dead. This is my homeland and I know how to handle the matter once you're gone. Since you already have my daughter, I can use that. Some sort of extortion plot you'd concocted that went bad. It won't really matter. You won't care."

"I believe you'd actually prefer me dead."

"No question. Much easier, in every way."

Thorvaldsen heard the running steps at the same moment he spotted Gary bolt from the plants and tackle Alfred Hermann. The boy was tall, lanky, and solid. His momentum toppled the older man from his feet and caused Hermann to lose the gun.

Gary rolled off his opponent and snatched up the weapon.

Hermann seemed stunned by the attack and came to his knees, searching for breath.

Thorvaldsen stood and grabbed the gun from Gary. He wrapped his hand around the weapon and, not giving Hermann time to rise, slammed the butt into the side of his head.

The dazed Austrian crumpled to the dirt.

"That was foolish," he said to Gary. "I would have handled it."

"How? He was pointing the gun at you."

He didn't want to say that he was indeed running out of options, so he simply clasped the boy's shoulder. "Good point, lad. But don't do that again."

"Sure, Henrik. No problem. Next time I'll let whoever shoot you."

He smiled. "You're just like your father."

"What now? There's another guy outside."

He led Gary near the exit and said in a soft voice, "Go out and tell him Herr Hermann needs him. Then let him enter first. I'll take care of things."

MALONE FOLLOWED THE TUNNEL MARKED BY THE LETTER D. The route was narrow, two people wide, and extended deep into the bowels of the rock. The path turned twice. Light came from more low-wattage sconces. The chilled, mysterious air carried an acrid quality that stung his eyes. After another few twists, they entered a chamber decorated with magnificent murals. He marveled at their brilliance. The Last Judgment, hell mouthing flames in the river, a Tree of Jesse. Cut into the wall from which they entered were seven doorways, above each of which was a single Roman letter. On the opposite wall seven more doorways, a solitary letter above each, too.

D M V S O A I.

"We take the O, right?" Pam said.

He smiled. "You catch on fast. That arbor is the way through this maze. There's going to be seven more of these junctures. V O S V A V V. That's what's left. Thomas Bainbridge left an important clue—but one that makes no sense until you get here. That's why the Guardians left it alone for three hundred years. It's meaningless."

"Unless you're in this rat maze."

They kept moving forward through the puzzle of passageways, misleading corridors, and dead ends. The time and energy required to construct the tunnels staggered Malone's imagination. But the Guardians had been at their task for two-thousand-plus years—plenty of time to be both innovative and thorough.

Seven more junctions appeared and he was pleased to see that each time a letter from the arbor appeared above a door. He kept his gun ready but heard nothing ahead of them. Each juncture contained a different marvel of hieroglyphs, cartouches, alphabet engravings, and cuneiform symbols.

Past the seventh intersection and into another tunnel, he knew that the final path lay ahead.

They turned a corner, and the light from the exit ahead was clearly brighter than the other junctures. McCollum could be there waiting, so he positioned Pam behind him and crept forward.

At the end, he stayed in the shadows and peered inside.

The room was large, maybe forty feet square, with overhead chandeliers. The walls towered twenty feet and were covered in mosaic maps. Egypt. Palestine. Jerusalem. Mesopotamia. The Mediterranean. Detail was minimal, coastlines tapered off into the unknown, and the writing was in Greek, Arabic, and Hebrew. On the opposite wall were seven more doors. The one with the letter M above it surely opened into the library itself.

They stepped inside the chamber.

"Welcome, Mr. Malone," a male voice said.

Two men took form from the darkness of one of the other doorways. One was the Guardian whom McCollum had earlier held at gunpoint, minus his straw hat. The other was Adam from Haddad's apartment and the monastery in Lisbon.

Malone aimed his weapon.

Neither the Guardian nor Adam moved. Both men simply stared at him with concerned expressions.

"I'm not your enemy," Adam said.

"How did you find us?" Pam asked.

"I didn't. You found me."

Malone thought about how the man standing across from him had gunned down George Haddad. Then he noticed that Adam was dressed similarly to the younger Guardian—baggy pants, cloak tucked into his waistband, rope belt, and sandals.

Neither man was armed.

He lowered his gun.

"You're a Guardian?" he asked Adam.

"A faithful servant."

"Why did you kill George Haddad?"

"I didn't."

Movement behind the two men caught Malone's attention. He saw a third figure step from the doorway.

Eve from Haddad's apartment. Alive and well.

"Mr. Malone," she said. "I'm the assistant librarian and we owe you an explanation, but it must be quick."

He kept his composure.

"We were there in London to create an illusion. It was imperative that you continue forward, and the Librarian believed the ruse was the best way to accomplish that goal."

"The Librarian?"

She nodded. "He leads us. We aren't many, but have always been enough to protect this place. Many Guardians have served. I'm sure you saw their bones in the church. But the world is changing. It's becoming increasingly difficult for us to continue our mission. We are about to be without funds, and our recruitment, of late, has been dismal. Then there is the threat."

He waited for her to explain.

"For the past several years someone has been seeking us. They've even involved governments. The incident five years ago with George Haddad—where you were able to secrete him away—left an invitee both known and exposed. That has *never* happened before. All the invitees from the past kept their pledge of secrecy, save one—Thomas Bainbridge. We're fortunate, though, in that his transgression proved useful. Your quest was made possible by Bainbridge's lack of character."

"You knew we were coming?" Pam asked.

"Most of your journey was stimulated by us, except that the Israelis have been quite aggressive in trying to find you. Even the Americans were involved. But it seems for different reasons. Everyone was willing to bargain us away. The Librarian decided to set into motion events that we controlled, ones that could lead the relevant players straight here."

"How is that possible?" he asked.

"You're here, aren't you?"

"We were in London," Adam said, "to move you. We used

some theatrical special effects to convince you of the shootings." Adam faced Pam. "Shooting you was an accident. I didn't expect you to be outside."

"That makes two of us," Malone said. But there was something else. He faced Eve. "George shot you. I took his gun. It was loaded with live ammunition."

"Yes, thank goodness he has good aim. I'm still sore, but the vest did its job."

"We went to Lisbon," Adam said, "to keep you moving forward, along with diverting the Israelis. We needed the three of you to come here alone. The others, in the abbey, were part of a Mossad assassination unit. But you eliminated them."

Malone glanced at Pam. "Looks like you definitely weren't the only one played."

"The man who came here with you is named Dominick Sabre," Eve said, "though his birth name is James McCollum. He works for an organization known as the Order of the Golden Fleece. He's come to take the library."

"And I brought him," Malone said.

"No," Adam said. "*We* allowed you to bring him."

"Where is this Librarian?" Pam asked.

Adam motioned at the doorways. "In there. He went with Sabre. At gunpoint."

"Cotton," Pam said. "You realize what they're saying? If Eve wasn't killed then—"

"The Librarian is George Haddad."

Eve nodded, tears forming in her eyes. "He's going to die."

"He's taken Sabre inside," the younger Guardian said, "knowing that he will not return."

"How does he know that?" Malone asked.

"Either the Order or Sabre wants this site for themselves. Which one? That remains to be seen. But we will all be killed, regardless. Since we're but a few, that will not be difficult to accomplish."

"No weapons in this place?"

Adam shook his head. "Not allowed here."

"Is what's back there worth dying for?" Pam asked.

"Without question," Adam said.

Malone knew what was happening. "Your Librarian was responsible for the death of a Guardian long ago. He thinks his death will be an atonement for that sin."

"I know," Eve said. "This morning he watched as you parachuted and knew this was his final day. He told me what he had to do." She stepped forward. Tears now streaked her cheeks. "He said you would stop what was happening. So save him. He need not die. Save us all."

Malone faced the doorway marked M and gripped the gun tight. He dropped his pack to the floor and told Pam, "Stay here."

"No," she said. "I'm going."

He faced her. This woman, whom he'd both loved and hated, seemed, like Haddad, at a crossroads herself.

"I want to help," she said.

He had no idea what would happen in there. "Gary needs at least one parent."

Her gaze locked on him. "That old man needs us, too."

77

MARYLAND

STEPHANIE LISTENED TO FOX NEWS RADIO. THE CAR BOMBING had been reported, the vehicle's registration run, and Daley identified. Patrons inside the restaurant had corroborated his physical identification, along with describing a woman who'd been sitting with him. Witnesses had told how the woman and another dark-skinned female fled the scene before police arrived.

Not surprisingly, no press reported that armed men had been found dead a few miles from the scene of the explosion. The Secret Service's cleanup had been fast and thorough.

They were driving another government car, a Chevy Tahoe, supplied by Daniels. The president wanted them away from Camp David before she made the call. They were now seventy miles south, on the outskirts of northern Washington. She grabbed her cell phone and dialed Green's mobile number.

"I've been waiting," Green said when he answered. "Have you heard about Daley?"

"We had a front-row seat." And she told him what happened at the restaurant.

"What were you doing there?"

"Having breakfast. He was buying."

"Any reason why you're being flippant?"

"Watching a man die has a way of jading your attitude."

"What's happening?" Green asked.

"The same people who killed Daley tried to kill Cassiopeia and me. But we managed to get away. They were apparently on Daley's tail, and they moved on us right after we left the restaurant."

"You seem to have a number of lives, Stephanie."

"Daley told me things, Brent. There's a lot going on. He was privy to it. He also has proof."

"Was he the traitor?"

"Hardly. The vice president gets that crown. Daley had amassed quite a lot on the VP."

She kept the car on the road and listened to the silence on the other end of the phone.

"Solid evidence?"

"Good enough for *The Washington Post*. He was terrified. That's why he met with me. He wanted help. He gave some stuff to me."

"Then your life is at risk, Stephanie."

"We've already figured that one out. Now we need your help."

"Of course. You'll have it. What do you want me to do?"

"Those flash drives from Daley's house. They relate to the evidence I have. Together they're enough to take the VP down. Once he goes, then we'll learn the rest, since I doubt he'll graciously take the fall alone. Treason comes with a harsh penalty. Death *is* one of the options for the jury."

More silence.

"Do you know if Cotton has checked in?" she asked.

"I haven't been told if he has. I've heard from no one. How about Thorvaldsen? Has he contacted Cassiopeia?"

"Not a word."

Her heart sank as she realized that Brent Green was part of what was happening. The pain on her face conveyed to Cassiopeia his betrayal.

"We need to meet, Brent. Privately. Just you, me, and Cassiopeia. How's your schedule?"

"Nothing I can't change."

"Good. Daley has more proof. Stuff he said would conclusively show who else is involved. He's been amassing it for a while. Those flash drives you have contain taped conversations of the VP's chief of staff talking about succession after the president is dead. But there's more. We need to meet at Daley's house. Can you get there?"

"Of course. You know where the information is hidden?"

"He told me."

"Then let's deal with this."

"That's the plan. See you there in half an hour."

She clicked off.

"I'm sorry," Cassiopeia said.

She wasn't going to dwell on someone else's failure. "We have to stay sharp. Green had Daley killed. We know that now. He's also plotting to kill the president."

"And us," Cassiopeia said. "Those men were working for the Saudis. The Saudis apparently think Green and the vice president are on their side. But the VP is also dealing with the Order. Which means the Saudis will never see a thing. The Order will get it all, to use however they want."

The interstate congealed as they approached central Washington. Stephanie slowed the Tahoe and said, "Let's hope the Arabs understand that before they decide to deal with us."

78

SINAI PENINSULA

GEORGE HADDAD LED HIS EXECUTIONER INTO THE LIBRARY OF Alexandria. The brightly lit subterranean chamber could dazzle at first sight. The walls were alive with mosaics fashioned in the spirit of everyday life—a barber shaving, a chiropodist, a painter, men crafting linen. He still recalled his first visit, but his assailant did not seem impressed.

"Where's the power come from?"

"Do you have a name?" Haddad asked.

"That's not an answer."

He knit his heavy eyebrows in a puzzled manner. "I'm an old man, hardly a threat to you. I'm simply curious."

"Name's Dominick Sabre."

"Have you come for yourself or others?"

"Myself. I've decided to become a librarian."

He smiled. "You'll find the job a challenge."

Sabre seemed to relax and stared around at the surroundings. The chamber was cathedral-like, with sloping walls and a barrel ceiling. The polished red granite shone like a gem. Columns rose from floor to ceiling, chiseled from the rock, each ornamented with letters, faces, plants, and animals. All of the chambers and tunnels were once the mines of pharaohs, abandoned for centuries by the time of Christ, re-crafted over the ensuing centuries by men obsessed with knowledge. Light came then by torches and lamps. Only in the past hundred years had technology allowed the soot to be cleaned away and the original beauty restored.

Sabre motioned to a mosaic emblem prominent on the far wall. "What's that?"

"The front of an Egyptian sledge, decorated with the head of a jackal, a heavy block on the sledge. The hieroglyph for wonder. Each of the library's rooms bears a symbol, which is the room's name. This is the Room of Wonder."

"You still never said where the power comes from."

"Solar. The electricity is low-voltage, but enough to power lights, computers, and communications equipment. Did you know that the concept for solar power was born more than two thousand years ago? Converting light into energy. But the idea was forgotten until the past fifty years, when someone once again thought of it."

Sabre motioned with his gun. "Where's that doorway lead?"

"The other four chambers. The Rooms of Province, Eternity, and Life, and the Reading Room. Each contains scrolls, as you can see. Approximately ten thousand are in this room."

Haddad casually moved to the center. Diamond-shaped stone bins, turned on edge, spanning long rows, held scrolls stacked loosely. "Many of these can no longer be read. Age has taken its toll. But there is much here. Works by Euclid the mathematician. Herophiles on medicine. The *Histories* of Manetho, about the early pharaohs. Callimachus the poet and grammarian."

"You talk a lot."

"I only thought that, since you intend to become the Librarian, you should begin to learn your charge."

"How did all these survive?"

"The original Guardians chose this location well. The mountain is dry. Moisture is rare in the Sinai, and water is the printed word's greatest enemy—other than, of course, fire." He motioned at extinguishers that rested at regular intervals around the room. "We're prepared for that."

"Let's see the other rooms."

"Of course. You should see it all."

He led Sabre toward the doorway, pleased.

Apparently his attacker had no idea who he was.

That should at least even the odds.

HERMANN OPENED HIS EYES. THREE BUTTERFLIES SAT PERCHED on his sleeve, his arm stretched out across the *schmetterlinghaus*'s putty-colored earth. His head ached and he recalled the blow from Thorvaldsen. He hadn't known the Dane was capable of such violence.

He pushed himself to his feet and spotted his chief of the guard lying prone twenty feet away.

His gun was gone.

He staggered to his employee, grateful no one was around. He glanced at his watch. He'd been down twenty minutes. His left temple throbbed and he gently traced the outline of a knot.

Thorvaldsen would pay for that assault.

The world was still unstable, but he caught hold of himself and brushed the dirt from his clothes. He bent down and shook the chief of the guard awake.

"We need to go," he said.

The other man rubbed his forehead and stood.

He steadied himself and commanded, "Not a word of this to anyone."

His minion nodded.

He walked over to the telephone box and lifted the receiver. "Please find Henrik Thorvaldsen."

He was surprised when the voice on the other end said he already knew the man's whereabouts.

"Out front. Preparing to leave."

79

SINAI PENINSULA

SABRE COULD NOT BELIEVE HIS GOOD FORTUNE. HE'D FOUND the Library of Alexandria. All around him were scrolls, papyri, parchments, and what the old man called codices—small, compact books, the pages brittle and brown, each one lying flat on the shelves beside the next, like bodies.

"Why is the air so fresh?" he wanted to know.

"Ventilation fans move the dry air from outside into here, where it's cooled by the mountain. Another innovation added in recent decades. The Guardians before me were ingenious. They took their charge seriously. Will you?"

They stood in the third room, named Eternity, another mosaic hieroglyph—a squatting man, his arms raised like a referee signaling a touchdown—high on the wall. More shelved codices spanned its length, with narrow aisles in between. The Librarian had explained that these were books from the seventh century, just before the original Library at Alexandria was sacked for the final time by Muslims.

"Much was retrieved in the months leading up to that change in political rule," the Librarian said. "These words exist nowhere else on this planet. Facts and events, what the world regards as history, would change if these were studied."

He liked what he was hearing. It all translated into one thing—power. He needed to know more, and quickly. Malone may well have forced another Guardian to show him through the maze. But his adversary could also just wait until he came out. That seemed more logical. Sabre had marked each of the doors they'd taken with an x scratched into the stone. Finding his way out would be easy. Then he'd deal with Malone.

But first he needed to know what Alfred Hermann would have asked.

"Are there manuscripts here about the Old Testament?"

HADDAD WAS PLEASED THAT HIS GUEST HAD FINALLY COME TO the point of his visit. He'd gone to a lot of trouble to make this happen. After his faked death in London, he'd waited, the apartment wired for sound and video, and watched to see if anyone else came. Sure enough, the man holding a gun on him had found the information left on the computer and the audiotape.

At Bainbridge Hall, Haddad had then waited for Malone, since the material he'd stashed beneath his bed had pointed straight there. Sabre's coming had been a bit of a surprise. His killing of the two men whom he'd sent into the mansion in the first place only confirmed the man's ill intentions.

One of the Guardians had managed to follow Malone to the Savoy Hotel and witnessed a breakfast with Sabre. Then those same eyes had watched as the two, plus Malone's ex-wife, boarded a flight to Lisbon. Since Haddad himself had fashioned the quest Malone was taking, he'd known exactly where the three were headed.

Which was why Adam and Eve were sent to Lisbon. To make sure that nothing prevented Malone and his new ally from making their way to the Sinai.

Haddad had thought the threat would be from governments —Israeli, Saudi, or American. But now he realized the greatest danger was from the man standing two meters away. He hoped Sabre was working for himself. And watching the expectancy in the other man's words and actions, he was now sure that the threat was containable.

"We have many texts concerning the Bible," he said. "That was a subject the library took a great interest in studying."

"The Old Testament. In Hebrew. Are there manuscripts here?"

"Three. Two supposedly copied from earlier texts. One an original."

"Where?"

He motioned to the doorway from which they'd entered. "Two rooms back. The Room of Province. If you intend to be the Librarian, you're going to have to learn where materials are stored."

"What do those Bibles say?"

He feigned ignorance. "What do you mean?"

"I've seen letters. From Jerome and Augustine. They talk of the Old Testament being changed. That the translations were altered. There were other invitees, four, who studied that, too. One, a man five years ago, a Palestinian, who said that the Old Testament was a record of the Jews not in Palestine, but somewhere else in Saudi Arabia. What do you know about that?"

"A great deal. And those men are correct. The translations of the accepted Bible are wrong. The Old Testament is indeed a record of the Jews in a place other than Palestine. West Arabia, in fact. I have read many manuscripts here in the library that prove the point. I have even seen maps of ancient Arabia that indicate biblical locations."

The gun came level and pointed straight at him. "Show me."

"Unless you're capable of reading Hebrew or Arabic, they will mean nothing."

"One more time, old man. Show me or I'll kill you and take my chances with your employees."

He shrugged. "Simply trying to be helpful."

SABRE HAD NO IDEA IF THE SHEETS AND CODICES SPREAD OUT before him were what Alfred Hermann sought. It didn't matter. He intended to control everything around him.

"These are treatises written in the second century by philosophers who studied at Alexandria," the Librarian said. "The Jews were just then beginning to become a political force in Palestine, asserting their supposed ancient presence, preaching an entitlement to the land. Sound familiar? These scholars determined that there was no ancient presence. They studied the Hebrew texts of the Old Testament, which the library maintained, and determined that the stories, as told at the time orally by the Jews, were far different in the texts, especially the oldest ones. Seems that as time progressed, the stories became more and more adapted to the Jews' then homeland, which had become Palestine. They'd simply forgotten their past in Arabia. If not for place-names, which remained constant, and the Old Testament written in its original Hebrew, that history would never have been discovered."

The Librarian pointed at one of the codices.

"That one is much later. Fifth century. When Christians decided they wanted the Old Testament to be included in their Bible. This treatise makes clear the translations were altered to conform the Old with the emerging New Testament. A conscious attempt to fashion a message using history, religion, and politics."

Sabre stared at the books.

The Librarian motioned to another stack of parchments contained within a clear plastic container. "This is the oldest Bible we have. Written four hundred years before Christ. All in Hebrew. The world has nothing like this. I believe the oldest Bible, outside this room, dates from nine hundred years *after* Christ. Is this what you seek?"

Sabre said nothing.

"You're an odd man," the Librarian suddenly said.

"What do you mean?"

"Do you know how many invitees have ventured here? Many thousands throughout the centuries. Our guest book is impressive. It started in the twelfth century with Averroës, the Arabic philosopher who wrote critically of Aristotle and challenged Augustine. He studied here. Those Guardians decided the time had come to share this knowledge, but selectively. Many of the names no one would recognize—just men and women of exceptional intelligence who came to the Guardians' attention. Minds that made their own individual contributions to our knowledge. In the days before radio, television, and computers, Guardians lived in major cities, always on the watch for invitees. Thomas Aquinas, Dante, Petrarch, Boccaccio, Poussin, Chaucer—men like that have all stood in this room. Montaigne wrote his *Essays* here. Francis Bacon conceived his famous statement *I take all knowledge for my province* here, in the Room of Province."

"Is all that supposed to mean something to me?"

The old man shrugged. "I'm trying to explain your charge.

You say you want to be the Librarian. If so, you will be granted quite a privilege. Those in the past who have served met Copernicus and Kepler and Descartes. Robespierre. Benjamin Franklin. Even Newton himself. All those learned souls benefited from this place, and the world benefited from their ability to comprehend and expand."

"And none of them ever said they were here?"

"Why would they? We seek no credit. In that way they obtain the recognition. If we assisted them? That was our charge. Quite an accomplishment, it has been, to keep this alive. Can you carry on that tradition?"

Since he had no intention of allowing anyone else to see this place, he asked what he really wanted to know. "How many Guardians are there?"

"Nine. Our ranks are greatly depleted."

"Where are they? I saw only two outside."

"The monastery is large. They were about their duties."

He motioned with the gun. "Let's go back to the first room. I want to see something else."

And the old man started walking.

He debated killing him here. But Malone should, by now, have figured out what was happening. He was either waiting at the other end of the maze or on his way through it.

Regardless, this old man would prove useful.

80

MALONE ROUNDED THE FINAL CORNER AND SPOTTED A DOOR-
way formed by two winged, human-headed lions. He knew
the symbolism. The mind of a man, the strength of an animal, the ubiquity of a bird. Marble doors hung open on
bronze hinges.

They stepped inside and stared at the opulence.

He marveled at how long it must have taken to create
something so extraordinary. Rows of diagonal bins lined the
tiled floor, broken by narrow aisles, each brimming with
scrolls. He stepped to one of the bins and slid out the top
bundle. The document was in remarkable condition, but he
dared not unroll it. He glanced inside the cylinder and saw
that the writing was still legible.

"I never knew something like this could exist," Pam said.
"It's beyond comprehension."

He'd seen amazing things, but nothing as wonderful as the
sight of all that this room held. He noticed high on one of the
shiny red walls more Latin words. *AD COMMUNEM DELECTA-*
TIONEM. For the enjoyment of all. "The Guardians accomplished something extraordinary."

He noticed a carving in one of the walls. He stepped close
and spied a ledger of what lay ahead, the rooms identified in
Latin. He translated each one out loud for Pam.

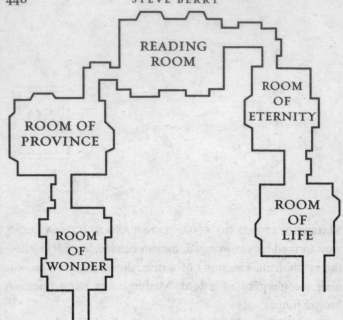

"Five rooms," he said. "They could be anywhere."

Movement at the far doorway caught his attention.

He saw George Haddad, then McCollum.

"Get down," he said to Pam, and he raised his weapon.

McCollum saw him and shoved Haddad to the ground, aiming across the chamber and firing. Malone dropped to the floor, using the shelves between them for cover. The bullet dinged off the granite columns behind him.

"You move fast," McCollum said from across the room.

"Didn't want you to be lonely."

"The Librarian kept me company."

"You and him get to know each other?"

"He talks too much, but he knows this place."

He wanted to know, "What now?"

"Afraid you and the ex have to die."

"I told you that you shouldn't get on my bad side."

"Bring it on, Malone. I've come this far, I don't plan to lose now. Tell you what, let's make it a fair game. Me against you. Right here. If you win, the old man and the ex are safe. Deal?"

"You're making the terms. Act on them."

HADDAD LISTENED TO THE EXCHANGE BETWEEN SABRE AND Malone. These two needed to settle their differences, and he needed to repay his debt. He thought again about the Guardian from all those decades ago when the young man had stared up at him with eyes full of resolve. He simply hadn't understood. But now, having seen the library, having become its Librarian, he knew what that fateful soul from 1948 knew.

He'd killed that good man for no reason.

And regretted it all his life.

"STAND UP," SABRE SAID TO THE LIBRARIAN, AND HE WATCHED as the old man rose. "All right, Malone. I'm acting. Here he comes." He motioned with the gun. "Go."

The Librarian walked slowly down the aisle between the diagonal bins. Sabre held his position, crouched behind the end of one of the rows.

Thirty feet away the Librarian stopped and turned.

The eyes that stared back penetrated him. He wondered about the old man. Something about him signaled danger, as if the soul behind the eyes had faced this scenario before and was not afraid. He debated killing the Librarian, but that might spur Malone on.

And that he did not want to do.

Not yet.

Malone was the only obstacle left. Once he was gone, the library was his.

So he was relieved when the old man finally walked away.

81

WASHINGTON, DC

STEPHANIE PARKED DOWN THE STREET FROM LARRY DALEY'S house, and she and Cassiopeia walked the remainder of the way. No sign of Brent Green or anyone else. They approached the front door, where Cassiopeia again picked the locks and Stephanie disarmed the alarm. She noticed that the pass code had not changed. Daley had left it alone, even after they'd gained entrance. Either foolishness or more evidence that she'd misjudged the man.

The interior was quiet. Cassiopeia swept each room to make sure they were alone. Stephanie made a stop in the office alcove where they'd found the flash drives. Then they both waited by the front door.

Ten minutes later a car parked outside.

Stephanie peered past the curtains and saw Green emerge from behind the wheel and walk toward the front door.

Alone.

She nodded at Cassiopeia, then opened the door.

Green was dressed in his typical dark suit and tie. Once

the attorney general was inside, she closed and locked the door. Cassiopeia took up a position near one of the windows.

"All right, Stephanie. Can you tell me what's happening?"

"Did you bring the flash drives?"

He reached into his jacket pocket and removed them.

"You listen to the recordings?"

He nodded. "Of course. The conversations are interesting, but in no way incriminating. There's talk of the Twenty-fifth Amendment, but it's just that. Talk. Certainly no conspiracy is either discussed or implied."

"That's why Daley gathered more," she said. "He told me that he's been looking at this for some time."

"Looking at what?"

And she noticed a flare of irritation.

"The conspiracy, Brent. The vice president is planning on killing Daniels. He's set the whole thing up to happen during a surprise visit Daniels will make next week to Afghanistan." She watched as the words, which would confirm that she knew what she was talking about, took hold.

Green remained stoic. "What proof did Daley find?"

"More conversations. He actually bugged the VP's private office. Not all that hard, since he was the one charged with making sure it wasn't being monitored. Seems the VP is connected to the Order of the Golden Fleece. Its head, Alfred Hermann, has arranged for the president's plane to be missile-attacked. Made the deal with bin Laden's people himself."

"Stephanie, I hope Daley amassed some impressive proof. Those are incredible charges."

"You said the whole administration was a cesspool. You said you wanted to get them. Here's your chance."

"How do we prove this?"

"The recordings are here. Daley told me about them. He

said they indicated everyone who's involved. We were leaving to drive back here when the car exploded."

Green stood in the foyer before the stairway where Daley and Heather Dixon had been yesterday. He seemed deep in thought. His game face. Of course, though the man had lied to her about Thorvaldsen, and he hadn't passed along to the president anything that Henrik had discovered, they needed concrete proof of his treachery.

"I know where he hid the recordings," she said.

Finally Green's eyes communicated interest. Cassiopeia stayed near the window, out of the way.

Stephanie led Green to the office alcove with the small desk and narrow bookshelves. One shelf held a row of CDs in their plastic cases. The music was all instrumental and from a variety of nations, even some Gregorian chants, which she found curious. She reached for one of the cases— *Tibetan Wonders*—and opened it. Inside, instead of the music CD, another disk filled the case. She popped it from the holder and said, "He liked to hide his stuff close by."

"What exactly is on there?"

"He says it's proof of who's part of this conspiracy. He said it reached to a level no one would ever suspect." Her nerves throbbed with excitement. "Want to listen?"

Green said nothing.

"Why'd you leak the Alexandria Link file?" she asked.

"I told you. To find the traitor. It led us several places. That's how we discovered the Israeli connection to Pam Malone. Leaking that file set everything in motion."

"And you had access?"

"Why the questions, Stephanie?"

"Because I was unaware you even knew about the Alexandria Link, much less knew enough details about it to think it would be bait for Israel."

Green cocked his head sideways in a quizzical fashion. "This is unexpected. A cross-examination."

She wasn't going to cut him any slack. Not now. "When we first talked about all this, you made it clear that you leaked the file on purpose, that it contained little other than a reference that Malone knew where George Haddad lived. Yet you specifically mentioned the Abrahamic covenant. How did you know?"

"The file wasn't all that secret."

"Really? That's not what Daley said. He insisted the information inside it was sparse and relatively unknown outside a handful of top people." She laced her words with insolence. "You weren't on the list. Yet you knew an awful lot."

Green stepped from the alcove and made his way back toward the den.

She followed.

Cassiopeia was gone.

Stephanie glanced around, concerned.

"My associates took care of her," Green said.

She did not like the sound of that. "And who takes care of me?"

Green reached beneath his jacket and produced a gun. "I have that duty. But I needed to speak with you alone first."

"To see how much I know? How much Cassiopeia knows? And who else knows?"

"I doubt you have help. After all, Stephanie, you aren't the best-liked person in this government. Daley tried to latch on to you, but that didn't work out."

"Your doing?"

Green nodded. "We wired the car with explosives and waited for the right time. All part of the terrorist attack on this nation that will start with Daley and end with Daniels. This country will be worked into a frenzy."

"Which the VP will exploit, after being sworn in. Then he'll need a vice president, and that's where you come in."

"Not all that many opportunities to advance anymore, Stephanie. You have to take what comes along. I'll be the perfect choice for the crisis. My confirmation will be unanimous."

"You're pathetic."

He threw her a self-deprecating expression. "I'll accept that. After all, you have only a few more minutes to live. By the way, you were supposed to become part of the attack. When you showed up at that restaurant I decided to add another layer, but you somehow managed to avoid the men that were sent. I still haven't learned how you accomplished that one."

"Good training. Makes all the difference."

He threw her a cold smile. "I'll miss that wit."

"Do you realize what you're doing? The violent overthrow of a duly elected president?"

"I believe it's called treason. But Danny Daniels is a weak, inept man who doesn't know what's best for this country. He's Israel's friend, no matter what, and that alone has crippled us in the Middle East. It's time for American favoritism to shift. The Arabs have so much more to offer."

"And the Alexandria Link will do that?"

He shrugged. "I don't know. That's the new president's problem, and he says he has it under control."

"You want to hang around that bad?"

"I wouldn't call being vice president of the United States *hanging around.* Since I aided the transition of power in such a critical way, I'll have a unique relationship. Lots of responsibility and little visibility."

She motioned at the gun. "You going to kill me?"

"No choice. That CD you have surely incriminates me. I can't let it go, and I can't let you go."

She wondered where Cassiopeia had been taken. This was not unfolding according to plan. And she hadn't expected Green himself to be toting a weapon. One thought flashed through her mind.

Stall.

"The attorney general of the United States is going to shoot me?"

"I've thought about it all day and, unfortunately, there's little choice."

"What about all those Christian values I've heard you talk about so much?"

"This is the heat of battle and the rules are different. It's a matter of survival, Stephanie. As I said, I did listen to the recordings Daley saved on the flash drives. The VP's chief of staff talked a lot about presidential succession. Too much. It's not incriminating, but it would raise questions. Daley was obviously investigating. That disk you're holding contains even more. It has to stop here. Of course, your body will never be found. There's a coffin waiting at the Saudi Arabian embassy. One of their envoys died and wants to be buried at home. You'll share a ride back to Arabia with him on a diplomatic flight."

"Got it all figured out, don't you?"

"Friends can be a good thing. I'm learning that. I went it alone for a long time, but I like being part of a team. The Saudis want only the destruction of Israel. We've promised that it can be done. The Israelis think the Saudis are working with them on this one. They aren't. They're working with us. Have been from the start."

"They have no idea what double-dealing pieces of crap all of you are. It's all about money and power. Nothing more."

"Anything else you'd like to say?"

She shook her head.

And the gun fired.

82

VIENNA

THORVALDSEN STOOD WITH GARY. HE'D CALLED JESPER JUST AS they'd left the *schmetterlinghaus* and told him to send a car and driver. As soon as he and Gary were on their way back to Copenhagen, he'd instruct his aide to release Margarete. He hadn't bothered to retrieve their clothes. No time. Instead, all he held was the atlas from the library that contained the letters of St. Jerome and St. Augustine.

Cars were coming and going from the lane that led through the trees to the front gate. Not all Order members stayed on the estate. Many chose to visit with friends or enjoy their favorite hotels in Vienna. He recognized some of those arriving and took a moment to chat. That also allowed him to blend with what was happening. But they needed to leave, with the letters, before Hermann awoke.

"Are we in trouble?" Gary asked.

"I'm not sure." And he wasn't.

"You whacked both those guys pretty hard."

He saw the boy was impressed. "I did, didn't I?"

"Don't want to be here when they wake up."

Neither did he. "We must keep these letters, and I'm afraid our host will never allow that."

"What about his daughter? He didn't seem to care about her."

"I don't believe he ever did. Taking her was just something unexpected that caused him to pause long enough for us to act." He thought of his own dead son. "Men like Alfred care little for family."

And how awful that must be. He missed his wife and his son. Seeing Gary Malone rush to his defense had both frightened and pleased him. He patted the boy on his shoulder.

"What is it?" Gary asked.

"Your daddy would be proud."

"Hope he's all right."

"Me, too."

Three cars sped down the main drive and rounded the paved lane. They stopped at the château, and men emerged from the first and third vehicles, each dressed in a dark suit. A quick survey of the surroundings and one of the men opened the rear door of the middle car.

The vice president of the United States climbed out into the afternoon sunshine, dressed casually in a pullover shirt beneath a navy blazer.

Thorvaldsen and Gary stood twenty yards away and watched as security men flanked the vice president and they all strolled toward the château's main entrance. Halfway, the vice president stopped and changed directions.

Heading straight for them.

Thorvaldsen watched the man with a mixture of anger and disgust. This ambitious fool seemed willing to do anything.

"Not a word, lad," he said to Gary. "Remember, ears open, mouth shut."

"I've figured that out."

"You must be Henrik Thorvaldsen," the vice president said as he came close and introduced himself.

"I am. A pleasure to meet you, sir."

"None of that *sir* stuff, okay? You're one of the wealthiest men in the world and I'm just a politician."

"What is the saying? One heartbeat away from the presidency?"

The American chuckled. "That's it. But it's still a rather dull job. I do get to travel, though, and I enjoy coming to places like this."

"And what brings you here today?"

"Alfred Hermann and I are friends. I came to pay my respects."

Another car cruised down the drive. A light-colored BMW with a uniformed driver. Thorvaldsen motioned and the car headed his way.

"Are you leaving?" the vice president asked.

"We have to go into town."

The American motioned at Gary. "And who is this?"

Thorvaldsen introduced them, using Gary's real name, and they shook hands.

"Never met a vice president before," Gary said.

The BMW stopped and the driver emerged, rounding the car and opening the rear door for Thorvaldsen.

"And I never met the son of Cotton Malone," the vice president said.

Thorvaldsen now realized they were in trouble. Which was doubly confirmed when he spotted Alfred Hermann parading their way, his chief of the guard in tow.

The vice president said, "Brent Green sends his regards."

And Thorvaldsen saw Green's betrayal in the man's hard eyes.

"I'm afraid you're not going anywhere," the VP said in a low tone.

Hermann arrived and shoved the car's rear door shut. "Herr Thorvaldsen will not need the ride. You may go."

Thorvaldsen was going to protest, make a scene, but he noticed that the chief of the guard assumed a position beside Gary. A gun beneath the man's jacket was pointed straight at the boy.

The message was clear.

He faced the driver. "That's correct. Thanks for coming."

Hermann relieved him of the atlas. "Your options are rapidly fading, Henrik."

"I would say so," the vice president said.

Hermann seemed puzzled. "Why are you here? What's happening?"

"Bring them both inside and I'll tell you all about it."

SINAI PENINSULA

MALONE WAITED UNTIL GEORGE HADDAD WAS SAFE BEHIND the bookshelf's end cap, where he and Pam had assumed a defensive position.

"Back from the dead?" he said to Haddad.

"Resurrection can be glorious."

"George, that man wants to kill all of you."

"I gathered. Lucky you're here."

"And what if I don't stop him?"

"Then this entire endeavor would have been a waste."

He needed to know, "What's back there?"

"Three more halls and the Reading Room. Each like this one. Not many places to hide."

He recalled the directory. "I'm just supposed to shoot it out with him?"

"I got you here. Now don't disappoint me."

Anger swelled in him. "There were simpler ways of doing this. He could be bringing reinforcements."

"I doubt that. But I have eyes outside watching to see if anyone else enters the *farsh*. I'm betting he's alone and will stay that way."

"How do you know that? The Israelis have been all over us."

"They're gone." Haddad pointed across the hall. "He's all that remains."

Malone caught sight of McCollum dashing through the archway and disappearing deeper into the library. Three more halls and the Reading Room. He was about to violate a multitude of the rules that had kept him alive for twelve years with the Magellan Billet. One was clear—*Never go in unless you know how you're going to get out.* But something else he'd learned also occurred to him. *When things go bad, anything can hurt you, including doing nothing.*

"Know this," Haddad said. "That man was responsible for your son being taken. He also destroyed your bookshop. He's as much to blame for you being here as I am. He would have killed Gary, if need be. And he'll gladly kill you."

"How do you know that about Gary?" Pam asked.

"The Guardians have access to a wealth of information."

"And how did you get to be Librarian?" Malone asked.

"Complicated story."

"I bet it is. You and I are going to have a long talk when this is over."

Haddad grinned. "Yes, my old friend, we'll have that long talk."

Malone pointed at Pam and spoke to Haddad. "Keep her here. She doesn't follow orders well at all."

"Go on," she said. "We'll be fine."

He decided to quit arguing and rushed forward down the aisle. At the exit, he stopped to one side. Twenty feet ahead another chamber opened. More towering walls, rows of stone shelving, letters, images, and mosaics from floor to ceiling. He crept forward, but hugged the corridor's polished sides. He entered the second hall and again took cover at the end of one of the shelf rows. The room was more square than the first, and he noticed a mixture of scrolls and codices.

No sign of movement. This was damn foolish. He was being drawn deeper. At some point McCollum would turn and fight, and on his terms.

But when?

HADDAD WATCHED PAM MALONE. BACK IN LONDON HE'D tried to assess her personality, wondering what she was even doing there. The Guardians had assembled personal information on Cotton Malone, things Haddad knew little about— Malone rarely talked about his wife and family. Theirs had been an academic friendship, spurred by a love of books and a respect for knowledge. But he knew enough, and the time had come to use that knowledge.

"We have to go back there," he said.

"Cotton said to stay here."

He allowed his gaze to bore into her. "We have to go back there." And to prove his point, he removed a pistol from beneath his cloak.

Surprisingly, she did not flinch. "I saw when you looked at McCollum."

"That the name he gave you?"

She nodded.

"His name is Sabre and he's a killer. I meant what I said in my apartment in London. I have a debt to pay, and I don't plan for Cotton to pay it for me."

"I saw it in your eyes. You wanted him to shoot. But you knew he wouldn't."

"Men like Sabre are stingy with their courage. They save it for when it's really needed. Like right now."

"You knew all this was going to happen?"

He shrugged. "Knew, thought, hoped. I don't know. We've been watching for Sabre. We knew he was planning something in Copenhagen, and when he took Gary we realized he was trying to find me. That's when I decided to involve myself. My second call to the West Bank was discovered by Israel's spies, which finally spurred them to move. Then, in Lisbon, I saw how I could lead all three of you here without the Israelis."

"You did this all so you could die?"

"I did this to protect the library. Sabre works for an organization that surely wants this knowledge for its own political and economic uses. They've been investigating us for some time. But you heard him. He's here for himself. Not them. Stop him and we stop everything."

"What are you going to do?"

"Not me. You have to do this, too."

"Me?"

"Cotton needs you. You going to walk away?"

He watched as she rolled the inquiry through her mind. He knew she was smart, gutsy, and brash. But also vulnerable. And prone to mistakes. He'd spent a lifetime reading people, and he hoped that he'd read Pam Malone correctly.

"No way," she said.

SABRE FLED THE ROOM OF PROVINCE AND ENTERED THE READ-
ing Room, which was filled with more tables and fewer shelves.
He knew from his first excursion that the next hall, the Room
of Eternity, led to the last hall, the entire library U-shaped.
Fake windows and alcoves adorned with faraway landscape
paintings and special lighting created an outdoor effect. He had
to keep reminding himself that he was underground.

Inside the Reading Room, he stopped.

Time to make use of what he'd noticed earlier.

MALONE KEPT ADVANCING, GUN READY. HE'D CHANGED THE
magazine for his last fresh one, but at least he had nine shots.
Three more remained in the one in his pocket, so he now had
twelve chances to stop McCollum.

His gaze darted from wall to wall and ceiling to floor, his
senses alert. His chest and spine were damp with perspiration, and the subterranean air chilled him. He passed through
the second hall and started down the corridor to the next
lighted room, which right-angled. He heard nothing and the
silence unnerved him. What kept him moving forward was
what Haddad had said—McCollum had been the one who
took Gary. The son of a bitch had touched his son. Taken him
away. Forced Malone to kill a man. No way those violations
were going unanswered. McCollum wanted a fight. He was
about to get one.

He came to the entrance to the third hall.

The Reading Room.

Maybe twenty tables of thick, rough-hewn planks, dark
and worn, dotted the room amid the shelving.

He spotted the exit on the opposite wall.

The room was larger than the other two, rectangular and
maybe sixty feet along its length. The walls supported slabs

and lintels of Byzantine origin, along with mosaics, this time scenes devoted to women, some spinning and weaving, others engaged in athletics. He ripped his gaze from the artistry and concentrated on the problem.

He expected McCollum, at any moment, to spring up from between the tables. He was ready. But nothing happened.

He stopped.

Something was wrong.

Then, across the room, at the base of the far wall, he spotted a dark reflection in the shiny red granite. A shadowy image, like looking through a soda bottle, rippling across the mirrorlike qualities of the finish.

From the floor.

Beneath the tables.

And then he realized.

84

WASHINGTON, DC

STEPHANIE HEARD THE GUNFIRE, BUT NO BULLET STRUCK HER. Then she saw the hole in the side of Brent Green's head and realized what had happened.

She turned.

Heather Dixon stood, gun in hand.

Green's body thudded to the hardwood floor, but she continued to watch Dixon, who lowered her weapon.

Cassiopeia walked up behind the Israeli.

"That's the end of that," Dixon said.

Stephanie caught Cassiopeia's attention. "What happened?"

"When you and Green went back to the office, she appeared. We were right. Green brought a few friends, who were waiting out back. The Secret Service grabbed them and then"—Cassiopeia pointed at Dixon—"she came inside."

Stephanie understood. "You're working with the president?"

"Had to be done. This bastard was going to sell us all out. He and your vice president could well have started a world war with what they planned."

She sensed something from the tone and wanted to know, "What about you and Daley?"

"I liked Larry. He approached us for help, told us what was happening, and he and I got to be close. Believe it or not, he was trying to stop things. You have to give him that."

"Been a whole lot easier if you both had just come to me with what you had."

Dixon shook her head. "That's your problem, Stephanie. You live in this idealistic bubble. You hated Larry. You didn't like Green. You thought the White House didn't like you. How were you going to be able to do anything?"

"But she made the perfect bait," Cassiopeia said. "Didn't she?"

"Every line needs a lure, and you two were this one's."

Stephanie still held the CD she'd planted in Daley's office. The disk was blank. Just something to get Green to react. "They get everything on tape out there?" She'd been wired before they left Camp David.

Cassiopeia nodded. "All of it."

"What about the Saudis?" she asked Dixon. "You were working with them when we first talked."

"Typical Arabs. Playing both sides. They were originally in league with the vice president, thinking he was going to help stop anything relating to the Alexandria Link. Then they figured out that was bullshit. So they back-channeled to us and we made a deal. On the mall that day, they were there just to spur you on, nothing more. Of course, none of us was aware that you'd acquired a partner." Dixon motioned with the gun at Cassiopeia. "I still owe you one for that dart."

"Maybe one day you'll get the chance to repay me."

Dixon smiled. "Maybe."

Stephanie stared at the body of Brent Green. She recalled how he'd suggested that he might be interested in her and how, for a moment, she'd liked the possibility. He'd actually defended her, supposedly been willing to resign in order to stand with her, and she'd found herself questioning all the doubts she'd harbored about him.

But it had all been an act.

"The president sent me to end this," Dixon said, interrupting her thoughts. "No trials. No press. The attorney general was a troubled man who took his own life. His body will be cremated and a death certificate issued by military medical examiners. Suicide. He'll be given a lavish burial and remembered fondly. End of story."

"And the Alexandria Link?" she asked.

"George Haddad has disappeared. We're hoping Malone has him. Haddad called Palestine months ago, then again a few days ago. After the first time, and after Larry told me things, we latched on to Pam Malone. The Mossad planned to take Gary Malone. But our prime minister balked. Then the Order beat us to it. With Pam Malone tagged, we just followed. But that didn't work out so well. Then all this happened. Daniels has assured us that nothing will come of anything. My government trusts him."

"Has anyone heard from Cotton?"

Dixon shook her head. "The last we heard he parachuted down somewhere in the Sinai. But it doesn't matter. If anything is found, the deal is we never hear about it."

"And once Daniels is no longer president?" Cassiopeia asked.

"Should be forgotten by then. If not, Israel will do what it's done for centuries. Fight like hell. We've managed and we'll continue."

And Stephanie believed that. But there was one other point. "The vice president. What about him?"

"From all we know, only Green, the VP, and Alfred Hermann understood exactly what was going to happen. When Green heard the conversation Larry recorded with the VP's chief of staff, he panicked and asked the Saudis to take Daley out. In typical fashion, they never mentioned that to us or we would have stopped them. But you can't trust an Arab." Dixon paused. "You two showing up, meeting with Larry, panicked Green, and he convinced the Saudis to move on you, too. After Daniels stopped the attack, killing all the hired help, and now with Green gone, it's all over for the Saudis."

Stephanie pointed to Green. "What about this?"

"We have people waiting to take this piece of crap back to his house, where his body will be found later today. Larry's death will not be attributed to any terrorist attack, as Green had planned."

"That could prove tough. The car did explode."

"The case will simply go down as unsolved. But it will have undertones, ones Daniels can exploit, like what these idiots had planned. I think Larry might actually like that one. He can still be of help, even from the grave."

"You haven't explained," Cassiopeia said, "how this can be contained with the VP still around?"

Dixon shrugged. "That's Daniels's problem." Then the Israeli found her cell phone, hit a button, and said, "Mr. President, Green's dead, just as you wanted."

85

SINAI PENINSULA

SABRE FIRED AT MALONE'S LEGS FORTY FEET AWAY. NONE OF the tables accommodated chairs, so his line of sight was clear. He wanted to cut the legs out from beneath his adversary, making the final kill easy.

He sent three bullets Malone's way.

But the legs were gone.

Damn.

He rolled out from beneath the table to the next one, inched up to the top edge to find Malone, and saw nothing.

Then he knew.

MALONE HAD REALIZED THAT MCCOLLUM INTENDED TO SHOOT his legs and had leaped onto the nearest table an instant before three shots popped through the hall. Paperweights of golden quartz clattered to the floor. McCollum would almost instantly deduce what Malone had done, so he decided to turn the advantage his way.

He waited an instant, then rolled off and saw McCollum

crouched behind one of the tables. He aimed and ticked off two shots, but McCollum shifted his position and used one of the thick pedestals for protection.

This shooting gallery was too open.

He darted behind a row of shelves that stood to his left.

"Not bad, Malone," his adversary said from across the room.

"I try."

"You're not getting out of here."

"We'll see."

"I've killed men better than you."

He wondered if the talk was bravado or mind games. Neither impressed him.

HADDAD LED PAM MALONE THROUGH THE LIBRARY, HEADING in the opposite direction from where Sabre and Malone had gone. They'd already heard shots. He needed to hurry. They entered the fifth hall, aptly named the Room of Life, symbolized by a mosaic cross with its upper vertical replaced by an egg-shaped oval.

He swept through and found the Room of Eternity, stopping at the exit doorway. Voices came down the corridor past the ninety-degree turn. Apparently the showdown was occurring in the Reading Room. Lots of tables, fewer shelves, more open space. Sabre's walk-through earlier had been for reconnaissance, and his opponent had noticed all the right things. He'd once done the same when fighting Jews. *Always know your battlefield.*

He knew this one intimately.

Five years ago he'd secretly completed the hero's quest, just before he'd called Cotton Malone for help. When he'd first arrived, gained access to the library, and learned that all he suspected about the Bible was true, he'd been over-whelmed. But when the Guardians asked for his help, he'd been thrilled. Many Guardians had been recruited from invitees, and all of the Guardians there then believed he should be their Librarian. They'd explained about the threats closing in and he'd agreed to solve their problem. But in the end he'd needed help, too. Which was why Malone had been involved.

Patience and knowledge had served him well.

He only hoped he hadn't miscalculated.

He stood still at the doorway leading from the Room of Eternity, Pam Malone behind him.

"Wait here," he whispered.

He eased forward through the corridor, turned its corner, and stole a peek into the Reading Room. He saw movement left and right. One man behind the shelves, the other using the tables for cover.

He crept back to Pam Malone and handed her his gun.

"I have to go in there," he said in a soft voice.

"And you're not coming back out."

He shook his head. "This is the end."

"You promised Cotton a long talk."

"I lied." He paused. "And you knew it."

"It's the lawyer in me."

"No, it's the human being in you. We all do things we regret. I've done my share. But at least, at the end of my life I was able to keep this library alive." He saw something in her eyes. "You know what I mean, don't you?"

She nodded.

"Then you know what you have to do."

He saw her confusion and patted her shoulder. "You'll know, when the moment arrives." He pointed at the gun. "Have you ever fired one before?"

She quickly shook her head no.

"Just point and pull the trigger. It kicks, so hold it steady."

She said nothing, but he was satisfied that she understood.

"Have a prosperous life. Tell Cotton he always had my respect."

And he turned and walked toward the Reading Room.

"WE CAN SIT HERE ALL DAY," MALONE called out.

"You're in way over your head," McCollum said. "A bit out of practice, aren't you?"

"I can kick *your* ass."

McCollum chuckled. "Tell you what I'm going to do. Think I'll double back and kill that ex-wife of yours. I would have killed your boy, too, if you hadn't taken out those idiots I hired. And by the way, did you think that was your doing? I set up that whole thing and you followed like a hound dog after the fox. Plan B was to kill the boy. Either way, I'd have found George Haddad."

He knew what McCollum was doing. Trying to work him up. Piss him off. Get him to react. But he wondered about something. "You ever find Haddad?"

"Nope. You were there when the Israelis killed him. I heard the whole thing."

Heard it? McCollum had no idea about the Librarian. So he asked, "Where'd you get that quest?"

"I gave it to him."

The new voice was George Haddad's.

Malone saw the Palestinian standing in the far doorway.

"Mr. Sabre, I manipulated you in the same way you did Cotton. I left the audiotape and the information on my computer for you to find, including the quest, which I created. I assure you, the journey I completed to originally find this place was much more difficult."

"You're full of crap," McCollum said.

"It had to be a challenge. Too easy and you might have thought it a trap. Too hard and you would have never made it. But you were anxious. I even left you a flash drive beside my computer, and you thought nothing of it. More of the bait for this trap."

Malone noticed that, from where Haddad stood, a clear line of sight existed to McCollum's position. But both of Haddad's hands were empty. Something that had surely been noticed.

"George, what are you doing?" he called out.

"Finishing what I started."

Haddad stepped toward McCollum.

"Trust what you know, Cotton. She won't let you down."

And his friend kept walking.

SABRE WATCHED THE LIBRARIAN MARCH TOWARD HIM. THIS man was George Haddad? All of what happened had been planned? He'd been led?

What had the old man called it? *A trap?* Hardly.

So he fired one shot.

To the Librarian's head.

MALONE SCREAMED "NO" AS THE BULLET PLOWED INTO George Haddad. He had so many questions he wanted to ask him, so much he hadn't understood. How had the Palestinian found his way from the West Bank, to London, to here? What was happening? What was it Haddad knew that was worth all this?

Anger surged through him and he clicked off two shots McCollum's way, but they only damaged the far wall.

Haddad lay motionless, a lake of blood forming around his head.

"The old man had guts," McCollum called out. "I was going to kill him anyway. Maybe he knew that?"

"You're dead" was all Malone said in response.

A chuckle from the other side of the hall. "Like you said about yourself. You might find that hard to accomplish."

He knew he had to end this. The Guardians were counting on him. Haddad had been counting on him.

Then he saw Pam.

Inside the doorway leading out. Just in the shadows, the angle making her invisible to McCollum.

She held a gun.

Trust what you know.

Haddad's last words.

He and Pam had spent most of their lives together, the past five hating each other. But she was a part of him, and he of her, and they always would be linked. If not by Gary, then by something neither one of them could explain. Not necessarily love, but a bond. He wouldn't allow anything to happen to her, and he had to trust that she wouldn't to him.

She won't let you down.

He popped the magazine from his gun, then aimed toward McCollum and pulled the trigger. The bullet already in the chamber thudded into one of the tabletops.

Then a click. And another.

One more to make the point.

"End of the line, Malone," McCollum said.

He stood, hoping his adversary would want to savor the kill. If McCollum chose to fire from his concealed position, he and Pam were both dead. But he knew his enemy. McCollum stood, gun pointed, and advanced from behind the table, weaving a path close to where Malone stood. Now his back was to the doorway. Not even his peripheral vision would help.

He needed to stall. "Your name Sabre?"

"The name I use over here. My real name is McCollum."

"What are you going to do?"

"Kill everyone here and keep this all to myself. Real simple."

"You don't have a clue as to what's here. What are you going to do with it?"

"I'll get people who know. My bet is there's plenty. Just the Old Testament thing is enough to make my mark on the world."

Pam had not moved. She'd certainly heard the clicks and knew that he was at McCollum's mercy. He imagined her fear. Over the past few days she'd seen people die. Now the terror of her killing another person must be surging through her. He'd felt that uncertainty himself. Pulling the trigger was never easy. The act came with consequences, the fear of which could absolutely paralyze. He only hoped her instincts would win out over her terror.

McCollum raised his gun. "Say hello to Haddad for me."

Pam rushed from the archway and her footsteps momentarily distracted McCollum. His head jerked right and he apparently caught sight of movement in the corner of his eye. Malone used that instant to kick the gun from McCollum's hand. He then jammed a fist into the other man's face, sending McCollum staggering back. He lunged to pound the bastard, but McCollum recovered and propelled himself forward. Together they slammed onto one of the tables and rolled off the other side. He brought a knee into the stomach and heard the breath leave his opponent.

He stood and grabbed McCollum off the floor, expecting

him to be winded. Instead, McCollum rammed his fists into Malone's chest and face.

The room winked in and out and he shook the pain from his brain.

He whirled and saw a knife in McCollum's hand.

The same knife from Lisbon.

He readied himself.

But never got the chance to do anything.

One shot.

McCollum acted surprised. Then blood flowed from a hole in his right side. Another shot and his arms went into the air and he staggered backward. A third, then a fourth, and the body tilted forward, the eyes rolled skyward, blood spurted from his mouth with each exhale, then he thudded face-first to the floor.

Malone turned.

Pam lowered the gun.

"About time," he said.

But she said nothing, her eyes wide at what she'd done. He stepped close and lowered her arm. She stared at him with a blank expression.

Figures emerged from the shadows of the doorway.

Nine men and women quietly approached.

Adam and Straw Hat were among the group. Eve was crying as she knelt beside Haddad's body.

The others knelt with her.

Pam stood still and watched.

So did he.

Finally he had to interrupt their mourning. "I assume you have communications equipment?"

Adam stared up at him and nodded.

"I need to use it."

86

VIENNA

THORVALDSEN WAS BACK IN THE LIBRARY WITH GARY—BUT this time Hermann and the vice president knew he was there. They were alone with the door closed, the security men just outside.

"They were here last night," the vice president said, clearly agitated. "Had to be there somewhere." He motioned to the upper shelves. "Damn place is like a concert hall. He called the attorney general and told him everything."

"Is that a problem?" Hermann asked.

"Thank God, no. Brent will be my vice president once all this happens. He's been handling things in Washington while I'm gone. So at least it's controlled on that end."

"This one," Hermann said, pointing at Thorvaldsen, "took my daughter yesterday. He did that *before* he heard anything last night."

The vice president grew even more agitated. "Which begs a whole host of questions. Alfred, I didn't question what you were doing here. You wanted the Alexandria Link, and you got it. I was the one who managed that. I don't know what you did with that information and I don't want to know, but it's obviously become a problem."

Hermann was rubbing the side of his head. "Henrik, you will pay dearly for striking me. No man has ever done that."

Thorvaldsen was not impressed. "Maybe it was about time."

"And you, young man."

A knot clenched in Thorvaldsen's throat. He hadn't planned to place Gary in jeopardy.

"Alfred," the vice president said, "everything is in motion. You're going to have to handle this situation."

Sweat beaded on Thorvaldsen's brow as he realized what those words meant.

"These two will never breathe a word of what they know."

"You'd kill the boy?" Thorvaldsen asked.

"You'd kill my daughter? So what? Yes, I'd kill the boy." Hermann's nostrils flared and his eyes bristled with the rage that clearly coursed through him.

"Not accustomed to this, are you, Alfred?"

"Taunting me will accomplish nothing."

But it would buy Thorvaldsen time, and that was about the only play he knew. He turned to the vice president. "Brent Green was a good man. What happened to him?"

"I'm not his priest, so I don't know. I assume he saw the benefits of taking my job. America needs strong leadership, people in power who aren't afraid to use it. Brent's that way. I'm that way."

"What about men of character?"

"That's a relative term. I prefer to see it as the United States partnering with the worldwide business community to accomplish goals of a mutually beneficial nature."

"You're a murderer," Gary said.

A soft knock came from the door and Hermann stepped across to answer. One of the vice president's security men whispered to Hermann. A puzzled look came to the Austrian's face, then he nodded and the security man left.

"The president is on the telephone," Hermann said.

Surprise flooded the vice president's face. "What the hell?"

"He tracked you here from the Secret Service. Your detail reported that you were in here with me and two others, one a boy. The president wants to talk to us all."

Thorvaldsen realized they'd have no choice. The president clearly knew a lot.

"He also wanted to know if I had a speakerphone," Hermann said as he walked to his desk and punched two buttons.

"Good day, Mr. President," Hermann said.

"I don't think you and I have ever met. Danny Daniels calling from Washington."

"No, sir. We haven't. It's a pleasure."

"Is my vice president there?"

"I'm here, Mr. President."

"And Thorvaldsen, you there? With the Malone boy?"

"He's here with me," Thorvaldsen said.

"First, I have some tragic news. I'm still reeling from it. Brent Green is dead."

Thorvaldsen caught the instant of shock on the vice president's face. Even Hermann flinched.

"Suicide," Daniels said. "Shot himself in the head. I was just told a few minutes ago. Awful. We're working up a press release now before the story explodes."

"How did this happen?" the vice president asked.

"I don't know, but it did and he's gone. Also, Larry Daley is dead. Car bomb. We have no idea about the culprits there."

More dismay invaded the vice president's expression and his shoulders seemed to sag an inch.

"Here's the situation," Daniels said. "Under the circumstances, I'm not going to be able to travel to Afghanistan next week. America needs me here and I need my vice president to take my place."

The vice president stayed silent.

"Anybody there?" Daniels said in a loud voice.

"Yes, sir," the vice president said. "I'm here."

"Great. Get your tail back here today and be ready to go next week. Of course, if you don't want to make that trip to see the troops, you can tender your resignation. Your choice. But I actually prefer you make the trip."

"What are you saying?"

"This isn't a secure line, so I doubt you want me to say what I really think. Let me say it with a story. One my daddy used to tell. There was a bird flying south for the winter, but he got caught in an ice storm and fell to the ground. He froze, but a cow came along and crapped on him. The warm poop unthawed him and he liked it so much he started to sing. A cat came along to see what the commotion was about, asked if he could help, saw it was a meal, and ate the bird. Here are the morals of the story. Everybody who shits on you ain't your enemy. Everybody who comes along to help ain't your friend. And if you're warm and happy, even in a pile of shit, keep your mouth shut. That make my point?"

"Perfectly, sir," the vice president said. "How do you suggest I explain my resignation?"

"Tough to use the always popular *Spend more time with my family.* No one in our position quits for that reason. Let's see, the last VP to resign was facing indictment. Can't use that one. Of course, you can't tell the truth, that you got caught committing high treason. How about, *The president and I seem no longer capable of working together*? Being the consummate politician that you are, I'm sure you will choose your words real careful because if I hear one thing I don't like, then I'm going to tell the truth. Talk issues, debate our differences, tell people I'm an asshole. All fine. But nothing I don't want to hear."

Thorvaldsen watched the vice president. The man seemed

to want to protest but wisely realized the effort would do no good.

"Mr. President," Thorvaldsen said. "Stephanie and Cassiopeia okay?"

"They're fine, Henrik. Can I call you that?"

"Nothing else."

"They were instrumental in working things through on this end."

"What about my mom and dad?" Gary blurted out.

"That must be Cotton's boy. Nice to meet you, Gary. Your mom and dad are fine. I talked with your dad just a few minutes ago. Which brings me to you, Herr Hermann."

Thorvaldsen caught the disdain in the president's voice.

"Your man Sabre found the Library of Alexandria. Actually, Cotton did that for him, but he did try to steal it away. Sabre's dead. So you lose. We have the library and, I assure you, not a soul will ever know where it is. As for you, Herr Hermann, Henrik and the boy better have no problems leaving your château, and I don't want to hear another word out of you or I'll let the Israelis *and* the Saudis know who orchestrated all this. Your problems then will be beyond comprehension. There will be no place good for you to hide."

The vice president slumped into one of the chairs.

"One more thing, Hermann. Not a word to bin Laden and his people. We want to meet them next week while they wait for my plane. If they're not there with missiles ready, I'm sending my commandos to take you out."

Hermann said nothing.

"I'll take your silence to mean you understand. You see, that's the great thing about being the leader of the free world. I have a lot of people willing to do what I want. People with a wide variety of talents. You got money. I got power."

Thorvaldsen had never met the American president, but he already liked him.

"Gary," the president said. "Your dad will be back in Copenhagen in a couple of days. And Henrik, thanks for all you did."

"I'm not sure I really helped."

"We won, didn't we? And that's what counts in this game." The line clicked off.

Hermann stood silent.

Thorvaldsen pointed to the atlas. "Those letters are useless, Alfred. You can't prove anything."

"Get out."

"Gladly."

Daniels was right.

Game over.

87

WASHINGTON, DC
MONDAY, OCTOBER 10
8:30 AM

STEPHANIE SAT IN THE OVAL OFFICE. SHE'D BEEN THERE MANY times, mostly feeling uncomfortable. But not today. She and Cassiopeia had come to meet with President Daniels.

Brent Green had been buried yesterday in Vermont with honors. The press had lauded his character and achievements. Democrats and Republicans said he would be missed. Daniels himself had delivered the eulogy, a moving tribute.

Larry Daley had been buried, too, in Florida, without fanfare. Only some family and a few friends. Stephanie and Cassiopeia had both attended.

Interesting how she'd read both men wrong. Daley wasn't a saint by any means, but he wasn't a murderer or a traitor. He'd tried to stop what was happening. Unfortunately, what was happening had stopped him.

"I want you back at the Magellan Billet," Daniels said to her.

"You might find that hard to explain."

"I don't have to explain myself. I never wanted you to go, but I had no choice at the time."

She wanted her job back. She liked what she did. But there was another matter. "What about bribing Congress?"

"I told you, Stephanie. I knew nothing about that. But it stops here and now. Just like with Green, though, the country won't benefit from that kind of scandal. Let's end it and move on."

She wasn't necessarily sure of Daniels's lack of complicity, but she agreed. That was the better course.

"No one will ever know anything that happened?" Cassiopeia asked.

Daniels was sitting behind his desk, feet propped on the edge, his tall frame leaning back in his chair. "Not a word."

The vice president had resigned Saturday, citing differences over policy with the administration. The press had been clamoring to get him on camera but had so far been unsuccessful.

"I imagine," Daniels said, "my ex–vice president will be trying to make a name for himself. There'll be a few public squabbles between us over policy, things like that. He might even make a try for the next election. But I'm not afraid of that fight. And speaking of fights, I need you to keep an eye on the Order of the Golden Fleece. Those folks are trouble.

We've cut their legs out from under them for now, but they'll stand up again."

"And Israel?" Cassiopeia asked. "What about them?"

"They have my pledge that nothing from the library will ever be released. Only Cotton and his ex-wife know where it is, but I'm not even going to note that anywhere. Let the damn thing stay hidden." Daniels looked at Stephanie. "You and Heather make peace?"

"Yesterday at the funeral. She truly liked Daley. She told me some things about Larry I never knew."

"See, you shouldn't be so judgmental. Green ordered Daley's death after he studied those flash drives. They pointed to leaks in the dike and he moved to plug them. Heather's a good agent. She does her job. Green and the vice president would have destroyed Israel. They didn't give a damn about nothing except themselves. And you thought I was a problem."

Stephanie smiled. "I was wrong about that, too, Mr. President."

Daniels motioned at Cassiopeia. "Back to building your castle in France?"

"I've been absent for a while. My employees are probably wondering about me."

"If yours are like mine, as long as the paychecks keep coming, they're happy." Daniels stood. "Thanks to both of you for what you did."

Stephanie stayed seated. She sensed something. "What is it you're not saying?"

Daniels's eyes gleamed. "Probably a whole bunch."

"It's the library. You were awfully cavalier about it a moment ago. You're not going to let it stay hidden, are you?"

"Not for me to decide. Somebody else is in charge of that one and we all know who he is."

MALONE LISTENED AS THE BELLS OF COPENHAGEN BANGED
loud for three PM. Højbro Plads was busy with its usual midday crowd. He, Pam, and Gary sat at an outdoor table, having just finished lunch. He and Pam had flown back from
Egypt yesterday, after spending Saturday with the Guardians
while they honored George Haddad.

He motioned for the check.

Thorvaldsen stood fifty yards away, supervising the re-
modeling of Malone's shop, which had started last week
while they were away. Scaffolding now embraced the four-
story façade, and workers were busy inside and out.

"I'm going to tell Henrik goodbye," Gary said, and the
boy rushed from the table through the crowd.

"That was sad Saturday with George," Pam said.

He knew there was still a lot on her mind. They hadn't
talked much about what had happened in the library.

"You all right?" he asked.

"I killed a man. He was a sorry piece of crap, but I still
killed him."

He said nothing.

"You stood up," she said. "Faced him, knowing I was back
there. You knew I'd shoot."

"I wasn't sure what you'd do. But I knew you'd do something, and that's all I needed."

"I've never fired a gun before. When Haddad gave it to
me, he told me to just point and shoot. He knew I'd do it,
too."

"Pam, you can't sweat it. You did what you had to."

"Like you did all those years." She paused. "I want to say
something, and it's not easy."

He waited.

"I'm sorry. I really am, for everything. I never knew what you went through out there. I thought it was ego, macho male stuff. I just didn't get it. But now I do. I was wrong. About a great many things."

"That makes two of us. I'm sorry, too. For everything that went wrong all those years."

She held up her hands in surrender. "Okay, I think that's enough emotion for us both."

He extended his hand. "Peace?"

She accepted the gesture. "Peace."

But then she bent close and gently kissed him on the lips. He hadn't expected that, and the sensation chilled his nerves.

"What was that for?"

"Don't get any ideas. I think we're both better off divorced, but that's not to say I don't remember."

"So how about neither one of us forgetting?"

"Fair enough," she said. After a pause she added, "What about Gary? What do we do? He needs to know the truth."

He'd thought about that dilemma. "And he will. Let's give it a little time and then we'll all three have a talk. I'm not sure it's going to matter much, from any of our points of view. But you're right, he's entitled to the truth."

He paid the check and they walked over to Thorvaldsen and Gary.

"I'll miss this boy," Henrik said. "He and I make a good team."

Malone and Pam had heard all about what happened in Austria.

"I think he's had more than enough intrigue," Pam said.

Malone agreed. "Back to school for you. Bad enough all the stuff you were into." He saw that Thorvaldsen understood his meaning. They'd talked about that yesterday. And though he was upset at the thought of Gary tackling a man holding a gun, secretly he was proud. No Malone blood coursed through the boy's veins, but enough of the father had seeped into the son to make him his in every way that counted. "Time for you guys to go."

The three of them walked to where the square ended and Jesper waited with Thorvaldsen's car.

"You had enough intrigue, too?" Malone asked Jesper.

The man only smiled and nodded. Thorvaldsen had said yesterday that two days with Margarete Hermann had been about all Jesper could stand. She'd been released on Saturday when Thorvaldsen and Gary flew back to Denmark. From what Thorvaldsen had said about Hermann, their father–daughter relationship was not to be envied. Blood did indeed tie them, but not much else.

He hugged his son and said, "I love you. Take care of your mother."

"She doesn't need me to do that."

"Don't be so sure."

He faced Pam. "If you ever need me, you know where I am."

"Same for you. If nothing else, we do know how to watch each other's backs."

They hadn't told Gary about what had happened in the Sinai, and they never would. Thorvaldsen had agreed to take the Guardians under his wing and provide funds to maintain the monastery and library. Already plans were in the works to electronically archive the manuscripts. Also, some recruitment would occur and the Guardians' ranks would be restored to a respectable number. The Dane had been thrilled at the prospect of aiding and was looking forward to visiting the site soon.

But it would all remain secret.

Thorvaldsen had assured Israel that the matter was contained and, with the United States likewise providing assurances, the Jews seemed satisfied.

Pam and Gary climbed into the car. Malone waved as the vehicle disappeared into traffic, headed for the airport. He then wove through the crowd to where Thorvaldsen watched as workmen cleared rubble from his building.

"All put to rest?" Henrik asked.

He knew what his friend meant. "That demon's gone."

"The past can really eat your soul."

He agreed.

"Or be your best friend."

He knew what Thorvaldsen meant. "It will be amazing to see what's in that library."

"No telling what treasures await."

He watched men on the scaffolding as they steam-cleaned the sixteenth-century exterior of soot.

"It'll look as good as it once did," Thorvaldsen said. "Up to you to restore the inventory. Lots of books to buy."

He was looking forward to it. That's what he did. A bookseller. But there was a point to be made from the lessons he'd learned over the past few days. He considered again how all three Malones had been threatened, and what really mattered. He pointed to the building.

"None of this is all that important."

The Dane cast him an understanding smile.

"It's just stuff, Henrik. That's all. Just stuff."

WRITER'S NOTE

This book involved lots of travel. Trips were made to Denmark, England, Germany, Austria, Washington, D.C., and Portugal. The basic concept was born during a dinner in Camden, South Carolina, when one of the hosts, Kenneth Harvey, asked me if I'd ever heard of a Lebanese scholar named Kamal Salibi. When I said no, Ken offered me four of Salibi's books. About a year later the idea for this novel blossomed. As always, though, the final story is a blend of fact and fiction.

Now it's time to know where the line was drawn.

As to the *nakba*, first described in the prologue, that tragedy was all too real and continues to haunt Middle East relations.

The monument described in chapters 8 and 34 is based on an actual marble arbor that exists at Shugborough Hall in England. New Agers and conspiratorialists have debated its meaning for decades. The press conference in chapter 8 actually happened at Shugborough Hall, and the offered interpretations of the monument are the ones the actual experts expounded. The concept of the Roman letters being a map is my invention.

As mentioned, the idea of the Old Testament being a record of ancient Jews in a place other than Palestine is not mine. In 1985 Salibi detailed this theory in a book titled *The*

Bible Came from Arabia. Salibi expounded on his ideas in three other works, *Who Was Jesus* (1988), *Secrets of the Bible People* (1988), and *The Historicity of Biblical Israel* (1998). George Haddad's experiences in how he noticed a connection between west Arabia and the Bible, detailed in chapter 52, mimic Salibi's. Also, the Saudi government did in fact bulldoze entire villages after the publication of Salibi's first book; to this day the Saudis refuse to allow any scientific digging in Asir.

The maps in chapters 57 and 68 are from Salibi's research. The idea that the land promised by God in the Abrahamic covenant lies in a region far removed from what we regard as Palestine is, to say the least, controversial. But as Salibi and George Haddad both noted, the matter could be easily proven, or dismissed, through archaeology. One point on language. Throughout the book, the term "Old Hebrew" is used to refer to the language of the original Hebrew Bible. Little is known of its orthography, grammar, syntax, or idiom. It was a language of learning, rarely spoken, and passed from common usage in the sixth or the fifth century B.C.E. "Old Hebrew," as opposed to Biblical or Rabbinical Hebrew or some other descriptive label, was chosen simply for reader convenience.

The Old Testament inconsistencies noted in chapters 20, 23, and 57 are nothing new. Scholars have debated these points for centuries. The Bible, though, is, if nothing else, a fluid document, and each generation seems to leave a mark upon its interpretation.

The story of David Ben-Gurion in chapter 22 is accurate. The father of modern Israel did radically change his politics after 1965, becoming more conciliatory toward the Arabs. Thereafter, he was shut out of Israeli politics until his death in 1973. Of course, his visit to the library was my concoction.

The history of Nicolas Poussin in chapter 29 is true. His life also made a dramatic shift. The fate of his *Shepherds of Arcadia* is told correctly, and the excerpt from a letter that describes what Poussin may have secretly learned is real. Why Poussin created *The Shepherds of Arcadia II,* the reverse image of the first painting (which was chiseled on the monument at Shugborough Hall), is a mystery.

The Guardians are not real. Perhaps if they had existed, the Library of Alexandria might have been saved. The physical description of the library offered in chapter 21 is the best available. As to how more than half a million manuscripts vanished, the three explanations in chapter 21 are the experts' best guess. The learned men described in chapter 32 all lived, but sadly, thanks to the destruction of the Library of Alexandria, none of their writings have survived. The Piri Reis Map (chapter 32) does still exist and offers a fleeting glimpse of what might have been lost.

The hero's quest is fictional, adapted from a mysterious manuscript called *The Red Serpent.* I came across it in Rennes-le-Château while researching *The Templar Legacy.*

The Order of the Golden Fleece was a French medieval society created as detailed in chapter 18. A social order bearing that name still thrives in Austria, but my fictional group is no relation. The robes and ornamentation described for the Order were inspired by the fifteenth-century incarnation.

The Monastery of Santa Maria de Belém stands in Lisbon. I visited twice, and its history and magnificence—as described in chapters 46, 48, 51, 53, and 54—are accurate, though some of the building's internal geography was changed. It's a remarkable place, as is Lisbon.

The sacrarium that plays a pivotal role in the hero's quest stands in the monastery at Belém. The way sunlight changes its silver exterior to gold is a phenomenon noted centuries ago. Today, to keep the effect constant, floodlights bathe the silver. Of course, those were eliminated from this story.

The National Air and Space Museum is one of my favorite places, and I was glad it finally found its way into one of my tales. Kronborg Slot (chapter 9), Helsingør (chapters 11 and 14), the *Baumeisterhaus* in Rothenburg (chapter 22), and the Rhine Valley and bridge spanning the Mosel River in central Germany (chapter 27) are all real.

The letters between St. Jerome and St. Augustine (chapters 63 and 65) are my invention. Both were learned men, active in formulating the early church. The letters show how Jerome's translation of the Old Testament from Hebrew to Latin may have been manipulated to serve the emerging church's purposes. The noted inconsistencies in Jerome's translation are Salibi's, not mine, but they do raise fascinating questions.

I've never parachuted from a C130H, but Colonel Barry King has and he told me all about it.

The abbey in the Sinai (chapter 72) is a composite of many that dot that desolate region. Locating the preserved Library of Alexandria there, underground (chapter 78), is not beyond possibility. Ancient Egyptians mined those mountains extensively and their tunnels would have still existed after the time of Christ.

The tale of the Sinai Bible (chapter 63) happened as presented. The Aleppo Codex (chapter 23), dated from 900 CE, is on display in Jerusalem and remains the oldest surviving Old Testament manuscript. A Bible from a time before Christ, though—like the one noted in chapter 79—would certainly change everything that is known about the Old Testament.

The Middle East conflict rages on. Amazing how all three of the world's major religions—Judaism, Islam, and Christianity—chose to venerate the same spot in Jerusalem.

For two thousand years these conflicting ideologies have battled for supremacy but, as stated in chapter 7, at its most fundamental level that fight is not over land, freedom, or politics. Instead, it centers on something far more basic.

The Word of God.

Each of the three religions possesses its own version. Each fervently believes the other two are wrong.

And that, more than anything else, explains why the conflict endures.

An Interview with the Author

Question: The subject of *The Alexandria Link* is the Library of Alexandria. What exactly was it?

Steve Berry: The grandest collection of knowledge in the ancient world: part university, laboratory, research institute, and zoo. An impressive complex of buildings and gardens (situated in two separate locations), resembling a Greek temple, each with richly decorated lecture and banquet halls linked by colonnaded walks. Founded in the fourth century BCE, the library was staffed by Greek scientists, philosophers, artists, writers, and scholars, and contained a vast collection—more than 700,000 scrolls and papyri. If any book was found aboard a ship that visited Alexandria, the law required it to be taken to the library and copied, the tradition being that no manuscript should be unavailable in Alexandria.

Q: What was Alexander himself like?

SB: Complex, to say the least. He lived a short life, thirty-three years, from 356 to 323 BCE. He was first king of Macedonia, then conquered much of what was then the civilized world—Greece, Egypt, Asia Minor, and Asia all the way to western India. He's been physically depicted in a variety of conflicting ways, which seems to only add to his mystique. A warrior of the highest order, he possessed a shrewd political sense that enabled him to convert bitter enemies into long-lasting friends. He was also a visionary: a Greek who became a Persian, rejecting the petty nationalism that clouded much of his time's political thinking. Before Alexander, eastern ideas flourished. After him, western thoughts dominated. He ushered in the Hellenistic Age of Greek dominance which, together with the later Romans and Christianity, formed the foundation of what is now western civilization. An amazing legacy.

Q: What eventually became of the Library of Alexandria?

SB: One version holds that it burned when Julius Caesar fought Ptolemy XIII in 48 BCE. Caesar ordered the torching of the royal fleet, but the fire spread throughout the city and may have consumed the library. Another version blamed Christians, who supposedly destroyed both the main library in 272 CE and the secondary one, in the Serapeum, in 391 as part of their effort to rid the city of all pagan influences. A final account credited Arabs with the library's destruction after they conquered Alexandria in 642. The caliph Omar, when asked about books in the imperial treasury, was quoted as saying, "If what is written agrees with the Book of God, they are not required. If it disagrees, they are not desired. Destroy them." So for six months, scrolls supposedly fueled the baths of Alexandria. But no one knows which version is true. The more likely explanation is that as Egypt was confronted with growing unrest and foreign aggression, the library became victim to persecution, mob violence, and military occupation—no longer enjoying special privileges. As with so much that man creates, it simply faded away.

Q: Is there a chance that the library is actually still in existence?

SB: What a find that would be, but sadly, it's most probably gone. Still, we can imagine that it survived.

Q: Given the recent talk about efforts to bring all written material together into one comprehensive and accessible digital library, was the Library of Alexandria ahead of its time?

SB: No question. Even ancient man recognized the logic and convenience of having knowledge both assimilated and organized. Unfortunately, the Library of Alexandria represented one of the first and last attempts of that age to accomplish the task. After its demise, it was not until the Middle Ages, 800 years later, that man again managed to duplicate the endeavor.

Q: How did you become interested in the topic?

SB: I've had an interest in the Library of Alexandria for many years, and knew that I wanted to eventually do a book about it. Libraries are fascinating. I currently serve as chairman of the Board of Trustees for the Camden County library, so the institutions are near and dear to my heart.

Q: What about Poussin's strange painting, *The Shepherds of Arcadia II,* and the odd markings at Bainbridge Hall in England, which you also work into the novel? Any idea what those really mean?

SB: Impossible to say. Both are fascinating. Why Poussin painted the reverse image of one of his earlier works remains a mystery. But that curiosity, as well as Poussin's actual life, fit well into the plot. The markings (along with Poussin's reverse painting) at my fictional Bainbridge Hall are based on an actual monument which stands at Shugborough Hall in England. Many an expert has tried to decipher their meaning and none has offered any satisfactory explanation. I actually think my interpretation might make the most sense.

Q: The prologue of *The Alexandria Link* is set in Palestine in 1948—just as the state of Israel was being established. This was obviously a crucial time in the history of that war-torn area, but it is also a tough subject to address.

What led you to write about it? How did you research the time and place? And what were the challenges involved?
SB: I struggled with this prologue, debating whether to use ancient times or stay current. I settled on 1948 because what happened to the Arabs during the *nakba* has great relevance to what's happening in the world today. That's the thing about the Middle East conflict: History plays a pivotal role. Researching all those events was easy. There are countless books. The challenge came in balancing the many conflicting claims. And, believe me, there aren't two, but one hundred and two, sides to every story.

Q: For the first time in your career, you bring back characters in this novel. Cotton Malone and a few others return from your recent bestseller, *The Templar Legacy.* Was it easier to work with characters you already knew, or was it harder?
SB: A little of both. You can't assume that readers of this book will have read *The Templar Legacy,* so there's a certain amount of character development that has to be included with each story. What recurring characters offer, though, is an ability to grow. Readers can learn more about these personalities as they face different situations. Like old friends, the more you see them, the more you know about them. That's different from my first three novels, *The Amber Room, The Romanov Prophecy,* and *The Third Secret,* which were all stand-alones.

Q: I assume Cotton and the others will be back. Can you give any clues as to what adventure awaits them?
SB: All I can tell you is they will all be back in *The Venetian Betrayal.* Visit my website for details: www.steveberry.org.

Read on for an excerpt of
Steve Berry's newest thriller

THE VENETIAN BETRAYAL

Published by Ballantine Books

COPENHAGEN, DENMARK
SATURDAY, APRIL 18, THE PRESENT
11:55 PM

THE SMELL ROUSED COTTON MALONE TO CONSCIOUSNESS.
Sharp, acrid, with a hint of sulfur. And something else.
Sweet and sickening. Like death.

He opened his eyes.

He lay prone on the floor, arms extended, palms to the
hardwood, which he immediately noticed was sticky.

What happened?

He'd attended the April gathering of the Danish Antiquar-
ian Booksellers Society a few blocks west of his bookshop,
near the gaiety of Tivoli. He liked the monthly meetings and
this one had been no exception. A few drinks, some friends,
and lots of book chatter. Tomorrow morning he'd agreed to
meet Cassiopeia Vitt. Her call yesterday to arrange the meeting had surprised him. He'd not heard from her since Christmas, when she'd spent a few days in Copenhagen. He'd been
cruising back home on his bicycle, enjoying the comfortable
spring night, when he'd decided to check out the unusual
meeting location she'd chosen, the Museum of Greco-Roman
Culture—a preparatory habit from his former profession.
Cassiopeia rarely did anything on impulse, so a little advance preparation wasn't a bad idea.

HE'D FOUND THE ADDRESS, WHICH FACED THE FREDERIKS-holms canal, and noticed a half-open door to the pitch-dark building—a door that should normally be closed and alarmed. He'd parked his bike. The least he could do was close the door and phone the police when he returned home.

But the last thing he remembered was grasping the door-knob.

He was now inside the museum.

In the ambient light that filtered in through two plate-glass windows, he saw a space decorated in typical Danish style—a sleek mixture of steel, wood, glass, and aluminum. The right side of his head throbbed and he caressed a tender knot.

He shook the fog from his brain and stood.

He'd visited this museum once and had been unimpressed with its collection of Greek and Roman artifacts. Just one of a hundred or more private collections throughout Copen-hagen, their subject matter as varied as the city's population.

He steadied himself against a glass display case. His fin-gertips again came away sticky and smelly, with the same nauseating odor.

He noticed that his shirt and trousers were damp, as was his hair, face, and arms. Whatever covered the museum's in-terior coated him, too.

He stumbled toward the front entrance and tried the door. Locked. Double dead bolt. A key would be needed to open it from the inside.

He stared back into the interior. The ceiling soared thirty feet. A wood-and-chrome staircase led up to a second floor that dissolved into more darkness, the ground floor extend-ing out beneath.

He found a light switch. Nothing. He lumbered over to a desk phone. No dial tone.

A noise disturbed the silence. Clicks and whines, like gears working. Coming from the second floor.

His training as a Justice Department agent cautioned him to keep quiet, but also urged him to investigate.

So he silently climbed the stairs.

The chrome banister was damp, as were each of the laminated risers. Fifteen steps up, more glass-and-chrome display cases dotted the hardwood floor. Marble reliefs and partial bronzes on pedestals loomed like ghosts. Movement caught his eye twenty feet away. An object rolling across the floor. Maybe two feet wide with rounded sides, pale in color, tight to the ground, like one of those robotic lawn mowers he'd once seen advertised. When a display case or statue was encountered, the thing stopped, retreated, then darted in a different direction. A nozzle extended from its top and every few seconds a burst of aerosol spewed out.

He stepped close.

All movement stopped. As if it sensed his presence. The nozzle swung to face him. A cloud of mist soaked his pants.

What was this?

The machine seemed to lose interest and scooted deeper into the darkness, more odorous mist expelling along the way. He stared down over the railing to the ground floor and spotted another of the contraptions parked beside a display case.

Nothing about this seemed good.

He needed to leave. The stench was beginning to turn his stomach.

The machine ceased its roaming and he heard a new sound.

Two years ago, before his divorce, his retirement from the government, and his abrupt move to Copenhagen, when he'd lived in Atlanta, he'd spent a few hundred dollars on a stainless-steel grill. The unit came with a red button that, when pumped, sparked a gas flame. He recalled the sound the igniter made with each pump of the button.

The same clicking he heard right now.

Sparks flashed.

The floor burst to life, first sun yellow, then burnt orange, finally settling on pale blue as flames radiated outward, consuming the hardwood. Flames simultaneously roared up the walls. The temperature rose swiftly and he raised an arm to shield his face. The ceiling joined the conflagration, and in less than fifteen seconds the second floor was totally ablaze.

Overhead sprinklers sprang to life.

He partially retreated down the staircase and waited for the fire to be doused.

But he noticed something.

The water simply aggravated the flames.

The machine that started the disaster suddenly disintegrated in a muted flash, flames rolling out in all directions, like waves searching for shore.

A fireball drifted to the ceiling and seemed to be welcomed by the spraying water. Steam thickened the air, not with smoke but with a chemical that made his head spin.

He leaped down the stairs two at a time. Another swoosh racked the second floor. Followed by two more. Glass shattered. Something crashed.

He darted to the front of the building.

The other gizmo that had sat dormant sprang to life and started skirting the ground-floor display cases.

More aerosol spewed into the scorching air.

He needed to get out. But the locked front door opened to the inside. Metal frame, thick wood. No way to kick it open. He watched as fire eased down the staircase, consuming each riser, like the devil descending to greet him. Even the chrome was being devoured with a vengeance.

His breaths became labored, thanks to the chemical fog and the rapidly vanishing oxygen. Surely someone would call the fire department, but they'd be no help to him. If a spark touched his soaked clothes . . .

The blaze found the bottom of the staircase.

Ten feet away.